The Moon Pool

The Moon Pool

A. Merritt

MINT EDITIONS

The Moon Pool was first published in 1918.

This edition published by Mint Editions 2021.

ISBN 9781513289939 | E-ISBN 9781513292786

Published by Mint Editions®

 MINT
EDITIONS

minteditionbooks.com

Publishing Director: Jennifer Newens
Design & Production: Rachel Lopez Metzger
Project Manager: Micaela Clark
Typesetting: Westchester Publishing Services

Contents

I

The Thing on the Moon Path

For two months I had been on the d'Entrecasteaux Islands gathering data for the concluding chapters of my book upon the flora of the volcanic islands of the South Pacific. The day before I had reached Port Moresby and had seen my specimens safely stored on board the Southern Queen. As I sat on the upper deck I thought, with homesick mind, of the long leagues between me and Melbourne, and the longer ones between Melbourne and New York.

It was one of Papua's yellow mornings when she shows herself in her sombrest, most baleful mood. The sky was smouldering ochre. Over the island brooded a spirit sullen, alien, implacable, filled with the threat of latent, malefic forces waiting to be unleashed. It seemed an emanation out of the untamed, sinister heart of Papua herself—sinister even when she smiles. And now and then, on the wind, came a breath from virgin jungles, laden with unfamiliar odours, mysterious and menacing.

It is on such mornings that Papua whispers to you of her immemorial ancientness and of her power. And, as every white man must, I fought against her spell. While I struggled I saw a tall figure striding down the pier; a Kapa-Kapa boy followed swinging a new valise. There was something familiar about the tall man. As he reached the gangplank he looked up straight into my eyes, stared for a moment, then waved his hand.

And now I knew him. It was Dr. David Throckmartin—"Throck" he was to me always, one of my oldest friends and, as well, a mind of the first water whose power and achievements were for me a constant inspiration as they were, I know, for scores other.

Coincidentally with my recognition came a shock of surprise, definitely—unpleasant. It was Throckmartin—but about him was something disturbingly unlike the man I had known long so well and to whom and to whose little party I had bidden farewell less than a month before I myself had sailed for these seas. He had married only a few weeks before, Edith, the daughter of Professor William Frazier, younger by at least a decade than he but at one with him in his ideals and as much in love, if it were possible, as Throckmartin. By virtue of her father's training a wonderful assistant, by virtue of her own sweet, sound heart a—I use the word in its olden sense—lover. With his equally youthful associate Dr. Charles Stanton and a Swedish woman, Thora Halversen, who had been Edith Throckmartin's nurse from babyhood, they had set forth for the Nan-Matal, that extraordinary group of island ruins clustered along the eastern shore of Ponape in the Carolines.

I knew that he had planned to spend at least a year among these ruins, not only of Ponape but of Lele—twin centres of a colossal riddle of humanity, a weird flower of civilization that blossomed ages before the seeds of Egypt were sown; of whose arts we know little enough and of whose science nothing. He had carried with him unusually complete equipment for the work he had expected to do and which, he hoped, would be his monument.

What then had brought Throckmartin to Port Moresby, and what was that change I had sensed in him?

Hurrying down to the lower deck I found him with the purser. As I spoke he turned, thrust out to me an eager hand—and then I saw what was that difference that had so moved me. He knew, of course by my silence and involuntary shrinking the shock my closer look had given me. His eyes filled; he turned brusquely from the purser, hesitated—then hurried off to his stateroom.

"'E looks rather queer—eh?" said the purser. "Know 'im well, sir? Seems to 'ave given you quite a start."

I made some reply and went slowly up to my chair. There I sat, composed my mind and tried to define what it was that had shaken me so. Now it came to me. The old Throckmartin was on the eve of his venture just turned forty, lithe, erect, muscular; his controlling expression one of enthusiasm, of intellectual keenness, of—what shall I say—expectant search. His always questioning brain had stamped its vigor upon his face.

But the Throckmartin I had seen below was one who had borne some scaring shock of mingled rapture and horror; some soul cataclysm that in its climax had remoulded, deep from within, his face, setting on it seal of wedded ecstasy and despair; as though indeed these two had come to him hand in hand, taken possession of him and departing left behind, ineradicably, their linked shadows!

Yes—it was that which appalled. For how could rapture and horror, Heaven and Hell mix, clasp hands—kiss?

Yet these were what in closest embrace lay on Throckmartin's face!

Deep in thought, subconsciously with relief, I watched the shore line sink behind; welcomed the touch of the wind of the free seas. I had hoped, and within the hope was an inexplicable shrinking that I would meet Throckmartin at lunch. He did not come down, and I was sensible of deliverance within my disappointment. All that afternoon I lounged about uneasily but still he kept to his cabin—and within me was no strength to summon him. Nor did he appear at dinner.

Dusk and night fell swiftly. I was warm and went back to my deck-chair. The Southern Queen was rolling to a disquieting swell and I had the place to myself.

Over the heavens was a canopy of cloud, glowing faintly and testifying to the moon riding behind it. There was much phosphorescence. Fitfully before the ship and at her sides arose those stranger little swirls of mist that swirl up from the Southern Ocean like breath of sea monsters, whirl for an instant and disappear.

Suddenly the deck door opened and through it came Throckmartin. He paused uncertainly, looked up at the sky with a curiously eager, intent gaze, hesitated, then closed the door behind him.

"Throck," I called. "Come! It's Goodwin."

He made his way to me.

"Throck," I said, wasting no time in preliminaries. "What's wrong? Can I help you?"

I felt his body grow tense.

"I'm going to Melbourne, Goodwin," he answered. "I need a few things—need them urgently. And more men—white men—"

He stopped abruptly; rose from his chair, gazed intently toward the north. I followed his gaze. Far, far away the moon had broken through the clouds. Almost on the horizon, you could see the faint luminescence of it upon the smooth sea. The distant patch of light quivered and shook. The clouds thickened again and it was gone. The ship raced on southward, swiftly.

Throckmartin dropped into his chair. He lighted a cigarette with a hand that trembled; then turned to me with abrupt resolution.

"Goodwin," he said. "I do need help. If ever man needed it, I do. Goodwin—can you imagine yourself in another world, alien, unfamiliar, a world of terror, whose unknown joy is its greatest terror of all; you all alone there, a stranger! As such a man would need help, so I need—"

He paused abruptly and arose; the cigarette dropped from his fingers. The moon had again broken through the clouds, and this time much nearer. Not a mile away was the patch of light that it threw upon the waves. Back of it, to the rim of the sea was a lane of moonlight; a gigantic gleaming serpent racing over the edge of the world straight and surely toward the ship.

Throckmartin stiffened to it as a pointer does to a hidden covey. To me from him pulsed a thrill of horror—but horror tinged with an unfamiliar, an infernal joy. It came to me and passed away—leaving me trembling with its shock of bitter sweet.

He bent forward, all his soul in his eyes. The moon path swept closer, closer still. It was now less than half a mile away. From it the ship fled—almost as though pursued. Down upon it, swift and straight, a radiant torrent cleaving the waves, raced the moon stream.

"Good God!" breathed Throckmartin, and if ever the words were a prayer and an invocation they were.

And then, for the first time—I saw—*it*!

The moon path stretched to the horizon and was bordered by darkness. It was as though the clouds above had been parted to form a lane-drawn aside like curtains or as the waters of the Red Sea were held back to let the hosts of Israel through. On each side of the stream was the black shadow cast by the folds of the high canopies And straight as a road between the opaque walls gleamed, shimmered, and danced the shining, racing, rapids of the moonlight.

Far, it seemed immeasurably far, along this stream of silver fire I sensed, rather than saw, something coming. It drew first into sight as a deeper glow within the light. On and on it swept toward us—an opalescent mistiness that sped with the suggestion of some winged creature in arrowed flight. Dimly there crept into my mind memory of the Dyak legend of the winged messenger of Buddha—the Akla bird whose feathers are woven of the moon rays, whose heart is a living opal, whose wings in flight echo the crystal clear music of the white stars—but whose beak is of frozen flame and shreds the souls of unbelievers.

Closer it drew and now there came to me sweet, insistent tinklings—like pizzicati on violins of glass; crystal clear; diamonds melting into sounds!

Now the Thing was close to the end of the white path; close up to the barrier of darkness still between the ship and the sparkling head of the moon stream. Now it beat up against that barrier as a bird against the bars of its cage. It whirled with shimmering plumes, with

A. MERRITT

swirls of lacy light, with spirals of living vapour. It held within it odd, unfamiliar gleams as of shifting mother-of-pearl. Coruscations and glittering atoms drifted through it as though it drew them from the rays that bathed it.

Nearer and nearer it came, borne on the sparkling waves, and ever thinner shrank the protecting wall of shadow between it and us. Within the mistiness was a core, a nucleus of intenser light—veined, opaline, effulgent, intensely alive. And above it, tangled in the plumes and spirals that throbbed and whirled were seven glowing lights.

Through all the incessant but strangely ordered movement of the—*thing*—these lights held firm and steady. They were seven—like seven little moons. One was of a pearly pink, one of a delicate nacreous blue, one of lambent saffron, one of the emerald you see in the shallow waters of tropic isles; a deathly white; a ghostly amethyst; and one of the silver that is seen only when the flying fish leap beneath the moon.

The tinkling music was louder still. It pierced the ears with a shower of tiny lances; it made the heart beat jubilantly—and checked it dolorously. It closed the throat with a throb of rapture and gripped it tight with the hand of infinite sorrow!

Came to me now a murmuring cry, stilling the crystal notes. It was articulate—but as though from something utterly foreign to this world. The ear took the cry and translated with conscious labour into the sounds of earth. And even as it compassed, the brain shrank from it irresistibly, and simultaneously it seemed reached toward it with irresistible eagerness.

Throckmartin strode toward the front of the deck, straight toward the vision, now but a few yards away from the stern. His face had lost all human semblance. Utter agony and utter ecstasy—there they were side by side, not resisting each other; unholy inhuman companions blending into a look that none of God's creatures should wear—and deep, deep as his soul! A devil and a God dwelling harmoniously side by side! So must Satan, newly fallen, still divine, seeing heaven and contemplating hell, have appeared.

And then—swiftly the moon path faded! The clouds swept over the sky as though a hand had drawn them together. Up from the south came a roaring squall. As the moon vanished what I had seen vanished with it—blotted out as an image on a magic lantern; the tinkling ceased abruptly—leaving a silence like that which follows an abrupt thunder clap. There was nothing about us but silence and blackness!

Through me passed a trembling as one who has stood on the very verge of the gulf wherein the men of the Louisades says lurks the fisher of the souls of men, and has been plucked back by sheerest chance.

Throckmartin passed an arm around me.

"It is as I thought," he said. In his voice was a new note; the calm certainty that has swept aside a waiting terror of the unknown. "Now I know! Come with me to my cabin, old friend. For now that you too have seen I can tell you"—he hesitated—"what it was you saw," he ended.

As we passed through the door we met the ship's first officer. Throckmartin composed his face into at least a semblance of normality.

"Going to have much of a storm?" he asked.

"Yes," said the mate. "Probably all the way to Melbourne."

Throckmartin straightened as though with a new thought. He gripped the officer's sleeve eagerly.

"You mean at least cloudy weather—for"—he hesitated—"for the next three nights, say?"

"And for three more," replied the mate.

"Thank God!" cried Throckmartin, and I think I never heard such relief and hope as was in his voice.

The sailor stood amazed. "Thank God?" he repeated. "Thank—what d'ye mean?"

But Throckmartin was moving onward to his cabin. I started to follow. The first officer stopped me.

"Your friend," he said, "is he ill?"

"The sea!" I answered hurriedly. "He's not used to it. I am going to look after him."

Doubt and disbelief were plain in the seaman's eyes but I hurried on. For I knew now that Throckmartin was ill indeed—but with a sickness the ship's doctor nor any other could heal.

II

"Dead! All Dead!"

He was sitting, face in hands, on the side of his berth as I entered. He had taken off his coat.

"Throck," I cried. "What was it? What are you flying from, man? Where is your wife—and Stanton?"

"Dead!" he replied monotonously. "Dead! All dead!" Then as I recoiled from him—"All dead. Edith, Stanton, Thora—dead—or worse. And Edith in the Moon Pool—with them—drawn by what you saw on the moon path—that has put its brand upon me—and follows me!"

He ripped open his shirt.

"Look at this," he said. Around his chest, above his heart, the skin was white as pearl. This whiteness was sharply defined against the healthy tint of the body. It circled him with an even cincture about two inches wide.

"Burn it!" he said, and offered me his cigarette. I drew back. He gestured—peremptorily. I pressed the glowing end of the cigarette into the ribbon of white flesh. He did not flinch nor was there odour of burning nor, as I drew the little cylinder away, any mark upon the whiteness.

"Feel it!" he commanded again. I placed my fingers upon the band. It was cold—like frozen marble.

He drew his shirt around him.

"Two things you have seen," he said. "*It*—and its mark. Seeing, you must believe my story. Goodwin, I tell you again that my wife is dead—or worse—I do not know; the prey of—what you saw; so, too, is Stanton; so Thora. How—"

Tears rolled down the seared face.

"Why did God let it conquer us? Why did He let it take my Edith?" he cried in utter bitterness. "Are there things stronger than God, do you think, Walter?"

I hesitated.

"Are there? Are there?" His wild eyes searched me.

"I do not know just how you define God," I managed at last through my astonishment to make answer. "If you mean the will to know, working through science—"

He waved me aside impatiently.

"Science," he said. "What is our science against—that? Or against the science of whatever devils that made it—or made the way for it to enter this world of ours?"

With an effort he regained control.

"Goodwin," he said, "do you know at all of the ruins on the Carolines; the cyclopean, megalithic cities and harbours of Ponape and Lele, of Kusaie, of Ruk and Hogolu, and a score of other islets there? Particularly, do you know of the Nan-Matal and the Metalanim?"

"Of the Metalanim I have heard and seen photographs," I said. "They call it, don't they, the Lost Venice of the Pacific?"

"Look at this map," said Throckmartin. "That," he went on, "is Christian's chart of Metalanim harbour and the Nan-Matal. Do you see the rectangles marked Nan-Tauach?"

"Yes," I said.

"There," he said, "under those walls is the Moon Pool and the seven gleaming lights that raise the Dweller in the Pool, and the altar and shrine of the Dweller. And there in the Moon Pool with it lie Edith and Stanton and Thora."

"The Dweller in the Moon Pool?" I repeated half-incredulously.

"The Thing you saw," said Throckmartin solemnly.

A solid sheet of rain swept the ports, and the Southern Queen began to roll on the rising swells. Throckmartin drew another deep breath of relief, and drawing aside a curtain peered out into the night. Its blackness seemed to reassure him. At any rate, when he sat again he was entirely calm.

"There are no more wonderful ruins in the world," he began almost casually. "They take in some fifty islets and cover with their intersecting canals and lagoons about twelve square miles. Who built them? None knows. When were they built? Ages before the memory of present man, that is sure. Ten thousand, twenty thousand, a hundred thousand years ago—the last more likely.

"All these islets, Walter, are squared, and their shores are frowning seawalls of gigantic basalt blocks hewn and put in place by the hands of ancient man. Each inner water-front is faced with a terrace of those basalt blocks which stand out six feet above the shallow canals that meander between them. On the islets behind these walls are time-shattered fortresses, palaces, terraces, pyramids; immense courtyards strewn with ruins—and all so old that they seem to wither the eyes of those who look on them.

"There has been a great subsidence. You can stand out of Metalanim harbour for three miles and look down upon the tops of similar monolithic structures and walls twenty feet below you in the water.

"And all about, strung on their canals, are the bulwarked islets with their enigmatic walls peering through the dense growths of mangroves—dead, deserted for incalculable ages; shunned by those who live near.

"You as a botanist are familiar with the evidence that a vast shadowy continent existed in the Pacific—a continent that was not rent asunder by volcanic forces as was that legendary one of Atlantis in the Eastern Ocean.[1] My work in Java, in Papua, and in the Ladrones had set my mind upon this Pacific lost land. Just as the Azores are believed to be the last high peaks of Atlantis, so hints came to me steadily that Ponape and Lele and their basalt bulwarked islets were the last points of the slowly sunken western land clinging still to the sunlight, and had been the last refuge and sacred places of the rulers of that race which had lost their immemorial home under the rising waters of the Pacific.

"I believed that under these ruins I might find the evidence that I sought.

"My—my wife and I had talked before we were married of making this our great work. After the honeymoon we prepared for the expedition. Stanton was as enthusiastic as ourselves. We sailed, as you know, last May for fulfilment of my dreams.

"At Ponape we selected, not without difficulty, workmen to help us—diggers. I had to make extraordinary inducements before I could get together my force. Their beliefs are gloomy, these Ponapeans. They people their swamps, their forests, their mountains, and shores, with malignant spirits—ani they call them. And they are afraid—bitterly afraid of the isles of ruins and what they think the ruins hide. I do not wonder—now!

"When they were told where they were to go, and how long we expected to stay, they murmured. Those who, at last, were tempted made what I thought then merely a superstitious proviso that they were

---

1. For more detailed observations on these points refer to G. Volkens, Uber die Karolinen Insel Yap, in Verhandlungen Gesellschaft Erdkunde Berlin, xxvii (1901); J. S. Kubary, Ethnographische Beitrage zur Kentniss des Karolinen Archipel (Leiden, 1889–1892); De Abrade Historia del Conflicto de las Carolinas, etc. (Madrid, 1886).—W. T. G.

to be allowed to go away on the three nights of the full moon. Would to God we had heeded them and gone too!"

"We passed into Metalanim harbour. Off to our left—a mile away arose a massive quadrangle. Its walls were all of forty feet high and hundreds of feet on each side. As we drew by, our natives grew very silent; watched it furtively, fearfully. I knew it for the ruins that are called Nan-Tauach, the 'place of frowning walls.' And at the silence of my men I recalled what Christian had written of this place; of how he had come upon its 'ancient platforms and tetragonal enclosures of stonework; its wonder of tortuous alleyways and labyrinth of shallow canals; grim masses of stonework peering out from behind verdant screens; cyclopean barricades,' and of how, when he had turned 'into its ghostly shadows, straight-way the merriment of guides was hushed and conversation died down to whispers.'"

He was silent for a little time.

"Of course I wanted to pitch our camp there," he went on again quietly, "but I soon gave up that idea. The natives were panic-stricken—threatened to turn back. 'No,' they said, 'too great ani there. We go to any other place—but not there.'

"We finally picked for our base the islet called Uschen-Tau. It was close to the isle of desire, but far enough away from it to satisfy our men. There was an excellent camping-place and a spring of fresh water. We pitched our tents, and in a couple of days the work was in full swing."

III

The Moon Rock

"I do not intend to tell you now," Throckmartin continued, "the results of the next two weeks, nor of what we found. Later—if I am allowed, I will lay all that before you. It is sufficient to say that at the end of those two weeks I had found confirmation for many of my theories.

"The place, for all its decay and desolation, had not infected us with any touch of morbidity—that is not Edith, Stanton, or myself. But Thora was very unhappy. She was a Swede, as you know, and in her blood ran the beliefs and superstitions of the Northland—some of them so strangely akin to those of this far southern land; beliefs of spirits of mountain and forest and water werewolves and beings malign. From the first she showed a curious sensitivity to what, I suppose, may be called the 'influences' of the place. She said it 'smelled' of ghosts and warlocks.

"I laughed at her then—

"Two weeks slipped by, and at their end the spokesman for our natives came to us. The next night was the full of the moon, he said. He reminded me of my promise. They would go back to their village in the morning; they would return after the third night, when the moon had begun to wane. They left us sundry charms for our 'protection,' and solemnly cautioned us to keep as far away as possible from Nan-Tauach during their absence. Half-exasperated, half-amused I watched them go.

"No work could be done without them, of course, so we decided to spend the days of their absence junketing about the southern islets of the group. We marked down several spots for subsequent exploration, and on the morning of the third day set forth along the east face of the breakwater for our camp on Uschen-Tau, planning to have everything in readiness for the return of our men the next day.

"We landed just before dusk, tired and ready for our cots. It was only a little after ten o'clock that Edith awakened me.

"'Listen!' she said. 'Lean over with your ear close to the ground!'

"I did so, and seemed to hear, far, far below, as though coming up from great distances, a faint chanting. It gathered strength, died down, ended; began, gathered volume, faded away into silence.

"'It's the waves rolling on rocks somewhere,' I said. 'We're probably over some ledge of rock that carries the sound.'

"'It's the first time I've heard it,' replied my wife doubtfully. We listened again. Then through the dim rhythms, deep beneath us, another sound came. It drifted across the lagoon that lay between us and Nan-Tauach in little tinkling waves. It was music—of a sort; I won't describe the strange effect it had upon me. You've felt it—"

"You mean on the deck?" I asked. Throckmartin nodded.

"I went to the flap of the tent," he continued, "and peered out. As I did so Stanton lifted his flap and walked out into the moonlight, looking over to the other islet and listening. I called to him.

"'That's the queerest sound!' he said. He listened again. 'Crystalline! Like little notes of translucent glass. Like the bells of crystal on the sistrums of Isis at Dendarah Temple,' he added half-dreamily. We gazed intently at the island. Suddenly, on the sea-wall, moving slowly, rhythmically, we saw a little group of lights. Stanton laughed.

"'The beggars!' he exclaimed. 'That's why they wanted to get away, is it? Don't you see, Dave, it's some sort of a festival—rites of some kind that they hold during the full moon! That's why they were so eager to have us *keep* away, too.'

"The explanation seemed good. I felt a curious sense of relief, although I had not been sensible of any oppression.

"'Let's slip over,' suggested Stanton—but I would not.

"'They're a difficult lot as it is,' I said. 'If we break into one of their religious ceremonies they'll probably never forgive us. Let's keep out of any family party where we haven't been invited.'

"'That's so,' agreed Stanton.

"The strange tinkling rose and fell, rose and fell—

"'There's something—something very unsettling about it,' said Edith at last soberly. 'I wonder what they make those sounds with. They frighten me half to death, and, at the same time, they make me feel as though some enormous rapture were just around the corner.'

"'It's devilish uncanny!' broke in Stanton.

"And as he spoke the flap of Thora's tent was raised and out into the moonlight strode the old Swede. She was the great Norse type—tall, deep-breasted, moulded on the old Viking lines. Her sixty years had slipped from her. She looked like some ancient priestess of Odin.

"She stood there, her eyes wide, brilliant, staring. She thrust her head forward toward Nan-Tauach, regarding the moving lights; she listened. Suddenly she raised her arms and made a curious gesture to the moon. It was—an archaic—movement; she seemed to drag it from remote antiquity—yet in it was a strange suggestion of power, Twice she repeated this gesture and—the tinklings died away! She turned to us.

"'Go!' she said, and her voice seemed to come from far distances. 'Go from here—and quickly! Go while you may. It has called—' She pointed to the islet. 'It knows you are here. It waits!' she wailed. 'It beckons—the—the—'

"She fell at Edith's feet, and over the lagoon came again the tinklings, now with a quicker note of jubilance—almost of triumph.

"We watched beside her throughout the night. The sounds from Nan-Tauach continued until about an hour before moon-set. In the morning Thora awoke, none the worse, apparently. She had had bad dreams, she said. She could not remember what they were—except that they had warned her of danger. She was oddly sullen, and throughout the morning her gaze returned again and again half-fascinatedly, half-wonderingly to the neighbouring isle.

"That afternoon the natives returned. And that night on Nan-Tauach the silence was unbroken nor were there lights nor sign of life.

"You will understand, Goodwin, how the occurrences I have related would excite the scientific curiosity. We rejected immediately, of course, any explanation admitting the supernatural.

"Our—symptoms let me call them—could all very easily be accounted for. It is unquestionable that the vibrations created by certain musical instruments have definite and sometimes extraordinary effect upon the nervous system. We accepted this as the explanation of the reactions we had experienced, hearing the unfamiliar sounds. Thora's nervousness, her superstitious apprehensions, had wrought her up to a condition of semi-somnambulistic hysteria. Science could readily explain her part in the night's scene.

"We came to the conclusion that there must be a passage-way between Ponape and Nan-Tauach known to the natives—and used by them during their rites. We decided that on the next departure of our labourers we would set forth immediately to Nan-Tauach. We would investigate during the day, and at evening my wife and Thora would go back to camp, leaving Stanton and me to spend the night on the island, observing from some safe hiding-place what might occur.

"The moon waned; appeared crescent in the west; waxed slowly toward the full. Before the men left us they literally prayed us to accompany them. Their importunities only made us more eager to see what it was that, we were now convinced, they wanted to conceal from us. At least that was true of Stanton and myself. It was not true of Edith. She was thoughtful, abstracted—reluctant.

"When the men were out of sight around the turn of the harbour, we took our boat and made straight for Nan-Tauach. Soon its mighty sea-wall towered above us. We passed through the water-gate with its gigantic hewn prisms of basalt and landed beside a half-submerged pier. In front of us stretched a series of giant steps leading into a vast court strewn with fragments of fallen pillars. In the centre of the court, beyond the shattered pillars, rose another terrace of basalt blocks, concealing, I knew, still another enclosure.

"And now, Walter, for the better understanding of what follows— and—and—" he hesitated. "Should you decide later to return with me or, if I am taken, to—to—follow us—listen carefully to my description of this place: Nan-Tauach is literally three rectangles. The first rectangle is the sea-wall, built up of monoliths—hewn and squared, twenty feet wide at the top. To get to the gateway in the sea-wall you pass along the canal marked on the map between Nan-Tauach and the islet named Tau. The entrance to the canal is bidden by dense thickets of mangroves; once through these the way is clear. The steps lead up from the landing of the sea-gate through the entrance to the courtyard.

"This courtyard is surrounded by another basalt wall, rectangular, following with mathematical exactness the march of the outer barricades. The sea-wall is from thirty to forty feet high—originally it must have been much higher, but there has been subsidence in parts. The wall of the first enclosure is fifteen feet across the top and its height varies from twenty to fifty feet—here, too, the gradual sinking of the land has caused portions of it to fall.

"Within this courtyard is the second enclosure. Its terrace, of the same basalt as the outer walls, is about twenty feet high. Entrance is gained to it by many breaches which time has made in its stonework. This is the inner court, the heart of Nan-Tauach! There lies the great central vault with which is associated the one name of living being that has come to us out of the mists of the past. The natives say it was the treasure-house of Chau-te-leur, a mighty king who reigned long 'before their fathers.' As Chan is the ancient Ponapean word both for sun and king, the name means, without doubt, 'place of the sun king.' It is a memory of a dynastic name of the race that ruled the Pacific continent, now vanished—just as the rulers of ancient Crete took the name of Minos and the rulers of Egypt the name of Pharaoh.

"And opposite this place of the sun king is the moon rock that hides the Moon Pool.

"It was Stanton who discovered the moon rock. We had been inspecting the inner courtyard; Edith and Thora were getting together our lunch. I came out of the vault of Chau-te-leur to find Stanton before a part of the terrace studying it wonderingly.

"'What do you make of this?' he asked me as I came up. He pointed to the wall. I followed his finger and saw a slab of stone about fifteen feet high and ten wide. At first all I noticed was the exquisite nicety with which its edges joined the blocks about it. Then I realized that its colour was subtly different—tinged with grey and of a smooth, peculiar—deadness.

"'Looks more like calcite than basalt,' I said. I touched it and withdrew my hand quickly for at the contact every nerve in my arm tingled as though a shock of frozen electricity had passed through it. It was not cold as we know cold. It was a chill force—the phrase I have used—frozen electricity—describes it better than anything else. Stanton looked at me oddly.

"'So you felt it too,' he said. 'I was wondering whether I was developing hallucinations like Thora. Notice, by the way, that the blocks beside it are quite warm beneath the sun.'

"We examined the slab eagerly. Its edges were cut as though by an engraver of jewels. They fitted against the neighbouring blocks in almost a hair-line. Its base was slightly curved, and fitted as closely as top and sides upon the huge stones on which it rested. And then we noted that these stones had been hollowed to follow the line of the grey stone's foot. There was a semicircular depression running from one side of the slab to the other. It was as though the grey rock stood in the centre of a shallow cup—revealing half, covering half. Something about this hollow attracted me. I reached down and felt it. Goodwin, although the balance of the stones that formed it, like all the stones of the courtyard, were rough and age-worn—this was as smooth, as even surfaced as though it had just left the hands of the polisher.

"'It's a door!' exclaimed Stanton. 'It swings around in that little cup. That's what makes the hollow so smooth.'

"'Maybe you're right,' I replied. 'But how the devil can we open it?'

"We went over the slab again—pressing upon its edges, thrusting against its sides. During one of those efforts I happened to look up—and cried out. A foot above and on each side of the corner of the grey rock's lintel was a slight convexity, visible only from the angle at which my gaze struck it.

"We carried with us a small scaling-ladder and up this I went. The bosses were apparently nothing more than chiseled curvatures in the stone. I laid my hand on the one I was examining, and drew it back sharply. In my palm, at the base of my thumb, I had felt the same shock that I had in touching the slab below. I put my hand back. The impression came from a spot not more than an inch wide. I went carefully over the entire convexity, and six times more the chill ran through my arm. There were seven circles an inch wide in the curved place, each of which communicated the precise sensation I have described. The convexity on the opposite side of the slab gave exactly the same results. But no amount of touching or of pressing these spots singly or in any combination gave the slightest promise of motion to the slab itself.

"'And yet—they're what open it,' said Stanton positively.

"'Why do you say that?' I asked.

"'I—don't know,' he answered hesitatingly. 'But something tells me so. Throck,' he went on half earnestly, half laughingly, 'the purely scientific part of me is fighting the purely human part of me. The scientific part is urging me to find some way to get that slab either down or open. The human part is just as strongly urging me to do nothing of the sort and get away while I can!'

"He laughed again—shamefacedly.

"'Which shall it be?' he asked—and I thought that in his tone the human side of him was ascendant.

"'It will probably stay as it is—unless we blow it to bits,' I said.

"'I thought of that,' he answered, 'and I wouldn't dare,' he added soberly enough. And even as I had spoken there came to me the same feeling that he had expressed. It was as though something passed out of the grey rock that struck my heart as a hand strikes an impious lip. We turned away—uneasily, and faced Thora coming through a breach on the terrace.

"'Miss Edith wants you quick,' she began—and stopped. Her eyes went past me to the grey rock. Her body grew rigid; she took a few stiff steps forward and then ran straight to it. She cast herself upon its breast, hands and face pressed against it; we heard her scream as though her

A. MERRITT

very soul were being drawn from her—and watched her fall at its foot. As we picked her up I saw steal from her face the look I had observed when first we heard the crystal music of Nan-Tauach—that unhuman mingling of opposites!"

IV

The First Vanishings

W e carried Thora back, down to where Edith was waiting. We told her what had happened and what we had found. She listened gravely, and as we finished Thora sighed and opened her eyes.

"'I would like to see the stone,' she said. 'Charles, you stay here with Thora.' We passed through the outer court silently—and stood before the rock. She touched it, drew back her hand as I had; thrust it forward again resolutely and held it there. She seemed to be listening. Then she turned to me.

"'David,' said my wife, and the wistfulness in her voice hurt me— 'David, would you be very, very disappointed if we went from here— without trying to find out anymore about it—would you?'

"Walter, I never wanted anything so much in my life as I wanted to learn what that rock concealed. Nevertheless, I tried to master my desire, and I answered—'Edith, not a bit if you want us to do it.'

"She read my struggle in my eyes. She turned back toward the grey rock. I saw a shiver pass through her. I felt a tinge of remorse and pity!

"'Edith,' I exclaimed, 'we'll go!'

"She looked at me again. 'Science is a jealous mistress,' she quoted. 'No, after all it may be just fancy. At any rate, you can't run away. No! But, Dave, I'm going to stay too!'

"And there was no changing her decision. As we neared the others she laid a hand on my arm.

"'Dave,' she said, 'if there should be something—well—inexplicable tonight—something that seems—too dangerous—will you promise to go back to our own islet tomorrow, if we can—and wait until the natives return?'

"I promised eagerly—the desire to stay and see what came with the night was like a fire within me.

"We picked a place about five hundred feet away from the steps leading into the outer court.

"The spot we had selected was well hidden. We could not be seen, and yet we had a clear view of the stairs and the gateway. We settled down just before dusk to wait for whatever might come. I was nearest the giant steps; next me Edith; then Thora, and last Stanton.

"Night fell. After a time the eastern sky began to lighten, and we knew that the moon was rising; grew lighter still, and the orb peeped over the sea; swam into full sight. I glanced at Edith and then at Thora. My wife was intently listening. Thora sat, as she had since we had placed ourselves, elbows on knees, her hands covering her face.

"And then from the moonlight flooding us there dripped down on me a great drowsiness. Sleep seemed to seep from the rays and fall upon my eyes, closing them—closing them inexorably. Edith's hand in mine relaxed. Stanton's head fell upon his breast and his body swayed drunkenly. I tried to rise—to fight against the profound desire for slumber that pressed on me.

"And as I fought, Thora raised her head as though listening; and turned toward the gateway. There was infinite despair in her face—and expectancy. I tried again to rise—and a surge of sleep rushed over me. Dimly, as I sank within it, I heard a crystalline chiming; raised my lids once more with a supreme effort.

"Thora, bathed in light, was standing at the top of the stairs.

"Sleep took me for its very own—swept me into the heart of oblivion!

"Dawn was breaking when I wakened. Recollection rushed back; I thrust a panic-stricken hand out toward Edith; touched her and my heart gave a great leap of thankfulness. She stirred, sat up, rubbing dazed eyes. Stanton lay on his side, back toward us, head in arms.

"Edith looked at me laughingly. 'Heavens! What sleep!' she said. Memory came to her.

"'What happened?' she whispered. 'What made us sleep like that?'

"Stanton awoke.

"'What's the matter!' he exclaimed. 'You look as though you've been seeing ghosts.'

"Edith caught my hands.

"'Where's Thora?' she cried. Before I could answer she had run out into the open, calling.

"'Thora was taken,' was all I could say to Stanton, 'together we went to my wife, now standing beside the great stone steps, looking up fearfully at the gateway into the terraces. There I told them what I had seen before sleep had drowned me. And together then we ran up the stairs, through the court and to the grey rock.

"The slab was closed as it had been the day before, nor was there trace of its having opened. No trace? Even as I thought this Edith dropped to her knees before it and reached toward something lying at its foot. It was a little piece of gay silk. I knew it for part of the kerchief Thora wore about her hair. She lifted the fragment. It had been cut from the kerchief as though by a razor-edge; a few threads ran from it—down toward the base of the slab; ran on to the base of the grey rock and—under it!

"The grey rock was a door! And it had opened and Thora had passed through it!

"I think that for the next few minutes we all were a little insane. We beat upon that portal with our hands, with stones and sticks. At last reason came back to us.

"Goodwin, during the next two hours we tried every way in our power to force entrance through the slab. The rock resisted our drills. We tried explosions at the base with charges covered by rock. They made not the slightest impression on the surface, expending their force, of course, upon the slighter resistance of their coverings.

"Afternoon found us hopeless. Night was coming on and we would have to decide our course of action. I wanted to go to Ponape for help. But Edith objected that this would take hours and after we had reached there it would be impossible to persuade our men to return with us that night, if at all. What then was left? Clearly only one of two choices: to go back to our camp, wait for our men, and on their return try to persuade them to go with us to Nan-Tauach. But this would mean the abandonment of Thora for at least two days. We could not do it; it would have been too cowardly.

"The other choice was to wait where we were for night to come; to wait for the rock to open as it had the night before, and to make a sortie through it for Thora before it could close again.

"Our path lay clear before us. We had to spend that night on Nan-Tauach!

"We had, of course, discussed the sleep phenomena very fully. If our theory that lights, sounds, and Thora's disappearance were linked with secret religious rites of the natives, the logical inference was that the slumber had been produced by them, perhaps by vapours—you know as well as I, what extraordinary knowledge these Pacific peoples have of such things. Or the sleep might have been simply a coincidence and produced by emanations either gaseous or from plants, natural causes which had happened to coincide in their effects with the other manifestations. We made some rough and ready but effective respirators.

"As dusk fell we looked over our weapons. Edith was an excellent shot with both rifle and pistol. We had decided that my wife was to remain in the hiding-place. Stanton would take up a station on the far side of the stairway and I would place myself opposite him on the side near Edith. The place I picked out was less than two hundred feet from her, and I could reassure myself now and then as to her safety as it looked down upon the hollow wherein she crouched. From our respective stations Stanton and I could command the gateway entrance. His position gave him also a glimpse of the outer courtyard.

"A faint glow in the sky heralded the moon. Stanton and I took our places. The moon dawn increased rapidly; the disk swam up, and in a moment it was shining in full radiance upon ruins and sea.

"As it rose there came a curious little sighing sound from the inner terrace. Stanton straightened up and stared intently through the gateway, rifle ready.

"'Stanton, what do you see?' I called cautiously. He waved a silencing hand. I turned my head to look at Edith. A shock ran through me. She lay upon her side. Her face, grotesque with its nose and mouth covered by the respirator, was turned full toward the moon. She was again in deepest sleep!

"As I turned again to call to Stanton, my eyes swept the head of the steps and stopped, fascinated. For the moonlight had thickened. It seemed to be—curdled—there; and through it ran little gleams and veins of shimmering white fire. A languor passed through me. It was not the ineffable drowsiness of the preceding night. It was a sapping of all will to move. I tried to cry out to Stanton. I had not even the will to move my lips. Goodwin—I could not even move my eyes!

"Stanton was in the range of my fixed vision. I watched him leap up the steps and move toward the gateway. The curdled radiance seemed to await him. He stepped into it—and was lost to my sight.

"For a dozen heart beats there was silence. Then a rain of tinklings that set the pulses racing with joy and at once checked them with tiny fingers of ice—and ringing through them Stanton's voice from the courtyard—a great cry—a scream—filled with ecstasy insupportable and horror unimaginable! And once more there was silence. I strove to burst the bonds that held me. I could not. Even my eyelids were fixed. Within them my eyes, dry and aching, burned.

"Then Goodwin—I first saw the—inexplicable! The crystalline music swelled. Where I sat I could take in the gateway and its basalt portals, rough and broken, rising to the top of the wall forty feet above, shattered, ruined portals—unclimbable. From this gateway an intenser light began to flow. It grew, it gushed, and out of it walked Stanton.

"Stanton! But—God! What a vision!"

A deep tremor shook him. I waited—waited.

V

Into the Moon Pool

"G oodwin," Throckmartin went on at last, "I can describe him only as a thing of living light. He radiated light; was filled with light; overflowed with it. A shining cloud whirled through and around him in radiant swirls, shimmering tentacles, luminescent, coruscating spirals.

"His face shone with a rapture too great to be borne by living man, and was shadowed with insuperable misery. It was as though it had been remoulded by the hand of God and the hand of Satan, working together and in harmony. You have seen that seal upon my own. But you have never seen it in the degree that Stanton bore it. The eyes were wide open and fixed, as though upon some inward vision of hell and heaven!

"The light that filled and surrounded him had a nucleus, a core—something shiftingly human shaped—that dissolved and changed, gathered itself, whirled through and beyond him and back again. And as its shining nucleus passed through him Stanton's whole body pulsed radiance. As the luminescence moved, there moved above it, still and serene always, seven tiny globes of seven colors, like seven little moons.

"Then swiftly Stanton was lifted—levitated—up the unscalable wall and to its top. The glow faded from the moonlight, the tinkling music grew fainter. I tried again to move. The tears were running down now from my rigid lids and they brought relief to my tortured eyes.

"I have said my gaze was fixed. It was. But from the side, peripherally, it took in a part of the far wall of the outer enclosure. Ages seemed to pass and a radiance stole along it. Soon drifted into sight the figure that was Stanton. Far away he was—on the gigantic wall. But still I could see the shining spirals whirling jubilantly around and through him; felt rather than saw his tranced face beneath the seven moons. A swirl of crystal notes, and he had passed. And all the time, as though from some opened well of light, the courtyard gleamed and sent out silver fires that dimmed the moonrays, yet seemed strangely to be a part of them.

"At last the moon neared the horizon. There came a louder burst of sound; the second, and last, cry of Stanton, like an echo of his first! Again the soft sighing from the inner terrace. Then—utter silence!

"The light faded; the moon was setting and with a rush life and power to move returned to me. I made a leap for the steps, rushed up them, through the gateway and straight to the grey rock. It was closed—as I knew it would be. But did I dream it or did I hear, echoing through it as though from vast distances a triumphant shouting?

"I ran back to Edith. At my touch she wakened; looked at me wanderingly; raised herself on a hand.

"'Dave!' she said, 'I slept—after all.' She saw the despair on my face and leaped to her feet. 'Dave!' she cried. 'What is it? Where's Charles?'

"I lighted a fire before I spoke. Then I told her. And for the balance of that night we sat before the flames, arms around each other—like two frightened children."

Abruptly Throckmartin held his hands out to me appealingly.

"Walter, old friend!" he cried. "Don't look at me as though I were mad. It's truth, absolute truth. Wait—" I comforted him as well as I could. After a little time he took up his story.

"Never," he said, "did man welcome the sun as we did that morning. As soon as it had risen we went back to the courtyard. The walls whereon I had seen Stanton were black and silent. The terraces were as they had been. The grey slab was in its place. In the shallow hollow at its base was—nothing. Nothing—nothing was there anywhere on the islet of Stanton—not a trace.

"What were we to do? Precisely the same arguments that had kept us there the night before held good now—and doubly good. We could not abandon these two; could not go as long as there was the faintest hope of finding them—and yet for love of each other how could we remain? I loved my wife,—how much I never knew until that day; and she loved me as deeply.

"'It takes only one each night,' she pleaded. 'Beloved, let it take me.'

"I wept, Walter. We both wept.

"'We will meet it together,' she said. And it was thus at last that we arranged it."

"That took great courage indeed, Throckmartin," I interrupted. He looked at me eagerly.

"You do believe then?" he exclaimed.

"I believe," I said. He pressed my hand with a grip that nearly crushed it.

"Now," he told me. "I do not fear. If I—fail, you will follow with help?"

I promised.

"We talked it over carefully," he went on, "bringing to bear all our power of analysis and habit of calm, scientific thought. We considered minutely the time element in the phenomena. Although the deep chanting began at the very moment of moonrise, fully five minutes had passed between its full lifting and the strange sighing sound from the inner terrace. I went back in memory over the happenings of the night before. At least ten minutes had intervened between the first heralding sigh and the intensification of the moonlight in the courtyard. And this glow grew for at least ten minutes more before the first burst of the crystal notes. Indeed, more than half an hour must have elapsed, I calculated, between the moment the moon showed above the horizon and the first delicate onslaught of the tinklings.

"'Edith!' I cried. 'I think I have it! The grey rock opens five minutes after upon the moonrise. But whoever or whatever it is that comes through it must wait until the moon has risen higher, or else it must come from a distance. The thing to do is not to wait for it, but to surprise it before it passes out the door. We will go into the inner court early. You will take your rifle and pistol and hide yourself where you can command the opening—if the slab does open. The instant it opens I will enter. It's our best chance, Edith. I think it's our only one.'

"My wife demurred strongly. She wanted to go with me. But I convinced her that it was better for her to stand guard without, prepared to help me if I were forced again into the open by what lay behind the rock.

"At the half-hour before moonrise we went into the inner court. I took my place at the side of the grey rock. Edith crouched behind a broken pillar twenty feet away; slipped her rifle-barrel over it so that it would cover the opening.

"The minutes crept by. The darkness lessened and through the breaches of the terrace I watched the far sky softly lighten. With the first pale flush the silence of the place intensified. It deepened; became unbearably—expectant. The moon rose, showed the quarter, the half, then swam up into full sight like a great bubble.

"Its rays fell upon the wall before me and suddenly upon the convexities I have described seven little circles of light sprang out. They gleamed, glimmered, grew brighter—shone. The gigantic slab before me glowed with them, silver wavelets of phosphorescence pulsed over its surface and then—it turned as though on a pivot, sighing softly as it moved!

"With a word to Edith I flung myself through the opening. A tunnel stretched before me. It glowed with the same faint silvery radiance. Down it I raced. The passage turned abruptly, passed parallel to the walls of the outer courtyard and then once more led downward.

"The passage ended. Before me was a high vaulted arch. It seemed to open into space; a space filled with lambent, coruscating, many-coloured mist whose brightness grew even as I watched. I passed through the arch and stopped in sheer awe!

"In front of me was a pool. It was circular, perhaps twenty feet wide. Around it ran a low, softly curved lip of glimmering silvery stone. Its water was palest blue. The pool with its silvery rim was like a great blue eye staring upward.

"Upon it streamed seven shafts of radiance. They poured down upon the blue eye like cylindrical torrents; they were like shining pillars of light rising from a sapphire floor.

"One was the tender pink of the pearl; one of the aurora's green; a third a deathly white; the fourth the blue in mother-of-pearl; a shimmering column of pale amber; a beam of amethyst; a shaft of molten silver. Such are the colours of the seven lights that stream upon the Moon Pool. I drew closer, awestricken. The shafts did not illumine the depths. They played upon the surface and seemed there to diffuse, to melt into it. The Pool drank them?

"Through the water tiny gleams of phosphorescence began to dart, sparkles and coruscations of pale incandescence. And far, far below I sensed a movement, a shifting glow as of a radiant body slowly rising.

"I looked upward, following the radiant pillars to their source. Far above were seven shining globes, and it was from these that the rays poured. Even as I watched their brightness grew. They were like seven moons set high in some caverned heaven. Slowly their splendour increased, and with it the splendour of the seven beams streaming from them.

"I tore my gaze away and stared at the Pool. It had grown milky, opalescent. The rays gushing into it seemed to be filling it; it was alive with sparklings, scintillations, glimmerings. And the luminescence I had seen rising from its depths was larger, nearer!

"A swirl of mist floated up from its surface. It drifted within the embrace of the rosy beam and hung there for a moment. The beam seemed to embrace it, sending through it little shining corpuscles, tiny rosy spiralings. The mist absorbed the rays, was strengthened by them, gained substance. Another swirl sprang into the amber shaft, clung and fed there, moved swiftly toward the first and mingled with it. And now other swirls arose, here and there, too fast to be counted; hung poised in the embrace of the light streams; flashed and pulsed into each other.

"Thicker and thicker still they arose until over the surface of the Pool was a pulsating pillar of opalescent mist steadily growing stronger; drawing within it life from the seven beams falling upon it; drawing to it from below the darting, incandescent atoms of the Pool. Into its centre was passing the luminescence rising from the far depths. And the pillar glowed, throbbed—began to send out questing swirls and tendrils—

"There forming before me was That which had walked with Stanton, which had taken Thora—the thing I had come to find!

"My brain sprang into action. My hand threw up the pistol and I fired shot after shot into the shining core.

"As I fired, it swayed and shook; gathered again. I slipped a second clip into the automatic and another idea coming to me took careful aim at one of the globes in the roof. From thence I knew came the force that shaped this Dweller in the Pool—from the pouring rays came its strength. If I could destroy them I could check its forming. I fired again and again. If I hit the globes I did no damage. The little motes in their beams danced with the motes in the mist, troubled. That was all.

"But up from the Pool like little bells, like tiny bursting bubbles of glass, swarmed the tinkling sounds—their pitch higher, all their sweetness lost, angry.

"And out from the Inexplicable swept a shining spiral.

"It caught me above the heart; wrapped itself around me. There rushed through me a mingled ecstasy and horror. Every atom of me quivered with delight and shrank with despair. There was nothing loathsome in it. But it was as though the icy soul of evil and the fiery soul of good had stepped together within me. The pistol dropped from my hand.

"So I stood while the Pool gleamed and sparkled; the streams of light grew more intense and the radiant Thing that held me gleamed and strengthened. Its shining core had shape—but a shape that my eyes and brain could not define. It was as though a being of another sphere should assume what it might of human semblance, but was not able to conceal that what human eyes saw was but a part of it. It was neither man nor woman; it was unearthly and androgynous. Even as I found its human semblance it changed. And still the mingled rapture and terror held me. Only in a little corner of my brain dwelt something untouched; something that held itself apart and watched. Was it the soul? I have never believed—and yet—

"Over the head of the misty body there sprang suddenly out seven little lights. Each was the colour of the beam beneath which it rested. I knew now that the Dweller was—complete!

"I heard a scream. It was Edith's voice. It came to me that she had heard the shots and followed me. I felt every faculty concentrate into a mighty effort. I wrenched myself free from the gripping tentacle and it swept back. I turned to catch Edith, and as I did so slipped—fell.

"The radiant shape above the Pool leaped swiftly—and straight into it raced Edith, arms outstretched to shield me from it! God!

"She threw herself squarely within its splendour," he whispered. "It wrapped its shining self around her. The crystal tinklings burst forth jubilantly. The light filled her, ran through and around her as it had with Stanton; and dropped down upon her face—the look!

"But her rush had taken her to the very verge of the Moon Pool. She tottered; she fell—with the radiance still holding her, still swirling and winding around and through her—into the Moon Pool! She sank, and with her went—the Dweller!

"I dragged myself to the brink. Far down was a shining, many-coloured nebulous cloud descending; out of it peered Edith's face, disappearing; her eyes stared up at me—and she vanished!

"'Edith!' I cried again. 'Edith, come back to me!'

"And then a darkness fell upon me. I remember running back through the shimmering corridors and out into the courtyard. Reason had left me. When it returned I was far out at sea in our boat wholly estranged from civilization. A day later I was picked up by the schooner in which I came to Port Moresby.

"I have formed a plan; you must hear it, Goodwin—" He fell upon his berth. I bent over him. Exhaustion and the relief of telling his story had been too much for him. He slept like the dead.

All that night I watched over him. When dawn broke I went to my room to get a little sleep myself. But my slumber was haunted.

The next day the storm was unabated. Throckmartin came to me at lunch. He had regained much of his old alertness.

"Come to my cabin," he said. There, he stripped his shirt from him. "Something is happening," he said. "The mark is smaller." It was as he said.

"I'm escaping," he whispered jubilantly, "Just let me get to Melbourne safely, and then we'll see who'll win! For, Walter, I'm not at all sure that Edith is dead—as we know death—nor that the others are. There is something outside experience there—some great mystery."

And all that day he talked to me of his plans.

"There's a natural explanation, of course," he said. "My theory is that the moon rock is of some composition sensitive to the action of moon rays; somewhat as the metal selenium is to sun rays. The little circles over the top are, without doubt, its operating agency. When the light strikes them they release the mechanism that opens the slab, just as you can open doors with sun or electric light by an ingenious arrangement of selenium-cells. Apparently it takes the strength of the full moon both to do this and to summon the Dweller in the Pool. We will first try a concentration of the rays of the waning moon upon these circles to see whether that will open the rock. If it does we will be able to investigate the Pool without interruption from—from—what emanates.

"Look, here on the chart are their locations. I have made this in duplicate for you in the event—of something happening—to me. And if I lose—you'll come after us, Goodwin, with help—won't you?"

And again I promised.

A little later he complained of increasing sleepiness.

"But it's just weariness," he said. "Not at all like that other drowsiness. It's an hour till moonrise still," he yawned at last. "Wake me up a good fifteen minutes before."

He lay upon the berth. I sat thinking. I came to myself with a guilty start. I had completely lost myself in my deep preoccupation. What time was it? I looked at my watch and jumped to the port-hole. It was full moonlight; the orb had been up for fully half an hour. I strode over to Throckmartin and shook him by the shoulder.

"Up, quick, man!" I cried. He rose sleepily. His shirt fell open at the neck and I looked, in amazement, at the white band around his chest. Even under the electric light it shone softly, as though little flecks of light were in it.

Throckmartin seemed only half-awake. He looked down at his breast, saw the glowing cincture, and smiled.

"Yes," he said drowsily, "it's coming—to take me back to Edith! Well, I'm glad."

"Throckmartin!" I cried. "Wake up! Fight!"

"Fight!" he said. "No use; come after us!"

He went to the port and sleepily drew aside the curtain. The moon traced a broad path of light straight to the ship. Under its rays the band around his chest gleamed brighter and brighter; shot forth little rays; seemed to writhe.

The lights went out in the cabin; evidently also throughout the ship, for I heard shoutings above.

Throckmartin still stood at the open port. Over his shoulder I saw a gleaming pillar racing along the moon path toward us. Through the window cascaded a blinding radiance. It gathered Throckmartin to it, clothed him in a robe of living opalescence. Light pulsed through and from him. The cabin filled with murmurings—

A wave of weakness swept over me, buried me in blackness. When consciousness came back, the lights were again burning brightly.

But of Throckmartin there was no trace!

VI

"The Shining Devil Took Them!"

My colleagues of the Association, and you others who may read
this my narrative, for what I did and did not when full realization
returned I must offer here, briefly as I can, an explanation; a defense—if
you will.

My first act was to spring to the open port. The coma had lasted
hours, for the moon was now low in the west! I ran to the door to
sound the alarm. It resisted under my frantic hands; would not open.
Something fell tinkling to the floor. It was the key and I remembered
then that Throckmartin had turned it before we began our vigil. With
memory a hope died that I had not known was in me, the hope that he
had escaped from the cabin, found refuge elsewhere on the ship.

And as I stooped, fumbling with shaking fingers for the key, a
thought came to me that drove again the blood from my heart,
held me rigid. I could sound no alarm on the Southern Queen for
Throckmartin!

Conviction of my appalling helplessness was complete. The ensemble
of the vessel from captain to cabin boy was, to put it conservatively,
average. None, I knew, save Throckmartin and myself had seen the first
apparition of the Dweller. Had they witnessed the second? I did not
know, nor could I risk speaking, not knowing. And not seeing, how
could they believe? They would have thought me insane—or worse;
even, it might be, his murderer.

I snapped off the electrics; waited and listened; opened the door with
infinite caution and slipped, unseen, into my own stateroom. The hours
until the dawn were eternities of waking nightmare. Reason, resuming
sway at last, steadied me. Even had I spoken and been believed where
in these wastes after all the hours could we search for Throckmartin?
Certainly the captain would not turn back to Port Moresby. And even
if he did, of what use for me to set forth for the Nan-Matal without the
equipment which Throckmartin himself had decided was necessary if
one hoped to cope with the mystery that lurked there?

There was but one thing to do—follow his instructions; get the
paraphernalia in Melbourne or Sydney if it were possible; if not sail to

America as swiftly as might be, secure it there and as swiftly return to Ponape. And this I determined to do.

Calmness came back to me after I had made this decision. And when I went up on deck I knew that I had been right. They had not seen the Dweller. They were still discussing the darkening of the ship, talking of dynamos burned out, wires short circuited, a half dozen explanations of the extinguishment. Not until noon was Throckmartin's absence discovered. I told the captain that I had left him early in the evening; that, indeed, I knew him but slightly, after all. It occurred to none to doubt me, or to question me minutely. Why should it have? His strangeness had been noted, commented upon; all who had met him had thought him half mad. I did little to discourage the impression. And so it came naturally that on the log it was entered that he had fallen or leaped from the vessel sometime during the night.

A report to this effect was made when we entered Melbourne. I slipped quietly ashore and in the press of the war news Throckmartin's supposed fate won only a few lines in the newspapers; my own presence on the ship and in the city passed unnoticed.

I was fortunate in securing at Melbourne everything I needed except a set of Becquerel ray condensers—but these were the very keystone of my equipment. Pursuing my search to Sydney I was doubly fortunate in finding a firm who were expecting these very articles in a consignment due them from the States within a fortnight. I settled down in strictest seclusion to await their arrival.

And now it will occur to you to ask why I did not cable, during this period of waiting, to the Association; demand aid from it. Or why I did not call upon members of the University staffs of either Melbourne or Sydney for assistance. At the least, why I did not gather, as Throckmartin had hoped to do, a little force of strong men to go with me to the Nan-Matal.

To the first two questions I answer frankly—I did not dare. And this reluctance, this inhibition, every man jealous of his scientific reputation will understand. The story of Throckmartin, the happenings I had myself witnessed, were incredible, abnormal, outside the facts of all known science. I shrank from the inevitable disbelief, perhaps ridicule—nay, perhaps even the graver suspicion that had caused me to seal my lips while on the ship. Why I myself could only half believe! How then could I hope to convince others?

And as for the third question—I could not take men into the range of such a peril without first warning them of what they might encounter; and if I did warn them—

It was checkmate! If it also was cowardice—well, I have atoned for it. But I do not hold it so; my conscience is clear.

That fortnight and the greater part of another passed before the ship I awaited steamed into port. By that time, between my straining anxiety to be after Throckmartin, the despairing thought that every moment of delay might be vital to him and his, and my intensely eager desire to know whether that shining, glorious horror on the moon path did exist or had been hallucination, I was worn almost to the edge of madness.

At last the condensers were in my hands. It was more than a week later, however, before I could secure passage back to Port Moresby and it was another week still before I started north on the Suwarna, a swift little sloop with a fifty-horsepower auxiliary, heading straight for Ponape and the Nan-Matal.

We sighted the Brunhilda some five hundred miles south of the Carolines. The wind had fallen soon after Papua had dropped astern. The Suwarna's ability to make her twelve knots an hour without it had made me very fully forgive her for not being as fragrant as the Javan flower for which she was named. Da Costa, her captain, was a garrulous Portuguese; his mate was a Canton man with all the marks of long and able service on some pirate junk; his engineer was a half-breed China-Malay who had picked up his knowledge of power plants, Heaven alone knew where, and, I had reason to believe, had transferred all his religious impulses to the American built deity of mechanism he so faithfully served. The crew was made up of six huge, chattering Tonga boys.

The Suwarna had cut through Finschafen Huon Gulf to the protection of the Bismarcks. She had threaded the maze of the archipelago tranquilly, and we were then rolling over the thousand-mile stretch of open ocean with New Hanover far behind us and our boat's bow pointed straight toward Nukuor of the Monte Verdes. After we had rounded Nukuor we should, barring accident, reach Ponape in not more than sixty hours.

It was late afternoon, and on the demure little breeze that marched behind us came far-flung sighs of spice-trees and nutmeg flowers. The slow prodigious swells of the Pacific lifted us in gentle, giant hands and sent us as gently down the long, blue wave slopes to the next broad, upward slope. There was a spell of peace over the ocean, stilling even the Portuguese captain who stood dreamily at the wheel, slowly swaying to the rhythmic lift and fall of the sloop.

There came a whining hail from the Tonga boy lookout draped lazily over the bow.

"Sail he b'long port side!"

Da Costa straightened and gazed while I raised my glass. The vessel was a scant mile away, and must have been visible long before the sleepy watcher had seen her. She was a sloop about the size of the Suwarna, without power. All sails set, even to a spinnaker she carried, she was making the best of the little breeze. I tried to read her name, but the vessel jibed sharply as though the hands of the man at the wheel had suddenly dropped the helm—and then with equal abruptness swung back to her course. The stern came in sight, and on it I read Brunhilda.

I shifted my glasses to the man at wheel. He was crouching down over the spokes in a helpless, huddled sort of way, and even as I looked the vessel veered again, abruptly as before. I saw the helmsman straighten up and bring the wheel about with a vicious jerk.

He stood so for a moment, looking straight ahead, entirely oblivious of us, and then seemed again to sink down within himself. It came to me that his was the action of a man striving vainly against a weariness unutterable. I swept the deck with my glasses. There was no other sign of life. I turned to find the Portuguese staring intently and with puzzled air at the sloop, now separated from us by a scant half mile.

"Something veree wrong I think there, sair," he said in his curious English. "The man on deck I know. He is captain and owner of the Br-rwun'ild. His name Olaf Huldricksson, what you say—Norwegian. He is eithair veree sick or veree tired—but I do not undweerstand where is the crew and the starb'd boat is gone—"

He shouted an order to the engineer and as he did so the faint breeze failed and the sails of the Brunhilda flapped down inert. We were now nearly abreast and a scant hundred yards away. The engine of the Suwarna died and the Tonga boys leaped to one of the boats.

"You Olaf Huldricksson!" shouted Da Costa. "What's a matter wit' you?"

The man at the wheel turned toward us. He was a giant; his shoulders enormous, thick chested, strength in every line of him, he towered like a viking of old at the rudder bar of his shark ship.

I raised the glass again; his face sprang into the lens and never have

I seen a visage lined and marked as though by ages of unsleeping misery as was that of Olaf Huldricksson!

The Tonga boys had the boat alongside and were waiting at the oars. The little captain was dropping into it.

"Wait!" I cried. I ran into my cabin, grasped my emergency medical kit and climbed down the rope ladder. The Tonga boys bent to the oars. We reached the side and Da Costa and I each seized a lanyard dangling from the stays and swung ourselves on board. Da Costa approached Huldricksson softly.

"What's the matter, Olaf?" he began—and then was silent, looking down at the wheel. The hands of Huldricksson were lashed fast to the spokes by thongs of thin, strong cord; they were swollen and black and the thongs had bitten into the sinewy wrists till they were hidden in the outraged flesh, cutting so deeply that blood fell, slow drop by drop, at his feet! We sprang toward him, reaching out hands to his fetters to loose them. Even as we touched them, Huldricksson aimed a vicious kick at me and then another at Da Costa which sent the Portuguese tumbling into the scuppers.

"Let be!" croaked Huldricksson; his voice was thick and lifeless as though forced from a dead throat; his lips were cracked and dry and his parched tongue was black. "Let be! Go! Let be!"

The Portuguese had picked himself up, whimpering with rage and knife in hand, but as Huldricksson's voice reached him he stopped. Amazement crept into his eyes and as he thrust the blade back into his belt they softened with pity.

"Something veree wrong wit' Olaf," he murmured to me. "I think he crazee!" And then Olaf Huldricksson began to curse us. He did not speak—he howled from that hideously dry mouth his imprecations. And all the time his red eyes roamed the seas and his hands, clenched and rigid on the wheel, dropped blood.

"I go below," said Da Costa nervously. "His wife, his daughter—" he darted down the companionway and was gone.

Huldricksson, silent once more, had slumped down over the wheel.

Da Costa's head appeared at the top of the companion steps.

"There is nobody, nobody," he paused—then—"nobody—nowhere!" His hands flew out in a gesture of hopeless incomprehension. "I do not understan'."

Then Olaf Huldricksson opened his dry lips and as he spoke a chill ran through me, checking my heart.

"The sparkling devil took them!" croaked Olaf Huldricksson, "the sparkling devil took them! Took my Helma and my little Freda! The sparkling devil came down from the moon and took them!"

He swayed; tears dripped down his cheeks. Da Costa moved toward him again and again Huldricksson watched him, alertly, wickedly, from his bloodshot eyes.

I took a hypodermic from my case and filled it with morphine. I drew Da Costa to me.

"Get to the side of him," I whispered, "talk to him." He moved over toward the wheel.

"Where is your Helma and Freda, Olaf?" he said.

Huldricksson turned his head toward him. "The shining devil took them," he croaked. "The moon devil that spark—"

A yell broke from him. I had thrust the needle into his arm just above one swollen wrist and had quickly shot the drug through. He struggled to release himself and then began to rock drunkenly. The morphine, taking him in his weakness, worked quickly. Soon over his face a peace dropped. The pupils of the staring eyes contracted. Once, twice, he swayed and then, his bleeding, prisoned hands held high and still gripping the wheel, he crumpled to the deck.

With utmost difficulty we loosed the thongs, but at last it was done. We rigged a little swing and the Tonga boys slung the great inert body over the side into the dory. Soon we had Huldricksson in my bunk. Da Costa sent half his crew over to the sloop in charge of the Cantonese. They took in all sail, stripping Huldricksson's boat to the masts and then with the Brunhilda nosing quietly along after us at the end of a long hawser, one of the Tonga boys at her wheel, we resumed the way so enigmatically interrupted.

I cleansed and bandaged the Norseman's lacerated wrists and sponged the blackened, parched mouth with warm water and a mild antiseptic.

Suddenly I was aware of Da Costa's presence and turned. His unease was manifest and held, it seemed to me, a queer, furtive anxiety.

"What you think of Olaf, sair?" he asked. I shrugged my shoulders. "You think he killed his woman and his babee?" He went on. "You think he crazee and killed all?"

"Nonsense, Da Costa," I answered. "You saw the boat was gone. Most probably his crew mutinied and to torture him tied him up the way you saw. They did the same thing with Hilton of the Coral Lady; you'll remember."

"No," he said. "No. The crew did not. Nobody there on board when Olaf was tied."

"What!" I cried, startled. "What do you mean?"

"I mean," he said slowly, "that Olaf tie himself!"

"Wait!" he went on at my incredulous gesture of dissent. "Wait, I show you." He had been standing with hands behind his back and now I saw that he held in them the cut thongs that had bound Huldricksson. They were blood-stained and each ended in a broad leather tip skilfully spliced into the cord. "Look," he said, pointing to these leather ends. I looked and saw in them deep indentations of teeth. I snatched one of the thongs and opened the mouth of the unconscious man on the bunk. Carefully I placed the leather within it and gently forced the jaws shut on it. It was true. Those marks were where Olaf Huldricksson's jaws had gripped.

"Wait!" Da Costa repeated, "I show you." He took other cords and rested his hands on the supports of a chair back. Rapidly he twisted one of the thongs around his left hand, drew a loose knot, shifted the cord up toward his elbow. This left wrist and hand still free and with them he twisted the other cord around the right wrist; drew a similar knot. His hands were now in the exact position that Huldricksson's had been on the Brunhilda but with cords and knots hanging loose. Then Da Costa reached down his head, took a leather end in his teeth and with a jerk drew the thong that noosed his left hand tight; similarly he drew tight the second.

He strained at his fetters. There before my eyes he had pinioned himself so that without aid he could not release himself. And he was exactly as Huldricksson had been!

"You will have to cut me loose, sair," he said. "I cannot move them. It is an old trick on these seas. Sometimes it is necessary that a man stand at the wheel many hours without help, and he does this so that if he sleep the wheel wake him, yes, sair."

I looked from him to the man on the bed.

"But why, sair," said Da Costa slowly, "did Olaf have to tie his hands?"

I looked at him, uneasily.

"I don't know," I answered. "Do you?"

He fidgeted, avoided my eyes, and then rapidly, almost surreptitiously crossed himself.

"No," he replied. "I know nothing. Some things I have heard—but they tell many tales on these seas."

He started for the door. Before he reached it he turned. "But this I do know," he half whispered, "I am damned glad there is no full moon tonight." And passed out, leaving me staring after him in amazement. What did the Portuguese know?

I bent over the sleeper. On his face was no trace of that unholy mingling of opposites the Dweller stamped upon its victims.

And yet—what was it the Norseman had said?

"The sparkling devil took them!" Nay, he had been even more explicit—"The sparkling devil that came down from the moon!"

Could it be that the Dweller had swept upon the Brunhilda, drawing down the moon path Olaf Huldricksson's wife and babe even as it had drawn Throckmartin?

As I sat thinking the cabin grew suddenly dark and from above came a shouting and patter of feet. Down upon us swept one of the abrupt, violent squalls that are met with in those latitudes. I lashed Huldricksson fast in the berth and ran up on deck.

The long, peaceful swells had changed into angry, choppy waves from the tops of which the spindrift streamed in long stinging lashes.

A half-hour passed; the squall died as quickly as it had arisen. The sea quieted. Over in the west, from beneath the tattered, flying edge of the storm, dropped the red globe of the setting sun; dropped slowly until it touched the sea rim.

I watched it—and rubbed my eyes and stared again. For over its flaming portal something huge and black moved, like a gigantic beckoning finger!

Da Costa had seen it, too, and he turned the Suwarna straight toward the descending orb and its strange shadow. As we approached we saw it was a little mass of wreckage and that the beckoning finger was a wing of canvas, sticking up and swaying with the motion of the waves. On the highest point of the wreckage sat a tall figure calmly smoking a cigarette.

We brought the Suwarna to, dropped a boat, and with myself as coxswain pulled toward a wrecked hydroairplane. Its occupant took a long puff at his cigarette, waved a cheerful hand, shouted a greeting. And just as he did so a great wave raised itself up behind him, took the wreckage, tossed it high in a swelter of foam, and passed on. When we had steadied our boat, where wreck and man had been was—nothing.

There came a tug at the side—, two muscular brown hands gripped it close to my left, and a sleek, black, wet head showed its top between them. Two bright, blue eyes that held deep within them a laughing deviltry looked into mine, and a long, lithe body drew itself gently over the thwart and seated its dripping self at my feet.

"Much obliged," said this man from the sea. "I knew somebody was sure to come along when the O'Keefe banshee didn't show up."

"The what?" I asked in amazement.

"The O'Keefe banshee—I'm Larry O'Keefe. It's a far way from Ireland, but not too far for the O'Keefe banshee to travel if the O'Keefe was going to click in."

I looked again at my astonishing rescue. He seemed perfectly serious.

"Have you a cigarette? Mine went out," he said with a grin, as he reached a moist hand out for the little cylinder, took it, lighted it.

I saw a lean, intelligent face whose fighting jaw was softened by the wistfulness of the clean-cut lips and the honesty that lay side by side with the deviltry in the laughing blue eyes; nose of a thoroughbred with the suspicion of a tilt; long, well-knit, slender figure that I knew must have all the strength of fine steel; the uniform of a lieutenant in the Royal Flying Corps of Britain's navy.

He laughed, stretched out a firm hand, and gripped mine.

"Thank you really ever so much, old man," he said.

I liked Larry O'Keefe from the beginning—but I did not dream as the Tonga boys pulled us back to the Suwarna bow that liking was to be forged into man's strong love for man by fires which souls such as his and mine—and yours who read this—could never dream.

Larry! Larry O'Keefe, where are you now with your leprechauns and banshee, your heart of a child, your laughing blue eyes, and your fearless soul? Shall I ever see you again, Larry O'Keefe, dear to me as some best beloved younger brother? Larry!

VII

LARRY O'KEEFE

Pressing back the questions I longed to ask, I introduced myself. Oddly enough, I found that he knew me, or rather my work. He had bought, it appeared, my volume upon the peculiar vegetation whose habitat is disintegrating lava rock and volcanic ash, that I had entitled, somewhat loosely, I could now perceive, Flora of the Craters. For he explained naively that he had picked it up, thinking it an entirely different sort of a book, a novel in fact—something like Meredith's Diana of the Crossways, which he liked greatly.

He had hardly finished this explanation when we touched the side of the Suwarna, and I was forced to curb my curiosity until we reached the deck.

"That thing you saw me sitting on," he said, after he had thanked the bowing little skipper for his rescue, "was all that was left of one of his Majesty's best little hydroairplanes after that cyclone threw it off as excess baggage. And by the way, about where are we?"

Da Costa gave him our approximate position from the noon reckoning.

O'Keefe whistled. "A good three hundred miles from where I left the H.M.S. Dolphin about four hours ago," he said. "That squall I rode in on was some whizzer!

"The Dolphin," he went on, calmly divesting himself of his soaked uniform, "was on her way to Melbourne. I'd been yearning for a joy ride and went up for an alleged scouting trip. Then that blow shot out of nowhere, picked me up, and insisted that I go with it.

"About an hour ago I thought I saw a chance to zoom up and out of it, I turned, and *blick* went my right wing, and down I dropped."

"I don't know how we can notify your ship, Lieutenant O'Keefe," I said. "We have no wireless."

"Doctair Goodwin," said Da Costa, "we could change our course, sair—perhaps—"

"Thanks—but not a bit of it," broke in O'Keefe. "Lord alone knows where the Dolphin is now. Fancy she'll be nosing around looking for me. Anyway, she's just as apt to run into you as you into her. Maybe we'll strike something with a wireless, and I'll trouble you to put me aboard." He hesitated. "Where are you bound, by the way?" he asked.

"For Ponape," I answered.

"No wireless there," mused O'Keefe. "Beastly hole. Stopped a week ago for fruit. Natives seemed scared to death at us—or something. What are you going there for?"

Da Costa darted a furtive glance at me. It troubled me.

O'Keefe noted my hesitation.

"Oh, I beg your pardon," he said. "Maybe I oughn't to have asked that?"

"It's no secret, Lieutenant," I replied. "I'm about to undertake some exploration work—a little digging among the ruins on the Nan-Matal."

I looked at the Portuguese sharply as I named the place. A pallor crept beneath his skin and again he made swiftly the sign of the cross, glancing as he did so fearfully to the north. I made up my mind then to question him when opportunity came. He turned from his quick scrutiny of the sea and addressed O'Keefe.

"There's nothing on board to fit you, Lieutenant."

"Oh, just give me a sheet to throw around me, Captain," said O'Keefe and followed him. Darkness had fallen, and as the two disappeared into Da Costa's cabin I softly opened the door of my own and listened. Huldricksson was breathing deeply and regularly.

I drew my electric-flash, and shielding its rays from my face, looked at him. His sleep was changing from the heavy stupor of the drug into one that was at least on the borderland of the normal. The tongue had lost its arid blackness and the mouth secretions had resumed action. Satisfied as to his condition I returned to deck.

O'Keefe was there, looking like a spectre in the cotton sheet he had wrapped about him. A deck table had been cleated down and one of the Tonga boys was setting it for our dinner. Soon the very creditable larder of the Suwarna dressed the board, and O'Keefe, Da Costa, and I attacked it. The night had grown close and oppressive. Behind us the forward light of the Brunhilda glided and the binnacle lamp threw up a faint glow in which her black helmsman's face stood out mistily. O'Keefe had looked curiously a number of times at our tow, but had asked no questions.

"You're not the only passenger we picked up today," I told him. "We found the captain of that sloop, lashed to his wheel, nearly dead with exhaustion, and his boat deserted by everyone except himself."

"What was the matter?" asked O'Keefe in astonishment.

"We don't know," I answered. "He fought us, and I had to drug him before we could get him loose from his lashings. He's sleeping down in my berth now. His wife and little girl ought to have been on board, the captain here says, but—they weren't."

"Wife and child gone!" exclaimed O'Keefe.

"From the condition of his mouth he must have been alone at the wheel and without water at least two days and nights before we found him," I replied. "And as for looking for anyone on these waters after such a time—it's hopeless."

"That's true," said O'Keefe. "But his wife and baby! Poor, poor devil!"

He was silent for a time, and then, at my solicitation, began to tell us more of himself. He had been little more than twenty when he had won his wings and entered the war. He had been seriously wounded at Ypres during the third year of the struggle, and when he recovered the war was over. Shortly after that his mother had died. Lonely and restless, he had re-entered the Air Service, and had remained in it ever since.

"And though the war's long over, I get homesick for the lark's land with the German planes playing tunes on their machine guns and their Archies tickling the soles of my feet," he sighed. "If you're in love, love to the limit; and if you hate, why hate like the devil and if it's a fight you're in, get where it's hottest and fight like hell—if you don't life's not worth the living," sighed he.

I watched him as he talked, feeling my liking for him steadily increasing. If I could but have a man like this beside me on the path of unknown peril upon which I had set my feet I thought, wistfully. We sat and smoked a bit, sipping the strong coffee the Portuguese made so well.

Da Costa at last relieved the Cantonese at the wheel. O'Keefe and I drew chairs up to the rail. The brighter stars shone out dimly through a hazy sky; gleams of phosphorescence tipped the crests of the waves and sparkled with an almost angry brilliance as the bow of the Suwarna tossed them aside. O'Keefe pulled contentedly at a cigarette. The glowing spark lighted the keen, boyish face and the blue eyes, now black and brooding under the spell of the tropic night.

"Are you American or Irish, O'Keefe?" I asked suddenly.

"Why?" he laughed.

"Because," I answered, "from your name and your service I would suppose you Irish—but your command of pure Americanese makes me doubtful."

He grinned amiably.

"I'll tell you how that is," he said. "My mother was an American—a Grace, of Virginia. My father was the O'Keefe, of Coleraine. And these two loved each other so well that the heart they gave me is half Irish and half American. My father died when I was sixteen. I used to go to the States with my mother every other year for a month or two. But after my father died we used to go to Ireland every other year. And there you are—I'm as much American as I am Irish.

"When I'm in love, or excited, or dreaming, or mad I have the brogue. But for the everyday purpose of life I like the United States talk, and I know Broadway as well as I do Binevenagh Lane, and the Sound as well as St. Patrick's Channel; educated a bit at Eton, a bit at Harvard; always too much money to have to make any; in love lots of times, and never a heartache after that wasn't a pleasant one, and never a real purpose in life until I took the king's shilling and earned my wings; something over thirty—and that's me—Larry O'Keefe."

"But it was the Irish O'Keefe who sat out there waiting for the banshee," I laughed.

"It was that," he said somberly, and I heard the brogue creep over his voice like velvet and his eyes grew brooding again. "There's never an O'Keefe for these thousand years that has passed without his warning. An' twice have I heard the banshee calling—once it was when my younger brother died an' once when my father lay waiting to be carried out on the ebb tide."

He mused a moment, then went on: "An' once I saw an Annir Choille, a girl of the green people, flit like a shade of green fire through Carntogher woods, an' once at Dunchraig I slept where the ashes of the Dun of Cormac MacConcobar are mixed with those of Cormac an' Eilidh the Fair, all burned in the nine flames that sprang from the harping of Cravetheen, an' I heard the echo of his dead harpings—"

He paused again and then, softly, with that curiously sweet, high voice that only the Irish seem to have, he sang:

Woman of the white breasts, Eilidh;
Woman of the gold-brown hair, and lips of the red, red rowan,
Where is the swan that is whiter, with breast more soft,
Or the wave on the sea that moves as thou movest, Eilidh.

VIII

Olaf's Story

There was a little silence. I looked upon him with wonder. Clearly he was in deepest earnest. I know the psychology of the Gael is a curious one and that deep in all their hearts their ancient traditions and beliefs have strong and living roots. And I was both amused and touched.

Here was this soldier, who had faced war and its ugly realities open-eyed and fearless, picking, indeed, the most dangerous branch of service for his own, a modern if ever there was one, appreciative of most unmystical Broadway, and yet soberly and earnestly attesting to his belief in banshee, in shadowy people of the woods, and phantom harpers! I wondered what he would think if he could see the Dweller and then, with a pang, that perhaps his superstitions might make him an easy prey.

He shook his head half impatiently and ran a hand over his eyes; turned to me and grinned:

"Don't think I'm cracked, Professor," he said. "I'm not. But it takes me that way now and then. It's the Irish in me. And, believe it or not, I'm telling you the truth."

I looked eastward where the moon, now nearly a week past the full, was mounting.

"You can't make me see what you've seen, Lieutenant," I laughed. "But you can make me hear. I've always wondered what kind of a noise a disembodied spirit could make without any vocal cords or breath or any other earthly sound-producing mechanism. How does the banshee sound?"

O'Keefe looked at me seriously.

"All right," he said. "I'll show you." From deep down in his throat came first a low, weird sobbing that mounted steadily into a keening whose mournfulness made my skin creep. And then his hand shot out and gripped my shoulder, and I stiffened like stone in my chair—for from behind us, like an echo, and then taking up the cry, swelled a wail that seemed to hold within it a sublimation of the sorrows of centuries! It gathered itself into one heartbroken, sobbing note and died away! O'Keefe's grip loosened, and he rose swiftly to his feet.

"It's all right, Professor," he said. "It's for me. It found me—all this way from Ireland."

Again the silence was rent by the cry. But now I had located it. It came from my room, and it could mean only one thing—Huldricksson had wakened.

"Forget your banshee!" I gasped, and made a jump for the cabin.

Out of the corner of my eye I noted a look of half-sheepish relief flit over O'Keefe's face, and then he was beside me. Da Costa shouted an order from the wheel, the Cantonese ran up and took it from his hands and the little Portuguese pattered down toward us. My hand on the door, ready to throw it open, I stopped. What if the Dweller were within—what if we had been wrong and it was not dependent for its power upon that full flood of moon ray which Throckmartin had thought essential to draw it from the blue pool!

From within, the sobbing wail began once more to rise. O'Keefe pushed me aside, threw open the door and crouched low within it. I saw an automatic flash dully in his hand; saw it cover the cabin from side to side, following the swift sweep of his eyes around it. Then he straightened and his face, turned toward the berth, was filled with wondering pity.

Through the window streamed a shaft of the moonlight. It fell upon Huldricksson's staring eyes; in them great tears slowly gathered and rolled down his cheeks; from his opened mouth came the woe-laden wailing. I ran to the port and drew the curtains. Da Costa snapped the lights.

The Norseman's dolorous crying stopped as abruptly as though cut. His gaze rolled toward us. And at one bound he broke through the leashes I had buckled round him and faced us, his eyes glaring, his yellow hair almost erect with the force of the rage visibly surging through him. Da Costa shrunk behind me. O'Keefe, coolly watchful, took a quick step that brought him in front of me.

"Where do you take me?" said Huldricksson, and his voice was like the growl of a beast. "Where is my boat?"

I touched O'Keefe gently and stood before the giant.

"Listen, Olaf Huldricksson," I said. "We take you to where the sparkling devil took your Helma and your Freda. We follow the sparkling devil that came down from the moon. Do you hear me?" I spoke slowly, distinctly, striving to pierce the mists that I knew swirled around the strained brain. And the words did pierce.

He thrust out a shaking hand.

"You say you follow?" he asked falteringly. "You know where to follow? Where it took my Helma and my little Freda?"

"Just that, Olaf Huldricksson," I answered. "Just that! I pledge you my life that I know."

Da Costa stepped forward. "He speaks true, Olaf. You go faster on the Suwarna than on the Br-rw-un'ilda, Olaf, yes."

The giant Norseman, still gripping my hand, looked at him. "I know you, Da Costa," he muttered. "You are all right. Ja! You are a fair man. Where is the Brunhilda?"

"She follow be'ind on a big rope, Olaf," soothed the Portuguese. "Soon you see her. But now lie down an' tell us, if you can, why you tie yourself to your wheel an' what it is that happen, Olaf."

"If you'll tell us how the sparkling devil came it will help us all when we get to where it is, Huldricksson," I said.

On O'Keefe's face there was an expression of well-nigh ludicrous doubt and amazement. He glanced from one to the other. The giant shifted his own tense look from me to the Irishman. A gleam of approval lighted in his eyes. He loosed me, and gripped O'Keefe's arm. "Staerk!" he said. "Ja—strong, and with a strong heart. A man—ja! He comes too—we shall need him—ja!"

"I tell," he muttered, and seated himself on the side of the bunk. "It was four nights ago. My Freda"—his voice shook—"Mine Yndling! She loved the moonlight. I was at the wheel and my Freda and my Helma they were behind me. The moon was behind us and the Brunhilda was like a swanboat sailing down with the moonlight sending her, ja.

"I heard my Freda say: 'I see a nisse coming down the track of the moon.' And I hear her mother laugh, low, like a mother does when her Yndling dreams. I was happy—that night—with my Helma and my Freda, and the Brunhilda sailing like a swan-boat, ja. I heard the child say, 'The nisse comes fast!' And then I heard a scream from my Helma, a great scream—like a mare when her foal is torn from her. I spun around fast, ja! I dropped the wheel and spun fast! I saw—" He covered his eyes with his hands.

The Portuguese had crept close to me, and I heard him panting like a frightened dog.

"I saw a white fire spring over the rail," whispered Olaf Huldricksson. "It whirled round and round, and it shone like—like stars in a whirlwind mist. There was a noise in my ears. It sounded like bells—little bells, ja!

Like the music you make when you run your finger round goblets. It made me sick and dizzy—the hell noise.

"My Helma was—indeholde—what you say—in the middle of the white fire. She turned her face to me and she turned it on the child, and my Helma's face burned into my heart. Because it was full of fear, and it was full of happiness—of glaede. I tell you that the fear in my Helma's face made me ice here"—he beat his breast with clenched hand—"but the happiness in it burned on me like fire. And I could not move—I could not move.

"I said in here"—he touched his head—"I said, 'It is Loki come out of Helvede. But he cannot take my Helma, for Christ lives and Loki has no power to hurt my Helma or my Freda! Christ lives! Christ lives!' I said. But the sparkling devil did not let my Helma go. It drew her to the rail; half over it. I saw her eyes upon the child and a little she broke away and reached to it. And my Freda jumped into her arms. And the fire wrapped them both and they were gone! A little I saw them whirling on the moon track behind the Brunhilda—and they were gone!

"The sparkling devil took them! Loki was loosed, and he had power. I turned the Brunhilda, and I followed where my Helma and mine Yndling had gone. My boys crept up and asked me to turn again. But I would not. They dropped a boat and left me. I steered straight on the path. I lashed my hands to the wheel that sleep might not loose them. I steered on and on and on—

"Where was the God I prayed when my wife and child were taken?" cried Olaf Huldricksson—and it was as though I heard Throckmartin asking that same bitter question. "I have left Him as He left me, ja! I pray now to Thor and to Odin, who can fetter Loki." He sank back, covering again his eyes.

"Olaf," I said, "what you have called the sparkling devil has taken ones dear to me. I, too, was following it when we found you. You shall go with me to its home, and there we will try to take from it your wife and your child and my friends as well. But now that you may be strong for what is before us, you must sleep again."

Olaf Huldricksson looked upon me and in his eyes was that something which souls must see in the eyes of Him the old Egyptians called the Searcher of Hearts in the Judgment Hall of Osiris.

"You speak truth!" he said at last slowly. "I will do what you say!"

He stretched out an arm at my bidding. I gave him a second injection. He lay back and soon he was sleeping. I turned toward Da

Costa. His face was livid and sweating, and he was trembling pitiably. O'Keefe stirred.

"You did that mighty well, Dr. Goodwin," he said. "So well that I almost believed you myself."

"What did you think of his story, Mr. O'Keefe?" I asked.

His answer was almost painfully brief and colloquial.

"Nuts!" he said. I was a little shocked, I admit. "I think he's crazy, Dr. Goodwin," he corrected himself, quickly. "What else could I think?"

I turned to the little Portuguese without answering.

"There's no need for any anxiety tonight, Captain," I said. "Take my word for it. You need some rest yourself. Shall I give you a sleeping draft?"

"I do wish you would, Dr. Goodwin, sair," he answered gratefully. "Tomorrow, when I feel bettair—I would have a talk with you."

I nodded. He did know something then! I mixed him an opiate of considerable strength. He took it and went to his own cabin.

I locked the door behind him and then, sitting beside the sleeping Norseman, I told O'Keefe my story from end to end. He asked few questions as I spoke. But after I had finished he cross-examined me rather minutely upon my recollections of the radiant phases upon each appearance, checking these with Throckmartin's observations of the same phenomena in the Chamber of the Moon Pool.

"And now what do you think of it all?" I asked.

He sat silent for a while, looking at Huldricksson.

"Not what you seem to think, Dr. Goodwin," he answered at last, gravely. "Let me sleep over it. One thing of course is certain—you and your friend Throckmartin and this man here saw—something. But—" he was silent again and then continued with a kindness that I found vaguely irritating—"but I've noticed that when a scientist gets superstitious it—er—takes very hard!

"Here's a few things I can tell you now though," he went on while I struggled to speak—"I pray in my heart that we'll meet neither the Dolphin nor anything with wireless on board going up. Because, Dr. Goodwin, I'd dearly love to take a crack at your Dweller.

"And another thing," said O'Keefe. "After this—cut out the trimmings, Doc, and call me plain Larry, for whether I think you're crazy or whether I don't, you're there with the nerve, Professor, and I'm for *you*.

A. MERRITT

"Goodnight!" said Larry and took himself out to the deck hammock he had insisted upon having slung for him, refusing the captain's importunities to use his own cabin.

And it was with extremely mixed emotions as to his compliment that I watched him go. Superstitious. I, whose pride was my scientific devotion to fact and fact alone! Superstitious—and this from a man who believed in banshees and ghostly harpers and Irish wood nymphs and no doubt in leprechauns and all their tribe!

Half laughing, half irritated, and wholly happy in even the part promise of Larry O'Keefe's comradeship on my venture, I arranged a couple of pillows, stretched myself out on two chairs and took up my vigil beside Olaf Huldricksson.

IX

A Lost Page of Earth

When I awakened the sun was streaming through the cabin porthole. Outside a fresh voice lilted. I lay on my two chairs and listened. The song was one with the wholesome sunshine and the breeze blowing stiffly and whipping the curtains. It was Larry O'Keefe at his matins:

> *The little red lark is shaking his wings,*
> *Straight from the breast of his love he springs*

Larry's voice soared.

> *His wings and his feathers are sunrise red,*
> *He hails the sun and his golden head,*
> *Good morning, Doc, you are long abed.*

This last was a most irreverent interpolation, I well knew. I opened my door. O'Keefe stood outside laughing. The Suwarna, her engines silent, was making fine headway under all sail, the Brunhilda skipping in her wake cheerfully with half her canvas up.

The sea was crisping and dimpling under the wind. Blue and white was the world as far as the eye could reach. Schools of little silvery green flying fish broke through the water rushing on each side of us; flashed for an instant and were gone. Behind us gulls hovered and dipped. The shadow of mystery had retreated far over the rim of this wide awake and beautiful world and if, subconsciously, I knew that somewhere it was brooding and waiting, for a little while at least I was consciously free of its oppression.

"How's the patient?" asked O'Keefe.

He was answered by Huldricksson himself, who must have risen just as I left the cabin. The Norseman had slipped on a pair of pajamas and, giant torso naked under the sun, he strode out upon us. We all of us looked at him a trifle anxiously. But Olaf's madness had left him. In his eyes was much sorrow, but the berserk rage was gone.

He spoke straight to me: "You said last night we follow?"

I nodded.

"It is where?" he asked again.

"We go first to Ponape and from there to Metalanim Harbour—to the Nan-Matal. You know the place?"

Huldricksson bowed—a white gleam as of ice showing in his blue eyes.

"It is there?" he asked.

"It is there that we must first search," I answered.

"Good!" said Olaf Huldricksson. "It is good!"

He looked at Da Costa inquiringly and the little Portuguese, following his thought, answered his unspoken question.

"We should be at Ponape tomorrow morning early, Olaf."

"Good!" repeated the Norseman. He looked away, his eyes tear-filled.

A restraint fell upon us; the embarrassment all men experience when they feel a great sympathy and a great pity, to neither of which they quite know how to give expression. By silent consent we discussed at breakfast only the most casual topics.

When the meal was over Huldricksson expressed a desire to go aboard the Brunhilda.

The Suwarna hove to and Da Costa and he dropped into the small boat. When they reached the Brunhilda's deck I saw Olaf take the wheel and the two fall into earnest talk. I beckoned to O'Keefe and we stretched ourselves out on the bow hatch under cover of the foresail. He lighted a cigarette, took a couple of leisurely puffs, and looked at me expectantly.

"Well?" I asked.

"Well," said O'Keefe, "suppose you tell me what you think—and then I'll proceed to point out your scientific errors." His eyes twinkled mischievously.

"Larry," I replied, somewhat severely, "you may not know that I have a scientific reputation which, putting aside all modesty, I may say is an enviable one. You used a word last night to which I must interpose serious objection. You more than hinted that I hid—superstitions. Let me inform you, Larry O'Keefe, that I am solely a seeker, observer, analyst, and synthesist of facts. I am not"—and I tried to make my tone as pointed as my words—"I am not a believer in phantoms or spooks, leprechauns, banshees, or ghostly harpers."

O'Keefe leaned back and shouted with laughter.

"Forgive me, Goodwin," he gasped. "But if you could have seen yourself solemnly disclaiming the banshee"—another twinkle showed in his eyes—"and then with all this sunshine and this wide-open world"—he shrugged his shoulders—"it's hard to visualize anything such as you and Huldricksson have described."

"I know how hard it is, Larry," I answered. "And don't think I have any idea that the phenomenon is supernatural in the sense spiritualists and table turners have given that word. I do think it is supernormal; energized by a force unknown to modern science—but that doesn't mean I think it outside the radius of science."

"Tell me your theory, Goodwin," he said. I hesitated—for not yet had I been able to put into form to satisfy myself any explanation of the Dweller.

"I think," I hazarded finally, "it is possible that some members of that race peopling the ancient continent which we know existed here in the Pacific, have survived. We know that many of these islands are honeycombed with caverns and vast subterranean spaces, literally underground lands running in some cases far out beneath the ocean floor. It is possible that for some reason survivors of this race sought refuge in the abysmal spaces, one of whose entrances is on the islet where Throckmartin's party met its end.

"As for their persistence in these caverns—we know they possessed a high science. They may have gone far in the mastery of certain universal forms of energy—especially that we call light. They may have developed a civilization and a science far more advanced than ours. What I call the Dweller may be one of the results of this science. Larry—it may well be that this lost race is planning to emerge again upon earth's surface!"

"And is sending out your Dweller as a messenger, a scientific dove from their Ark?" I chose to overlook the banter in his question.

"Did you ever hear of the Chamats?" I asked him. He shook his head.

"In Papua," I explained, "there is a wide-spread and immeasurably old tradition that 'imprisoned under the hills' is a race of giants who once ruled this region 'when it stretched from sun to sun before the moon god drew the waters over it'—I quote from the legend. Not only in Papua but throughout Malaysia you find this story. And, so the tradition runs, these people—the Chamats—will one day break through the hills and rule the world; 'make over the world' is the literal translation of the constant phrase in the tale. It was Herbert Spencer who pointed out that there is a basis of fact in every myth and legend of

A. MERRITT

man. It is possible that these survivors I am discussing form Spencer's fact basis for the Malaysian legend.[1]

"This much is sure—the moon door, which is clearly operated by the action of moon rays upon some unknown element or combination and the crystals through which the moon rays pour down upon the pool their prismatic columns, are humanly made mechanisms. So long as they are humanly made, and so long as it *is* this flood of moonlight from which the Dweller draws its power of materialization, the Dweller itself, if not the product of the human mind, is at least dependent upon the product of the human mind for its appearance."

"Wait a minute, Goodwin," interrupted O'Keefe. "Do you mean to say you think that this thing is made of—well—of moonshine?"

"Moonlight," I replied, "is, of course, reflected sunlight. But the rays which pass back to earth after their impact on the moon's surface are profoundly changed. The spectroscope shows that they lose practically all the slower vibrations we call red and infra-red, while the extremely rapid vibrations we call the violet and ultra-violet are accelerated and altered. Many scientists hold that there is an unknown element in the moon—perhaps that which makes the gigantic luminous trails that radiate in all directions from the lunar crater Tycho—whose energies are absorbed by and carried on the moon rays.

"At any rate, whether by the loss of the vibrations of the red or by the addition of this mysterious force, the light of the moon becomes something entirely different from mere modified sunlight—just as the addition or subtraction of one other chemical in a compound of several makes the product a substance with entirely different energies and potentialities.

"Now these rays, Larry, are given perhaps still another mysterious activity by the globes through which Throckmartin said they passed in the Chamber of the Moon Pool. The result is the necessary factor in the formation of the Dweller. There would be nothing scientifically improbable in such a process. Kubalski, the great Russian physicist, produced crystalline forms exhibiting every faculty that we call vital by subjecting certain combinations of chemicals to the action of highly

---

1. William Beebe, the famous American naturalist and ornithologist, recently fighting in France with America's air force, called attention to this remarkable belief in an article printed not long ago in the Atlantic Monthly. Still more significant was it that he noted a persistent rumour that the breaking out of the buried race was close.—W.J. B., Pres. I. A. of S.

concentrated rays of various colours. Something in light and nothing else produced their pseudo-vitality. We do not begin to know how to harness the potentialities of that magnetic vibration of the ether we call light."

"Listen, Doc," said Larry earnestly, "I'll take everything you say about this lost continent, the people who used to live on it, and their caverns, for granted. But by the sword of Brian Boru, you'll never get me to fall for the idea that a bunch of moonshine can handle a big woman such as you say Throckmartin's Thora was, nor a two-fisted man such as you say Throckmartin was, nor Huldricksson's wife—and I'll bet she was one of those strapping big northern women too—you'll never get me to believe that any bunch of concentrated moonshine could handle them and take them waltzing off along a moonbeam back to wherever it goes. No, Doc, not on your life, even Tennessee moonshine couldn't do that—nix!"

"All right, O'Keefe," I answered, now very much irritated indeed. "What's your theory?" And I could not resist adding: "Fairies?"

"Professor," he grinned, "if that Thing's a fairy it's Irish and when it sees me it'll be so glad there'll be nothing to it. 'I was lost, strayed, or stolen, Larry avick,' it'll say, 'an' I was so homesick for the old sod I was desp'rit,' it'll say, an' 'take me back quick before I do anymore har-rm!' it'll tell me—an' that's the truth.

"Now don't get me wrong. I believe you all saw something all right. But what I think you saw was some kind of gas. All this region is volcanic and islands and things are constantly poking up from the sea. It's probably gas; a volcanic emanation; something new to us and that drives you crazy—lots of kinds of gas do that. It hit the Throckmartin party on that island and they probably were all more or less delirious all the time; thought they saw things; talked it over and—collective hallucination—just like the Angels of Mons and other miracles of the war. Somebody sees something that looks like something else. He points it out to the man next him. 'Do you see it?' asks he. 'Sure I see it,' says the other. And there you are—collective hallucination.

"When your friends got it bad they most likely jumped overboard one by one. Huldricksson sails into a place where it is and it hits his wife. She grabs the child and jumps over. Maybe the moon rays make it luminous! I've seen gas on the front under the moon that looked like a thousand whirling dervish devils. Yes, and you could see the devil's faces in it. And if it got into your lungs nothing could ever make you think you hadn't seen real devils."

For a time I was silent.

"Larry," I said at last, "whether you are right or I am right, I must go to the Nan-Matal. Will you go with me, Larry?"

"Goodwin," he replied, "I surely will. I'm as interested as you are. If we don't run across the Dolphin I'll stick. I'll leave word at Ponape, to tell them where I am should they come along. If they report me dead for a while there's nobody to care. So that's all right. Only old man, be reasonable. You've thought over this so long, you're going bug, honestly you are."

And again, the gladness that I might have Larry O'Keefe with me, was so great that I forgot to be angry.

X

THE MOON POOL

D a Costa, who had come aboard unnoticed by either of us, now tapped me on the arm.

"Doctair Goodwin," he said, "can I see you in my cabin, sair?"

At last, then, he was going to speak. I followed him.

"Doctair," he said, when we had entered, "this is a veree strange thing that has happened to Olaf. Veree strange. An' the natives of Ponape, they have been very much excite' lately.

"Of what they fear I know nothing, nothing!" Again that quick, furtive crossing of himself. "But this I have to tell you. There came to me from Ranaloa last month a man, a Russian, a doctair, like you. His name it was Marakinoff. I take him to Ponape an' the natives there they will not take him to the Nan-Matal where he wish to go—no! So I take him. We leave in a boat, wit' much instrument carefully tied up. I leave him there wit' the boat an' the food. He tell me to tell no one an' pay me not to. But you are a friend an' Olaf he depend much upon you an' so I tell you, sair."

"You know nothing more than this, Da Costa?" I asked. "Nothing of another expedition?"

"No," he shook his head vehemently. "Nothing more."

"Hear the name Throckmartin while you were there?" I persisted.

"No," his eyes were steady as he answered but the pallor had crept again into his face.

I was not so sure. But if he knew more than he had told me why was he afraid to speak? My anxiety deepened and later I sought relief from it by repeating the conversation to O'Keefe.

"A Russian, eh," he said. "Well, they can be damned nice, or damned—otherwise. Considering what you did for me, I hope I can look him over before the Dolphin shows up."

Next morning we raised Ponape, without further incident, and before noon the Suwarna and the Brunhilda had dropped anchor in the harbour. Upon the excitement and manifest dread of the natives, when we sought among them for carriers and workmen to accompany us, I will not dwell. It is enough to say that no payment we offered could induce a single one of them to go to the Nan-Matal. Nor would they say why.

Finally it was agreed that the Brunhilda should be left in charge of a half-breed Chinaman, whom both Da Costa and Huldricksson knew and trusted. We piled her long-boat up with my instruments and food and camping equipment. The Suwarna took us around to Metalanim Harbour, and there, with the tops of ancient sea walls deep in the blue water beneath us, and the ruins looming up out of the mangroves, a scant mile from us, left us.

Then with Huldricksson manipulating our small sail, and Larry at the rudder, we rounded the titanic wall that swept down into the depths, and turned at last into the canal that Throckmartin, on his map, had marked as that which, running between frowning Nan-Tauach and its satellite islet, Tau, led straight to the gate of the place of ancient mysteries.

And as we entered that channel we were enveloped by a silence; a silence so intense, so—weighted that it seemed to have substance; an alien silence that clung and stifled and still stood aloof from us—the living. It was a stillness, such as might follow the long tramping of millions into the grave; it was—paradoxical as it may be—filled with the withdrawal of life.

Standing down in the chambered depths of the Great Pyramid I had known something of such silence—but never such intensity as this. Larry felt it and I saw him look at me askance. If Olaf, sitting in the bow, felt it, too, he gave no sign; his blue eyes, with again the glint of ice within them, watched the channel before us.

As we passed, there arose upon our left sheer walls of black basalt blocks, cyclopean, towering fifty feet or more, broken here and there by the sinking of their deep foundations.

In front of us the mangroves widened out and filled the canal. On our right the lesser walls of Tau, sombre blocks smoothed and squared and set with a cold, mathematical nicety that filled me with vague awe, slipped by. Through breaks I caught glimpses of dark ruins and of great fallen stones that seemed to crouch and menace us, as we passed. Somewhere there, hidden, were the seven globes that poured the moon fire down upon the Moon Pool.

Now we were among the mangroves and, sail down, the three of us pushed and pulled the boat through their tangled roots and branches. The noise of our passing split the silence like a profanation, and from the ancient bastions came murmurs—forbidding, strangely sinister. And now we were through, floating on a little open space of shadow-filled water. Before us lifted the gateway of Nan-Tauach, gigantic, broken, incredibly old; shattered portals through which had passed men and women of earth's dawn; old with a weight of years that pressed leadenly upon the eyes that looked upon it, and yet was in some curious indefinable way—menacingly defiant.

Beyond the gate, back from the portals, stretched a flight of enormous basalt slabs, a giant's stairway indeed; and from each side of it marched the high walls that were the Dweller's pathway. None of us spoke as we grounded the boat and dragged it upon a half-submerged pier. And when we did speak it was in whispers.

"What next?" asked Larry.

"I think we ought to take a look around," I replied in the same low tones. "We'll climb the wall here and take a flash about. The whole place ought to be plain as day from that height."

Huldricksson, his blue eyes alert, nodded. With the greatest difficulty we clambered up the broken blocks.

To the east and south of us, set like children's blocks in the midst of the sapphire sea, lay dozens of islets, none of them covering more than two square miles of surface; each of them a perfect square or oblong within its protecting walls.

On none was there sign of life, save for a few great birds that hovered here and there, and gulls dipping in the blue waves beyond.

We turned our gaze down upon the island on which we stood. It was, I estimated, about three-quarters of a mile square. The sea wall enclosed it. It was really an enormous basalt-sided open cube, and within it two other open cubes. The enclosure between the first and second wall was stone paved, with here and there a broken pillar and long stone benches. The hibiscus, the aloe tree, and a number of small shrubs had found place, but seemed only to intensify its stark loneliness.

"Wonder where the Russian can be?" asked Larry.

I shook my head. There was no sign of life here. Had Marakinoff gone—or had the Dweller taken him, too? Whatever had happened, there was no trace of him below us or on any of the islets within our range of vision. We scrambled down the side of the gateway. Olaf looked at me wistfully.

"We start the search now, Olaf," I said. "And first, O'Keefe, let us see whether the grey stone is really here. After that we will set up camp, and while I unpack, you and Olaf search the island. It won't take long."

Larry gave a look at his service automatic and grinned. "Lead on, Macduff," he said. We made our way up the steps, through the outer enclosures and into the central square, I confess to a fire of scientific curiosity and eagerness tinged with a dread that O'Keefe's analysis might be true. Would we find the moving slab and, if so, would it be as Throckmartin had described? If so, then even Larry would have to admit that here was something that theories of gases and luminous emanations would not explain; and the first test of the whole amazing story would be passed. But if not—And there before us, the faintest tinge of grey setting it apart from its neighbouring blocks of basalt, was the moon door!

There was no mistaking it. This was, in very deed, the portal through which Throckmartin had seen pass that gloriously dreadful apparition he called the Dweller. At its base was the curious, seemingly polished cup-like depression within which, my lost friend had told me, the opening door swung.

What was that portal—more enigmatic than was ever sphinx? And what lay beyond it? What did that smooth stone, whose wan deadness whispered of ages-old corridors of time opening out into alien, unimaginable vistas, hide? It had cost the world of science Throckmartin's great brain—as it had cost Throckmartin those he loved. It had drawn me to it in search of Throckmartin—and its shadow had fallen upon the soul of Olaf the Norseman; and upon what thousands upon thousands more I wondered, since the brains that had conceived it had vanished with their secret knowledge?

What lay beyond it?

I stretched out a shaking hand and touched the surface of the slab. A faint thrill passed through my hand and arm, oddly unfamiliar and as oddly unpleasant; as of electric contact holding the very essence of cold. O'Keefe, watching, imitated my action. As his fingers rested on the stone his face filled with astonishment.

"It's the door?" he asked. I nodded. There was a low whistle from him and he pointed up toward the top of the grey stone. I followed the gesture and saw, above the moon door and on each side of it, two gently curving bosses of rock, perhaps a foot in diameter.

"The moon door's keys," I said.

"It begins to look so," answered Larry. "If we can find them," he added.

"There's nothing we can do till moonrise," I replied. "And we've none too much time to prepare as it is. Come!"

A little later we were beside our boat. We lightered it, set up the tent, and as it was now but a short hour to sundown I bade them leave me and make their search. They went off together, and I busied myself with opening some of the paraphernalia I had brought with me.

First of all I took out the two Becquerel ray-condensers that I had bought in Sydney. Their lenses would collect and intensify to the fullest extent any light directed upon them. I had found them most useful in making spectroscopic analysis of luminous vapours, and I knew that at Yerkes Observatory splendid results had been obtained from them in collecting the diffused radiance of the nebulae for the same purpose.

If my theory of the grey slab's mechanism were correct, it was practically certain that with the satellite only a few nights past the full we could concentrate enough light on the bosses to open the rock. And as the ray streams through the seven globes described by Throckmartin would be too weak to energize the Pool, we could enter the chamber free from any fear of encountering its tenant, make our preliminary observations and go forth before the moon had dropped so far that the concentration in the condensers would fall below that necessary to keep the portal from closing.

I took out also a small spectroscope, and a few other instruments for the analysis of certain light manifestations and the testing of metal and liquid. Finally, I put aside my emergency medical kit.

I had hardly finished examining and adjusting these before O'Keefe and Huldricksson returned. They reported signs of a camp at least ten days old beside the northern wall of the outer court, but beyond that no evidence of others beyond ourselves on Nan-Tauach.

We prepared supper, ate and talked a little, but for the most part were silent. Even Larry's high spirits were not in evidence; half a dozen times I saw him take out his automatic and look it over. He was more thoughtful than I had ever seen him. Once he went into the tent, rummaged about a bit and brought out another revolver which, he said, he had got from Da Costa, and a half-dozen clips of cartridges. He passed the gun over to Olaf.

At last a glow in the southeast heralded the rising moon. I picked up my instruments and the medical kit; Larry and Olaf shouldered each a short ladder that was part of my equipment, and, with our electric flashes pointing the way, walked up the great stairs, through the enclosures, and straight to the grey stone.

By this time the moon had risen and its clipped light shone full upon the slab. I saw faint gleams pass over it as of fleeting phosphorescence—but so faint were they that I could not be sure of the truth of my observation.

We set the ladders in place. Olaf I assigned to stand before the door and watch for the first signs of its opening—if open it should. The Becquerels were set within three-inch tripods, whose feet I had equipped with vacuum rings to enable them to hold fast to the rock.

I scaled one ladder and fastened a condenser over the boss; descended; sent Larry up to watch it, and, ascending the second ladder, rapidly fixed the other in its place. Then, with O'Keefe watchful on his perch, I on mine, and Olaf's eyes fixed upon the moon door, we began our vigil. Suddenly there was an exclamation from Larry.

"Seven little lights are beginning to glow on this stone!" he cried.

But I had already seen those beneath my lens begin to gleam out with a silvery lustre. Swiftly the rays within the condenser began to thicken and increase, and as they did so the seven small circles waxed like stars growing out of the dusk, and with a queer—curdled is the best word I can find to define it—radiance entirely strange to me.

Beneath me I heard a faint, sighing murmur and then the voice of Huldricksson:

"It opens—the stone turns—"

I began to climb down the ladder. Again came Olaf's voice:

"The stone—it is open—" And then a shriek, a wail of blended anguish and pity, of rage and despair—and the sound of swift footsteps racing through the wall beneath me!

I dropped to the ground. The moon door was wide open, and through it I caught a glimpse of a corridor filled with a faint, pearly vaporous light like earliest misty dawn. But of Olaf I could see—nothing! And even as I stood, gaping, from behind me came the sharp crack of a rifle; the glass of the condenser at Larry's side flew into fragments; he dropped swiftly to the ground, the automatic in his hand flashed once, twice, into the darkness.

And the moon door began to pivot slowly, slowly back into its place!

I rushed toward the turning stone with the wild idea of holding it open. As I thrust my hands against it there came at my back a snarl and an oath and Larry staggered under the impact of a body that had flung itself straight at his throat. He reeled at the lip of the shallow cup at the base of the slab, slipped upon its polished curve, fell and rolled with that which had attacked him, kicking and writhing, straight through the narrowing portal into the passage!

Forgetting all else, I sprang to his aid. As I leaped I felt the closing edge of the moon door graze my side. Then, as Larry raised a fist, brought it down upon the temple of the man who had grappled with him and rose from the twitching body unsteadily to his feet, I heard shuddering past me a mournful whisper; spun about as though some giant's hand had whirled me—

The end of the corridor no longer opened out into the moonlit square of ruined Nan-Tauach. It was barred by a solid mass of glimmering stone. The moon door had closed!

O'Keefe took a stumbling step toward the barrier behind us. There was no mark of juncture with the shining walls; the slab fitted into the sides as closely as a mosaic.

"It's shut all right," said Larry. "But if there's a way in, there's a way out. Anyway, Doc, we're right in the pew we've been heading for— so why worry?" He grinned at me cheerfully. The man on the floor groaned, and he dropped to his knees beside him.

"Marakinoff!" he cried.

At my exclamation he moved aside, turning the face so I could see it. It was clearly Russian, and just as clearly its possessor was one of unusual force and intellect.

The strong, massive brow with orbital ridge unusually developed, the dominant, high-bridged nose, the straight lips with their more than suggestion of latent cruelty, and the strong lines of the jaw beneath a black, pointed beard all gave evidence that here was a personality beyond the ordinary.

"Couldn't be anybody else," said Larry, breaking in on my thoughts. "He must have been watching us over there from Chau-ta-leur's vault all the time."

Swiftly he ran practised hands over his body; then stood erect, holding out to me two wicked-looking magazine pistols and a knife. "He got one of my bullets through his right forearm, too," he said. "Just a flesh wound, but it made him drop his rifle. Some arsenal, our little Russian scientist, what?"

I opened my medical kit. The wound was a slight one, and Larry stood looking on as I bandaged it.

"Got another one of those condensers?" he asked, suddenly. "And do you suppose Olaf will know enough to use it?"

"Larry," I answered, "Olaf's not outside! He's in here somewhere!"

His jaw dropped.

"The hell you say!" he whispered.

"Didn't you hear him shriek when the stone opened?" I asked.

"I heard him yell, yes," he said. "But I didn't know what was the matter. And then this wildcat jumped me—" He paused and his eyes widened. "Which way did he go?" he asked swiftly. I pointed down the faintly glowing passage.

"There's only one way," I said.

"Watch that bird close," hissed O'Keefe, pointing to Marakinoff— and pistol in hand stretched his long legs and raced away. I looked down at the Russian. His eyes were open, and he reached out a hand to me. I lifted him to his feet.

"I have heard," he said. "We follow, quick. If you will take my arm, please, I am shaken yet, yes—" I gripped his shoulder without a word, and the two of us set off down the corridor after O'Keefe. Marakinoff was gasping, and his weight pressed upon me heavily, but he moved with all the will and strength that were in him.

As we ran I took hasty note of the tunnel. Its sides were smooth and polished, and the light seemed to come not from their surfaces, but from far within them—giving to the walls an illusive aspect of distance and depth; rendering them in a peculiarly weird way—spacious. The passage turned, twisted, ran down, turned again. It came to me that the light that illumined the tunnel was given out by tiny points deep within the stone, sprang from the points ripplingly and spread upon their polished faces.

There was a cry from Larry far ahead.

"Olaf!"

I gripped Marakinoff's arm closer and we sped on. Now we were coming fast to the end of the passage. Before us was a high arch, and through it I glimpsed a dim, shifting luminosity as of mist filled with rainbows. We reached the portal and I looked into a chamber that might have been transported from that enchanted palace of the Jinn King that rises beyond the magic mountains of Kaf.

Before me stood O'Keefe and a dozen feet in front of him, Huldricksson, with something clasped tightly in his arms. The Norseman's feet were at the verge of a shining, silvery lip of stone within whose oval lay a blue pool. And down upon this pool staring upward like a gigantic eye, fell seven pillars of phantom light—one of them amethyst, one of rose, another of white, a fourth of blue, and three of emerald, of silver, and of amber. They fell each upon the azure surface, and I knew that these were the seven streams of radiance, within which the Dweller took shape—now but pale ghosts of their brilliancy when the full energy of the moon stream raced through them.

Huldricksson bent and placed on the shining silver lip of the Pool that which he held—and I saw that it was the body of a child! He set it there so gently, bent over the side and thrust a hand down into the water. And as he did so he moaned and lurched against the little body that lay before him. Instantly the form moved—and slipped over the verge into the blue. Huldricksson threw his body over the stone, hands clutching, arms thrust deep down—and from his lips issued a long-drawn, heart-shrivelling wail of pain and of anguish that held in it nothing human!

Close on its wake came a cry from Marakinoff.

"Catch him!" shouted the Russian. "Drag him back! Quick!"

He leaped forward, but before he could half clear the distance, O'Keefe had leaped too, had caught the Norseman by the shoulders and toppled him backward, where he lay whimpering and sobbing. And as I rushed behind Marakinoff I saw Larry lean over the lip of the Pool and cover his eyes with a shaking hand; saw the Russian peer into it with real pity in his cold eyes.

Then I stared down myself into the Moon Pool, and there, sinking, was a little maid whose dead face and fixed, terror-filled eyes looked straight into mine; and ever sinking slowly, slowly—vanished! And I knew that this was Olaf's Freda, his beloved yndling!

But where was the mother, and where had Olaf found his babe?

The Russian was first to speak.

"You have nitroglycerin there, yes?" he asked, pointing toward my medical kit that I had gripped unconsciously and carried with me during the mad rush down the passage. I nodded and drew it out.

"Hypodermic," he ordered next, curtly; took the syringe, filled it accurately with its one one-hundredth of a grain dosage, and leaned over Huldricksson. He rolled up the sailor's sleeves half-way to the shoulder. The arms were white with somewhat of that weird semitranslucence that I had seen on Throckmartin's breast where a tendril of the Dweller had touched him; and his hands were of the same whiteness—like a baroque pearl. Above the line of white, Marakinoff thrust the needle.

"He will need all his heart can do," he said to me.

Then he reached down into a belt about his waist and drew from it a small, flat flask of what seemed to be lead. He opened it and let a few drops of its contents fall on each arm of the Norwegian. The liquid sparkled and instantly began to spread over the skin much as oil or gasoline dropped on water does—only far more rapidly. And as it spread it drew a sparkling film over the marbled flesh and little wisps of vapour rose from it. The Norseman's mighty chest heaved with agony. His hands clenched. The Russian gave a grunt of satisfaction at this, dropped a little more of the liquid, and then, watching closely, grunted again and leaned back. Huldricksson's laboured breathing ceased, his head dropped upon Larry's knee, and from his arms and hands the whiteness swiftly withdrew.

Marakinoff arose and contemplated us—almost benevolently.

"He will all right be in five minutes," he said. "I know. I do it to pay for that shot of mine, and also because we will need him. Yes." He turned to Larry. "You have a poonch like a mule kick, my young friend," he said. "Sometime you pay me for that, too, eh?" He smiled; and the quality of the grimace was not exactly reassuring. Larry looked him over quizzically.

"You're Marakinoff, of course," he said. The Russian nodded, betraying no surprise at the recognition.

"And you?" he asked.

"Lieutenant O'Keefe of the Royal Flying Corps," replied Larry, saluting. "And this gentleman is Dr. Walter T. Goodwin."

Marakinoff's face brightened.

"The American botanist?" he queried. I nodded.

"Ah," cried Marakinoff eagerly, "but this is fortunate. Long I have desired to meet you. Your work, for an American, is most excellent; surprising. But you are wrong in your theory of the development of the Angiospermae from Cycadeoidea dacotensis. Da—all wrong—"

I was interrupting him with considerable heat, for my conclusions from the fossil Cycadeoidea I knew to be my greatest triumph, when Larry broke in upon me rudely.

"Say," he spluttered, "am I crazy or are you? What in damnation kind of a place and time is this to start an argument like that?

"Angiospermae, is it?" exclaimed Larry. "Hell!"

Marakinoff again regarded him with that irritating air of benevolence.

"You have not the scientific mind, young friend," he said. "The poonch, yes! But so has the mule. You must learn that only the fact is important—not you, not me, not this"—he pointed to Huldricksson— "or its sorrows. Only the fact, whatever it is, is real, yes. But"—he turned to me—"another time—"

Huldricksson interrupted him. The big seaman had risen stiffly to his feet and stood with Larry's arm supporting him. He stretched out his hands to me.

"I saw her," he whispered. "I saw mine Freda when the stone swung. She lay there—just at my feet. I picked her up and I saw that mine Freda was dead. But I hoped—and I thought maybe mine Helma was somewhere here, too, So I ran with mine yndling—here—" His voice broke. "I thought maybe she was *not* dead," he went on. "And I saw that"—he pointed to the Moon Pool—"and I thought I would bathe her face and she might live again. And when I dipped my hands within—the life left them, and cold, deadly cold, ran up through them into my heart. And mine Freda—she fell—" he covered his eyes, and dropping his head on O'Keefe's shoulder, stood, racked by sobs that seemed to tear at his very soul.

XI

The Flame-Tipped Shadows

Marakinoff nodded his head solemnly as Olaf finished.
"Da!" he said. "That which comes from here took them both—
the woman and the child. Da! They came clasped within it and the stone
shut upon them. But why it left the child behind I do not understand."

"How do you know that?" I cried in amazement.

"Because I saw it," answered Marakinoff simply. "Not only did I see
it, but hardly had I time to make escape through the entrance before
it passed whirling and murmuring and its bell sounds all joyous. Da! It
was what you call the squeak close, that."

"Wait a moment," I said—stilling Larry with a gesture. "Do I
understand you to say that you were within this place?"

Marakinoff actually beamed upon me.

"Da, Dr. Goodwin," he said, "I went in when that which comes from
it went out!"

I gaped at him, stricken dumb; into Larry's bellicose attitude crept a
suggestion of grudging respect; Olaf, trembling, watched silently.

"Dr. Goodwin and my impetuous young friend, you," went on
Marakinoff after a moment's silence and I wondered vaguely why he
did not include Huldricksson in his address—"it is time that we have
an understanding. I have a proposal to make to you also. It is this; we
are what you call a bad boat, and all of us are in it. Da! We need all
hands, is it not so? Let us put together our knowledge and our brains
and resources—and even a poonch of a mule is a resource," he looked
wickedly at O'Keefe, "and pull our boat into quiet waters again. After
that—"

"All very well, Marakinoff," interjected Larry, "but I don't feel very
safe in any boat with somebody capable of shooting me through the
back."

Marakinoff waved a deprecatory hand.

"It was natural that," he said, "logical, da! Here is a very great secret,
perhaps many secrets to my country invaluable—" He paused, shaken by
some overpowering emotion; the veins in his forehead grew congested,
the cold eyes blazed and the guttural voice harshened.

"I do not apologize and I do not explain," rasped Marakinoff. "But I will tell you, da! Here is my country sweating blood in an experiment to liberate the world. And here are the other nations ringing us like wolves and waiting to spring at our throats at the least sign of weakness. And here are you, Lieutenant O'Keefe of the English wolves, and you Dr. Goodwin of the Yankee pack—and here in this place may be that will enable my country to win its war for the worker. What are the lives of you two and this sailor to that? Less than the flies I crush with my hand, less than midges in the sunbeam!"

He suddenly gripped himself.

"But that is not now the important thing," he resumed, almost coldly. "Not that nor my shooting. Let us squarely the situation face. My proposal is so: that we join interests, and what you call see it through together; find our way through this place and those secrets learn of which I have spoken, if we can. And when that is done we will go our ways, to his own land each, to make use of them for our lands as each of us may. On my part, I offer my knowledge—and it is very valuable, Dr. Goodwin—and my training. You and Lieutenant O'Keefe do the same, and this man Olaf, what he can of his strength, for I do not think his usefulness lies in his brains, no."

"In effect, Goodwin," broke in Larry as I hesitated, "the professor's proposition is this: he wants to know what's going on here but he begins to realize it's no one man's job and besides we have the drop on him. We're three to his one, and we have all his hardware and cutlery. But also we can do better with him than without him—just as he can do better with us than without us. It's an even break—for a while. But once he gets that information he's looking for, then look out. You and Olaf and I are the wolves and the flies and the midges again—and the strafing will be about due. Nevertheless, with three to one against him, if he can get away with it he deserves to. I'm for taking him up, if you are."

There was almost a twinkle in Marakinoff's eyes.

"It is not just as I would have put it, perhaps," he said, "but in its skeleton he has right. Nor will I turn my hand against you while we are still in danger here. I pledge you my honor on this."

Larry laughed.

"All right, Professor," he grinned. "I believe you mean every word you say. Nevertheless, I'll just keep the guns."

Marakinoff bowed, imperturbably.

"And now," he said, "I will tell you what I know. I found the secret of the door mechanism even as you did, Dr. Goodwin. But by carelessness, my condensers were broken. I was forced to wait while I sent for others—and the waiting might be for months. I took certain precautions, and on the first night of this full moon I hid myself within the vault of Chau-ta-leur."

An involuntary thrill of admiration for the man went through me at the manifest heroism of this leap in the dark. I could see it reflected in Larry's face.

"I hid in the vault," continued Marakinoff, "and I saw that which comes from here come out. I waited—long hours. At last, when the moon was low, it returned—ecstatically—with a man, a native, in embrace enfolded. It passed through the door, and soon then the moon became low and the door closed.

"The next night more confidence was mine, yes. And after that which comes had gone, I looked through its open door. I said, 'It will not return for three hours. While it is away, why shall I not into its home go through the door it has left open?' So I went—even to here. I looked at the pillars of light and I tested the liquid of the Pool on which they fell. That liquid, Dr. Goodwin, is not water, and it is not any fluid known on earth." He handed me a small vial, its neck held in a long thong.

"Take this," he said, "and see."

Wonderingly, I took the bottle; dipped it down into the Pool. The liquid was extraordinarily light; seemed, in fact, to give the vial buoyancy. I held it to the light. It was striated, streaked, as though little living, pulsing veins ran through it. And its blueness, even in the vial, held an intensity of luminousness.

"Radioactive," said Marakinoff. "Some liquid that is intensely radioactive; but what it is I know not at all. Upon the living skin it acts like radium raised to the nth power and with an element most mysterious added. The solution with which I treated him," he pointed to Huldricksson, "I had prepared before I came here, from certain information I had. It is largely salts of radium and its base is Loeb's formula for the neutralization of radium and X-ray burns. Taking this man at once, before the degeneration had become really active, I could negative it. But after two hours I could have done nothing."

He paused a moment.

"Next I studied the nature of these luminous walls. I concluded that whoever had made them, knew the secret of the Almighty's manufacture of light from the ether itself! Colossal! Da! But the substance of these blocks confines an atomic—how would you say—atomic manipulation, a conscious arrangement of electrons, light-emitting and perhaps indefinitely so. These blocks are lamps in which oil and wick are electrons drawing light waves from ether itself! A Prometheus, indeed, this discoverer! I looked at my watch and that little guardian warned me that it was time to go. I went. That which comes forth returned—this time empty-handed.

"And the next night I did the same thing. Engrossed in research, I let the moments go by to the danger point, and scarcely was I replaced within the vault when the shining thing raced over the walls, and in its grip the woman and child.

"Then you came—and that is all. And now—what is it you know?"

Very briefly I went over my story. His eyes gleamed now and then, but he did not interrupt me.

"A great secret! A colossal secret!" he muttered, when I had ended. "We cannot leave it hidden."

"The first thing to do is to try the door," said Larry, matter of fact.

"There is no use, my young friend," assured Marakinoff mildly.

"Nevertheless we'll try," said Larry. We retraced our way through the winding tunnel to the end, but soon even O'Keefe saw that any idea of moving the slab from within was hopeless. We returned to the Chamber of the Pool. The pillars of light were fainter, and we knew that the moon was sinking. On the world outside before long dawn would be breaking. I began to feel thirst—and the blue semblance of water within the silvery rim seemed to glint mockingly as my eyes rested on it.

"Da!" it was Marakinoff, reading my thoughts uncannily. "Da! We will be thirsty. And it will be very bad for him of us who loses control and drinks of that, my friend. Da!"

Larry threw back his shoulders as though shaking a burden from them.

"This place would give an angel of joy the willies," he said. "I suggest that we look around and find something that will take us somewhere. You can bet the people that built it had more ways of getting in than that once-a-month family entrance. Doc, you and Olaf take the left wall; the professor and I will take the right."

He loosened one of his automatics with a suggestive movement.

"After you, Professor," he bowed, politely, to the Russian. We parted and set forth.

The chamber widened out from the portal in what seemed to be the arc of an immense circle. The shining walls held a perceptible curve, and from this curvature I estimated that the roof was fully three hundred feet above us.

The floor was of smooth, mosaic-fitted blocks of a faintly yellow tinge. They were not light-emitting like the blocks that formed the walls. The radiance from these latter, I noted, had the peculiar quality of *thickening* a few yards from its source, and it was this that produced the effect of misty, veiled distances. As we walked, the seven columns of rays streaming down from the crystalline globes high above us waned steadily; the glow within the chamber lost its prismatic shimmer and became an even grey tone somewhat like moonlight in a thin cloud.

Now before us, out from the wall, jutted a low terrace. It was all of a pearly rose-coloured stone, slender, graceful pillars of the same hue. The face of the terrace was about ten feet high, and all over it ran a bas-relief of what looked like short-trailing vines, surmounted by five stalks, on the tip of each of which was a flower.

We passed along the terrace. It turned in an abrupt curve. I heard a hail, and there, fifty feet away, at the curving end of a wall identical with that where we stood, were Larry and Marakinoff. Obviously the left side of the chamber was a duplicate of that we had explored. We joined. In front of us the columned barriers ran back a hundred feet, forming an alcove. The end of this alcove was another wall of the same rose stone, but upon it the design of vines was much heavier.

We took a step forward—there was a gasp of awe from the Norseman, a guttural exclamation from Marakinoff. For on, or rather within, the wall before us, a great oval began to glow, waxed almost to a flame and then shone steadily out as though from behind it a light was streaming through the stone itself!

And within the roseate oval two flame-tipped shadows appeared, stood for a moment, and then seemed to float out upon its surface. The shadows wavered; the tips of flame that nimbused them with flickering points of vermilion pulsed outward, drew back, darted forth again, and once more withdrew themselves—and as they did so the shadows thickened—and suddenly there before us stood two figures!

One was a girl—a girl whose great eyes were golden as the fabled lilies of Kwan-Yung that were born of the kiss of the sun upon the amber goddess the demons of Lao-Tz'e carved for him; whose softly curved lips were red as the royal coral, and whose golden-brown hair reached to her knees!

And the second was a gigantic frog—A *woman* frog, head helmeted with carapace of shell around which a fillet of brilliant yellow jewels shone; enormous round eyes of blue circled with a broad iris of green; monstrous body of banded orange and white girdled with strand upon strand of the flashing yellow gems; six feet high if an inch, and with one webbed paw of its short, powerfully muscled forelegs resting upon the white shoulder of the golden-eyed girl!

Moments must have passed as we stood in stark amazement, gazing at that incredible apparition. The two figures, although as real as any of those who stood beside me, unphantomlike as it is possible to be, had a distinct suggestion of—projection.

They were there before us—golden-eyed girl and grotesque frog-woman—complete in every line and curve; and still it was as though their bodies passed back through distances; as though, to try to express the wellnigh inexpressible, the two shapes we were looking upon were the end of an infinite number stretching in fine linked chain far away, of which the eyes saw only the nearest, while in the brain some faculty higher than sight recognized and registered the unseen others.

The gigantic eyes of the frog-woman took us all in—unwinkingly. Little glints of phosphorescence shone out within the metallic green of the outer iris ring. She stood upright, her great legs bowed; the monstrous slit of a mouth slightly open, revealing a row of white teeth sharp and pointed as lancets; the paw resting on the girl's shoulder, half covering its silken surface, and from its five webbed digits long yellow claws of polished horn glistened against the delicate texture of the flesh.

But if the frog-woman regarded us all, not so did the maiden of the rosy wall. Her eyes were fastened upon Larry, drinking him in with extraordinary intentness. She was tall, far over the average of women, almost as tall, indeed, as O'Keefe himself; not more than twenty years old, if that, I thought. Abruptly she leaned forward, the golden eyes softened and grew tender; the red lips moved as though she were speaking.

Larry took a quick step, and his face was that of one who after countless births comes at last upon the twin soul lost to him for ages. The frog-woman turned her eyes upon the girl; her huge lips moved, and I knew that she was talking! The girl held out a warning hand to

O'Keefe, and then raised it, resting each finger upon one of the five flowers of the carved vine close beside her. Once, twice, three times, she pressed upon the flower centres, and I noted that her hand was curiously long and slender, the digits like those wonderful tapering ones the painters we call the primitive gave to their Virgins.

Three times she pressed the flowers, and then looked intently at Larry once more. A slow, sweet smile curved the crimson lips. She stretched both hands out toward him again eagerly; a burning blush rose swiftly over white breasts and flowerlike face.

Like the clicking out of a cinematograph, the pulsing oval faded and golden-eyed girl and frog-woman were gone!

And thus it was that Lakla, the handmaiden of the Silent Ones, and Larry O'Keefe first looked into each other's hearts!

Larry stood rapt, gazing at the stone.

"Eilidh," I heard him whisper; "Eilidh of the lips like the red, red rowan and the golden-brown hair!"

"Clearly of the Ranadae," said Marakinoff, "a development of the fossil Labyrinthodonts: you saw her teeth, da?"

"Ranadae, yes," I answered. "But from the Stegocephalia; of the order Ecaudata—"

Never such a complete indignation as was in O'Keefe's voice as he interrupted.

"What do you mean—fossils and Stego whatever it is?" he asked. "She was a girl, a wonder girl—a real girl, and Irish, or I'm not an O'Keefe!"

"We were talking about the frog-woman, Larry," I said, conciliatingly.

His eyes were wild as he regarded us.

"Say," he said, "if you two had been in the Garden of Eden when Eve took the apple, you wouldn't have had time to give her a look for counting the scales on the snake!"

He strode swiftly over to the wall. We followed. Larry paused, stretched his hand up to the flowers on which the tapering fingers of the golden-eyed girl had rested.

"It was here she put up her hand," he murmured. He pressed caressingly the carved calyxes, once, twice, a third time even as she had—and silently and softly the wall began to split; on each side a great stone pivoted slowly, and before us a portal stood, opening into a narrow corridor glowing with the same rosy lustre that had gleamed around the flame-tipped shadows!

"Have your gun ready, Olaf!" said Larry. "We follow Golden Eyes," he said to me.

"Follow?" I echoed stupidly.

"Follow!" he said. "She came to show us the way! Follow? I'd follow her through a thousand hells!"

And with Olaf at one end, O'Keefe at the other, both of them with automatics in hand, and Marakinoff and I between them, we stepped over the threshold.

At our right, a few feet away, the passage ended abruptly in a square of polished stone, from which came faint rose radiance. The roof of the place was less than two feet over O'Keefe's head.

A yard at left of us lifted a four-foot high, gently curved barricade, stretching from wall to wall—and beyond it was blackness; an utter and appalling blackness that seemed to gather itself from infinite depths. The rose-glow in which we stood was cut off by the blackness as though it had substance; it shimmered out to meet it, and was checked as though by a blow; indeed, so strong was the suggestion of sinister, straining force within the rayless opacity that I shrank back, and Marakinoff with me. Not so O'Keefe. Olaf beside him, he strode to the wall and peered over. He beckoned us.

"Flash your pocket-light down there," he said to me, pointing into the thick darkness below us. The little electric circle quivered down as though afraid, and came to rest upon a surface that resembled nothing so much as clear, black ice. I ran the light across—here and there. The floor of the corridor was of a substance so smooth, so polished, that no man could have walked upon it; it sloped downward at a slowly increasing angle.

"We'd have to have non-skid chains and brakes on our feet to tackle that," mused Larry. Abstractedly be ran his hands over the edge on which he was leaning. Suddenly they hesitated and then gripped tightly.

"That's a queer one!" he exclaimed. His right palm was resting upon a rounded protuberance, on the side of which were three small circular indentations.

"A queer one—" he repeated—and pressed his fingers upon the circles.

There was a sharp click; the slabs that had opened to let us through swung swiftly together; a curiously rapid vibration thrilled through us, a wind arose and passed over our heads—a wind that grew and grew until it became a whistling shriek, then a roar and then a mighty humming, to which every atom in our bodies pulsed in rhythm painful almost to disintegration!

The rosy wall dwindled in a flash to a point of light and disappeared!

Wrapped in the clinging, impenetrable blackness we were racing, dropping, hurling at a frightful speed—where?

And ever that awful humming of the rushing wind and the lightning cleaving of the tangible dark—so, it came to me oddly, must the newly released soul race through the sheer blackness of outer space up to that Throne of Justice, where God sits high above all suns!

I felt Marakinoff creep close to me; gripped my nerve and flashed my pocket-light; saw Larry standing, peering, peering ahead, and Huldricksson, one strong arm around his shoulders, bracing him. And then the speed began to slacken.

Millions of miles, it seemed, below the sound of the unearthly hurricane I heard Larry's voice, thin and ghostlike, beneath its clamour.

"Got it!" shrilled the voice. "Got it! Don't worry!"

The wind died down to the roar, passed back into the whistling shriek and diminished to a steady whisper. In the comparative quiet O'Keefe's tones now came in normal volume.

"Some little shoot-the-chutes, what?" he shouted. "Say—if they had this at Coney Island or the Crystal Palace! Press all the way in these holes and she goes top-high. Diminish pressure—diminish speed. The curve of this—dashboard—here sends the wind shooting up over our heads—like a windshield. What's behind you?"

I flashed the light back. The mechanism on which we were ended in another wall exactly similar to that over which O'Keefe crouched.

"Well, we can't fall out, anyway," he laughed. "Wish to hell I knew where the brakes were! Look out!"

We dropped dizzily down an abrupt, seemingly endless slope; fell— fell as into an abyss—then shot abruptly out of the blackness into a throbbing green radiance. O'Keefe's fingers must have pressed down upon the controls, for we leaped forward almost with the speed of light. I caught a glimpse of luminous immensities on the verge of which we flew; of depths inconceivable, and flitting through the incredible spaces—gigantic shadows as of the wings of Israfel, which are so wide, say the Arabs, the world can cower under them like a nestling—and then—again the living blackness!

"What was that?" This from Larry, with the nearest approach to awe that he had yet shown.

"Trolldom!" croaked the voice of Olaf.

"Chert!" This from Marakinoff. "What a space!"

"Have you considered, Dr. Goodwin," he went on after a pause, "a curious thing? We know, or, at least, is it not that nine out of ten astronomers believe, that the moon was hurled out of this same region we now call the Pacific when the earth was yet like molasses; almost molten, I should say. And is it not curious that that which comes from the Moon Chamber needs the moon-rays to bring it forth; is it not? And is it not significant again that the stone depends upon the moon for operating? Da! And last—such a space in mother earth as we just glimpsed, how else could it have been torn but by some gigantic birth— like that of the moon? Da! I do not put forward these as statements of fact—no! But as suggestions—"

I started; there was so much that this might explain—an unknown element that responded to the moon-rays in opening the moon door; the blue Pool with its weird radioactivity, and the force within it that reacted to the same light stream—

It was not inconceivable that a film had drawn over the world wound, a film of earth-flesh which drew itself over that colossal abyss after our planet had borne its satellite—that world womb did not close when her shining child sprang forth—it was possible; and all that we know of earth depth is four miles of her eight thousand.

What is there at the heart of earth? What of that radiant unknown element upon the moon mount Tycho? What of that element unknown to us as part of earth which is seen only in the corona of the sun at eclipse that we call coronium? Yet the earth is child of the sun as the moon is earth's daughter. And what of that other unknown element we find glowing green in the far-flung nebulae—green as that we had just passed through—and that we call nebulium? Yet the sun is child of the nebulae as the earth is child of the sun and the moon is child of the earth.

And what miracles are there in coronium and nebulium which, as the child of nebula and sun, we inherit? Yes—and in Tycho's enigma which came from earth heart?

We were flashing down to earth heart! And what miracles were hidden there?

XII

The End of the Journey

S ay Doc!" It was Larry's voice flung back at me. "I was thinking about that frog. I think it was her pet. Damn me if I see any difference between a frog and a snake, and one of the nicest women I ever knew had two pet pythons that followed her around like kittens. Not such a devilish lot of choice between a frog and a snake—except on the side of the frog? What? Anyway, any pet that girl wants is hers, I don't care if it's a leaping twelve-toed lobster or a whale-bodied scorpion. Get me?"

By which I knew that our remarks upon the frog woman were still bothering O'Keefe.

"He thinks of foolish nothings like the foolish sailor!" grunted Marakinoff, acid contempt in his words. "What are their women to— this?" He swept out a hand and as though at a signal the car poised itself for an instant, then dipped, literally dipped down into sheer space; skimmed forward in what was clearly curved flight, rose as upon a sweeping upgrade and then began swiftly to slacken its fearful speed.

Far ahead a point of light showed; grew steadily; we were within it—and softly all movement ceased. How acute had been the strain of our journey I did not realize until I tried to stand—and sank back, leg-muscles too shaky to bear my weight. The car rested in a slit in the centre of a smooth walled chamber perhaps twenty feet square. The wall facing us was pierced by a low doorway through which we could see a flight of steps leading downward.

The light streamed through a small opening, the base of which was twice a tall man's height from the floor. A curving flight of broad, low steps led up to it. And now it came to my steadying brain that there was something puzzling, peculiar, strangely unfamiliar about this light. It was silvery, shaded faintly with a delicate blue and flushed lightly with a nacreous rose; but a rose that differed from that of the terraces of the Pool Chamber as the rose within the opal differs from that within the pearl. In it were tiny, gleaming points like the motes in a sunbeam, but sparkling white like the dust of diamonds, and with a quality of vibrant vitality; they were as though they were alive. The light cast no shadows!

A little breeze came through the oval and played about us. It was laden with what seemed the mingled breath of spice flowers and pines. It was curiously vivifying, and in it the diamonded atoms of light shook and danced.

I stepped out of the car, the Russian following, and began to ascend the curved steps toward the opening, at the top of which O'Keefe and Olaf already stood. As they looked out I saw both their faces change—Olaf's with awe, O'Keefe's with incredulous amaze. I hurried to their side.

At first all that I could see was space—a space filled with the same coruscating effulgence that pulsed about me. I glanced upward, obeying that instinctive impulse of earth folk that bids them seek within the sky for sources of light. There was no sky—at least no sky such as we know—all was a sparkling nebulosity rising into infinite distances as the azure above the day-world seems to fill all the heavens—through it ran pulsing waves and flashing javelin rays that were like shining shadows of the aurora; echoes, octaves lower, of those brilliant arpeggios and chords that play about the poles. My eyes fell beneath its splendour; I stared outward.

Miles away, gigantic luminous cliffs sprang sheer from the limits of a lake whose waters were of milky opalescence. It was from these cliffs that the spangled radiance came, shimmering out from all their lustrous surfaces. To left and to right, as far as the eye could see, they stretched—and they vanished in the auroral nebulosity on high!

"Look at that!" exclaimed Larry. I followed his pointing finger. On the face of the shining wall, stretched between two colossal columns, hung an incredible veil; prismatic, gleaming with all the colours of the spectrum. It was like a web of rainbows woven by the fingers of the daughters of the Jinn. In front of it and a little at each side was a semi-circular pier, or, better, a plaza of what appeared to be glistening, pale-yellow ivory. At each end of its half-circle clustered a few low-walled, rose-stone structures, each of them surmounted by a number of high, slender pinnacles.

We looked at each other, I think, a bit helplessly—and back again through the opening. We were standing, as I have said, at its base. The wall in which it was set was at least ten feet thick, and so, of course, all that we could see of that which was without were the distances that revealed themselves above the outer ledge of the oval.

"Let's take a look at what's under us," said Larry.

He crept out upon the ledge and peered down, the rest of us following. A hundred yards beneath us stretched gardens that must have been like those of many-columned Iram, which the ancient Addite King had built for his pleasure ages before the deluge, and which Allah, so the Arab legend tells, took and hid from man, within the Sahara, beyond all hope of finding—jealous because they were more beautiful than his in paradise. Within them flowers and groves of laced, fernlike trees, pillared pavilions nestled.

The trunks of the trees were of emerald, of vermilion, and of azure-blue, and the blossoms, whose fragrance was borne to us, shone like jewels. The graceful pillars were tinted delicately. I noted that the pavilions were double—in a way, two-storied—and that they were oddly splotched with circles, with squares, and with oblongs of—opacity; noted too that over many this opacity stretched like a roof; yet it did not seem material; rather was it—impenetrable shadow!

Down through this city of gardens ran a broad shining green thoroughfare, glistening like glass and spanned at regular intervals with graceful, arched bridges. The road flashed to a wide square, where rose, from a base of that same silvery stone that formed the lip of the Moon Pool, a titanic structure of seven terraces; and along it flitted objects that bore a curious resemblance to the shell of the Nautilus. Within them were—human figures! And upon tree-bordered promenades on each side walked others!

Far to the right we caught the glint of another emerald-paved road.

And between the two the gardens grew sweetly down to the hither side of that opalescent water across which were the radiant cliffs and the curtain of mystery.

Thus it was that we first saw the city of the Dweller; blessed and accursed as no place on earth, or under or above earth has ever been—or, that force willing which some call God, ever again shall be!

"Chert!" whispered Marakinoff. "Incredible!"

"Trolldom!" gasped Olaf Huldricksson. "It is Trolldom!"

"Listen, Olaf!" said Larry. "Cut out that Trolldom stuff! There's no Trolldom, or fairies, outside Ireland. Get that! And this isn't Ireland. And, buck up, Professor!" This to Marakinoff. "What you see down there are people—*just plain people*. And wherever there's people is where I live. Get me?

"There's no way in but in—and no way out but out," said O'Keefe. "And there's the stairway. Eggs are eggs no matter how they're cooked—

and people are just people, fellow travellers, no matter what dish they are in," he concluded. "Come on!"

With the three of us close behind him, he marched toward the entrance.

XIII

Yolara, Priestess of the Shining One

"Y ou'd better have this handy, Doc." O'Keefe paused at the head of the stairway and handed me one of the automatics he had taken from Marakinoff.

"Shall I not have one also?" rather anxiously asked the latter.

"When you need it you'll get it," answered O'Keefe. "I'll tell you frankly, though, Professor, that you'll have to show me before I trust you with a gun. You shoot too straight—from cover."

The flash of anger in the Russian's eyes turned to a cold consideration.

"You say always just what is in your mind, Lieutenant O'Keefe," he mused. "Da—that I shall remember!" Later I was to recall this odd observation—and Marakinoff was to remember indeed.

In single file, O'Keefe at the head and Olaf bringing up the rear, we passed through the portal. Before us dropped a circular shaft, into which the light from the chamber of the oval streamed liquidly; set in its sides the steps spiralled, and down them we went, cautiously. The stairway ended in a circular well; silent—with no trace of exit! The rounded stones joined each other evenly—hermetically. Carved on one of the slabs was one of the five flowered vines. I pressed my fingers upon the calyxes, even as Larry had within the Moon Chamber.

A crack—horizontal, four feet wide—appeared on the wall; widened, and as the sinking slab that made it dropped to the level of our eyes, we looked through a hundred-feet-long rift in the living rock! The stone fell steadily—and we saw that it was a Cyclopean wedge set within the slit of the passageway. It reached the level of our feet and stopped. At the far end of this tunnel, whose floor was the polished rock that had, a moment before, fitted hermetically into its roof, was a low, narrow triangular opening through which light streamed.

"Nowhere to go but out!" grinned Larry. "And I'll bet Golden Eyes is waiting for us with a taxi!" He stepped forward. We followed, slipping, sliding along the glassy surface; and I, for one, had a lively apprehension of what our fate would be should that enormous mass rise before we had emerged! We reached the end; crept out of the narrow triangle that was its exit.

We stood upon a wide ledge carpeted with a thick yellow moss. I looked behind—and clutched O'Keefe's arm. The door through which we had come had vanished! There was only a precipice of pale rock, on whose surfaces great patches of the amber moss hung; around whose base our ledge ran, and whose summits, if summits it had, were hidden, like the luminous cliffs, in the radiance above us.

"Nowhere to go but ahead—and Golden Eyes hasn't kept her date!" laughed O'Keefe—but somewhat grimly.

We walked a few yards along the ledge and, rounding a corner, faced the end of one of the slender bridges. From this vantage point the oddly shaped vehicles were plain, and we could see they were, indeed, like the shell of the Nautilus and elfinly beautiful. Their drivers sat high upon the forward whorl. Their bodies were piled high with cushions, upon which lay women half-swathed in gay silken webs. From the pavilioned gardens smaller channels of glistening green ran into the broad way, much as automobile runways do on earth; and in and out of them flashed the fairy shells.

There came a shout from one. Its occupants had glimpsed us. They pointed; others stopped and stared; one shell turned and sped up a runway—and quickly over the other side of the bridge came a score of men. They were dwarfed—none of them more than five feet high, prodigiously broad of shoulder, clearly enormously powerful.

"Trolde!" muttered Olaf, stepping beside O'Keefe, pistol swinging free in his hand.

But at the middle of the bridge the leader stopped, waved back his men, and came toward us alone, palms outstretched in the immemorial, universal gesture of truce. He paused, scanning us with manifest wonder; we returned the scrutiny with interest. The dwarf's face was as white as Olaf's—far whiter than those of the other three of us; the features clean-cut and noble, almost classical; the wide set eyes of a curious greenish grey and the black hair curling over his head like that on some old Greek statue.

Dwarfed though he was, there was no suggestion of deformity about him. The gigantic shoulders were covered with a loose green tunic that looked like fine linen. It was caught in at the waist by a broad girdle studded with what seemed to be amazonites. In it was thrust a long curved poniard resembling the Malaysian kris. His legs were swathed in the same green cloth as the upper garment. His feet were sandalled.

My gaze returned to his face, and in it I found something subtly disturbing; an expression of half-malicious gaiety that underlay the wholly prepossessing features like a vague threat; a mocking deviltry that hinted at entire callousness to suffering or sorrow; something of the spirit that was vaguely alien and disquieting.

He spoke—and, to my surprise, enough of the words were familiar to enable me clearly to catch the meaning of the whole. They were Polynesian, the Polynesian of the Samoans which is its most ancient form, but in some indefinable way—archaic. Later I was to know that the tongue bore the same relation to the Polynesian of today as does *not* that of Chaucer, but of the Venerable Bede, to modern English. Nor was this to be so astonishing, when with the knowledge came the certainty that it was from it the language we call Polynesian sprang.

"From whence do you come, strangers—and how found you your way here?" said the green dwarf.

I waved my hand toward the cliff behind us. His eyes narrowed incredulously; he glanced at its drop, upon which even a mountain goat could not have made its way, and laughed.

"We came through the rock," I answered his thought. "And we come in peace," I added.

"And may peace walk with you," he said half-derisively—"if the Shining One wills it!"

He considered us again.

"Show me, strangers, where you came through the rock," he commanded. We led the way to where we had emerged from the well of the stairway.

"It was here," I said, tapping the cliff.

"But I see no opening," he said suavely.

"It closed behind us," I answered; and then, for the first time, realized how incredible the explanation sounded. The derisive gleam passed through his eyes again. But he drew his poniard and gravely sounded the rock.

"You give a strange turn to our speech," he said. "It sounds strangely, indeed—as strange as your answers." He looked at us quizzically. "I wonder where you learned it! Well, all that you can explain to the Afyo Maie." His head bowed and his arms swept out in a wide salaam. "Be pleased to come with me!" he ended abruptly.

"In peace?" I asked.

"In peace," he replied—then slowly—"with me at least."

"Oh, come on, Doc!" cried Larry. "As long as we're here let's see the sights. Allons mon vieux!" he called gaily to the green dwarf. The latter, understanding the spirit, if not the words, looked at O'Keefe with a twinkle of approval; turned then to the great Norseman and scanned him with admiration; reached out and squeezed one of the immense biceps.

"Lugur will welcome you, at least," he murmured as though to himself. He stood aside and waved a hand courteously, inviting us to pass. We crossed. At the base of the span one of the elfin shells was waiting.

Beyond, scores had gathered, their occupants evidently discussing us in much excitement. The green dwarf waved us to the piles of cushions and then threw himself beside us. The vehicle started off smoothly, the now silent throng making way, and swept down the green roadway at a terrific pace and wholly without vibration, toward the seven-terraced tower.

As we flew along I tried to discover the source of the power, but I could not—then. There was no sign of mechanism, but that the shell responded to some form of energy was certain—the driver grasping a small lever which seemed to control not only our speed, but our direction.

We turned abruptly and swept up a runway through one of the gardens, and stopped softly before a pillared pavilion. I saw now that these were much larger than I had thought. The structure to which we had been carried covered, I estimated, fully an acre. Oblong, with its slender, vari-coloured columns spaced regularly, its walls were like the sliding screens of the Japanese—shoji.

The green dwarf hurried us up a flight of broad steps flanked by great carved serpents, winged and scaled. He stamped twice upon mosaicked stones between two of the pillars, and a screen rolled aside, revealing an immense hall scattered about with low divans on which lolled a dozen or more of the dwarfish men, dressed identically as he.

They sauntered up to us leisurely; the surprised interest in their faces tempered by the same inhumanly gay malice that seemed to be characteristic of all these people we had as yet seen.

"The Afyo Maie awaits them, Rador," said one.

The green dwarf nodded, beckoned us, and led the way through the great hall and into a smaller chamber whose far side was covered with the opacity I had noted from the aerie of the cliff. I examined the—blackness—with lively interest.

It had neither substance nor texture; it was not matter—and yet it suggested solidity; an entire cessation, a complete absorption of light; an ebon veil at once immaterial and palpable. I stretched, involuntarily, my hand out toward it, and felt it quickly drawn back.

"Do you seek your end so soon?" whispered Rador. "But I forget—you do not know," he added. "On your life touch not the blackness, ever. It—"

He stopped, for abruptly in the density a portal appeared; swinging out of the shadow like a picture thrown by a lantern upon a screen. Through it was revealed a chamber filled with a soft rosy glow. Rising from cushioned couches, a woman and a man regarded us, half leaning over a long, low table of what seemed polished jet, laden with flowers and unfamiliar fruits.

About the room—that part of it, at least, that I could see—were a few oddly shaped chairs of the same substance. On high, silvery tripods three immense globes stood, and it was from them that the rose glow emanated. At the side of the woman was a smaller globe whose roseate gleam was tempered by quivering waves of blue.

"Enter Rador with the strangers!" a clear, sweet voice called.

Rador bowed deeply and stood aside, motioning us to pass. We entered, the green dwarf behind us, and out of the corner of my eye I saw the doorway fade as abruptly as it had appeared and again the dense shadow fill its place.

"Come closer, strangers. Be not afraid!" commanded the bell-toned voice.

We approached.

The woman, sober scientist that I am, made the breath catch in my throat. Never had I seen a woman so beautiful as was Yolara of the Dweller's city—and none of so perilous a beauty. Her hair was of the colour of the young tassels of the corn and coiled in a regal crown above her broad, white brows; her wide eyes were of grey that could change to a cornflower blue and in anger deepen to purple; grey or blue, they had little laughing devils within them, but when the storm of anger darkened them—they were not laughing, no! The silken webs that half covered, half revealed her did not hide the ivory whiteness of her flesh nor the sweet curve of shoulders and breasts. But for all her amazing beauty, she was—sinister! There was cruelty about the curving mouth, and in the music of her voice—not conscious cruelty, but the more terrifying, careless cruelty of nature itself.

The girl of the rose wall had been beautiful, yes! But her beauty was human, understandable. You could imagine her with a babe in her arms—but you could not so imagine this woman. About her loveliness hovered something unearthly. A sweet feminine echo of the Dweller was Yolara, the Dweller's priestess—and as gloriously, terrifyingly evil!

XIV

The Justice of Lora

As I looked at her the man arose and made his way round the table
toward us. For the first time my eyes took in Lugur. A few inches
taller than the green dwarf, he was far broader, more filled with the
suggestion of appalling strength.

The tremendous shoulders were four feet wide if an inch, tapering
down to mighty thewed thighs. The muscles of his chest stood out
beneath his tunic of red. Around his forehead shone a chaplet of
bright-blue stones, sparkling among the thick curls of his silver-ash
hair.

Upon his face pride and ambition were written large—and power
still larger. All the mockery, the malice, the hint of callous indifference
that I had noted in the other dwarfish men were there, too—but
intensified, touched with the satanic.

The woman spoke again.

"Who are you strangers, and how came you here?" She turned to
Rador. "Or is it that they do not understand our tongue?"

"One understands and speaks it—but very badly, O Yolara," answered
the green dwarf.

"Speak, then, that one of you," she commanded.

But it was Marakinoff who found his voice first, and I marvelled at
the fluency, so much greater than mine, with which he spoke.

"We came for different purposes. I to seek knowledge of a kind; he"—
pointing to me "of another. This man"—he looked at Olaf—"to find a
wife and child."

The grey-blue eyes had been regarding O'Keefe steadily and with
plainly increasing interest.

"And why did *you* come?" she asked him. "Nay—I would have him
speak for himself, if he can," she stilled Marakinoff peremptorily.

When Larry spoke it was haltingly, in the tongue that was strange
to him, searching for the proper words.

"I came to help these men—and because something I could not then
understand called me, O lady, whose eyes are like forest pools at dawn,"
he answered; and even in the unfamiliar words there was a touch of the

Irish brogue, and little merry lights danced in the eyes Larry had so apostrophized.

"I could find fault with your speech, but none with its burden," she said. "What forest pools are I know not, and the dawn has not shone upon the people of Lora these many sais of laya.[1] But I sense what you mean!"

The eyes deepened to blue as she regarded him. She smiled.

"Are there many like you in the world from which you come?" she asked softly. "Well, we soon shall—"

Lugur interrupted her almost rudely and glowering.

"Best we should know how they came hence," he growled.

She darted a quick look at him, and again the little devils danced in her wondrous eyes.

"Yes, that is true," she said. "How came you here?"

Again it was Marakinoff who answered—slowly, considering every word.

"In the world above," he said, "there are ruins of cities not built by any of those who now dwell there. To us these places called, and we sought for knowledge of the wise ones who made them. We found a passageway. The way led us downward to a door in yonder cliff, and through it we came here."

---

1. Later I was to find that Murian reckoning rested upon the extraordinary increased luminosity of the cliffs at the time of full moon on earth—this action, to my mind, being linked either with the effect of the light streaming globes upon the Moon Pool, whose source was in the shining cliffs, or else upon some mysterious affinity of their radiant element with the flood of moonlight on earth—the latter, most probably, because even when the moon must have been clouded above, it made no difference in the phenomenon. Thirteen of these shinings forth constituted a laya, one of them a lat. Ten was sa; ten times ten times ten a said, or thousand; ten times a thousand was a sais. A sais of laya was then literally ten thousand years. What we would call an hour was by them called a va. The whole time system was, of course, a mingling of time as it had been known to their remote, surface-dwelling ancestors, and the peculiar determining factors in the vast cavern.

(Unquestionably there is a subtle difference between time as we know it and time in this subterranean land—its progress there being slower. This, however, is only in accord with the well-known doctrine of relativity, which predicates both space and time as necessary inventions of the human mind to orient itself to the conditions under which it finds itself. I tried often to measure this difference, but could never do so to my entire satisfaction. The closest I can come to it is to say that an hour of our time is the equivalent of an hour and five-eighths in Muria. For further information upon this matter of relativity the reader may consult any of the numerous books upon the subject.—W. T. G.)

"Then have you found what you sought?" spoke she. "For we are of those who built the cities. But this gateway in the rock—where is it?"

"After we passed, it closed upon us; nor could we after find trace of it," answered Marakinoff.

The incredulity that had shown upon the face of the green dwarf fell upon theirs; on Lugur's it was clouded with furious anger.

He turned to Rador.

"I could find no opening, lord," said the green dwarf quickly.

And there was so fierce a fire in the eyes of Lugur as he swung back upon us that O'Keefe's hand slipped stealthily down toward his pistol.

"Best it is to speak truth to Yolara, priestess of the Shining One, and to Lugur, the Voice," he cried menacingly.

"It is the truth," I interposed. "We came down the passage. At its end was a carved vine, a vine of five flowers"—the fire died from the red dwarf's eyes, and I could have sworn to a swift pallor. "I rested a hand upon these flowers, and a door opened. But when we had gone through it and turned, behind us was nothing but unbroken cliff. The door had vanished."

I had taken my cue from Marakinoff. If he had eliminated the episode of car and Moon Pool, he had good reason, I had no doubt; and I would be as cautious. And deep within me something cautioned me to say nothing of my quest; to stifle all thought of Throckmartin— something that warned, peremptorily, finally, as though it were a message from Throckmartin himself!

"A vine with five flowers!" exclaimed the red dwarf. "Was it like this, say?"

He thrust forward a long arm. Upon the thumb of the hand was an immense ring, set with a dull-blue stone. Graven on the face of the jewel was the symbol of the rosy walls of the Moon Chamber that had opened to us their two portals. But cut over the vine were seven circles, one about each of the flowers and two larger ones covering, intersecting them.

"This is the same," I said; "but these were not there"—I indicated the circles.

The woman drew a deep breath and looked deep into Lugur's eyes.

"The sign of the Silent Ones!" he half whispered.

It was the woman who first recovered herself.

"The strangers are weary, Lugur," she said. "When they are rested they shall show where the rocks opened."

I sensed a subtle change in their attitude toward us; a new intentness; a doubt plainly tinged with apprehension. What was it they feared? Why had the symbol of the vine wrought the change? And who or what were the Silent Ones?

Yolara's eyes turned to Olaf, hardened, and grew cold grey. Subconsciously I had noticed that from the first the Norseman had been absorbed in his regard of the pair; had, indeed, never taken his gaze from them; had noticed, too, the priestess dart swift glances toward him.

He returned her scrutiny fearlessly, a touch of contempt in the clear eyes—like a child watching a snake which he did not dread, but whose danger be well knew.

Under that look Yolara stirred impatiently, sensing, I know, its meaning.

"Why do you look at me so?" she cried.

An expression of bewilderment passed over Olaf's face.

"I do not understand," he said in English.

I caught a quickly repressed gleam in O'Keefe's eyes. He knew, as I knew, that Olaf must have understood. But did Marakinoff?

Apparently he did not. But why was Olaf feigning ignorance?

"This man is a sailor from what we call the North," thus Larry haltingly. "He is crazed, I think. He tells a strange tale of a something of cold fire that took his wife and babe. We found him wandering where we were. And because he is strong we brought him with us. That is all, O lady, whose voice is sweeter than the honey of the wild bees!"

"A shape of cold fire?" she repeated.

"A shape of cold fire that whirled beneath the moon, with the sound of little bells," answered Larry, watching her intently.

She looked at Lugur and laughed.

"Then he, too, is fortunate," she said. "For he has come to the place of his something of cold fire—and tell him that he shall join his wife and child, in time; that I promise him."

Upon the Norseman's face there was no hint of comprehension, and at that moment I formed an entirely new opinion of Olaf's intelligence; for certainly it must have been a prodigious effort of the will, indeed, that enabled him, understanding, to control himself.

"What does she say?" he asked.

Larry repeated.

"Good!" said Olaf. "Good!"

He looked at Yolara with well-assumed gratitude. Lugur, who had been scanning his bulk, drew close. He felt the giant muscles which Huldricksson accommodatingly flexed for him.

"But he shall meet Valdor and Tahola before he sees those kin of his," he laughed mockingly. "And if he bests them—for reward—his wife and babe!"

A shudder, quickly repressed, shook the seaman's frame. The woman bent her supremely beautiful head.

"These two," she said, pointing to the Russian and to me, "seem to be men of learning. They may be useful. As for this man,"—she smiled at Larry—"I would have him explain to me somethings." She hesitated. "What 'hon-ey of 'e wild bees-s' is." Larry had spoken the words in English, and she was trying to repeat them. "As for this man, the sailor, do as you please with him, Lugur; always remembering that I have given my word that he shall join that wife and babe of his!" She laughed sweetly, sinisterly. "And now—take them, Rador—give them food and drink and let them rest till we shall call them again."

She stretched out a hand toward O'Keefe. The Irishman bowed low over it, raised it softly to his lips. There was a vicious hiss from Lugur; but Yolara regarded Larry with eyes now all tender blue.

"You please me," she whispered.

And the face of Lugur grew darker.

We turned to go. The rosy, azure-shot globe at her side suddenly dulled. From it came a faint bell sound as of chimes far away. She bent over it. It vibrated, and then its surface ran with little waves of dull colour; from it came a whispering so low that I could not distinguish the words—if words they were.

She spoke to the red dwarf.

"They have brought the three who blasphemed the Shining One," she said slowly. "Now it is in my mind to show these strangers the justice of Lora. What say you, Lugur?"

The red dwarf nodded, his eyes sparkling with a malicious anticipation.

The woman spoke again to the globe. "Bring them here!"

And again it ran swiftly with its film of colours, darkened, and shone rosy once more. From without there came a rustle of many feet upon the rugs. Yolara pressed a slender hand upon the base of the pedestal of the globe beside her. Abruptly the light faded from all, and on the same instant the four walls of blackness vanished, revealing on two sides the lovely, unfamiliar garden through the guarding rows of pillars; at our backs soft draperies hid what lay beyond; before us, flanked by flowered screens, was the corridor through which we had entered, crowded now by the green dwarfs of the great hall.

The dwarfs advanced. Each, I now noted, had the same clustering black hair of Rador. They separated, and from them stepped three figures—a youth of not more than twenty, short, but with the great shoulders of all the males we had seen of this race; a girl of seventeen, I judged, white-faced, a head taller than the boy, her long, black hair dishevelled; and behind these two a stunted, gnarled shape whose head was sunk deep between the enormous shoulders, whose white beard fell like that of some ancient gnome down to his waist, and whose eyes were a white flame of hate. The girl cast herself weeping at the feet of the priestess; the youth regarded her curiously.

"You are Songar of the Lower Waters?" murmured Yolara almost caressingly. "And this is your daughter and her lover?"

The gnome nodded, the flame in his eyes leaping higher.

"It has come to me that you three have dared blaspheme the Shining One, its priestess, and its Voice," went on Yolara smoothly. "Also that you have called out to the three Silent Ones. Is it true?"

"Your spies have spoken—and have you not already judged us?" The voice of the old dwarf was bitter.

A flicker shot through the eyes of Yolara, again cold grey. The girl reached a trembling hand out to the hem of the priestess's veils.

"Tell us why you did these things, Songar," she said. "Why you did them, knowing full well what your—reward—would be."

The dwarf stiffened; he raised his withered arms, and his eyes blazed.

"Because evil are your thoughts and evil are your deeds," he cried. "Yours and your lover's, there"—he levelled a finger at Lugur. "Because of the Shining One you have made evil, too, and the greater wickedness you contemplate—you and he with the Shining One. But I tell you that your measure of iniquity is full; the tale of your sin near ended! Yea—the Silent Ones have been patient, but soon they will speak." He pointed at us. "A sign are *they*—a warning—harlot!" He spat the word.

In Yolara's eyes, grown black, the devils leaped unrestrained.

"Is it even so, Songar?" her voice caressed. "Now ask the Silent Ones to help you! They sit afar—but surely they will hear you." The sweet voice was mocking. "As for these two, they shall pray to the Shining

One for forgiveness—and surely the Shining One will take them to its bosom! As for you—you have lived long enough, Songar! Pray to the Silent Ones, Songar, and pass out into the nothingness—you!"

She dipped down into her bosom and drew forth something that resembled a small cone of tarnished silver. She levelled it, a covering clicked from its base, and out of it darted a slender ray of intense green light.

It struck the old dwarf squarely over the heart, and spread swift as light itself, covering him with a gleaming, pale film. She clenched her hand upon the cone, and the ray disappeared. She thrust the cone back into her breast and leaned forward expectantly; so Lugur and so the other dwarfs. From the girl came a low wail of anguish; the boy dropped upon his knees, covering his face.

For the moment the white beard stood rigid; then the robe that had covered him seemed to melt away, revealing all the knotted, monstrous body. And in that body a vibration began, increasing to incredible rapidity. It wavered before us like a reflection in a still pond stirred by a sudden wind. It grew and grew—to a rhythm whose rapidity was intolerable to watch and that still chained the eyes.

The figure grew indistinct, misty. Tiny sparks in infinite numbers leaped from it—like, I thought, the radiant shower of particles hurled out by radium when seen under the microscope. Mistier still it grew—there trembled before us for a moment a faintly luminous shadow which held, here and there, tiny sparkling atoms like those that pulsed in the light about us! The glowing shadow vanished, the sparkling atoms were still for a moment—and shot away, joining those dancing others.

Where the gnomelike form had been but a few seconds before—there was nothing!

O'Keefe drew a long breath, and I was sensible of a prickling along my scalp.

Yolara leaned toward us.

"You have seen," she said. Her eyes lingered tigerishly upon Olaf's pallid face. "Heed!" she whispered. She turned to the men in green, who were laughing softly among themselves.

"Take these two, and go!" she commanded.

"The justice of Lora," said the red dwarf. "The justice of Lora and the Shining One under Thanaroa!"

Upon the utterance of the last word I saw Marakinoff start violently. The hand at his side made a swift, surreptitious gesture, so fleeting that

I hardly caught it. The red dwarf stared at the Russian, and there was amazement upon his face.

Swiftly as Marakinoff, he returned it.

"Yolara," the red dwarf spoke, "it would please me to take this man of wisdom to my own place for a time. The giant I would have, too."

The woman awoke from her brooding; nodded.

"As you will, Lugur," she said.

And as, shaken to the core, we passed out into the garden into the full throbbing of the light, I wondered if all the tiny sparkling diamond points that shook about us had once been men like Songar of the Lower Waters—and felt my very soul grow sick!

XV

The Angry, Whispering Globe

Our way led along a winding path between banked masses of softly radiant blooms, groups of feathery ferns whose plumes were starred with fragrant white and blue flowerets, slender creepers swinging from the branches of the strangely trunked trees, bearing along their threads orchid-like blossoms both delicately frail and gorgeously flamboyant.

The path we trod was an exquisite mosaic—pastel greens and pinks upon a soft grey base, garlands of nimbused forms like the flaming rose of the Rosicrucians held in the mouths of the flying serpents. A smaller pavilion arose before us, single-storied, front wide open.

Upon its threshold Rador paused, bowed deeply, and motioned us within. The chamber we entered was large, closed on two sides by screens of grey; at the back gay, concealing curtains. The low table of blue stone, dressed with fine white cloths, stretched at one side flanked by the cushioned divans.

At the left was a high tripod bearing one of the rosy globes we had seen in the house of Yolara; at the head of the table a smaller globe similar to the whispering one. Rador pressed upon its base, and two other screens slid into place across the entrance, shutting in the room.

He clapped his hands; the curtains parted, and two girls came through them. Tall and willow lithe, their bluish-black hair falling in ringlets just below their white shoulders, their clear eyes of forget-me-not blue, and skins of extraordinary fineness and purity—they were singularly attractive. Each was clad in an extremely scanty bodice of silken blue, girdled above a kirtle that came barely to their very pretty knees.

"Food and drink," ordered Rador.

They dropped back through the curtains.

"Do you like them?" he asked us.

"Some chickens!" said Larry. "They delight the heart," he translated for Rador.

The green dwarf's next remark made me gasp.

"They are yours," he said.

Before I could question him further upon this extraordinary statement the pair re-entered, bearing a great platter on which were small loaves, strange fruits, and three immense flagons of rock crystal—two filled with a slightly sparkling yellow liquid and the third with a purplish drink. I became acutely sensible that it had been hours since I had either eaten or drunk. The yellow flagons were set before Larry and me, the purple at Rador's hand.

The girls, at his signal, again withdrew. I raised my glass to my lips and took a deep draft. The taste was unfamiliar but delightful.

Almost at once my fatigue disappeared. I realized a clarity of mind, an interesting exhilaration and sense of irresponsibility, of freedom from care, that were oddly enjoyable. Larry became immediately his old gay self.

The green dwarf regarded us whimsically, sipping from his great flagon of rock crystal.

"Much do I desire to know of that world you came from," he said at last—"through the rocks," he added, slyly.

"And much do we desire to know of this world of yours, O Rador," I answered.

Should I ask him of the Dweller; seek from him a clue to Throckmartin? Again, clearly as a spoken command, came the warning to forbear, to wait. And once more I obeyed.

"Let us learn, then, from each other." The dwarf was laughing. "And first—are all above like you—drawn out"—he made an expressive gesture—"and are there many of you?"

"There are—" I hesitated, and at last spoke the Polynesian that means tens upon tens multiplied indefinitely—"there are as many as the drops of water in the lake we saw from the ledge where you found us," I continued; "many as the leaves on the trees without. And they are all like us—varyingly."

He considered skeptically, I could see, my remark upon our numbers.

"In Muria," he said at last, "the men are like me or like Lugur. Our women are as you see them—like Yolara or those two who served you." He hesitated. "And there is a third; but only one."

Larry leaned forward eagerly.

"Brown-haired with glints of ruddy bronze, golden-eyed, and lovely as a dream, with long, slender, beautiful hands?" he cried.

"Where saw you *her*?" interrupted the dwarf, starting to his feet.

"Saw her?" Larry recovered himself. "Nay, Rador, perhaps, I only dreamed that there was such a woman."

"See to it, then, that you tell not your dream to Yolara," said the dwarf grimly. "For her I meant and her you have pictured is Lakla, the hand-maiden to the Silent Ones, and neither Yolara nor Lugur, nay, nor the Shining One, love her overmuch, stranger."

"Does she dwell here?" Larry's face was alight.

The dwarf hesitated, glanced about him anxiously.

"Nay," he answered, "ask me no more of her." He was silent for a space. "And what do you who are as leaves or drops of water do in that world of yours?" he said, plainly bent on turning the subject.

"Keep off the golden-eyed girl, Larry," I interjected. "Wait till we find out why she's tabu."

"Love and battle, strive and accomplish and die; or fail and die," answered Larry—to Rador—giving me a quick nod of acquiescence to my warning in English.

"In that at least your world and mine differ little," said the dwarf.

"How great is this world of yours, Rador?" I spoke.

He considered me gravely.

"How great indeed I do not know," he said frankly at last. "The land where we dwell with the Shining One stretches along the white waters for—" He used a phrase of which I could make nothing. "Beyond this city of the Shining One and on the hither shores of the white waters dwell the mayia ladala—the common ones." He took a deep draft from his flagon. "There are, first, the fair-haired ones, the children of the ancient rulers," he continued. "There are, second, we the soldiers; and last, the mayia ladala, who dig and till and weave and toil and give our rulers and us their daughters, and dance with the Shining One!" he added.

"Who rules?" I asked.

"The fair-haired, under the Council of Nine, who are under Yolara, the Priestess and Lugur, the Voice," he answered, "who are in turn beneath the Shining One!" There was a ring of bitter satire in the last.

"And those three who were judged?"—this from Larry.

"They were of the mayia ladala," he replied, "like those two I gave you. But they grow restless. They do not like to dance with the Shining One—the blasphemers!" He raised his voice in a sudden great shout of mocking laughter.

In his words I caught a fleeting picture of the race—an ancient, luxurious, close-bred oligarchy clustered about some mysterious deity;

a soldier class that supported them; and underneath all the toiling, oppressed hordes.

"And is that all?" asked Larry.

"No," he answered. "There is the Sea of Crimson where—"

Without warning the globe beside us sent out a vicious note, Rador turned toward it, his face paling. Its surface crawled with whisperings—angry, peremptory!

"I hear!" he croaked, gripping the table. "I obey!"

He turned to us a face devoid for once of its malice.

"Ask me no more questions, strangers," he said. "And now, if you are done, I will show you where you may sleep and bathe."

He arose abruptly. We followed him through the hangings, passed through a corridor and into another smaller chamber, roofless, the sides walled with screens of dark grey. Two cushioned couches were there and a curtained door leading into an open, outer enclosure in which a fountain played within a wide pool.

"Your bath," said Rador. He dropped the curtain and came back into the room. He touched a carved flower at one side. There was a tiny sighing from overhead and instantly across the top spread a veil of blackness, impenetrable to light but certainly not to air, for through it pulsed little breaths of the garden fragrances. The room filled with a cool twilight, refreshing, sleep-inducing. The green dwarf pointed to the couches.

"Sleep!" he said. "Sleep and fear nothing. My men are on guard outside." He came closer to us, the old mocking gaiety sparkling in his eyes.

"But I spoke too quickly," he whispered. "Whether it is because the Afyo Maie fears their tongues—or—" he laughed at Larry. "The maids are *not* yours!" Still laughing he vanished through the curtains of the room of the fountain before I could ask him the meaning of his curious gift, its withdrawal, and his most enigmatic closing remarks.

"Back in the great old days of Ireland," thus Larry breaking into my thoughts raptly, the brogue thick, "there was Cairill mac Cairill—Cairill Swiftspear. An' Cairill wronged Keevan of Emhain Abhlach, of the blood of Angus of the great people when he was sleeping in the likeness of a pale reed. Then Keevan put this penance on Cairill—that for a year Cairill should wear his body in Emhain Abhlach, which is the Land of Faery and for that year Keevan should wear the body of Cairill. And it was done.

"In that year Cairill met Emar of the Birds that are one white, one red, and one black—and they loved, and from that love sprang Ailill their son. And when Ailill was born he took a reed flute and first he played slumber on Cairill, and then he played old age so that Cairill grew white and withered; then Ailill played again and Cairill became a shadow—then a shadow of a shadow—then a breath; and the breath went out upon the wind!" He shivered. "Like the old gnome," he whispered, "that they called Songar of the Lower Waters!"

He shook his head as though he cast a dream from him. Then, all alert—

"But that was in Iceland ages agone. And there's nothing like that here, Doc!" He laughed. "It doesn't scare me one little bit, old boy. The pretty devil lady's got the wrong slant. When you've had a pal standing beside you one moment—full of life, and joy, and power, and potentialities, telling what he's going to do to make the world hum when he gets through the slaughter, just running over with zip and pep of life, Doc—and the next instant, right in the middle of a laugh—a piece of damned shell takes off half his head and with it joy and power and all the rest of it"—his face twitched—"well, old man, in the face of *that* mystery a disappearing act such as the devil lady treated us to doesn't make much of a dent. Not on me. But by the brogans of Brian Boru—if we could have had some of that stuff to turn on during the war—oh, boy!"

He was silent, evidently contemplating the idea with vast pleasure. And as for me, at that moment my last doubt of Larry O'Keefe vanished, I saw that he did believe, really believed, in his banshees, his leprechauns and all the old dreams of the Gael—but only within the limits of Ireland.

In one drawer of his mind was packed all his superstition, his mysticism, and what of weakness it might carry. But face him with any peril or problem and the drawer closed instantaneously leaving a mind that was utterly fearless, incredulous, and ingenious; swept clean of all cobwebs by as fine a skeptic broom as ever brushed a brain.

"Some stuff!" Deepest admiration was in his voice. "If we'd only had it when the war was on—imagine half a dozen of us scooting over the enemy batteries and the gunners underneath all at once beginning to shake themselves to pieces! Wow!" His tone was rapturous.

"It's easy enough to explain, Larry," I said. "The effect, that is—for what the green ray is made of I don't know, of course. But what it does, clearly, is stimulate atomic vibration to such a pitch that the cohesion between the particles of matter is broken and the body flies to bits—just as a fly-wheel does when its speed gets so great that the particles of which *it* is made can't hold together."

"Shake themselves to pieces is right, then!" he exclaimed.

"Absolutely right," I nodded. "Everything in Nature vibrates. And all matter—whether man or beast or stone or metal or vegetable—is made up of vibrating molecules, which are made up of vibrating atoms which are made up of truly infinitely small particles of electricity called electrons, and electrons, the base of all matter, are themselves perhaps only a vibration of the mysterious ether.

"If a magnifying glass of sufficient size and strength could be placed over us we could see ourselves as sieves—our space lattice, as it is called. And all that is necessary to break down the lattice, to shake us into nothingness, is some agent that will set our atoms vibrating at such a rate that at last they escape the unseen cords and fly off.

"The green ray of Yolara is such an agent. It set up in the dwarf that incredibly rapid rhythm that you saw and—shook him not to atoms—but to electrons!"

"They had a gun on the West Front—a seventy-five," said O'Keefe, "that broke the eardrums of everybody who fired it, no matter what protection they used. It looked like all the other seventy-fives—but there was something about its sound that did it. They had to recast it."

"It's practically the same thing," I replied. "By some freak its vibratory qualities had that effect. The deep whistle of the sunken Lusitania would, for instance, make the Singer Building shake to its foundations; while the Olympic did not affect the Singer at all but made the Woolworth shiver all through. In each case they stimulated the atomic vibration of the particular building—"

I paused, aware all at once of an intense drowsiness. O'Keefe, yawning, reached down to unfasten his puttees.

"Lord, I'm sleepy!" he exclaimed. "Can't understand it—what you say—most—interesting—Lord!" he yawned again; straightened. "What made Reddy take such a shine to the Russian?" he asked.

"Thanaroa," I answered, fighting to keep my eyes open.

"What?"

"When Lugur spoke that name I saw Marakinoff signal him. Thanaroa is, I suspect, the original form of the name of Tangaroa, the greatest god of the Polynesians. There's a secret cult to him in the islands.

Marakinoff may belong to it—he knows it anyway. Lugur recognized the signal and despite his surprise answered it."

"So he gave him the high sign, eh?" mused Larry. "How could they both know it?"

"The cult is a very ancient one. Undoubtedly it had its origin in the dim beginnings before these people migrated here," I replied. "It's a link—one—of the few links between up there and the lost past—"

"Trouble then," mumbled Larry. "Hell brewing! I smell it—Say, Doc, is this sleepiness natural? Wonder where my—gas mask—is—" he added, half incoherently.

But I myself was struggling desperately against the drugged slumber pressing down upon me.

"Lakla!" I heard O'Keefe murmur. "Lakla of the golden eyes—no Eilidh—the Fair!" He made an immense effort, half raised himself, grinned faintly.

"Thought this was paradise when I first saw it, Doc," he sighed. "But I know now, if it is, No-Man's Land was the greatest place on earth for a honeymoon. They—they've got us, Doc—" He sank back. "Good luck, old boy, wherever you're going." His hand waved feebly. "Glad—knew—you. Hope—see—you—'gain—"

His voice trailed into silence. Fighting, fighting with every fibre of brain and nerve against the sleep, I felt myself being steadily overcome. Yet before oblivion rushed down upon me I seemed to see upon the grey-screened wall nearest the Irishman an oval of rosy light begin to glow; watched, as my falling lids inexorably fell, a flame-tipped shadow waver on it; thicken; condense—and there looking down upon Larry, her eyes great golden stars in which intensest curiosity and shy tenderness struggled, sweet mouth half smiling, was the girl of the Moon Pool's Chamber, the girl whom the green dwarf had named—Lakla: the vision Larry had invoked before that sleep which I could no longer deny had claimed him—

Closer she came—closer—the eyes were over us.

Then oblivion indeed!

XVI

Yolara of Muria vs. the O'Keefe

I awakened with all the familiar, homely sensation of a shade having been pulled up in a darkened room. I thrilled with a wonderful sense of deep rest and restored resiliency. The ebon shadow had vanished from above and down into the room was pouring the silvery light. From the fountain pool came a mighty splashing and shouts of laughter. I jumped and drew the curtain. O'Keefe and Rador were swimming a wild race; the dwarf like an otter, out-distancing and playing around the Irishman at will.

Had that overpowering sleep—and now I confess that my struggle against it had been largely inspired by fear that it was the abnormal slumber which Throckmartin had described as having heralded the approach of the Dweller before it had carried away Thora and Stanton—had that sleep been after all nothing but natural reaction of tired nerves and brains?

And that last vision of the golden-eyed girl bending over Larry? Had that also been a delusion of an overstressed mind? Well, it might have been, I could not tell. At any rate, I decided, I would speak about it to O'Keefe once we were alone again—and then giving myself up to the urge of buoyant well-being I shouted like a boy, stripped and joined the two in the pool. The water was warm and I felt the unwonted tingling of life in every vein increase; something from it seemed to pulse through the skin, carrying a clean vigorous vitality that toned every fibre. Tiring at last, we swam to the edge and drew ourselves out. The green dwarf quickly clothed himself and Larry rather carefully donned his uniform.

"The Afyo Maie has summoned us, Doc," he said. "We're to—well—I suppose you'd call it breakfast with her. After that, Rador tells me, we're to have a session with the Council of Nine. I suppose Yolara is as curious as any lady of—the upper world, as you might put it—and just naturally can't wait," he added.

He gave himself a last shake, patted the automatic hidden under his left arm, whistled cheerfully.

"After you, my dear Alphonse," he said to Rador, with a low bow. The dwarf laughed, bent in an absurd imitation of Larry's mocking courtesy and started ahead of us to the house of the priestess. When he had gone a little way on the orchid-walled path I whispered to O'Keefe:

"Larry, when you were falling off to sleep—did you think you saw anything?"

"See anything!" he grinned. "Doc, sleep hit me like a Hun shell. I thought they were pulling the gas on us. I—I had some intention of bidding you tender farewells," he continued, half sheepishly. "I think I did start 'em, didn't I?"

I nodded.

"But wait a minute—" he hesitated. "I had a queer sort of dream—"

"'What was it?" I asked eagerly,

"Well," he answered slowly, "I suppose it was because I'd been thinking of—Golden Eyes. Anyway, I thought she came through the wall and leaned over me—yes, and put one of those long white hands of hers on my head—I couldn't raise my lids—but in some queer way I could see her. Then it got real dreamish. Why do you ask?"

Rador turned back toward us,

"Later," I answered, "Not now. When we're alone."

But through me went a little glow of reassurance. Whatever the maze through which we were moving; whatever of menacing evil lurking there—the Golden Girl was clearly watching over us; watching with whatever unknown powers she could muster.

We passed the pillared entrance; went through a long bowered corridor and stopped before a door that seemed to be sliced from a monolith of pale jade—high, narrow, set in a wall of opal.

Rador stamped twice and the same supernally sweet, silver bell tones of—yesterday, I must call it, although in that place of eternal day the term is meaningless—bade us enter. The door slipped aside. The chamber was small, the opal walls screening it on three sides, the black opacity covering it, the fourth side opening out into a delicious little walled garden—a mass of the fragrant, luminous blooms and delicately colored fruit. Facing it was a small table of reddish wood and from the omnipresent cushions heaped around it arose to greet us—Yolara.

Larry drew in his breath with an involuntary gasp of admiration and bowed low. My own admiration was as frank—and the priestess was well pleased with our homage.

She was swathed in the filmy, half-revelant webs, now of palest blue. The corn-silk hair was caught within a wide-meshed golden net in which sparkled tiny brilliants, like blended sapphires and diamonds.

Her own azure eyes sparkled as brightly as they, and I noted again in their clear depths the half-eager approval as they rested upon O'Keefe's lithe, well-knit figure and his keen, clean-cut face. The high-arched, slender feet rested upon soft sandals whose gauzy withes laced the exquisitely formed leg to just below the dimpled knee.

"Some giddy wonder!" exclaimed Larry, looking at me and placing a hand over his heart. "Put her on a New York roof and she'd empty Broadway. Take the cue from me, Doc."

He turned to Yolara, whose face was somewhat puzzled.

"I said, O lady whose shining hair is a web for hearts, that in our world your beauty would dazzle the sight of men as would a little woman sun!" he said, in the florid imagery to which the tongue lends itself so well.

A flush stole up through the translucent skin. The blue eyes softened and she waved us toward the cushions. Black-haired maids stole in, placing before us the fruits, the little loaves and a steaming drink somewhat the colour and odor of chocolate. I was conscious of outrageous hunger.

"What are you named, strangers?" she asked.

"This man is named Goodwin," said O'Keefe. "As for me, call me Larry."

"Nothing like getting acquainted quick," he said to me—but kept his eyes upon Yolara as though he were voicing another honeyed phrase. And so she took it, for: "You must teach me your tongue," she murmured.

"Then shall I have two words where now I have one to tell you of your loveliness," he answered.

"And also that'll take time," he spoke to me. "Essential occupation out of which we can't be drafted to make these fun-loving folk any Roman holiday. Get me!"

"Larree," mused Yolara. "I like the sound. It is sweet—" and indeed it was as she spoke it.

"And what is your land named, Larree?" she continued. "And Goodwin's?" She caught the sound perfectly.

"My land, O lady of loveliness, is two—Ireland and America; his but one—America."

She repeated the two names—slowly, over and over. We seized the opportunity to attack the food; halting half guiltily as she spoke again.

"Oh, but you are hungry!" she cried. "Eat then." She leaned her chin upon her hands and regarded us, whole fountains of questions brimming up in her eyes.

"How is it, Larree, that you have two countries and Goodwin but one?" she asked, at last unable to keep silent longer.

"I was born in Ireland; he in America. But I have dwelt long in his land and my heart loves each," he said.

She nodded, understandingly.

"Are all the men of Ireland like you, Larree? As all the men here are like Lugur or Rador? I like to look at you," she went on, with naive frankness. "I am tired of men like Lugur and Rador. But they are strong," she added, swiftly. "Lugur can hold up ten in his two arms and raise six with but one hand."

We could not understand her numerals and she raised white fingers to illustrate.

"That is little, O lady, to the men of Ireland," replied O'Keefe. "Lo, I have seen one of my race hold up ten times ten of our—what call you that swift thing in which Rador brought us here?"

"Corial," said she.

"Hold up ten times twenty of our corials with but two fingers—and these corials of ours—"

"Coria," said she.

"And these coria of ours are each greater in weight than ten of yours. Yes, and I have seen another with but one blow of his hand raise hell!

"And so I have," he murmured to me. "And both at Forty-second and Fifth Avenue, N. Y.—U. S. A."

Yolara considered all this with manifest doubt.

"Hell?" she inquired at last. "I know not the word."

"Well," answered O'Keefe. "Say Muria then. In many ways they are, I gather, O heart's delight, one and the same."

Now the doubt in the blue eyes was strong indeed. She shook her head.

"None of our men can do *that*!" she answered, at length. "Nor do I think you could, Larree."

"Oh, no," said Larry easily. "I never tried to be that strong. I fly," he added, casually.

The priestess rose to her feet, gazing at him with startled eyes.

"Fly!" she repeated incredulously. "Like a *Zitia*? A bird?"

Larry nodded—and then seeing the dawning command in her eyes, went on hastily.

"Not with my own wings, Yolara. In a—a corial that moves through—what's the word for air, Doc—well, through this—" He made a wide gesture up toward the nebulous haze above us. He took a pencil and on a white cloth made a hasty sketch of an airplane. "In a—a corial like this—" She regarded the sketch gravely, thrust a hand down into her girdle and brought forth a keen-bladed poniard; cut Larry's markings out and placed the fragment carefully aside.

"That I can understand," she said.

"Remarkably intelligent young woman," muttered O'Keefe. "Hope I'm not giving anything away—but she had me."

"But what are your women like, Larree? Are they like me? And how many have loved you?" she whispered.

"In all Ireland and America there is none like you, Yolara," he answered. "And take that anyway you please," he muttered in English. She took it, it was evident, as it most pleased her.

"Do you have goddesses?" she asked.

"Every woman in Ireland and America, is a goddess"; thus Larry.

"Now that I do not believe." There was both anger and mockery in her eyes. "I know women, Larree—and if that were so there would be no peace for men."

"There isn't!" replied he. The anger died out and she laughed, sweetly, understandingly.

"And which goddess do you worship, Larree?"

"You!" said Larry O'Keefe boldly.

"Larry! Larry!" I whispered. "Be careful. It's high explosive."

But the priestess was laughing—little trills of sweet bell notes; and pleasure was in each note.

"You are indeed bold, Larree," she said, "to offer me your worship. Yet am I pleased by your boldness. Still—Lugur is strong; and you are not of those who—what did you say—have tried. And your wings are not here—Larree!"

Again her laughter rang out. The Irishman flushed; it was *touché* for Yolara!

"Fear not for me with Lugur," he said, grimly. "Rather fear for him!"

The laughter died; she looked at him searchingly; a little enigmatic smile about her mouth—so sweet and so cruel.

"Well—we shall see," she murmured. "You say you battle in your world. With what?"

"Oh, with this and with that," answered Larry, airily. "We manage—"

A. MERRITT

"Have you the Keth—I mean that with which I sent Songar into the nothingness?" she asked swiftly.

"See what she's driving at?" O'Keefe spoke to me, swiftly. "Well I do! But here's where the O'Keefe lands.

"I said," he turned to her, "O voice of silver fire, that your spirit is high even as your beauty—and searches out men's souls as does your loveliness their hearts. And now listen, Yolara, for what I speak is truth"—into his eyes came the far-away gaze; into his voice the Irish softness—"Lo, in my land of Ireland, this many of your life's length agone—see"—he raised his ten fingers, clenched and unclenched them times twenty—"the mighty men of my race, the Taitha-da-Dainn, could send men out into the nothingness even as do you with the Keth. And this they did by their harpings, and by words spoken—words of power, O Yolara, that have their power still—and by pipings and by slaying sounds.

"There was Cravetheen who played swift flames from his harp, flying flames that ate those they were sent against. And there was Dalua, of Hy Brasil, whose pipes played away from man and beast and all living things their shadows—and at last played them to shadows too, so that wherever Dalua went his shadows that had been men and beast followed like a storm of little rustling leaves; yea, and Bel the Harper, who could make women's hearts run like wax and men's hearts flame to ashes and whose harpings could shatter strong cliffs and bow great trees to the sod—"

His eyes were bright, dream-filled; she shrank a little from him, faint pallor under the perfect skin.

"I say to you, Yolara, that these things were and are—in Ireland." His voice rang strong. "And I have seen men as many as those that are in your great chamber this many times over"—he clenched his hands once more, perhaps a dozen times—"blasted into nothingness before your Keth could even have touched them. Yea—and rocks as mighty as those through which we came lifted up and shattered before the lids could fall over your blue eyes. And this is truth, Yolara—all truth! Stay—have you that little cone of the Keth with which you destroyed Songar?"

She nodded, gazing at him, fascinated, fear and puzzlement contending.

"Then use it." He took a vase of crystal from the table, placed it on the threshold that led into the garden. "Use it on this—and I will show you."

"I will use it upon one of the ladala—" she began eagerly.

The exaltation dropped from him; there was a touch of horror in the eyes he turned to her; her own dropped before it.

"It shall be as you say," she said hurriedly. She drew the shining cone from her breast; levelled it at the vase. The green ray leaped forth, spread over the crystal, but before its action could even be begun, a flash of light shot from O'Keefe's hand, his automatic spat and the trembling vase flew into fragments. As quickly as he had drawn it, he thrust the pistol back into place and stood there empty handed, looking at her sternly. From the anteroom came shouting, a rush of feet.

Yolara's face was white, her eyes strained—but her voice was unshaken as she called to the clamouring guards:

"It is nothing—go to your places!"

But when the sound of their return had ceased she stared tensely at the Irishman—then looked again at the shattered vase.

"It is true!" she cried, "but see, the Keth is—alive!"

I followed her pointing finger. Each broken bit of the crystal was vibrating, shaking its particles out into space. Broken it the bullet of Larry's had—but not released it from the grip of the disintegrating force. The priestess's face was triumphant.

"But what matters it, O shining urn of beauty—what matters it to the vase that is broken what happens to its fragments?" asked Larry, gravely—and pointedly.

The triumph died from her face and for a space she was silent; brooding.

"Next," whispered O'Keefe to me. "Lots of surprises in the little box; keep your eye on the opening and see what comes out."

We had not long to wait. There was a sparkle of anger about Yolara, something too of injured pride. She clapped her hands; whispered to the maid who answered her summons, and then sat back regarding us, maliciously.

"You have answered me as to your strength—but you have not proved it; but the Keth you have answered. Now answer this!" she said.

She pointed out into the garden. I saw a flowering branch bend and snap as though a hand had broken it—but no hand was there! Saw then another and another bend and break, a little tree sway and fall—and closer and closer to us came the trail of snapping boughs while down into the garden poured the silvery light revealing—nothing! Now a great ewer beside a pillar rose swiftly in air and hurled itself crashing at my feet. Cushions close to us swirled about as though in the vortex of a whirlwind.

And unseen hands held my arms in a mighty clutch fast to my sides, another gripped my throat and I felt a needle-sharp poniard point pierce my shirt, touch the skin just over my heart!

"Larry!" I cried, despairingly. I twisted my head; saw that he too was caught in this grip of the invisible. But his face was calm, even amused.

"Keep cool, Doc!" he said. "Remember—she wants to learn the language!"

Now from Yolara burst chime upon chime of mocking laughter. She gave a command—the hands loosened, the poniard withdrew from my heart; suddenly as I had been caught I was free—and unpleasantly weak and shaky.

"Have you *that* in Ireland, Larree!" cried the priestess—and once more trembled with laughter.

"A good play, Yolara." His voice was as calm as his face. "But they did that in Ireland even before Dalua piped away his first man's shadow. And in Goodwin's land they make ships—coria that go on water—so you can pass by them and see only sea and sky; and those water coria are each of them many times greater than this whole palace of yours."

But the priestess laughed on.

"It did get me a little," whispered Larry. "That wasn't quite up to my mark. But God! If we could find that trick out and take it back with us!"

"Not so, Larree!" Yolara gasped, through her laughter. "Not so! Goodwin's cry betrayed you!"

Her good humour had entirely returned; she was like a mischievous child pleased over some successful trick; and like a child she cried—"I'll show you!"—signalled again; whispered to the maid who, quickly returning, laid before her a long metal case. Yolara took from her girdle something that looked like a small pencil, pressed it and shot a thin stream of light for all the world like an electric flash, upon its hasp. The lid flew open. Out of it she drew three flat, oval crystals, faint rose in hue. She handed one to O'Keefe and one to me.

"Look!" she commanded, placing the third before her own eyes. I peered through the stone and instantly there leaped into sight, out of thin air—six grinning dwarfs! Each was covered from top of head to soles of feet in a web so tenuous that through it their bodies were plain. The gauzy stuff seemed to vibrate—its strands to run together like quick-silver. I snatched the crystal from my eyes and—the chamber was empty! Put it back—and there were the grinning six!

Yolara gave another sign and they disappeared, even from the crystals.

"It is what they wear, Larree," explained Yolara, graciously. "It is something that came to us from—the Ancient Ones. But we have so few"—she sighed.

"Such treasures must be two-edged swords, Yolara," commented O'Keefe. "For how know you that one within them creeps not to you with hand eager to strike?"

"There is no danger," she said indifferently. "I am the keeper of them."

She mused for a space, then abruptly:

"And now no more. You two are to appear before the Council at a certain time—but fear nothing. You, Goodwin, go with Rador about our city and increase your wisdom. But you, Larree, await me here in my garden—" she smiled at him, provocatively—maliciously, too. "For shall not one who has resisted a world of goddesses be given all chance to worship when at last he finds his own?"

She laughed—whole-heartedly and was gone. And at that moment I liked Yolara better than ever I had before and—alas—better than ever I was to in the future.

I noted Rador standing outside the open jade door and started to go, but O'Keefe caught me by the arm.

"Wait a minute," he urged. "About Golden Eyes—you were going to tell me something—it's been on my mind all through that little sparring match."

I told him of the vision that had passed through my closing lids. He listened gravely and then laughed.

"Hell of a lot of privacy in this place!" he grinned. "Ladies who can walk through walls and others with regular invisible cloaks to let 'em flit wherever they please. Oh, well, don't let it get on your nerves, Doc. Remember—everything's natural! That robe stuff is just camouflage of course. But Lord, if we could only get a piece of it!"

"The material simply admits all light-vibrations, or perhaps curves them, just as the opacities cut them off," I answered. "A man under the X-ray is partly invisible; this makes him wholly so. He doesn't register, as the people of the motion-picture profession say."

"Camouflage," repeated Larry. "And as for the Shining One—Say!" he snorted. "I'd like to set the O'Keefe banshee up against it. I'll bet that old resourceful Irish body would give it the first three bites and a

A. MERRITT

strangle hold and wallop it before it knew it had 'em. Oh! Wow! Boy Howdy!"

I heard him still chuckling gleefully over this vision as I passed along the opal wall with the green dwarf.

A shell was awaiting us. I paused before entering it to examine the polished surface of runway and great road. It was obsidian—volcanic glass of pale emerald, unflawed, translucent, with no sign of block or juncture. I examined the shell.

"What makes it go?" I asked Rador. At a word from him the driver touched a concealed spring and an aperture appeared beneath the control-lever, of which I have spoken in a preceding chapter. Within was a small cube of black crystal, through whose sides I saw, dimly, a rapidly revolving, glowing ball, not more than two inches in diameter. Beneath the cube was a curiously shaped, slender cylinder winding down into the lower body of the Nautilus whorl.

"Watch!" said Rador. He motioned me into the vehicle and took a place beside me. The driver touched the lever; a stream of coruscations flew from the ball down into the cylinder. The shell started smoothly, and as the tiny torrent of shining particles increased it gathered speed.

"The corial does not touch the road," explained Rador. "It is lifted so far"—he held his forefinger and thumb less than a sixteenth of an inch apart—"above it."

And perhaps here is the best place to explain the activation of the shells or coria. The force utilized was atomic energy. Passing from the whirling ball the ions darted through the cylinder to two bands of a peculiar metal affixed to the base of the vehicles somewhat like skids of a sled. Impinging upon these they produced a partial negation of gravity, lifting the shell slightly, and at the same time creating a powerful repulsive force or thrust that could be directed backward, forward, or sidewise at the will of the driver. The creation of this energy and the mechanism of its utilization were, briefly, as follows:

[Dr. Goodwin's lucid and exceedingly comprehensive description of this extraordinary mechanism has been deleted by the Executive Council of the International Association of Science as too dangerously suggestive to scientists of the Central European Powers with which we were so recently at war. It is allowable, however, to state that his observations are in the possession of experts in this country, who are, unfortunately, hampered in their research not only by the scarcity of the radioactive elements that we know, but also by the lack of the element or elements unknown to us that entered into the formation of the fiery ball within the cube of black crystal. Nevertheless, as the principle is so clear, it is believed that these difficulties will ultimately be overcome.—J. B. K., President, I. A. of S.]

The wide, glistening road was gay with the coria. They darted in and out of the gardens; within them the fair-haired, extraordinarily beautiful women on their cushions were like princesses of Elfland, caught in gorgeous fairy webs, resting within the hearts of flowers. In some shells were flaxen-haired dwarfish men of Lugur's type; sometimes black-polled brother officers of Rador; often raven-tressed girls, plainly hand-maidens of the women; and now and then beauties of the lower folk went by with one of the blond dwarfs.

We swept around the turn that made of the jewel-like roadway an enormous horseshoe and, speedily, upon our right the cliffs through which we had come in our journey from the Moon Pool began to march forward beneath their mantles of moss. They formed a gigantic abutment, a titanic salient. It had been from the very front of this salient's invading angle that we had emerged; on each side of it the precipices, faintly glowing, drew back and vanished into distance.

The slender, graceful bridges under which we skimmed ended at openings in the upflung, far walls of verdure. Each had its little garrison of soldiers. Through some of the openings a rivulet of the green obsidian river passed. These were roadways to the farther country, to the land of the ladala, Rador told me; adding that none of the lesser folk could cross into the pavilioned city unless summoned or with pass.

We turned the bend of the road and flew down that farther emerald ribbon we had seen from the great oval. Before us rose the shining cliffs and the lake. A half-mile, perhaps, from these the last of the bridges flung itself. It was more massive and about it hovered a spirit of ancientness lacking in the other spans; also its garrison was larger and at its base the tangent way was guarded by two massive structures, somewhat like blockhouses, between which it ran. Something about it aroused in me an intense curiosity.

"Where does that road lead, Rador?" I asked.

"To the one place above all of which I may not tell you, Goodwin," he answered. And again I wondered.

We skimmed slowly out upon the great pier. Far to the left was the prismatic, rainbow curtain between the Cyclopean pillars. On the white waters graceful shells—lacustrian replicas of the Elf chariots—swam, but none was near that distant web of wonder.

"Rador—what is that?" I asked.

"It is the Veil of the Shining One!" he answered slowly.

Was the Shining One that which we named the Dweller?

"What is the Shining One?" I cried, eagerly. Again he was silent. Nor did he speak until we had turned on our homeward way.

And lively as my interest, my scientific curiosity, were—I was conscious suddenly of acute depression. Beautiful, wondrously beautiful this place was—and yet in its wonder dwelt a keen edge of menace, of unease—of inexplicable, inhuman woe; as though in a secret garden of God a soul should sense upon it the gaze of some lurking spirit of evil which some way, somehow, had crept into the sanctuary and only bided its time to spring.

XVII

THE LEPRECHAUN

The shell carried us straight back to the house of Yolara. Larry was awaiting me. We stood again before the tenebrous wall where first we had faced the priestess and the Voice. And as we stood, again the portal appeared with all its disconcerting, magical abruptness.

But now the scene was changed. Around the jet table were grouped a number of figures—Lugur, Yolara beside him; seven others—all of them fair-haired and all men save one who sat at the left of the priestess—an old, old woman, how old I could not tell, her face bearing traces of beauty that must once have been as great as Yolara's own, but now ravaged, in some way awesome; through its ruins the fearful, malicious gaiety shining out like a spirit of joy held within a corpse!

Began then our examination, for such it was. And as it progressed I was more and more struck by the change in the O'Keefe. All flippancy was gone, rarely did his sense of humour reveal itself in any of his answers. He was like a cautious swordsman, fencing, guarding, studying his opponent; or rather, like a chess-player who keeps sensing some far-reaching purpose in the game: alert, contained, watchful. Always he stressed the power of our surface races, their multitudes, their solidarity.

Their questions were myriad. What were our occupations? Our system of government? How great were the waters? The land? Intensely interested were they in the World War, querying minutely into its causes, its effects. In our weapons their interest was avid. And they were exceedingly minute in their examination of us as to the ruins which had excited our curiosity; their position and surroundings—and if others than ourselves might be expected to find and pass through their entrance!

At this I shot a glance at Lugur. He did not seem unduly interested. I wondered if the Russian had told him as yet of the girl of the rosy wall of the Moon Pool Chamber and the real reasons for our search. Then I answered as briefly as possible—omitting all reference to these things. The red dwarf watched me with unmistakable amusement—and I knew Marakinoff had told him. But clearly Lugur had kept his information even from Yolara; and as clearly she had spoken to none of that episode when O'Keefe's automatic had shattered the Keth-smitten vase. Again I felt that sense of deep bewilderment—of helpless search for clue to all the tangle.

For two hours we were questioned and then the priestess called Rador and let us go.

Larry was sombre as we returned. He walked about the room uneasily.

"Hell's brewing here all right," he said at last, stopping before me. "I can't make out just the particular brand—that's all that bothers me. We're going to have a stiff fight, that's sure. What I want to do quick is to find the Golden Girl, Doc. Haven't seen her on the wall lately, have you?" he queried, hopefully fantastic.

"Laugh if you want to," he went on. "But she's our best bet. It's going to be a race between her and the O'Keefe banshee—but I put my money on her. I had a queer experience while I was in that garden, after you'd left." His voice grew solemn. "Did you ever see a leprechaun, Doc?" I shook my head again, as solemnly. "He's a little man in green," said Larry. "Oh, about as high as your knee. I saw one once—in Carntogher Woods. And as I sat there, half asleep, in Yolara's garden, the living spit of him stepped out from one of those bushes, twirling a little shillalah.

"'It's a tight box ye're gettin' in, Larry avick,' said he, 'but don't ye be downhearted, lad.'

"'I'm carrying on,' said I, 'but you're a long way from Ireland,' I said, or thought I did.

"'Ye've a lot o' friends there,' he answered. 'An' where the heart rests the feet are swift to follow. Not that I'm sayin' I'd like to live here, Larry,' said he.

"'I know where my heart is now,' I told him. 'It rests on a girl with golden eyes and the hair and swan-white breast of Eilidh the Fair—but me feet don't seem to get me to her,' I said."

The brogue thickened.

"An' the little man in green nodded his head an' whirled his shillalah.

"'It's what I came to tell ye,' says he. 'Don't ye fall for the Bhean-Nimher, the serpent woman wit' the blue eyes; she's a daughter of Ivor, lad—an' don't ye do nothin' to make the brown-haired coleen ashamed o' ye, Larry O'Keefe. I knew yer great, great grandfather an' his before him, aroon,' says he, 'an' wan o' the O'Keefe failin's is to think their hearts big enough to hold all the wimmen o' the world. A heart's built to hold only wan permanently, Larry,' he says, 'an' I'm warnin' ye a nice girl don't like to move into a place all cluttered up wid another's washin' an' mendin' an' cookin' an' other things pertainin' to general wife work. Not that I think the blue-eyed wan is keen for mendin' an' cookin'!' says he.

"'You don't have to be comin' all this way to tell me that,' I answer.

"'Well, I'm just a tellin' you,' he says. 'Ye've got some rough knocks comin', Larry. In fact, ye're in for a devil of a time. But, remember that ye're the O'Keefe,' says he. 'An' while the bhoys are all wid ye, avick, ye've got to be on the job yourself.'

"'I hope,' I tell him, 'that the O'Keefe banshee can find her way here in time—that is, if it's necessary, which I hope it won't be.'

"'Don't ye worry about that,' says he. 'Not that she's keen on leavin' the ould sod, Larry. The good ould soul's in quite a state o' mind about ye, aroon. I don't mind tellin' ye, lad, that she's mobilizing all the clan an' if she *has* to come for ye, avick, they'll be wid her an' they'll sweep this joint clean before ye go. What they'll do to it'll make the Big Wind look like a summer breeze on Lough Lene! An' that's about all, Larry. We thought a voice from the Green Isle would cheer ye. Don't fergit that ye're the O'Keefe an' I say it again—all the bhoys are wid ye. But we want t' kape bein' proud o' ye, lad!'

"An' I looked again and there was only a bush waving."

There wasn't a smile in my heart—or if there was it was a very tender one.

"I'm going to bed," he said abruptly. "Keep an eye on the wall, Doc!"

Between the seven sleeps that followed, Larry and I saw but little of each other. Yolara sought him more and more. Thrice we were called before the Council; once we were at a great feast, whose splendours and surprises I can never forget. Largely I was in the company of Rador. Together we two passed the green barriers into the dwelling-place of the ladala.

They seemed provided with everything needful for life. But everywhere was an oppressiveness, a gathering together of hate, that was spiritual rather than material—as tangible as the latter and far, far more menacing!

"They do not like to dance with the Shining One," was Rador's constant and only reply to my efforts to find the cause.

Once I had concrete evidence of the mood. Glancing behind me, I saw a white, vengeful face peer from behind a tree-trunk, a hand lift, a shining dart speed from it straight toward Rador's back. Instinctively I thrust him aside. He turned upon me angrily. I pointed to where the little missile lay, still quivering, on the ground. He gripped my hand.

"That, some day I will repay!" he said. I looked again at the thing. At its end was a tiny cone covered with a glistening, gelatinous substance.

Rador pulled from a tree beside us a fruit somewhat like an apple.

"Look!" he said. He dropped it upon the dart—and at once, before my eyes, in less than ten seconds, the fruit had rotted away!

"That's what would have happened to Rador but for you, friend!" he said.

Come now between this and the prelude to the latter half of the drama whose history this narrative is—only scattering and necessarily fragmentary observations.

First—the nature of the ebon opacities, blocking out the spaces between the pavilion-pillars or covering their tops like roofs, These were magnetic fields, light absorbers, negativing the vibrations of radiance; literally screens of electric force which formed as impervious a barrier to light as would have screens of steel.

They instantaneously made night appear in a place where no night was. But they interposed no obstacle to air or to sound. They were extremely simple in their inception—no more miraculous than is glass, which, inversely, admits the vibrations of light, but shuts out those coarser ones we call air—and, partly, those others which produce upon our auditory nerves the effects we call sound.

Briefly their mechanism was this:

[For the same reason that Dr. Goodwin's exposition of the mechanism of the atomic engines was deleted, his description of the light-destroying screens has been deleted by the Executive Council.—J. B. F., President, I. A. of S.]

There were two favoured classes of the ladala—the soldiers and the dream-makers. The dream-makers were the most astonishing social phenomena, I think, of all. Denied by their circumscribed environment the wider experiences of us of the outer world, the Murians had perfected an amazing system of escape through the imagination.

They were, too, intensely musical. Their favourite instruments were double flutes; immensely complex pipe-organs; harps, great and small. They had another remarkable instrument made up of a double octave of small drums which gave forth percussions remarkably disturbing to the emotional centres.

It was this love of music that gave rise to one of the few truly humorous incidents of our caverned life. Larry came to me—it was just after our fourth sleep, I remember.

"Come on to a concert," he said.

We skimmed off to one of the bridge garrisons. Rador called the two-score guards to attention; and then, to my utter stupefaction, the whole company, O'Keefe leading them, roared out the anthem, "God Save the King." They sang—in a closer approach to the English than might have been expected scores of miles below England's level. "Send him victorious! Happy and glorious!" they bellowed.

He quivered with suppressed mirth at my paralysis of surprise.

"Taught 'em that for Marakinoff's benefit!" he gasped. "Wait till that Red hears it. He'll blow up.

"Just wait until you hear Yolara lisp a pretty little thing I taught her," said Larry as we set back for what we now called home. There was an impish twinkle in his eyes.

And I did hear. For it was not many minutes later that the priestess condescended to command me to come to her with O'Keefe.

"Show Goodwin how much you have learned of our speech, O lady of the lips of honeyed flame!" murmured Larry.

She hesitated; smiled at him, and then from that perfect mouth, out of the exquisite throat, in the voice that was like the chiming of little silver bells, she trilled a melody familiar to me indeed:

"She's only a bird in a gilded cage,
A bee-yu-tiful sight to see—"

And so on to the bitter end.

"She thinks it's a love-song," said Larry when we had left. "It's only part of a repertoire I'm teaching her. Honestly, Doc, it's the only way I can keep my mind clear when I'm with her," he went on earnestly. "She's a devil-ess from hell—but a wonder. Whenever I find myself going I get her to sing that, or Take Back Your Gold! or some other ancient lay, and I'm back again—pronto—with the right perspective! Pop goes all the mystery! 'Hell!' I say, 'she's only a woman!'"

XVIII

The Amphitheatre of Jet

For hours the black-haired folk had been streaming across the bridges, flowing along the promenade by scores and by hundreds, drifting down toward the gigantic seven-terraced temple whose interior I had never as yet seen, and from whose towering exterior, indeed, I had always been kept far enough away—unobtrusively, but none the less decisively—to prevent any real observation. The structure, I had estimated, nevertheless, could not reach less than a thousand feet above its silvery base, and the diameter of its circular foundation was about the same.

I wondered what was bringing the *ladala* into Lora, and where they were vanishing. All of them were flower-crowned with the luminous, lovely blooms—old and young, slender, mocking-eyed girls, dwarfed youths, mothers with their babes, gnomed oldsters—on they poured, silent for the most part and sullen—a sullenness that held acid bitterness even as their subtle, half-sinister, half-gay malice seemed tempered into little keen-edged flames, oddly, menacingly defiant.

There were many of the green-clad soldiers along the way, and the garrison of the only bridge span I could see had certainly been doubled.

Wondering still, I turned from my point of observation and made my way back to our pavilion, hoping that Larry, who had been with Yolara for the past two hours, had returned. Hardly had I reached it before Rador came hurrying up, in his manner a curious exultance mingled with what in anyone else I would have called a decided nervousness.

"Come!" he commanded before I could speak. "The Council has made decision—and *Larree* is awaiting you."

"What has been decided?" I panted as we sped along the mosaic path that led to the house of Yolara. "And why is Larry awaiting me?"

And at his answer I felt my heart pause in its beat and through me race a wave of mingled panic and eagerness.

"The Shining One dances!" had answered the green dwarf. "And you are to worship!"

What was this dancing of the Shining One, of which so often he had spoken?

Whatever my forebodings, Larry evidently had none.

"Great stuff!" he cried, when we had met in the great antechamber now empty of the dwarfs. "Hope it will be worth seeing—have to be something damned good, though, to catch me, after what I've seen of shows at the front," he added.

And remembering, with a little shock of apprehension, that he had no knowledge of the Dweller beyond my poor description of it—for there are no words actually to describe what that miracle of interwoven glory and horror was—I wondered what Larry O'Keefe would say and do when he did behold it!

Rador began to show impatience.

"Come!" he urged. "There is much to be done—and the time grows short!"

He led us to a tiny fountain room in whose miniature pool the white waters were concentrated, pearl-like and opalescent in their circling rim.

"Bathe!" he commanded; and set the example by stripping himself and plunging within. Only a minute or two did the green dwarf allow us, and he checked us as we were about to don our clothing.

Then, to my intense embarrassment, without warning, two of the black-haired girls entered, bearing robes of a peculiar dull-blue hue. At our manifest discomfort Rador's laughter roared out. He took the garments from the pair, motioned them to leave us, and, still laughing, threw one around me. Its texture was soft, but decidedly metallic—like some blue metal spun to the fineness of a spider's thread. The garment buckled tightly at the throat, was girdled at the waist, and, below this cincture, fell to the floor, its folds being held together by a half-dozen looped cords; from the shoulders a hood resembling a monk's cowl.

Rador cast this over my head; it completely covered my face, but was of so transparent a texture that I could see, though somewhat mistily, through it. Finally he handed us both a pair of long gloves of the same material and high stockings, the feet of which were gloved—five-toed.

And again his laughter rang out at our manifest surprise.

"The priestess of the Shining One does not altogether trust the Shining One's Voice," he said at last. "And these are to guard against any sudden—errors. And fear not, Goodwin," he went on kindly. "Not for the Shining One itself would Yolara see harm come to *Larree* here— nor, because of him, to you. But I would not stake much on the great white one. And for him I am sorry, for him I do like well."

"Is he to be with us?" asked Larry eagerly.

"He is to be where we go," replied the dwarf soberly.

Grimly Larry reached down and drew from his uniform his automatic. He popped a fresh clip into the pocket fold of his girdle. The pistol he slung high up beneath his arm-pit.

The green dwarf looked at the weapon curiously. O'Keefe tapped it.

"This," said Larry, "slays quicker than the *Keth*—I take it so no harm shall come to the blue-eyed one whose name is Olaf. If I should raise it—be you not in its way, Rador!" he added significantly.

The dwarf nodded again, his eyes sparkling. He thrust a hand out to both of us.

"A change comes," he said. "What it is I know not, nor how it will fall. But this remember—Rador is more friend to you than you yet can know. And now let us go!" he ended abruptly.

He led us, not through the entrance, but into a sloping passage ending in a blind wall; touched a symbol graven there, and it opened, precisely as had the rosy barrier of the Moon Pool Chamber. And, just as there, but far smaller, was a passage end, a low curved wall facing a shaft not black as had been that abode of living darkness, but faintly luminescent. Rador leaned over the wall. The mechanism clicked and started; the door swung shut; the sides of the car slipped into place, and we swept swiftly down the passage; overhead the wind whistled. In a few moments the moving platform began to slow down. It stopped in a closed chamber no larger than itself.

Rador drew his poniard and struck twice upon the wall with its hilt. Immediately a panel moved away, revealing a space filled with faint, misty blue radiance. And at each side of the open portal stood four of the dwarfish men, grey-headed, old, clad in flowing garments of white, each pointing toward us a short silver rod.

Rador drew from his girdle a ring and held it out to the first dwarf. He examined it, handed it to the one beside him, and not until each had inspected the ring did they lower their curious weapons; containers of that terrific energy they called the *Keth*, I thought; and later was to know that I had been right.

We stepped out; the doors closed behind us. The place was weird enough. Its pave was a greenish-blue stone resembling lapis lazuli. On each side were high pedestals holding carved figures of the same material. There were perhaps a score of these, but in the mistiness I could not make out their outlines. A droning, rushing roar beat upon our ears; filled the whole cavern.

"I smell the sea," said Larry suddenly.

The roaring became deep-toned, clamorous, and close in front of us a rift opened. Twenty feet in width, it cut the cavern floor and vanished into the blue mist on each side. The cleft was spanned by one solid slab of rock not more than two yards wide. It had neither railing nor other protection.

The four leading priests marched out upon it one by one, and we followed. In the middle of the span they knelt. Ten feet beneath us was a torrent of blue sea-water racing with prodigious speed between polished walls. It gave the impression of vast depth. It roared as it sped by, and far to the right was a low arch through which it disappeared. It was so swift that its surface shone like polished blue steel, and from it came the blessed, *our worldly*, familiar ocean breath that strengthened my soul amazingly and made me realize how earth-sick I was.

Whence came the stream, I marvelled, forgetting for the moment, as we passed on again, all else. Were we closer to the surface of earth than I had thought, or was this some mighty flood falling through an opening in sea floor, Heaven alone knew how many miles above us, losing itself in deeper abysses beyond these? How near and how far this was from the truth I was to learn—and never did truth come to man in more dreadful guise!

The roaring fell away, the blue haze lessened. In front of us stretched a wide flight of steps, huge as those which had led us into the courtyard of Nan-Tauach through the ruined sea-gate. We scaled it; it narrowed; from above light poured through a still narrower opening. Side by side Larry and I passed out of it.

We had emerged upon an enormous platform of what seemed to be glistening ivory. It stretched before us for a hundred yards or more and then shelved gently into the white waters. Opposite—not a mile away—was that prodigious web of woven rainbows Rador had called the Veil of the Shining One. There it shone in all its unearthly grandeur, on each side of the Cyclopean pillars, as though a mountain should stretch up arms raising between them a fairy banner of auroral glories. Beneath it was the curved, scimitar sweep of the pier with its clustered, gleaming temples.

Before that brief, fascinated glance was done, there dropped upon my soul a sensation as of brooding weight intolerable; a spiritual oppression as though some vastness was falling, pressing, stifling me, I turned—and Larry caught me as I reeled.

"Steady! Steady, old man!" he whispered.

At first all that my staggering consciousness could realize was an immensity, an immeasurable uprearing that brought with it the same throat-gripping vertigo as comes from gazing downward from some great height—then a blur of white faces—intolerable shinings of hundreds upon thousands of eyes. Huge, incredibly huge, a colossal amphitheatre of jet, a stupendous semi-circle, held within its mighty arc the ivory platform on which I stood.

It reared itself almost perpendicularly hundreds of feet up into the sparkling heavens, and thrust down on each side its ebon bulwarks—like monstrous paws. Now, the giddiness from its sheer greatness passing, I saw that it was indeed an amphitheatre sloping slightly backward tier after tier, and that the white blur of faces against its blackness, the gleaming of countless eyes were those of myriads of the people who sat silent, flower-garlanded, their gaze focused upon the rainbow curtain and sweeping over me like a torrent—tangible, appalling!

Five hundred feet beyond, the smooth, high retaining wall of the amphitheatre raised itself—above it the first terrace of the seats, and above this, dividing the tiers for another half a thousand feet upward, set within them like a panel, was a dead-black surface in which shone faintly with a bluish radiance a gigantic disk; above it and around it a cluster of innumerable smaller ones.

On each side of me, bordering the platform, were scores of small pillared alcoves, a low wall stretching across their fronts; delicate, fretted grills shielding them, save where in each lattice an opening stared—it came to me that they were like those stalls in ancient Gothic cathedrals wherein for centuries had kneeled paladins and people of my own race on earth's fair face. And within these alcoves were gathered, score upon score, the elfin beauties, the dwarfish men of the fair-haired folk. At my right, a few feet from the opening through which we had come, a passageway led back between the fretted stalls. Half-way between us and the massive base of the amphitheatre a dais rose. Up the platform to it a wide ramp ascended; and on ramp and dais and along the centre of the gleaming platform down to where it kissed the white waters, a broad ribbon of the radiant flowers lay like a fairy carpet.

On one side of this dais, meshed in a silken web that hid no line or curve of her sweet body, white flesh gleaming through its folds, stood Yolara; and opposite her, crowned with a circlet of flashing blue stones, his mighty body stark bare, was Lugur!

O'Keefe drew a long breath; Rador touched my arm and, still dazed, I let myself be drawn into the aisle and through a corridor that ran behind the alcoves. At the back of one of these the green dwarf paused, opened a door, and motioned us within.

Entering, I found that we were exactly opposite where the ramp ran up to the dais—and that Yolara was not more than fifty feet away. She glanced at O'Keefe and smiled. Her eyes were ablaze with little dancing points of light; her body seemed to palpitate, the rounded delicate muscles beneath the translucent skin to run with joyful little eager waves!

Larry whistled softly.

"There's Marakinoff!" he said.

I looked where he pointed. Opposite us sat the Russian, clothed as we were, leaning forward, his eyes eager behind his glasses; but if he saw us he gave no sign.

"And there's Olaf!" said O'Keefe.

Beneath the carved stall in which sat the Russian was an aperture and within it was Huldricksson. Unprotected by pillars or by grills, opening clear upon the platform, near him stretched the trail of flowers up to the great dais which Lugur and Yolara the priestess guarded. He sat alone, and my heart went out to him.

O'Keefe's face softened.

"Bring him here," he said to Rador.

The green dwarf was looking at the Norseman, too, a shade of pity upon his mocking face. He shook his head.

"Wait!" he said. "You can do nothing now—and it may be there will be no need to do anything," he added; but I could feel that there was little of conviction in his words.

A. MERRITT

XIX

THE MADNESS OF OLAF

Yolara threw her white arms high. From the mountainous tiers came a mighty sigh; a rippling ran through them. And upon the moment, before Yolara's arms fell, there issued, apparently from the air around us, a peal of sound that might have been the shouting of some playful god hurling great suns through the net of stars. It was like the deepest notes of all the organs in the world combined in one; summoning, majestic, cosmic!

It held within it the thunder of the spheres rolling through the infinite, the birth-song of suns made manifest in the womb of space; echoes of creation's supernal chord! It shook the body like a pulse from the heart of the universe—pulsed—and died away.

On its death came a blaring as of all the trumpets of conquering hosts since the first Pharaoh led his swarms—triumphal, compelling! Alexander's clamouring hosts, brazen-throated wolf-horns of Caesar's legions, blare of trumpets of Genghis Khan and his golden horde, clangor of the locust levies of Tamerlane, bugles of Napoleon's armies—war-shout of all earth's conquerors! And it died!

Fast upon it, a throbbing, muffled tumult of harp sounds, mellownesses of myriads of wood horns, the subdued sweet shrilling of multitudes of flutes, Pandean pipings—inviting, carrying with them the calling of waterfalls in the hidden places, rushing brooks and murmuring forest winds—calling, calling, languorous, lulling, dripping into the brain like the very honeyed essence of sound.

And after them a silence in which the memory of the music seemed to beat, to beat ever more faintly, through every quivering nerve.

From me all fear, all apprehension, had fled. In their place was nothing but joyous anticipation, a supernal freedom from even the shadow of the shadow of care or sorrow; not now did anything matter—Olaf or his haunted, hate-filled eyes; Throckmartin or his fate—nothing of pain, nothing of agony, nothing of striving nor endeavour nor despair in that wide outer world that had turned suddenly to a troubled dream.

Once more the first great note pealed out! Once more it died and from the clustered spheres a kaleidoscopic blaze shot as though drawn from the majestic sound itself. The many-coloured rays darted across the white waters and sought the face of the irised Veil. As they touched, it sparkled, flamed, wavered, and shook with fountains of prismatic colour.

The light increased—and in its intensity the silver air darkened. Faded into shadow that white mosaic of flower-crowned faces set in the amphitheatre of jet, and vast shadows dropped upon the high-flung tiers and shrouded them. But on the skirts of the rays the fretted stalls in which we sat with the fair-haired ones blazed out, iridescent, like jewels.

I was sensible of an acceleration of every pulse; a wild stimulation of every nerve. I felt myself being lifted above the world—close to the threshold of the high gods—soon their essence and their power would stream out into me! I glanced at Larry. His eyes were—wild—with life!

I looked at Olaf—and in his face was none of this—only hate, and hate, and hate.

The peacock waves streamed out over the waters, cleaving the seeming darkness, a rainbow path of glory. And the Veil flashed as though all the rainbows that had ever shone were burning within it. Again the mighty sound pealed.

Into the centre of the Veil the light drew itself, grew into an intolerable brightness—and with a storm of tinklings, a tempest of crystalline notes, a tumult of tiny chimings, through it sped—the Shining One!

Straight down that radiant path, its high-flung plumes of feathery flame shimmering, its coruscating spirals whirling, its seven globes of seven colours shining above its glowing core, it raced toward us. The hurricane of bells of diamond glass were jubilant, joyous. I felt O'Keefe grip my arm; Yolara threw her white arms out in a welcoming gesture; I heard from the tier a sigh of rapture—and in it a poignant, wailing under-tone of agony!

Over the waters, down the light stream, to the end of the ivory pier, flew the Shining One. Through its crystal *pizzicati* drifted inarticulate murmurings—deadly sweet, stilling the heart and setting it leaping madly.

For a moment it paused, poised itself, and then came whirling down the flower path to its priestess, slowly, ever more slowly. It hovered for a moment between the woman and the dwarf, as though contemplating them; turned to her with its storm of tinklings softened, its murmurings infinitely caressing. Bent toward it, Yolara seemed to gather within herself pulsing waves of power; she was terrifying; gloriously, maddeningly evil; and as gloriously, maddeningly heavenly! Aphrodite and the Virgin! Tanith of the Carthaginians and St. Bride of the Isles! A queen of hell and a princess of heaven—in one!

Only for a moment did that which we had called the Dweller and which these named the Shining One, pause. It swept up the ramp to the dais, rested there, slowly turning, plumes and spirals lacing and unlacing, throbbing, pulsing. Now its nucleus grew plainer, stronger— human in a fashion, and all inhuman; neither man nor woman; neither god nor devil; subtly partaking of all. Nor could I doubt that whatever it was, within that shining nucleus was something sentient; something that had will and energy, and in some awful, supernormal fashion— intelligence!

Another trumpeting—a sound of stones opening—a long, low wail of utter anguish—something moved shadowy in the river of light, and slowly at first, then ever more rapidly, shapes swam through it. There were half a score of them—girls and youths, women and men. The Shining One poised itself, regarded them. They drew closer, and in the eyes of each and in their faces was the bud of that awful intermingling of emotions, of joy and sorrow, ecstasy and terror, that I had seen in full blossom on Throckmartin's.

The Thing began again its murmurings—now infinitely caressing, coaxing—like the song of a siren from some witched star! And the bell-sounds rang out—compellingly, calling—calling—calling—

I saw Olaf lean far out of his place; saw, half-consciously, at Lugur's signal, three of the dwarfs creep in and take places, unnoticed, behind him.

Now the first of the figures rushed upon the dais—and paused. It was the girl who had been brought before Yolara when the gnome named Songar was driven into the nothingness! With all the quickness of light a spiral of the Shining One stretched out and encircled her.

At its touch there was an infinitely dreadful shrinking and, it seemed, a simultaneous hurling of herself into its radiance. As it wrapped its swirls around her, permeated her—the crystal chorus burst forth— tumultuously; through and through her the radiance pulsed. Began then that infinitely dreadful, but infinitely glorious, rhythm they called the dance of the Shining One. And as the girl swirled within its sparkling mists another and another flew into its embrace, until, at last, the dais was an incredible vision; a mad star's Witches' Sabbath; an altar of white faces and bodies gleaming through living flame; transfused with rapture insupportable and horror that was hellish—and ever, radiant plumes and spirals expanding, the core of the Shining One waxed—growing greater—as it consumed, as it drew into and through itself the life-force of these lost ones!

So they spun, interlaced—and there began to pulse from them life, vitality, as though the very essence of nature was filling us. Dimly I recognized that what I was beholding was vampirism inconceivable! The banked tiers chanted. The mighty sounds pealed forth!

It was a Saturnalia of demigods!

Then, whirling, bell-notes storming, the Shining One withdrew slowly from the dais down the ramp, still embracing, still interwoven with those who had thrown themselves into its spirals. They drifted with it as though half-carried in dreadful dance; white faces sealed—forever—into that semblance of those who held within linked God and devil—I covered my eyes!

I heard a gasp from O'Keefe; opened my eyes and sought his; saw the wildness vanish from them as he strained forward. Olaf had leaned far out, and as he did so the dwarfs beside him caught him, and whether by design or through his own swift, involuntary movement, thrust him half into the Dweller's path. The Dweller paused in its gyrations—seemed to watch him. The Norseman's face was crimson, his eyes blazing. He threw himself back and, with one defiant shout, gripped one of the dwarfs about the middle and sent him hurtling through the air, straight at the radiant Thing! A whirling mass of legs and arms, the dwarf flew—then in midflight stopped as though some gigantic invisible hand had caught him, and—was dashed down upon the platform not a yard from the Shining One!

Like a broken spider he moved—feebly—once, twice. From the Dweller shot a shimmering tentacle—touched him—recoiled. Its crystal tinklings changed into an angry chiming. From all about—jewelled stalls and jet peak—came a sigh of incredulous horror.

Lugur leaped forward. On the instant Larry was over the low barrier between the pillars, rushing to the Norseman's side. And even as they ran there was another wild shout from Olaf, and he hurled himself out, straight at the throat of the Dweller!

But before he could touch the Shining One, now motionless—and never was the thing more horrible than then, with the purely human suggestion of surprise plain in its poise—Larry had struck him aside.

I tried to follow—and was held by Rador. He was trembling—but not with fear. In his face was incredulous hope, inexplicable eagerness.

"Wait!" he said. "Wait!"

The Shining One stretched out a slow spiral, and as it did so I saw the bravest thing man has ever witnessed. Instantly O'Keefe thrust himself between it and Olaf, pistol out. The tentacle touched him, and the dull blue of his robe flashed out into blinding, intense azure light. From the automatic in his gloved hand came three quick bursts of flame straight into the Thing. The Dweller drew back; the bell-sounds swelled.

Lugur paused, his hand darted up, and in it was one of the silver *Keth* cones. But before he could flash it upon the Norseman, Larry had unlooped his robe, thrown its fold over Olaf, and, holding him with one hand away from the Shining One, thrust with the other his pistol into the dwarf's stomach. His lips moved, but I could not hear what he said. But Lugur understood, for his hand dropped.

Now Yolara was there—all this had taken barely more than five seconds. She thrust herself between the three men and the Dweller. She spoke to it—and the wild buzzing died down; the gay crystal tinklings burst forth again. The Thing murmured to her—began to whirl—faster, faster—passed down the ivory pier, out upon the waters, bearing with it, meshed in its light, the sacrifices—swept on ever more swiftly, triumphantly and turning, turning, with its ghastly crew, vanished through the Veil!

Abruptly the polychromatic path snapped out. The silver light poured in upon us. From all the amphitheatre arose a clamour, a shouting. Marakinoff, his eyes staring, was leaning out, listening. Unrestrained now by Rador, I vaulted the wall and rushed forward. But not before I had heard the green dwarf murmur:

"There is something stronger than the Shining One! Two things—yea—a strong heart—and hate!"

Olaf, panting, eyes glazed, trembling, shrank beneath my hand.

"The devil that took my Helma!" I heard him whisper. "The Shining Devil!"

"Both these men," Lugur was raging, "they shall dance with the Shining one. And this one, too." He pointed at me malignantly.

"This man is mine," said the priestess, and her voice was menacing. She rested her hand on Larry's shoulder. "He shall not dance. No—

nor his friend. I have told you I dare not for this one!" She pointed to Olaf.

"Neither this man, nor this," said Larry, "shall be harmed. This is my word, Yolara!"

"Even so," she answered quietly, "my lord!"

I saw Marakinoff stare at O'Keefe with a new and curiously speculative interest. Lugur's eyes grew hellish; he raised his arms as though to strike her. Larry's pistol prodded him rudely enough.

"No rough stuff now, kid!" said O'Keefe in English. The red dwarf quivered, turned—caught a robe from a priest standing by, and threw it over himself. The *ladala*, shouting, gesticulating, fighting with the soldiers, were jostling down from the tiers of jet.

"Come!" commanded Yolara—her eyes rested upon Larry. "Your heart is great, indeed—my lord!" she murmured; and her voice was very sweet. "Come!"

"This man comes with us, Yolara," said O'Keefe pointing to Olaf.

"Bring him," she said. "Bring him—only tell him to look no more upon me as before!" she added fiercely.

Beside her the three of us passed along the stalls, where sat the fair-haired, now silent, at gaze, as though in the grip of some great doubt. Silently Olaf strode beside me. Rador had disappeared. Down the stairway, through the hall of turquoise mist, over the rushing sea-stream we went and stood beside the wall through which we had entered. The white-robed ones had gone.

Yolara pressed; the portal opened. We stepped upon the car; she took the lever; we raced through the faintly luminous corridor to the house of the priestess.

And one thing now I knew sick at heart and soul the truth had come to me—no more need to search for Throckmartin. Behind that Veil, in the lair of the Dweller, dead-alive like those we had just seen swim in its shining train was he, and Edith, Stanton and Thora and Olaf Huldricksson's wife!

The car came to rest; the portal opened; Yolara leaped out lightly, beckoned and flitted up the corridor. She paused before an ebon screen. At a touch it vanished, revealing an entrance to a small blue chamber, glowing as though cut from the heart of some gigantic sapphire; bare, save that in its centre, upon a low pedestal, stood a great globe fashioned from milky rock-crystal; upon its surface were faint tracings as of seas and continents, but, if so, either of some other world or of this world in

A. MERRITT

immemorial past, for in no way did they resemble the mapped coastlines of our earth.

Poised upon the globe, rising from it out into space, locked in each other's arms, lips to lips, were two figures, a woman and a man, so exquisite, so lifelike, that for the moment I failed to realize that they, too, were carved of the crystal. And before this shrine—for nothing else could it be, I knew—three slender cones raised themselves: one of purest white flame, one of opalescent water, and the third of—moonlight! There was no mistaking them, the height of a tall man each stood—but how water, flame and light were held so evenly, so steadily in their spire-shapes, I could not tell.

Yolara bowed lowly—once, twice, thrice. She turned to O'Keefe, nor by slightest look or gesture betrayed she knew others were there than he. The blue eyes wide, searching, unfathomable, she drew close; put white hands on his shoulders, looked down into his very soul.

"My lord," she murmured. "Now listen well for I, Yolara, give you three things—myself, and the Shining One, and the power that is the Shining One's—yea, and still a fourth thing that is all three—power over all upon that world from whence you came! These, my lord, ye shall have. I swear it"—she turned toward the altar—uplifted her arms—"by Siya and by Siyana, and by the flame, by the water, and by the light!"[1]

Her eyes grew purple dark.

"Let none dare to take you from me! Nor ye go from me unbidden!" she whispered fiercely.

Then swiftly, still ignoring us, she threw her arms about O'Keefe, pressed her white body to his breast, lips raised, eyes closed, seeking

---

1. I have no space here even to outline the eschatology of this people, nor to catalogue their pantheon. Siya and Siyana typified worldly love. Their ritual was, however, singularly free from those degrading elements usually found in love-cults. Priests and priestesses of all cults dwelt in the immense seven-terraced structure, of which the jet amphitheatre was the water side. The symbol, icon, representation, of Siya and Siyana—the globe and the up-striving figures—typified earthly love, feet bound to earth, but eyes among the stars. Hell or heaven I never heard formulated, nor their equivalents; unless that existence in the Shining One's domain could serve for either. Over all this was Thanaroa, remote; unheeding, but still maker and ruler of all—an absentee First Cause personified! Thanaroa seemed to be the one article of belief in the creed of the soldiers—Rador, with his reverence for the Ancient Ones, was an exception. Whatever there was, indeed, of high, truly religious impulse among the Murians, this far, High God had. I found this exceedingly interesting, because it had long been my theory—to put the matter in the shape of a geometrical formula—that the real attractiveness of gods to man increases uniformly according to the square of their distance—W. T. G.

his. O'Keefe's arms tightened around her, his head dropped lips seeking, finding hers—passionately! From Olaf came a deep indrawn breath that was almost a groan. But not in my heart could I find blame for the Irishman!

The priestess opened eyes now all misty blue, thrust him back, stood regarding him. O'Keefe, dead-white, raised a trembling hand to his face.

"And thus have I sealed my oath, O my lord!" she whispered. For the first time she seemed to recognize our presence, stared at us a moment, then through us, and turned to O'Keefe.

"Go, now!" she said. "Soon Rador shall come for you. Then—well, after that let happen what will!"

She smiled once more at him—so sweetly; turned toward the figures upon the great globe; sank upon her knees before them. Quietly we crept away; still silent, made our way to the little pavilion. But as we passed we heard a tumult from the green roadway; shouts of men, now and then a woman's scream. Through a rift in the garden I glimpsed a jostling crowd on one of the bridges: green dwarfs struggling with the *ladala*—and all about droned a humming as of a giant hive disturbed!

Larry threw himself down upon one of the divans, covered his face with his hands, dropped them to catch in Olaf's eyes troubled reproach, looked at me.

"*I* couldn't help it," he said, half defiantly—half-miserably. "God, what a woman! I *couldn't* help it!"

"Larry," I asked. "Why didn't you tell her you didn't love her—then?"

He gazed at me—the old twinkle back in his eye.

"Spoken like a scientist, Doc!" he exclaimed. "I suppose if a burning angel struck you out of nowhere and threw itself about you, you would most dignifiedly tell it you didn't want to be burned. For God's sake, don't talk nonsense, Goodwin!" he ended, almost peevishly.

"Evil! Evil!" The Norseman's voice was deep, nearly a chant. "All here is of evil: Trolldom and Helvede it is, Ja! And that she *djaevelsk* of beauty—what is she but harlot of that shining devil they worship. I, Olaf Huldricksson, know what she meant when she held out to you power over all the world, *Ja!*—as if the world had not devils enough in it now!"

"What?" The cry came from both O'Keefe and myself at once.

Olaf made a gesture of caution, relapsed into sullen silence. There were footsteps on the path, and into sight came Rador—but a Rador changed. Gone was every vestige of his mockery; curiously solemn, he saluted O'Keefe and Olaf with that salute which, before this, I had seen given only to Yolara and to Lugur. There came a swift quickening of the tumult—died away. He shrugged mighty shoulders.

"The *ladala* are awake!" he said. "So much for what two brave men can do!" He paused thoughtfully. "Bones and dust jostle not each other for place against the grave wall!" he added oddly. "But if bones and dust have revealed to them that they still—live—"

He stopped abruptly, eyes seeking the globe that bore and sent forth speech.[2]

"The *Afyo Maie* has sent me to watch over you till she summons you," he announced clearly. "There is to be a—feast. You, *Larree*, you Goodwin, are to come. I remain here with—Olaf."

"No harm to him!" broke in O'Keefe sharply. Rador touched his heart, his eyes.

"By the Ancient Ones, and by my love for you, and by what you twain did before the Shining One—I swear it!" he whispered.

Rador clapped palms; a soldier came round the path, in his grip a long flat box of polished wood. The green dwarf took it, dismissed him, threw open the lid.

"Here is your apparel for the feast, *Larree*," he said, pointing to the contents.

---

2. I find that I have neglected to explain the working of these interesting mechanisms that were telephonic, dictaphonic, telegraphic in one. I must assume that my readers are familiar with the receiving apparatus of wireless telegraphy, which must be "tuned" by the operator until its own vibratory quality is in exact harmony with the vibrations—the extremely rapid impacts—of those short electric wavelengths we call Hertzian, and which carry the wireless messages. I must assume also that they are familiar with the elementary fact of physics that the vibrations of light and sound are interchangeable. The hearing-talking globes utilize both these principles, and with consummate simplicity. The light with which they shone was produced by an atomic "motor" within their base, similar to that which activated the merely illuminating globes. The composition of the phonic spheres gave their surfaces an acute sensitivity and resonance. In conjunction with its energizing power, the metal set up what is called a "field of force," which linked it with every particle of its kind no matter how distant. When vibrations of speech impinged upon the resonant surface its rhythmic light-vibrations were broken, just as a telephone transmitter breaks an electric current. Simultaneously these light-vibrations were changed into sound—on the surfaces of all spheres tuned to that particular instrument. The "crawling" colours which showed themselves at these times were literally the voice of the speaker in its spectrum equivalent. While usually the sounds produced required considerable familiarity with the apparatus to be understood quickly, they could, on occasion, be made startlingly loud and clear—as I was soon to realize—W. T. G.

O'Keefe stared, reached down and drew out a white, shimmering, softly metallic, long-sleeved tunic, a broad, silvery girdle, leg swathings of the same argent material, and sandals that seemed to be cut out from silver. He made a quick gesture of angry dissent.

"Nay, *Larree*!" muttered the dwarf. "Wear them—I counsel it—I pray it—ask me not why," he went on swiftly, looking again at the globe.

O'Keefe, as I, was impressed by his earnestness. The dwarf made a curiously expressive pleading gesture. O'Keefe abruptly took the garments; passed into the room of the fountain.

"The Shining One dances not again?" I asked.

"No," he said. "No"—he hesitate—"it is the usual feast that follows the sacrament! Lugur—and Double Tongue, who came with you, will be there," he added slowly.

"Lugur—" I gasped in astonishment. "After what happened—he will be there?"

"Perhaps because of what happened, Goodwin, my friend," he answered—his eyes again full of malice; "and there will be others—friends of Yolara—friends of Lugur—and perhaps another"—his voice was almost inaudible—"one whom they have not called—" He halted, half-fearfully, glancing at the globe; put finger to lips and spread himself out upon one of the couches.

"Strike up the band"—came O'Keefe's voice—"here comes the hero!"

He strode into the room. I am bound to say that the admiration in Rador's eyes was reflected in my own, and even, if involuntarily, in Olaf's.

"A son of Siyana!" whispered Rador.

He knelt, took from his girdle-pouch a silk-wrapped something, unwound it—and, still kneeling, drew out a slender poniard of gleaming white metal, hilted with the blue stones; he thrust it into O'Keefe's girdle; then gave him again the rare salute.

"Come," he ordered and took us to the head of the pathway.

"Now," he said grimly, "let the Silent Ones show their power—if they still have it!"

And with this strange benediction, he turned back.

"For God's sake, Larry," I urged as we approached the house of the priestess, "you'll be careful!"

He nodded—but I saw with a little deadly pang of apprehension in my heart a puzzled, lurking doubt within his eyes.

As we ascended the serpent steps Marakinoff appeared. He gave a signal to our guards—and I wondered what influence the Russian had attained, for promptly, without question, they drew aside. At me he smiled amiably.

"Have you found your friends yet?" he went on—and now I sensed something deeply sinister in him. "No! It is too bad! Well, don't give up hope." He turned to O'Keefe.

"Lieutenant, I would like to speak to you—alone!"

"I've no secrets from Goodwin," answered O'Keefe.

"So?" queried Marakinoff, suavely. He bent, whispered to Larry.

The Irishman started, eyed him with a certain shocked incredulity, then turned to me.

"Just a minute, Doc!" he said, and I caught the suspicion of a wink. They drew aside, out of ear-shot. The Russian talked rapidly. Larry was all attention. Marakinoff's earnestness became intense; O'Keefe interrupted—appeared to question. Marakinoff glanced at me and as his gaze shifted from O'Keefe, I saw a flame of rage and horror blaze up in the latter's eyes. At last the Irishman appeared to consider gravely; nodded as though he had arrived at some decision, and Marakinoff thrust his hand to him.

And only I could have noticed Larry's shrinking, his microscopic hesitation before he took it, and his involuntary movement, as though to shake off something unclean, when the clasp had ended.

Marakinoff, without another look at me, turned and went quickly within. The guards took their places. I looked at Larry inquiringly.

"Don't ask a thing now, Doc!" he said tensely. "Wait till we get home. But we've got to get damned busy and quick—I'll tell you that now—"

XX

The Tempting of Larry

We paused before thick curtains, through which came the faint murmur of many voices. They parted; out came two—ushers, I suppose, they were—in cuirasses and kilts that reminded me somewhat of chain-mail—the first armour of any kind here that I had seen. They held open the folds.

The chamber, on whose threshold we stood, was far larger than either anteroom or hall of audience. Not less than three hundred feet long and half that in depth, from end to end of it ran two huge semi-circular tables, paralleling each other, divided by a wide aisle, and heaped with flowers, with fruits, with viands unknown to me, and glittering with crystal flagons, beakers, goblets of as many hues as the blooms. On the gay-cushioned couches that flanked the tables, lounging luxuriously, were scores of the fair-haired ruling class and there rose a little buzz of admiration, oddly mixed with a half-startled amaze, as their gaze fell upon O'Keefe in all his silvery magnificence. Everywhere the light-giving globes sent their roseate radiance.

The cuirassed dwarfs led us through the aisle. Within the arc of the inner half—circle was another glittering board, an oval. But of those seated there, facing us—I had eyes for only one—Yolara! She swayed up to greet O'Keefe—and she was like one of those white lily maids, whose beauty Hoang-Ku, the sage, says made the Gobi first a paradise, and whose lusts later the burned-out desert that it is. She held out hands to Larry, and on her face was passion—unashamed, unhiding.

She was Circe—but Circe conquered. Webs of filmiest white clung to the rose-leaf body. Twisted through the corn-silk hair a threaded circlet of pale sapphires shone; but they were pale beside Yolara's eyes. O'Keefe bent, kissed her hands, something more than mere admiration flaming from him. She saw—and, smiling, drew him down beside her.

It came to me that of all, only these two, Yolara and O'Keefe, were in white—and I wondered; then with a tightening of nerves ceased to wonder as there entered—Lugur! He was all in scarlet, and as he strode forward a silence fell a tense, strained silence.

A. MERRITT

His gaze turned upon Yolara, rested upon O'Keefe, and instantly his face grew—dreadful—there is no other word than that for it. Marakinoff leaned forward from the centre of the table, near whose end I sat, touched and whispered to him swiftly. With appalling effort the red dwarf controlled himself; he saluted the priestess ironically, I thought; took his place at the further end of the oval. And now I noted that the figures between were the seven of that Council of which the Shining One's priestess and Voice were the heads. The tension relaxed, but did not pass—as though a storm-cloud should turn away, but still lurk, threatening.

My gaze ran back. This end of the room was draped with the exquisitely coloured, graceful curtains looped with gorgeous garlands. Between curtains and table, where sat Larry and the nine, a circular platform, perhaps ten yards in diameter, raised itself a few feet above the floor, its gleaming surface half-covered with the luminous petals, fragrant, delicate.

On each side below it, were low carven stools. The curtains parted and softly entered girls bearing their flutes, their harps, the curiously emotion-exciting, octaved drums. They sank into their places. They touched their instruments; a faint, languorous measure throbbed through the rosy air.

The stage was set! What was to be the play?

Now about the tables passed other dusky-haired maids, fair bosoms bare, their scanty kirtles looped high, pouring out the wines for the feasters.

My eyes sought O'Keefe. Whatever it had been that Marakinoff had said, clearly it now filled his mind—even to the exclusion of the wondrous woman beside him. His eyes were stern, cold—and now and then, as he turned them toward the Russian, filled with a curious speculation. Yolara watched him, frowned, gave a low order to the Hebe behind her.

The girl disappeared, entered again with a ewer that seemed cut of amber. The priestess poured from it into Larry's glass a clear liquid that shook with tiny sparkles of light. She raised the glass to her lips, handed it to him. Half-smiling, half-abstractedly, he took it, touched his own lips where hers had kissed; drained it. A nod from Yolara and the maid refilled his goblet.

At once there was a swift transformation in the Irishman. His abstraction vanished; the sternness fled; his eyes sparkled. He leaned caressingly toward Yolara; whispered. Her blue eyes flashed triumphantly; her chiming laughter rang. She raised her own glass—but within it was not that clear drink that filled Larry's! And again he drained his own; and, lifting it, full once more, caught the baleful eyes of Lugur, and held it toward him mockingly. Yolara swayed close—alluring, tempting. He arose, face all reckless gaiety; rollicking deviltry.

"A toast!" he cried in English, "to the Shining One—and may the hell where it belongs soon claim it!"

He had used their own word for their god—all else had been in his own tongue, and so, fortunately, they did not understand. But the contempt in his action they did recognize—and a dead, a fearful silence fell upon them all. Lugur's eyes blazed, little sparks of crimson in their green. The priestess reached up, caught at O'Keefe. He seized the soft hand; caressed it; his gaze grew far away, sombre.

"The Shining One." He spoke low. "An' now again I see the faces of those who dance with it. It is the Fires of Mora—come, God alone knows how—from Erin—to this place. The Fires of Mora!" He contemplated the hushed folk before him; and then from his lips came that weirdest, most haunting of the lyric legends of Erin—the Curse of Mora:

> *"The fretted fires of Mora blew o'er him in the night;*
> *He thrills no more to loving, nor weeps for past delight.*
> *For when those flames have bitten, both grief and joy take flight—"*

Again Yolara tried to draw him down beside her; and once more he gripped her hand. His eyes grew fixed—he crooned:

> *"And through the sleeping silence his feet must track the tune,*
> *When the world is barred and speckled with silver of the moon—"*

He stood, swaying, for a moment, and then, laughing, let the priestess have her way; drained again the glass.

And now my heart was cold, indeed—for what hope was there left with Larry mad, wild drunk!

The silence was unbroken—elfin women and dwarfs glancing furtively at each other. But now Yolara arose, face set, eyes flashing grey.

"Hear you, the Council, and you, Lugur—and all who are here!" she cried. "Now I, the priestess of the Shining One, take, as is my right, my mate. And this is he!" She pointed down upon Larry. He glanced up at her.

"Can't quite make out what you say, Yolara," he muttered thickly. "But say anything—you like—I love your voice!"

I turned sick with dread. Yolara's hand stole softly upon the Irishman's curls caressingly.

"You know the law, Yolara." Lugur's voice was flat, deadly, "You may not mate with other than your own kind. And this man is a stranger—a barbarian—food for the Shining One!" Literally, he spat the phrase.

"No, not of our kind—Lugur—higher!" Yolara answered serenely. "Lo, a son of Siya and of Siyana!"

"A lie!" roared the red dwarf. "A lie!"

"The Shining One revealed it to me!" said Yolara sweetly. "And if ye believe not, Lugur—go ask of the Shining One if it be not truth!"

There was bitter, nameless menace in those last words—and whatever their hidden message to Lugur, it was potent. He stood, choking, face hell-shadowed—Marakinoff leaned out again, whispered. The red dwarf bowed, now wholly ironically; resumed his place and his silence. And again I wondered, icy-hearted, what was the power the Russian had so to sway Lugur.

"What says the Council?" Yolara demanded, turning to them.

Only for a moment they consulted among themselves. Then the woman, whose face was a ravaged shrine of beauty, spoke.

"The will of the priestess is the will of the Council!" she answered.

Defiance died from Yolara's face; she looked down at Larry tenderly. He sat swaying, crooning.

"Bid the priests come," she commanded, then turned to the silent room. "By the rites of Siya and Siyana, Yolara takes their son for her mate!" And again her hand stole down possessively, serpent soft, to the drunken head of the O'Keefe.

The curtains parted widely. Through them filed, two by two, twelve hooded figures clad in flowing robes of the green one sees in forest vistas of opening buds of dawning spring. Of each pair one bore clasped to breast a globe of that milky crystal in the sapphire shrine-room; the other a harp, small, shaped somewhat like the ancient clarsach of the Druids.

Two by two they stepped upon the raised platform, placed gently upon it each their globe; and two by two crouched behind them. They formed now a star of six points about the petalled dais, and, simultaneously, they drew from their faces the covering cowls.

I half-rose—youths and maidens these of the fair-haired; and youths and maids more beautiful than any of those I had yet seen—for upon their faces was little of that disturbing mockery to which I have been forced so often, because of the deep impression it made upon me, to refer. The ashen-gold of the maiden priestesses' hair was wound about their brows in shining coronals. The pale locks of the youths were clustered within circlets of translucent, glimmering gems like moonstones. And then, crystal globe alternately before and harp alternately held by youth and maid, they began to sing.

What was that song, I do not know—nor ever shall. Archaic, ancient beyond thought, it seemed—not with the ancientness of things that for uncounted ages have been but wind-driven dust. Rather was it the ancientness of the golden youth of the world, love lilts of earth younglings, with light of new-born suns drenching them, chorals of young stars mating in space; murmurings of April gods and goddesses. A languor stole through me. The rosy lights upon the tripods began to die away, and as they faded the milky globes gleamed forth brighter, ever brighter. Yolara rose, stretched a hand to Larry, led him through the sextuple groups, and stood face to face with him in the centre of their circle.

The rose-light died; all that immense chamber was black, save for the circle of the glowing spheres. Within this their milky radiance grew brighter—brighter. The song whispered away. A throbbing arpeggio dripped from the harps, and as the notes pulsed out, up from the globes, as though striving to follow, pulsed with them tips of moon-fire cones, such as I had seen before Yolara's altar. Weirdly, caressingly, compellingly the harp notes throbbed in repeated, re-repeated theme, holding within itself the same archaic golden quality I had noted in the singing. And over the moon flame pinnacles rose higher!

Yolara lifted her arms; within her hands were clasped O'Keefe's. She raised them above their two heads and slowly, slowly drew him with her into a circling, graceful step, tendrillings delicate as the slow spirallings of twilight mist upon some still stream.

As they swayed the rippling arpeggios grew louder, and suddenly the slender pinnacles of moon fire bent, dipped, flowed to the floor, crept in a shining ring around those two—and began to rise, a gleaming, glimmering, enchanted barrier—rising, ever rising—hiding them!

With one swift movement Yolara unbound her circlet of pale sapphires, shook loose the waves of her silken hair. It fell, a rippling, wondrous cascade, veiling both her and O'Keefe to their girdles—and now the shining coils of moon fire had crept to their knees—was circling higher—higher.

And ever despair grew deeper in my soul!

What was that! I started to my feet, and all around me in the darkness I heard startled motion. From without came a blaring of trumpets, the sound of running men, loud murmurings. The tumult drew closer. I heard cries of "Lakla! Lakla!" Now it was at the very threshold and within it, oddly, as though—punctuating—the clamour, a deep-toned, almost abysmal, booming sound—thunderously bass and reverberant.

Abruptly the harpings ceased; the moon fires shuddered, fell, and began to sweep back into the crystal globes; Yolara's swaying form grew rigid, every atom of it listening. She threw aside the veiling cloud of hair, and in the gleam of the last retreating spirals her face glared out like some old Greek mask of tragedy.

The sweet lips that even at their sweetest could never lose their delicate cruelty, had no sweetness now. They were drawn into a square—inhuman as that of the Medusa; in her eyes were the fires of the pit, and her hair seemed to writhe like the serpent locks of that Gorgon whose mouth she had borrowed; all her beauty was transformed into a nameless thing—hideous, inhuman, blasting! If this was the true soul of Yolara springing to her face, then, I thought, God help us in very deed!

I wrested my gaze away to O'Keefe. All drunkenness gone, himself again, he was staring down at her, and in his eyes were loathing and horror unutterable. So they stood—and the light fled.

Only for a moment did the darkness hold. With lightning swiftness the blackness that was the chamber's other wall vanished. Through a portal open between grey screens, the silver sparkling radiance poured.

And through the portal marched, two by two, incredible, nightmare figures—frog-men, giants, taller by nearly a yard than even tall O'Keefe! Their enormous saucer eyes were irised by wide bands of green-flecked red, in which the phosphorescence flickered. Their long muzzles, lips half-open in monstrous grin, held rows of glistening, slender, lancet sharp fangs. Over the glaring eyes arose a horny helmet, a carapace of black and orange scales, studded with foot-long lance-headed horns.

They lined themselves like soldiers on each side of the wide table aisle, and now I could see that their horny armour covered shoulders and backs, ran across the chest in a knobbed cuirass, and at wrists and heels jutted out into curved, murderous spurs. The webbed hands and feet ended in yellow, spade-shaped claws.

They carried spears, ten feet, at least, in length, the heads of which were pointed cones, glistening with that same covering, from whose touch of swift decay I had so narrowly saved Rador.

They were grotesque, yes—more grotesque than anything I had ever seen or dreamed, and they were—terrible!

And then, quietly, through their ranks came—a girl! Behind her, enormous pouch at his throat swelling in and out menacingly, in one paw a treelike, spike-studded mace, a frog-man, huger than any of the others, guarding. But of him I caught but a fleeting, involuntary impression—all my gaze was for her.

For it was she who had pointed out to us the way from the peril of the Dweller's lair on Nan-Tauach. And as I looked at her, I marvelled that ever could I have thought the priestess more beautiful. Into the eyes of O'Keefe rushed joy and an utter abasement of shame.

And from all about came murmurs—edged with anger, half-incredulous, tinged with fear:

"Lakla!"

"Lakla!"

"The handmaiden!"

She halted close beside me. From firm little chin to dainty buskined feet she was swathed in the soft robes of dull, almost coppery hue. The left arm was hidden, the right free and gloved. Wound tight about it was one of the vines of the sculptured wall and of Lugur's circled signet-ring. Thick, a vivid green, its five tendrils ran between her fingers, stretching out five flowered heads that gleamed like blossoms cut from gigantic, glowing rubies.

So she stood contemplating Yolara. Then drawn perhaps by my gaze, she dropped her eyes upon me; golden, translucent, with tiny flecks of amber in their aureate irises, the soul that looked through them was as far removed from that flaming out of the priestess as zenith is above nadir.

I noted the low, broad brow, the proud little nose, the tender mouth, and the soft—sunlight—glow that seemed to transfuse the delicate skin. And suddenly in the eyes dawned a smile—sweet, friendly, a touch of roguishness, profoundly reassuring in its all humanness. I felt my heart expand as though freed from fetters, a recrudescence of confidence in the essential reality of things—as though in nightmare the struggling consciousness should glimpse some familiar face and know the terrors with which it strove were but dreams. And involuntarily I smiled back at her.

She raised her head and looked again at Yolara, contempt and a certain curiosity in her gaze; at O'Keefe—and through the softened eyes drifted swiftly a shadow of sorrow, and on its fleeting wings deepest interest, and hovering over that a naive approval as reassuringly human as had been her smile.

She spoke, and her voice, deep-timbred, liquid gold as was Yolara's all silver, was subtly the synthesis of all the golden glowing beauty of her.

"The Silent Ones have sent me, O Yolara," she said. "And this is their command to you—that you deliver to me to bring before them three of the four strangers who have found their way here. For him there who plots with Lugur"—she pointed at Marakinoff, and I saw Yolara start—"they have no need. Into his heart the Silent Ones have looked; and Lugur and you may keep him, Yolara!"

There was honeyed venom in the last words.

Yolara was herself now; only the edge of shrillness on her voice revealed her wrath as she answered.

"And whence have the Silent Ones gained power to command, *choya?*"

This last, I knew, was a very vulgar word; I had heard Rador use it in a moment of anger to one of the serving maids, and it meant, approximately, "kitchen girl," "scullion." Beneath the insult and the acid disdain, the blood rushed up under Lakla's ambered ivory skin.

"Yolara"—her voice was low—"of no use is it to question me. I am but the messenger of the Silent Ones. And one thing only am I bidden to ask you—do you deliver to me the three strangers?"

Lugur was on his feet; eagerness, sardonic delight, sinister anticipation thrilling from him—and my same glance showed Marakinoff, crouched, biting his finger-nails, glaring at the Golden Girl.

"No!" Yolara spat the word. "No! Now by Thanaroa and by the Shining One, no!" Her eyes blazed, her nostrils were wide, in her fair throat a little pulse beat angrily. "You, Lakla—take you my message to the Silent Ones. Say to them that I keep this man"—she pointed to Larry—"because he is mine. Say to them that I keep the yellow-haired one and him"—she pointed to me—"because it pleases me.

"Tell them that upon their mouths I place my foot, so!"—she stamped upon the dais viciously—"and that in their faces I spit!"—and her action was hideously snakelike. "And say last to them, you handmaiden, that if *you* they dare send to Yolara again, she will feed *you* to the Shining One! Now—go!"

The handmaiden's face was white.

"Not unforeseen by the three was this, Yolara," she replied. "And did you speak as you have spoken then was I bidden to say this to you." Her voice deepened. "Three *tal* have you to take counsel, Yolara. And at the end of that time these things must you have determined—either to do or not to do: first, send the strangers to the Silent Ones; second, give up, you and Lugur and all of you, that dream you have of conquest of the world without; and, third, forswear the Shining One! And if you do not one and all these things, then are you done, your cup of life broken, your wine of life spilled. Yea, Yolara, for you and the Shining One, Lugur and the Nine and all those here and their kind shall pass! This say the Silent Ones, 'Surely shall all of ye pass and be as though never had ye been!'"

Now a gasp of rage and fear arose from all those around me—but the priestess threw back her head and laughed loud and long. Into the silver sweet chiming of her laughter clashed that of Lugur—and after a little the nobles took it up, till the whole chamber echoed with their mirth. O'Keefe, lips tightening, moved toward the Handmaiden, and almost imperceptibly, but peremptorily, she waved him back.

"Those *are* great words—great words indeed, *choya*," shrilled Yolara at last; and again Lakla winced beneath the word. "Lo, for *laya* upon *laya*, the Shining One has been freed from the Three; and for *laya* upon *laya* they have sat helpless, rotting. Now I ask you again—whence comes their power to lay their will upon me, and whence comes their strength to wrestle with the Shining One and the beloved of the Shining One?"

And again she laughed—and again Lugur and all the fairhaired joined in her laughter.

Into the eyes of Lakla I saw creep a doubt, a wavering; as though deep within her the foundations of her own belief were none too firm.

She hesitated, turning upon O'Keefe gaze in which rested more than suggestion of appeal! And Yolara saw, too, for she flushed with triumph, stretched a finger toward the handmaiden.

"Look!" she cried. "Look! Why, even *she* does not believe!" Her voice grew silk of silver—merciless, cruel. "Now am I minded to send another answer to the Silent Ones. Yea! But not by *you*, Lakla; by these"—she pointed to the frog-men, and, swift as light, her hand darted into her bosom, bringing forth the little shining cone of death.

But before she could level it the Golden Girl had released that hidden left arm and thrown over her face a fold of the metallic swathings. Swifter than Yolara, she raised the arm that held the vine—and now I knew this was no inert blossoming thing.

It was alive!

It writhed down her arm, and its five rubescent flower heads thrust out toward the priestess—vibrating, quivering, held in leash only by the light touch of the handmaiden at its very end.

From the swelling throat pouch of the monster behind her came a succession of the reverberant boomings. The frogmen wheeled, raised their lances, levelled them at the throng. Around the reaching ruby flowers a faint red mist swiftly grew.

The silver cone dropped from Yolara's rigid fingers; her eyes grew stark with horror; all her unearthly loveliness fled from her; she stood pale-lipped. The Handmaiden dropped the protecting veil—and now it was she who laughed.

"It would seem, then, Yolara, that there *is* a thing of the Silent Ones ye fear!" she said. "Well—the kiss of the *Yekta* I promise you in return for the embrace of your Shining One."

She looked at Larry, long, searchingly, and suddenly again with all that effect of sunlight bursting into dark places, her smile shone upon him. She nodded, half gaily; looked down upon me, the little merry light dancing in her eyes; waved her hand to me.

She spoke to the giant frog-man. He wheeled behind her as she turned, facing the priestess, club upraised, fangs glistening. His troop moved not a jot, spears held high. Lakla began to pass slowly—almost, I thought, tauntingly—and as she reached the portal Larry leaped from the dais.

"*Alanna!*" he cried. "You'll not be leavin' me just when I've found you!"

In his excitement he spoke in his own tongue, the velvet brogue appealing. Lakla turned, contemplated O'Keefe, hesitant, unquestionably longingly, irresistibly like a child making up her mind whether she dared or dared not take a delectable something offered her.

"I go with you," said O'Keefe, this time in her own speech. "Come on, Doc!" He reached out a hand to me.

But now Yolara spoke. Life and beauty had flowed back into her face, and in the purple eyes all her hosts of devils were gathered.

"Do you forget what I promised you before Siya and Siyana? And do you think that you can leave me—me—as though I were a *choya*—like *her*." She pointed to Lakla. "Do you—"

"Now, listen, Yolara," Larry interrupted almost plaintively. "No promise has passed from me to you—and why would you hold me?" He passed unconsciously into English. "Be a good sport, Yolara," he urged, "You *have* got a very devil of a temper, you know, and so have I; and we'd be really awfully uncomfortable together. And why don't you get rid of that devilish pet of yours, and be good!"

She looked at him, puzzled, Marakinoff leaned over, translated to Lugur. The red dwarf smiled maliciously, drew near the priestess; whispered to her what was without doubt as near as he could come in the Murian to Larry's own very colloquial phrases.

Yolara's lips writhed.

"Hear me, Lakla!" she cried. "Now would I not let you take this man from me were I to dwell ten thousand *laya* in the agony of the *Yekta's* kiss. This I swear to you—by Thanaroa, by my heart, and by my strength—and may my strength wither, my heart rot in my breast, and Thanaroa forget me if I do!"

"Listen, Yolara"—began O'Keefe again.

"Be silent, you!" It was almost a shriek. And her hand again sought in her breast for the cone of rhythmic death.

Lugur touched her arm, whispered again, The glint of guile shone in her eyes; she laughed softly, relaxed.

"The Silent Ones, Lakla, bade you say that they—allowed—me three *tal* to decide," she said suavely. "Go now in peace, Lakla, and say that Yolara has heard, and that for the three *tal* they—allow—her she will take council." The handmaiden hesitated.

"The Silent Ones have said it," she answered at last. "Stay you here, strangers"—the long lashes drooped as her eyes met O'Keefe's and a hint of blush was in her cheeks—"stay you here, strangers, till then. But, Yolara, see you on that heart and strength you have sworn by that they come to no harm—else that which you have invoked shall come upon you swiftly indeed—and that I promise you," she added.

Their eyes met, clashed, burned into each other—black flame from Abaddon and golden flame from Paradise.

"Remember!" said Lakla, and passed through the portal. The gigantic frog-man boomed a thunderous note of command, his grotesque guards turned and slowly followed their mistress; and last of all passed out the monster with the mace.

XXI

Larry's Defiance

A clamour arose from all the chambers; stilled in an instant by a motion of Yolara's hand. She stood silent, regarding O'Keefe with something other now than blind wrath; something half regretful, half beseeching. But the Irishman's control was gone.

"Yolara,"—his voice shook with rage, and he threw caution to the wind—"now hear *me*. I go where I will and when I will. Here shall we stay until the time she named is come. And then we follow her, whether you will or not. And if any should have thought to stop us—tell them of that flame that shattered the vase," he added grimly.

The wistfulness died out of her eyes, leaving them cold. But no answer made she to him.

"What Lakla has said, the Council must consider, and at once." The priestess was facing the nobles. "Now, friends of mine, and friends of Lugur, must all feud, all rancour, between us end." She glanced swiftly at Lugur. "The *ladala* are stirring, and the Silent Ones threaten. Yet fear not—for are we not strong under the Shining One? And now—leave us."

Her hand dropped to the table, and she gave, evidently, a signal, for in marched a dozen or more of the green dwarfs.

"Take these two to their place," she commanded, pointing to us.

The green dwarfs clustered about us. Without another look at the priestess O'Keefe marched beside me, between them, from the chamber. And it was not until we had reached the pillared entrance that Larry spoke.

"I hate to talk like that to a woman, Doc," he said, "and a pretty woman, at that. But first she played me with a marked deck, and then not only pinched all the chips, but drew a gun on me. What the hell! she nearly had me—*married*—to her. I don't know what the stuff was she gave me; but, take it from me, if I had the recipe for that brew I could sell it for a thousand dollars a jolt at Forty-second and Broadway.

"One jigger of it, and you forget there is a trouble in the world; three of them, and you forget there is a world. No excuse for it, Doc; and I don't care what you say or what Lakla may say—it wasn't my fault, and I don't hold it up against myself for a damn."

A. MERRITT

"I must admit that I'm a bit uneasy about her threats," I said, ignoring all this. He stopped abruptly.

"What're you afraid of?"

"Mostly," I answered dryly, "I have no desire to dance with the Shining One!"

"Listen to me, Goodwin," He took up his walk impatiently. "I've all the love and admiration for you in the world; but this place has got your nerve. Hereafter one Larry O'Keefe, of Ireland and the little old U. S. A., leads this party. Nix on the tremolo stop, nix on the superstition! I'm the works. Get me?"

"Yes, I get you!" I exclaimed testily enough. "But to use your own phrase, kindly can the repeated references to superstition."

"Why should I?" He was almost wrathful. "You scientific people build up whole philosophies on the basis of things you never saw, and you scoff at people who believe in other things that you think *they* never saw and that don't come under what you label scientific. You talk about paradoxes—why, your scientist, who thinks he is the most skeptical, the most materialistic aggregation of atoms ever gathered at the exact mathematical centre of Missouri, has more blind faith than a dervish, and more credulity, more superstition, than a cross-eyed smoke beating it past a country graveyard in the dark of the moon!"

"Larry!" I cried, dazed.

"Olaf's no better," he said. "But I can make allowances for him. He's a sailor. No, sir. What this expedition needs is a man without superstition. And remember this. The leprechaun promised that I'd have full warning before anything happened. And if we do have to go out, we'll see that banshee bunch clean up before we do, and pass in a blaze of glory. And don't forget it. Hereafter—I'm—in—charge!"

By this time we were before our pavilion; and neither of us in a very amiable mood I'm afraid. Rador was awaiting us with a score of his men.

"Let none pass in here without authority—and let none pass out unless I accompany them," he ordered bruskly. "Summon one of the swiftest of the *coria* and have it wait in readiness," he added, as though by afterthought.

But when we had entered and the screens were drawn together his manner changed; all eagerness he questioned us. Briefly we told him of the happenings at the feast, of Lakla's dramatic interruption, and of what had followed.

"Three *tal*," he said musingly; "three *tal* the Silent Ones have allowed—and Yolara agreed." He sank back, silent and thoughtful.[1]

"*Ja!* " It was Olaf. "*Ja!* I told you the Shining Devil's mistress was all evil. *Ja!* Now I begin again that tale I started when he came"—he glanced toward the preoccupied Rador. "And tell him not what I say should he ask. For I trust none here in Trolldom, save the *Jomfrau*—the White Virgin!

"After the oldster was *adsprede*"—Olaf once more used that expressive Norwegian word for the dissolving of Songar—"I knew that it was a time for cunning. I said to myself, 'If they think I have no ears to hear, they will speak; and it may be I will find a way to save my Helma and Dr. Goodwin's friends, too.' *Ja*, and they did speak.

"The red *Trolde* asked the Russian how came it he was a worshipper of Thanaroa." I could not resist a swift glance of triumph toward O'Keefe. "And the Russian," rumbled Olaf, "said that all his people worshipped Thanaroa and had fought against the other nations that denied him.

"And then we had come to Lugur's palace. They put me in rooms, and there came to me men who rubbed and oiled me and loosened my muscles. The next day I wrestled with a great dwarf they called Valdor. He was a mighty man, and long we struggled, and at last I broke his back. And Lugur was pleased, so that I sat with him at feast and with the Russian, too. And again, not knowing that I understood them, they talked.

"The Russian had gone fast and far. They talked of Lugur as emperor of all Europe, and Marakinoff under him. They spoke of the green light that shook life from the oldster; and Lugur said that the secret of it had been the Ancient Ones' and that the Council had not too much of it. But the Russian said that among his race were many wise men who could make more once they had studied it.

"And the next day I wrestled with a great dwarf named Tahola, mightier far than Valdor. Him I threw after a long, long time, and his back also I broke. Again Lugur was pleased. And again we sat at table, he and the Russian and I. This time they spoke of something these *Trolde* have which opens up a *Svaelc*—abysses into which all in its range drops up into the sky!"

"What!" I exclaimed.

"I know about them," said Larry. "Wait!"

---

1. A *tal* in Muria is the equivalent of thirty hours of earth surface time.—W. T. G.

"Lugur had drunk much," went on Olaf. "He was boastful. The Russian pressed him to show this thing. After a while the red one went out and came back with a little golden box. He and the Russian went into the garden. I followed them. There was a *lille Høj*—a mound—of stones in that garden on which grew flowers and trees.

"Lugur pressed upon the box, and a spark no bigger than a sand grain leaped out and fell beside the stones. Lugur pressed again, and a blue light shot from the box and lighted on the spark. The spark that had been no bigger than a grain of sand grew and grew as the blue struck it. And then there was a sighing, a wind blew—and the stones and the flowers and the trees were not. They were *forsvinde*—vanished!

"Then Lugur, who had been laughing, grew quickly sober; for he thrust the Russian back—far back. And soon down into the garden came tumbling the stones and the trees, but broken and shattered, and falling as though from a great height. And Lugur said that of *this* something they had much, for its making was a secret handed down by their own forefathers and not by the Ancient Ones.

"They feared to use it, he said, for a spark thrice as large as that he had used would have sent all that garden falling upward and might have opened a way to the outside before—he said just this—'*before we are ready to go out into it!*'

"The Russian questioned much, but Lugur sent for more drink and grew merrier and threatened him, and the Russian was silent through fear. Thereafter I listened when I could, and little more I learned, but that little enough. *Ja!* Lugur is hot for conquest; so Yolara and so the Council. They tire of it here and the Silent Ones make their minds not too easy, no, even though they jeer at them! And this they plan—to rule our world with their Shining Devil."

The Norseman was silent for a moment; then voice deep, trembling—

"Trolldom is awake; Helvede crouches at Earth Gate whining to be loosed into a world already devil ridden! And we are but three!"

I felt the blood drive out of my heart. But Larry's was the fighting face of the O'Keefes of a thousand years. Rador glanced at him, arose, stepped through the curtains; returned swiftly with the Irishman's uniform.

"Put it on," he said, bruskly; again fell back into his silence and whatever O'Keefe had been about to say was submerged in his wild and joyful whoop. He ripped from him glittering tunic and leg swathings.

"Richard is himself again!" he shouted; and each garment as he donned it, fanned his old devil-may-care confidence to a higher flame. The last scrap of it on, he drew himself up before us.

"Bow down, ye divils!" he cried. "Bang your heads on the floor and do homage to Larry the First, Emperor of Great Britain, Autocrat of all Ireland, Scotland, England, and Wales, and adjacent waters and islands! Kneel, ye scuts, kneel."

"Larry," I cried, "are you going crazy?"

"Not a bit of it," he said. "I'm that and more if Comrade Marakinoff is on the level. Whoop! Bring forth the royal jewels an' put a whole new bunch of golden strings in Tara's harp an' down with the Sassenach forever! Whoop!"

He did a wild jig.

"Lord how good the old togs feel," he grinned. "The touch of 'em has gone to my head. But it's straight stuff I'm telling you about my empire."

He sobered.

"Not that it's not serious enough at that. A lot that Olaf's told us I've surmised from hints dropped by Yolara. But I got the full key to it from the Red himself when he stopped me just before—before"—he reddened—"well, just before I acquired that brand-new brand of souse."

"Maybe he had a hint—maybe he just surmised that I knew a lot more than I did. And he thought Yolara and I were going to be loving little turtle doves. Also he figured that Yolara had a lot more influence with the Unholy Fireworks than Lugur. Also that being a woman she could be more easily handled. All this being so, what was the logical thing for himself to do? Sure, you get me, Steve! Throw down Lugur and make an alliance with me! So *he* calmly offered to ditch the red dwarf if I would deliver Yolara. My reward from Russia was to be said emperorship! Can you beat it? Good Lord!"

He went off into a perfect storm of laughter. But not to me in the light of what Russia has done and has proved herself capable, did this thing seem at all absurd; rather in it I sensed the dawn of catastrophe colossal.

"And yet," he was quiet enough now, "I'm a bit scared. They've got the *Keth* ray and those gravity-destroying bombs—"

"Gravity-destroying bombs!" I gasped.

"Sure," he said. "The little fairy that sent the trees and stones kiting up from Lugur's garden. Marakinoff licked his lips over them. They cut off gravity, just about as the shadow screens cut off light—and consequently whatever's in their range goes shooting just naturally up to the moon—

"They get my goat, why deny it?" went on Larry. "With them and the *Keth* and gentle invisible soldiers walking around assassinating at will—well, the worst Bolsheviki are only puling babes, eh, Doc?"

"I don't mind the Shining One," said O'Keefe, "one splash of a downtown New York high-pressure fire hose would do for it! But the others—are the goods! Believe me!"

But for once O'Keefe's confidence found no echo within me. Not lightly, as he, did I hold that dread mystery, the Dweller—and a vision passed before me, a vision of an Apocalypse undreamed by the Evangelist.

A vision of the Shining One swirling into our world, a monstrous, glorious flaming pillar of incarnate, eternal Evil—of peoples passing through its radiant embrace into that hideous, unearthly life-in-death which I had seen enfold the sacrifices—of armies trembling into dancing atoms of diamond dust beneath the green ray's rhythmic death—of cities rushing out into space upon the wings of that other demoniac force which Olaf had watched at work—of a haunted world through which the assassins of the Dweller's court stole invisible, carrying with them every passion of hell—of the rallying to the Thing of every sinister soul and of the weak and the unbalanced, mystics and carnivores of humanity alike; for well I knew that, once loosed, not any nation could hold this devil-god for long and that swiftly its blight would spread!

And then a world that was all colossal reek of cruelty and terror; a welter of lusts, of hatreds and of torment; a chaos of horror in which the Dweller waxing ever stronger, the ghastly hordes of those it had consumed growing ever greater, wreaked its inhuman will!

At the last a ruined planet, a cosmic plague, spinning through the shuddering heavens; its verdant plains, its murmuring forests, its meadows and its mountains manned only by a countless crew of soulless, mindless dead-alive, their shells illumined with the Dweller's infernal glory—and flaming over this vampirized earth like a flare from some hell far, infinitely far, beyond the reach of man's farthest flung imagining—the Dweller!

Rador jumped to his feet; walked to the whispering globe. He bent over its base; did something with its mechanism; beckoned to us. The globe swam rapidly, faster than ever I had seen it before. A low humming arose, changed into a murmur, and then from it I heard Lugur's voice clearly.

"It is to be war then?"

There was a chorus of assent—from the Council, I thought.

"I will take the tall one named—*Larree*." It was the priestess's voice. "After the three *tal*, you may have him, Lugur, to do with as you will."

"No!" it was Lugur's voice again, but with a rasp of anger. "All must die."

"He shall die," again Yolara. "But I would that first he see Lakla pass—and that she know what is to happen to him."

"No!" I started—for this was Marakinoff. "Now is no time, Yolara, for one's own desires. This is my counsel. At the end of the three *tal* Lakla will come for our answer. Your men will be in ambush and they will slay her and her escort quickly with the *Keth*. But not till that is done must the three be slain—and then quickly. With Lakla dead we shall go forth to the Silent Ones—and I promise you that I will find the way to destroy them!"

"It is well!" It was Lugur.

"It *is* well, Yolara." It was a woman's voice, and I knew it for that old one of ravaged beauty. "Cast from your mind whatever is in it for this stranger—either of love or hatred. In this the Council is with Lugur and the man of wisdom."

There was a silence. Then came the priestess's voice, sullen but—beaten.

"It is well!"

"Let the three be taken now by Rador to the temple and given to the High Priest Sator"—thus Lugur—"until what we have planned comes to pass."

Rador gripped the base of the globe; abruptly it ceased its spinning. He turned to us as though to speak and even as he did so its bell note sounded peremptorily and on it the colour films began to creep at their accustomed pace.

"I hear," the green dwarf whispered. "They shall be taken there at once." The globe grew silent. He stepped toward us.

"You have heard," he turned to us.

"Not on your life, Rador," said Larry. "Nothing doing!" And then in the Murian's own tongue. "We follow Lakla, Rador. And *you* lead the way." He thrust the pistol close to the green dwarf's side.

Rador did not move.

"Of what use, *Larree*?" he said, quietly. "Me you can slay—but in the end you will be taken. Life is not held so dear in Muria that my men out there or those others who can come quickly will let you by—even though you slay many. And in the end they will overpower you."

There was a trace of irresolution in O'Keefe's face.

"And," added Rador, "if I let you go I dance with the Shining One—or worse!"

O'Keefe's pistol hand dropped.

"You're a good sport, Rador, and far be it from me to get you in bad," he said. "Take us to the temple—when we get there—well, your responsibility ends, doesn't it?"

The green dwarf nodded; on his face a curious expression—was it relief? Or was it emotion higher than this?

He turned curtly.

"Follow," he said. We passed out of that gay little pavilion that had come to be home to us even in this alien place. The guards stood at attention.

"You, Sattoya, stand by the globe," he ordered one of them. "Should the *Afyo Maie* ask, say that I am on my way with the strangers even as she has commanded."

We passed through the lines to the *corial* standing like a great shell at the end of the runway leading into the green road.

"Wait you here," he said curtly to the driver. The green dwarf ascended to his seat, sought the lever and we swept on—on and out upon the glistening obsidian.

Then Rador faced us and laughed.

"*Larree*," he cried, "I love you for that spirit of yours! And did you think that Rador would carry to the temple prison a man who would take the chances of torment upon his own shoulders to save him? Or you, Goodwin, who saved him from the rotting death? For what did I take the *corial* or lift the veil of silence that I might hear what threatened you—"

He swept the *corial* to the left, away from the temple approach.

"I am done with Lugur and with Yolara and the Shining One!" cried Rador. "My hand is for you three and for Lakla and those to whom she is handmaiden!"

The shell leaped forward; seemed to fly.

XXII

THE CASTING OF THE SHADOW

Now we were racing down toward that last span whose ancientness had set it apart from all the other soaring arches. The shell's speed slackened; we approached warily.

"We pass there?" asked O'Keefe.

The green dwarf nodded, pointing to the right where the bridge ended in a broad platform held high upon two gigantic piers, between which ran a spur from the glistening road. Platform and bridge were swarming with men-at-arms; they crowded the parapets, looking down upon us curiously but with no evidence of hostility. Rador drew a deep breath of relief.

"We don't have to break our way through, then?" There was disappointment in the Irishman's voice.

"No use, *Larree!*" Smiling, Rador stopped the *corial* just beneath the arch and beside one of the piers. "Now, listen well. They have had no warning, hence does Yolara still think us on the way to the temple. This is the gateway of the Portal—and the gateway is closed by the Shadow. Once I commanded here and I know its laws. This must I do—by craft persuade Serku, the keeper of the gateway, to lift the Shadow; or raise it myself. And that will be hard and it may well be that in the struggle life will be stripped of us all. Yet is it better to die fighting than to dance with the Shining One!"

He swept the shell around the pier. Opened a wide plaza paved with the volcanic glass, but black as that down which we had sped from the chamber of the Moon Pool. It shone like a mirrored lakelet of jet; on each side of it arose what at first glance seemed towering bulwarks of the same ebon obsidian; at second, revealed themselves as structures hewn and set in place by men; polished faces pierced by dozens of high, narrow windows.

Down each facade a stairway fell, broken by small landings on which a door opened; they dropped to a broad ledge of greyish stone edging the lip of this midnight pool and upon it also fell two wide flights from either side of the bridge platform. Along all four stairways the guards were ranged; and here and there against the ledge stood the shells—in a curiously comforting resemblance to parked motors in our own world.

The sombre walls bulked high; curved and ended in two obelisked pillars from which, like a tremendous curtain, stretched a barrier of that tenebrous gloom which, though weightless as shadow itself, I now knew to be as impenetrable as the veil between life and death. In this murk, unlike all others I had seen, I sensed movement, a quivering, a tremor constant and rhythmic; not to be seen, yet caught by some subtle sense; as though through it beat a swift pulse of—black light.

The green dwarf turned the *corial* slowly to the edge at the right; crept cautiously on toward where, not more than a hundred feet from the barrier, a low, wide entrance opened in the fort. Guarding its threshold stood two guards, armed with broadswords, double-handed, terminating in a wide lunette mouthed with murderous fangs. These they raised in salute and through the portal strode a dwarf huge as Rador, dressed as he and carrying only the poniard that was the badge of office of Muria's captainry.

The green dwarf swept the shell expertly against the ledge; leaped out.

"Greeting, Serku!" he answered. "I was but looking for the *coria* of Lakla."

"Lakla!" exclaimed Serku. "Why, the handmaiden passed with her *Akka* nigh a *va* ago!"

"Passed!" The astonishment of the green dwarf was so real that half was I myself deceived. "You let her *pass?*"

"Certainly I let her pass—" But under the green dwarf's stern gaze the truculence of the guardian faded. "Why should I not?" he asked, apprehensively.

"Because Yolara commanded otherwise," answered Rador, coldly.

"There came no command to me." Little beads of sweat stood out on Serku's forehead.

"Serku," interrupted the green dwarf swiftly, "truly is my heart wrung for you. This is a matter of Yolara and of Lugur and the Council; yes, even of the Shining One! And the message was sent—and the fate, mayhap, of all Muria rested upon your obedience and the return of Lakla with these strangers to the Council. Now truly is my heart wrung, for there are few I would less like to see dance with the Shining One than you, Serku," he ended, softly.

Livid now was the gateway's guardian, his great frame shaking.

"Come with me and speak to Yolara," he pleaded. "There came no message—tell her—"

"Wait, Serku!" There was a thrill as of inspiration in Rador's voice. "This *corial* is of the swiftest—Lakla's are of the slowest. With Lakla scarce a *va* ahead we can reach her before she enters the Portal. Lift you the Shadow—we will bring her back, and this will I do for you, Serku."

Doubt tempered Serku's panic.

"Why not go alone, Rador, leaving the strangers here with me?" he asked—and I thought not unreasonably.

"Nay, then." The green dwarf was brusk. "Lakla will not return unless I carry to her these men as evidence of our good faith. Come—we will speak to Yolara and she shall judge you—" He started away—but Serku caught his arm.

"No, Rador, no!" he whispered, again panic-stricken. "Go you—as you will. But bring her back! Speed, Rador!" He sprang toward the entrance. "I lift the Shadow—"

Into the green dwarf's poise crept a curious, almost a listening, alertness. He leaped to Serku's side.

"I go with you," I heard. "Some little I can tell you—" They were gone.

"Fine work!" muttered Larry. "Nominated for a citizen of Ireland when we get out of this, one Rador of—"

The Shadow trembled—shuddered into nothingness; the obelisked outposts that had held it framed a ribbon of roadway, high banked with verdure, vanishing in green distances.

And then from the portal sped a shriek, a death cry! It cut through the silence of the ebon pit like a whimpering arrow. Before it had died, down the stairways came pouring the guards. Those at the threshold raised their swords and peered within. Abruptly Rador was between them. One dropped his hilt and gripped him—the green dwarf's poniard flashed and was buried in his throat. Down upon Rador's head swept the second blade. A flame leaped from O'Keefe's hand and the sword seemed to fling itself from its wielder's grasp—another flash and the soldier crumpled. Rador threw himself into the shell, darted to the high seat—and straight between the pillars of the Shadow we flew!

There came a crackling, a darkness of vast wings flinging down upon us. The *corial's* flight was checked as by a giant's hand. The shell swerved sickeningly; there was an oddly metallic splintering; it quivered; shot ahead. Dizzily I picked myself up and looked behind.

The Shadow had fallen—but too late, a bare instant too late. And shrinking as we fled from it, still it seemed to strain like some fettered Afrit from Eblis, throbbing with wrath, seeking with every malign power it possessed to break its bonds and pursue. Not until long after were we to know that it had been the dying hand of Serku, groping out of oblivion, that had cast it after us as a fowler upon an escaping bird.

"Snappy work, Rador!" It was Larry speaking. "But they cut the end off your bus all right!"

A full quarter of the hindward whorl was gone, sliced off cleanly. Rador noted it with anxious eyes.

"That is bad," he said, "but not too bad perhaps. All depends upon how closely Lugur and his men can follow us."

He raised a hand to O'Keefe in salute.

"But to you, *Larree*, I owe my life—not even the *Keth* could have been as swift to save me as that death flame of yours—friend!"

The Irishman waved an airy hand.

"Serku"—the green dwarf drew from his girdle the bloodstained poniard—"Serku I was forced to slay. Even as he raised the Shadow the globe gave the alarm. Lugur follows with twice ten times ten of his best—" He hesitated. "Though we have escaped the Shadow it has taken toll of our swiftness. May we reach the Portal before it closes upon Lakla—but if we do not—" He paused again. "Well—I know a way—but it is not one I am gay to follow—no!"

He snapped open the aperture that held the ball flaming within the dark crystal; peered at it anxiously. I crept to the torn end of the *corial*. The edges were crumbling, disintegrated. They powdered in my fingers like dust. Mystified still, I crept back where Larry, sheer happiness pouring from him, was whistling softly and polishing up his automatic. His gaze fell upon Olaf's grim, sad face and softened.

"Buck up, Olaf!" he said. "We've got a good fighting chance. Once we link up with Lakla and her crowd I'm betting that we get your wife—never doubt it! The baby—" he hesitated awkwardly. The Norseman's eyes filled; he stretched a hand to the O'Keefe.

"The *Yndling*—she is of the *de Dode*," he half whispered, "of the blessed dead. For her I have no fear and for her vengeance will be given me. *Ja!* But my Helma—she is of the dead-alive—like those we saw whirling like leaves in the light of the Shining Devil—and I would that she too were of *de Dode*—and at rest. I do not know how to fight the Shining Devil—no!"

His bitter despair welled up in his voice.

"Olaf," Larry's voice was gentle. "We'll come out on top—I know it. Remember one thing. All this stuff that seems so strange and—and, well, sort of supernatural, is just a lot of tricks we're not hep to as yet. Why, Olaf, suppose you took a Fijian when the war was on and set him suddenly down in London with autos rushing past, sirens blowing, Archies popping, a dozen enemy planes dropping bombs, and the searchlights shooting all over the sky—wouldn't he think he was among thirty-third degree devils in some exclusive circle of hell? Sure he would! And yet everything he saw would be natural—just as natural as all this is, once we get the answer to it. Not that we're Fijians, of course, but the principle is the same."

The Norseman considered this; nodded gravely.

"*Ja!* " he answered at last. "And at least we can fight. That is why I have turned to Thor of the battles, *Ja!* And *one* have I hope in for mine Helma—the white maiden. Since I have turned to the old gods it has been made clear to me that I shall slay Lugur and that the *Heks*, the evil witch Yolara, shall also die. But I would talk with the white maiden."

"All right," said Larry, "but just don't be afraid of what you don't understand. There's another thing"—he hesitated, nervously—"there's another thing that may startle you a bit when we meet up with Lakla—her—er—frogs!"

"Like the frog-woman we saw on the wall?" asked Olaf.

"Yes," went on Larry, rapidly. "It's this way—I figure that the frogs grow rather large where she lives, and they're a bit different too. Well, Lakla's got a lot of 'em trained. Carry spears and clubs and all that junk—just like trained seals or monkeys or so on in the circus. Probably a custom of the place. Nothing queer about that, Olaf. Why people have all kinds of pets—armadillos and snakes and rabbits, kangaroos and elephants and tigers."

Remembering how the frog-woman had stuck in Larry's mind from the outset, I wondered whether all this was not more to convince himself than Olaf.

"Why, I remember a nice girl in Paris who had four pet pythons—" he went on.

But I listened no more, for now I was sure of my surmise. The road had begun to thrust itself through high-flung, sharply pinnacled masses and rounded outcroppings of rock on which clung patches of the amber moss.

A. MERRITT

The trees had utterly vanished, and studding the moss-carpeted plains were only clumps of a willowy shrub from which hung, like grapes, clusters of white waxen blooms. The light too had changed; gone were the dancing, sparkling atoms and the silver had faded to a soft, almost ashen greyness. Ahead of us marched a rampart of coppery cliffs rising, like all these mountainous walls we had seen, into the immensities of haze. Something long drifting in my subconsciousness turned to startled realization. The speed of the shell was slackening! The aperture containing the ionizing mechanism was still open; I glanced within. The whirling ball of fire was not dimmed, but its coruscations, instead of pouring down through the cylinder, swirled and eddied and shot back as though trying to re-enter their source. Rador nodded grimly.

"The Shadow takes its toll," he said.

We topped a rise—Larry gripped my arm.

"Look!" he cried, and pointed. Far, far behind us, so far that the road was but a glistening thread, a score of shining points came speeding.

"Lugur and his men," said Rador.

"Can't you step on her?" asked Larry.

"Step on her?" repeated the green dwarf, puzzled.

"Give her more speed; push her," explained O'Keefe.

Rador looked about him. The coppery ramparts were close, not more than three or four miles distant; in front of us the plain lifted in a long rolling swell, and up this the *corial* essayed to go—with a terrifying lessening of speed. Faintly behind us came shootings, and we knew that Lugur drew close. Nor anywhere was there sign of Lakla nor her frogmen.

Now we were half-way to the crest; the shell barely crawled and from beneath it came a faint hissing; it quivered, and I knew that its base was no longer held above the glassy surface but rested on it.

"One last chance!" exclaimed Rador. He pressed upon the control lever and wrenched it from its socket. Instantly the sparkling ball expanded, whirling with prodigious rapidity and sending a cascade of coruscations into the cylinder. The shell rose; leaped through the air; the dark crystal split into fragments; the fiery ball dulled; died—but upon the impetus of that last thrust we reached the crest. Poised there for a moment, I caught a glimpse of the road dropping down the side of an enormous moss-covered, bowl-shaped valley whose sharply curved sides ended abruptly at the base of the towering barrier.

Then down the steep, powerless to guide or to check the shell, we plunged in a meteor rush straight for the annihilating adamantine breasts of the cliffs!

Now the quick thinking of Larry's air training came to our aid. As the rampart reared close he threw himself upon Rador; hurled him and himself against the side of the flying whorl. Under the shock the finely balanced machine swerved from its course. It struck the soft, low bank of the road, shot high in air, bounded on through the thick carpeting, whirled like a dervish and fell upon its side. Shot from it, we rolled for yards, but the moss saved broken bones or serious bruise.

"Quick!" cried the green dwarf. He seized an arm, dragged me to my feet, began running to the cliff base not a hundred feet away. Beside us raced O'Keefe and Olaf. At our left was the black road. It stopped abruptly—was cut off by a slab of polished crimson stone a hundred feet high, and as wide, set within the coppery face of the barrier. On each side of it stood pillars, cut from the living rock and immense, almost, as those which held the rainbow veil of the Dweller. Across its face weaved unnameable carvings—but I had no time for more than a glance. The green dwarf gripped my arm again.

"Quick!" he cried again. "The handmaiden has passed!"

At the right of the Portal ran a low wall of shattered rock. Over this we raced like rabbits. Hidden behind it was a narrow path. Crouching, Rador in the lead, we sped along it; three hundred, four hundred yards we raced—and the path ended in a *cul de sac*! To our ears was borne a louder shouting.

The first of the pursuing shells had swept over the lip of the great bowl, poised for a moment as we had and then began a cautious descent. Within it, scanning the slopes, I saw Lugur.

"A little closer and I'll get him!" whispered Larry viciously. He raised his pistol.

His hand was caught in a mighty grip; Rador, eyes blazing, stood beside him.

"No!" rasped the green dwarf. He heaved a shoulder against one of the boulders that formed the pocket. It rocked aside, revealing a slit.

"In!" ordered he, straining against the weight of the stone. O'Keefe slipped through. Olaf at his back, I following. With a lightning leap the dwarf was beside me, the huge rock missing him by a hair breadth as it swung into place!

We were in Cimmerian darkness. I felt for my pocket-flash and recalled with distress that I had left it behind with my medicine kit when we fled from the gardens. But Rador seemed to need no light.

"Grip hands!" he ordered. We crept, single file, holding to each other like children, through the black. At last the green dwarf paused.

"Await me here," he whispered. "Do not move. And for your lives— be silent!"

And he was gone.

XXIII

Dragon Worm and Moss Death

For a small eternity—to me at least—we waited. Then as silent as ever the green dwarf returned. "It is well," he said, some of the strain gone from his voice. "Grip hands again, and follow."

"Wait a bit, Rador," this was Larry. "Does Lugur know this side entrance? If he does, why not let Olaf and me go back to the opening and pick them off as they come in? We could hold the lot—and in the meantime you and Goodwin could go after Lakla for help."

"Lugur knows the secret of the Portal—if he dare use it," answered the captain, with a curious indirection. "And now that they have challenged the Silent Ones I think he *will* dare. Also, he will find our tracks—and it may be that he knows this hidden way."

"Well, for God's sake!" O'Keefe's appalled bewilderment was almost ludicrous. "If *he* knows all that, and *you* knew all that, why didn't you let me click him when I had the chance?"

"*Larree*," the green dwarf was oddly humble. "It seemed good to me, too—at first. And then I heard a command, heard it clearly, to stop you—that Lugur die not now, lest a greater vengeance fail!"

"Command? From whom?" The Irishman's voice distilled out of the blackness the very essence of bewilderment.

"I thought," Rador was whispering—"I thought it came from the Silent Ones!"

"Superstition!" groaned O'Keefe in utter exasperation. "Always superstition! What can you do against it!

"Never mind, Rador." His sense of humour came to his aid. "It's too late now, anyway. Where do we go from here, old dear?" he laughed.

"We tread the path of one I am not fain to meet," answered Rador. "But if meet we must, point the death tubes at the pale shield he bears upon his throat and send the flame into the flower of cold fire that is its centre—nor look into his eyes!"

Again Larry gasped, and I with him.

"It's getting too deep for me, Doc," he muttered dejectedly. "Can you make head or tail of it?"

"No," I answered, shortly enough, "but Rador fears something and that's his description of it."

"Sure," he replied, "only it's a code I don't understand." I could feel his grin. "All right for the flower of cold fire, Rador, and I won't look into his eyes," he went on cheerfully. "But hadn't we better be moving?"

"Come!" said the soldier; again hand in hand we went blindly on.

O'Keefe was muttering to himself.

"Flower of cold fire! Don't look into his eyes! Some joint! Damned superstition." Then he chuckled and carolled, softly:

> *"Oh, mama, pin a cold rose on me;*
> *Two young frog-men are in love with me;*
> *Shut my eyes so I can't see."*

"Sh!" Rador was warning; he began whispering. "For half a *va* we go along a way of death. From its peril we pass into another against whose dangers I can guard you. But in part this is in view of the roadway and it may be that Lugur will see us. If so, we must fight as best we can. If we pass these two roads safely, then is the way to the Crimson Sea clear, nor need we fear Lugur nor any. And there is another thing—that Lugur does not know—when he opens the Portal the Silent Ones will hear and Lakla and the *Akka* will be swift to greet its opener."

"Rador," I asked, "how know *you* all this?"

"The handmaiden is my own sister's child," he answered quietly.

O'Keefe drew a long breath.

"Uncle," he remarked casually in English, "meet the man who's going to be your nephew!"

And thereafter he never addressed the green dwarf except by the avuncular title, which Rador, humorously enough, apparently conceived to be one of respectful endearment.

For me a light broke. Plain now was the reason for his foreknowledge of Lakla's appearance at the feast where Larry had so narrowly escaped Yolara's spells; plain the determining factor that had cast his lot with ours, and my confidence, despite his discourse of mysterious perils, experienced a remarkable quickening.

Speculation as to the marked differences in pigmentation and appearance of niece and uncle was dissipated by my consciousness that we were now moving in a dim half-light. We were in a fairly wide tunnel. Not far ahead the gleam filtered, pale yellow like sunlight sifting through the leaves of autumn poplars. And as we drove closer to its source I saw that it did indeed pass through a leafy screen hanging over the passage end. This Rador drew aside cautiously, beckoned us and we stepped through.

It appeared to be a tunnel cut through soft green mould. Its base was a flat strip of pathway a yard wide from which the walls curved out in perfect cylindrical form, smoothed and evened with utmost nicety. Thirty feet wide they were at their widest, then drew toward each other with no break in their symmetry; they did not close. Above was, roughly, a ten-foot rift, ragged edged, through which poured light like that in the heart of pale amber, a buttercup light shot through with curiously evanescent bronze shadows.

"Quick!" commanded Rador, uneasily, and set off at a sharp pace.

Now, my eyes accustomed to the strange light, I saw that the tunnel's walls were of moss. In them I could trace fringe leaf and curly leaf, pressings of enormous bladder caps (Physcomitrium), immense splashes of what seemed to be the scarlet-crested Cladonia, traceries of huge moss veils, crushings of teeth (peristome) gigantic; spore cases brown and white, saffron and ivory, hot vermilions and cerulean blues, pressed into an astounding mosaic by some titanic force.

"Hurry!" It was Rador calling. I had lagged behind.

He quickened the pace to a half-run; we were climbing; panting. The amber light grew stronger; the rift above us wider. The tunnel curved; on the left a narrow cleft appeared. The green dwarf leaped toward it, thrust us within, pushed us ahead of him up a steep rocky fissure—well-nigh, indeed, a chimney. Up and up this we scrambled until my lungs were bursting and I thought I could climb no more. The crevice ended; we crawled out and sank, even Rador, upon a little leaf-carpeted clearing circled by lacy tree ferns.

Gasping, legs aching, we lay prone, relaxed, drawing back strength and breath. Rador was first to rise. Thrice he bent low as in homage, then—

"Give thanks to the Silent Ones—for their power has been over us!" he exclaimed.

Dimly I wondered what he meant. Something about the fern leaf at which I had been staring aroused me. I leaped to my feet and ran to its base. This was no fern, no! It was fern *moss*! The largest of its species I had ever found in tropic jungles had not been more than two inches high, and this was—twenty feet! The scientific fire I had experienced in the tunnel returned uncontrollable. I parted the fronds, gazed out—

My outlook commanded a vista of miles—and that vista! A *Fata Morgana* of plantdom! A land of flowered sorcery!

Forests of tree-high mosses spangled over with blooms of every conceivable shape and colour; cataracts and clusters, avalanches and nets of blossoms in pastels, in dulled metallics, in gorgeous flamboyant hues; some of them phosphorescent and shining like living jewels; some sparkling as though with dust of opals, of sapphires, of rubies and topazes and emeralds; thickets of convolvuli like the trumpets of the seven archangels of Mara, king of illusion, which are shaped from the bows of splendours arching his highest heaven!

And moss veils like banners of a marching host of Titans; pennons and bannerets of the sunset; gonfalons of the Jinn; webs of faery; oriflammes of elfland!

Springing up through that polychromatic flood myriads of pedicles—slender and straight as spears, or soaring in spirals, or curving with undulations gracile as the white serpents of Tanit in ancient Carthaginian groves—and all surmounted by a fantasy of spore cases in shapes of minaret and turret, domes and spires and cones, caps of Phrygia and bishops' mitres, shapes grotesque and unnameable— shapes delicate and lovely!

They hung high poised, nodding and swaying—like goblins hovering over *Titania's* court; cacophony of Cathay accenting the *Flower Maiden* music of "Parsifal"; *bizarrerie* of the angled, fantastic beings that people the Javan pantheon watching a bacchanal of houris in Mohammed's paradise!

Down upon it all poured the amber light; dimmed in the distances by huge, drifting darkenings lurid as the flying mantles of the hurricane.

And through the light, like showers of jewels, myriads of birds, darting, dipping, soaring, and still other myriads of gigantic, shimmering butterflies.

A sound came to us, reaching out like the first faint susurrus of the incoming tide; sighing, sighing, growing stronger—now its mournful whispering quivered all about us, shook us—then passing like a Presence, died away in far distances.

"The Portal!" said Rador. "Lugur has entered!"

He, too, parted the fronds and peered back along our path. Peering with him we saw the barrier through which we had come stretching verdure-covered walls for miles three or more away. Like a mole burrow in a garden stretched the trail of the tunnel; here and there we could look down within the rift at its top; far off in it I thought I saw the glint of spears.

"They come!" whispered Rador. "Quick! We must not meet them here!"

And then—

"Holy St. Brigid!" gasped Larry.

From the rift in the tunnel's continuation, nigh a mile beyond the cleft through which we had fled, lifted a crown of horns—of tentacles—erect, alert, of mottled gold and crimson; lifted higher—and from a monstrous scarlet head beneath them blazed two enormous, obloid eyes, their depths wells of purplish phosphorescence; higher still—noseless, earless, chinless; a livid, worm mouth from which a slender scarlet tongue leaped like playing flames! Slowly it rose—its mighty neck cuirassed with gold and scarlet scales from whose polished surfaces the amber light glinted like flakes of fire; and under this neck shimmered something like a palely luminous silvery shield, guarding it. The head of horror mounted—and in the shield's centre, full ten feet across, glowing, flickering, shining out—coldly, was a rose of white flame, a "flower of cold fire" even as Rador had said.

Now swiftly the Thing upreared, standing like a scaled tower a hundred feet above the rift, its eyes scanning that movement I had seen along the course of its lair. There was a hissing; the crown of horns fell, whipped and writhed like the tentacles of an octopus; the towering length dropped back.

"Quick!" gasped Rador and through the fern moss, along the path and down the other side of the steep we raced.

Behind us for an instant there was a rushing as of a torrent; a far-away, faint, agonized screaming—silence!

"No fear *now* from those who followed," whispered the green dwarf, pausing.

"Sainted St. Patrick!" O'Keefe gazed ruminatively at his automatic. "An' he expected me to kill *that* with this. Well, as Fergus O'Connor said when they sent him out to slaughter a wild bull with a potato knife: 'Ye'll niver rayilize how I appreciate the confidence ye show in me!'

"What was it, Doc?" he asked.

"The dragon worm!" Rador said.

"It was Helvede Orm—the hell worm!" groaned Olaf.

"There you go again—" blazed Larry; but the green dwarf was hurrying down the path and swiftly we followed, Larry muttering, Olaf mumbling, behind me.

The green dwarf was signalling us for caution. He pointed through a break in a grove of fifty-foot cedar mosses—we were skirting the glassy road! Scanning it we found no trace of Lugur and wondered whether he too had seen the worm and had fled. Quickly we passed on; drew away from the *coria* path. The mosses began to thin; less and less they grew, giving way to low clumps that barely offered us shelter. Unexpectedly another screen of fern moss stretched before us. Slowly Rador made his way through it and stood hesitating.

The scene in front of us was oddly weird and depressing; in some indefinable way—dreadful. Why, I could not tell, but the impression was plain; I shrank from it. Then, self-analyzing, I wondered whether it could be the uncanny resemblance the heaps of curious mossy fungi scattered about had to beast and bird—yes, and to man—that was the cause of it. Our path ran between a few of them. To the left they were thick. They were viridescent, almost metallic hued—verd-antique. Curiously indeed were they like distorted images of dog and deerlike forms, of birds—of *dwarfs* and here and there the simulacra of the giant frogs! Spore cases, yellowish green, as large as mitres and much resembling them in shape protruded from the heaps. My repulsion grew into a distinct nausea.

Rador turned to us a face whiter far than that with which he had looked upon the dragon worm.

"Now for your lives," he whispered, "tread softly here as I do—and speak not at all!"

He stepped forward on tiptoe, slowly with utmost caution. We crept after him; passed the heaps beside the path—and as I passed my skin crept and I shrank and saw the others shrink too with that unnameable loathing; nor did the green dwarf pause until he had reached the brow of a small hillock a hundred yards beyond. And he was trembling.

"Now what are we up against?" grumbled O'Keefe.

The green dwarf stretched a hand; stiffened; gazed over to the left of us beyond a lower hillock upon whose broad crest lay a file of the moss shapes. They fringed it, their mitres having a grotesque appearance of watching what lay below. The glistening road lay there—and from it came a shout. A dozen of the *coria* clustered, filled with Lugur's men and in one of them Lugur himself, laughing wickedly!

There was a rush of soldiers and up the low hillock raced a score of them toward us.

"Run!" shouted Rador.

"Not much!" grunted Larry—and took swift aim at Lugur. The automatic spat: Olaf's echoed. Both bullets went wild, for Lugur, still laughing, threw himself into the protection of the body of his shell. But following the shots, from the file of moss heaps on the crest, came a series of muffled explosions. Under the pistol's concussions the mitred caps had burst and instantly all about the running soldiers grew a cloud of tiny, glistening white spores—like a little cloud of puff-ball dust many times magnified. Through this cloud I glimpsed their faces, stricken with agony.

Some turned to fly, but before they could take a second step stood rigid.

The spore cloud drifted and eddied about them; rained down on their heads and half bare breasts, covered their garments—and swiftly they began to change! Their features grew indistinct—merged! The glistening white spores that covered them turned to a pale yellow, grew greenish, spread and swelled, darkened. The eyes of one of the soldiers glinted for a moment—and then were covered by the swift growth!

Where but a few moments before had been men were only grotesque heaps, swiftly melting, swiftly rounding into the semblance of the mounds that lay behind us—and already beginning to take on their gleam of ancient viridescence!

The Irishman was gripping my arm fiercely; the pain brought me back to my senses.

"Olaf's right," he gasped. "This *is* hell! I'm sick." And he was, frankly and without restraint. Lugur and his others awakened from their nightmare; piled into the *coria*, wheeled, raced away.

"On!" said Rador thickly. "Two perils have we passed—the Silent Ones watch over us!"

Soon we were again among the familiar and so unfamiliar moss giants. I knew what I had seen and this time Larry could not call me—superstitious. In the jungles of Borneo I had examined that other swiftly developing fungus which wreaks the vengeance of some of the hill tribes upon those who steal their women; gripping with its microscopic hooks into the flesh; sending quick, tiny rootlets through the skin down into the capillaries, sucking life and thriving and never to be torn away until the living thing it clings to has been sapped dry. Here was but another of the species in which the development's rate was incredibly accelerated. Some of this I tried to explain to O'Keefe as we sped along, reassuring him.

"But they turned to moss before our eyes!" he said.

Again I explained, patiently. But he seemed to derive no comfort at all from my assurances that the phenomena were entirely natural and, aside from their more terrifying aspect, of peculiar interest to the botanist.

"I know," was all he would say. "But suppose one of those things had burst while we were going through—God!"

I was wondering how I could with comparative safety study the fungus when Rador stopped; in front of us was again the road ribbon.

"Now is all danger passed," he said. "The way lies open and Lugur has fled—"

There was a flash from the road. It passed me like a little lariat of light. It struck Larry squarely between the eyes, spread over his face and drew itself within!

"Down!" cried Rador, and hurled me to the ground. My head struck sharply; I felt myself grow faint; Olaf fell beside me; I saw the green dwarf draw down the O'Keefe; he collapsed limply, face still, eyes staring. A shout—and from the roadway poured a host of Lugur's men; I could hear Lugur bellowing.

There came a rush of little feet; soft, fragrant draperies brushed my face; dimly I watched Lakla bend over the Irishman.

She straightened—her arms swept out and the writhing vine, with its tendrilled heads of ruby bloom, five flames of misty incandescence, leaped into the faces of the soldiers now close upon us. It darted at their throats, striking, coiling, and striking again; coiling and uncoiling with incredible rapidity and flying from leverage points of throats, of faces, of breasts like a spring endowed with consciousness, volition and hatred—and those it struck stood rigid as stone with faces masks of inhuman fear and anguish; and those still unstricken fled.

Another rush of feet—and down upon Lugur's forces poured the frog-men, their booming giant leading, thrusting with their lances, tearing and rending with talons and fangs and spurs.

Against that onslaught the dwarfs could not stand. They raced for the shells; I heard Lugur shouting, menacingly—and then Lakla's voice, pealing like a golden bugle of wrath.

"Go, Lugur!" she cried. "Go—that you and Yolara and your Shining One may die together! Death for you, Lugur—death for you all! Remember Lugur—death!"

There was a great noise within my head—no matter, Lakla was here—Lakla here—but too late—Lugur had outplayed us; moss death nor dragon worm had frightened him away—he had crept back to trap us—Lakla had come too late—Larry was dead—Larry! But I had heard no banshee wailing—and Larry had said he could not die without that warning—no, Larry was not dead. So ran the turbulent current of my mind.

A horny arm lifted me; two enormous, oddly gentle saucer eyes were staring into mine; my head rolled; I caught a glimpse of the Golden Girl kneeling beside the O'Keefe.

The noise in my head grew thunderous—was carrying me away on its thunder—swept me into soft, blind darkness.

XXIV

THE CRIMSON SEA

I was in the heart of a rose pearl, swinging, swinging; no, I was in a rosy dawn cloud, pendulous in space. Consciousness flooded me, in reality I was in the arms of one of the man frogs, carrying me as though I were a babe, and we were passing through some place suffused with glow enough like heart of pearl or dawn cloud to justify my awakening vagaries.

Just ahead walked Lakla in earnest talk with Rador, and content enough was I for a time to watch her. She had thrown off the metallic robes; her thick braids of golden brown hair with their flame glints of bronze were twined in a high coronal meshed in silken net of green; little clustering curls escaped from it, clinging to the nape of the proud white neck, shyly kissing it. From her shoulders fell a loose, sleeveless garment of shimmering green belted with a high golden girdle; skirt folds dropping barely below the knees.

She had cast aside her buskins, too, and the slender, high-arched feet were sandalled. Between the buckled edges of her kirtle I caught gleams of translucent ivory as exquisitely moulded, as delectably rounded, as those revealed so naively beneath the hem.

Something was knocking at the doors of my consciousness—some tragic thing. What was it? Larry! Where was Larry? I remembered; raised my head abruptly; saw at my side another frog-man carrying O'Keefe, and behind him, Olaf, step instinct with grief, following like some faithful, wistful dog who has lost a loved master. Upon my movement the monster bearing me halted, looked down inquiringly, uttered a deep, booming note that held the quality of interrogation.

Lakla turned; the clear, golden eyes were sorrowful, the sweet mouth drooping; but her loveliness, her gentleness, that undefinable synthesis of all her tender self that seemed always to circle her with an atmosphere of lucid normality, lulled my panic.

"Drink this," she commanded, holding a small vial to my lips.

Its contents were aromatic, unfamiliar but astonishingly effective, for as soon as they passed my lips I felt a surge of strength; consciousness was restored.

"Larry!" I cried. "Is he dead?"

Lakla shook her head; her eyes were troubled.

"No," she said; "but he is like one dead—and yet unlike—"

"Put me down," I demanded of my bearer.

He tightened his hold; round eyes upon the Golden Girl. She spoke—in sonorous, reverberating monosyllables—and I was set upon my feet; I leaped to the side of the Irishman. He lay limp, with a disquieting, abnormal sequacity, as though every muscle were utterly flaccid; the antithesis of the *rigor mortis*, thank God, but terrifyingly toward the other end of its arc; a syncope I had never known. The flesh was stone cold; the pulse barely perceptible, long intervalled; the respiration undiscoverable; the pupils of the eyes were enormously dilated; it was as though life had been drawn from every nerve.

"A light flashed from the road. It struck his face and seemed to sink in," I said.

"I saw," answered Rador; "but what it was I know not; and I thought I knew all the weapons of our rulers." He glanced at me curiously. "Some talk there has been that the stranger who came with you, Double Tongue, was making new death tools for Lugur," he ended.

Marakinoff! The Russian at work already in this storehouse of devastating energies, fashioning the weapons for his plots! The Apocalyptic vision swept back upon me—

"He is not dead." Lakla's voice was poignant. "He is not dead; and the Three have wondrous healing. They can restore him if they will—and they will, they *will*!" For a moment she was silent. "Now their gods help Lugur and Yolara," she whispered; "for come what may, whether the Silent Ones be strong or weak, if he dies, surely shall I fall upon them and I will slay those two—yea, though I, too, perish!"

"Yolara and Lugur shall both die." Olaf's eyes were burning. "But Lugur is mine to slay."

That pity I had seen before in Lakla's eyes when she looked upon the Norseman banished the white wrath from them. She turned, half hurriedly, as though to escape his gaze.

"Walk with us," she said to me, "unless you are still weak."

I shook my head, gave a last look at O'Keefe; there was nothing I could do; I stepped beside her. She thrust a white arm into mine protectingly, the wonderfully moulded hand with its long, tapering fingers catching about my wrist; my heart glowed toward her.

"Your medicine is potent, handmaiden," I answered. "And the touch of your hand would give me strength enough, even had I not drunk it," I added in Larry's best manner.

Her eyes danced, trouble flying.

"Now, that was well spoken for such a man of wisdom as Rador tells me you are," she laughed; and a little pang shot through me. Could not a lover of science present a compliment without it always seeming to be as unusual as plucking a damask rose from a cabinet of fossils?

Mustering my philosophy, I smiled back at her. Again I noted that broad, classic brow, with the little tendrils of shining bronze caressing it, the tilted, delicate, nut-brown brows that gave a curious touch of innocent *diablerie* to the lovely face—flowerlike, pure, high-bred, a touch of roguishness, subtly alluring, sparkling over the maiden Madonnaness that lay ever like a delicate, luminous suggestion beneath it; the long, black, curling lashes—the tender, rounded, bare left breast—

"I have always liked you," she murmured naively, "since first I saw you in that place where the Shining One goes forth into your world. And I am glad you like my medicine as well as that you carry in the black box that you left behind," she added swiftly.

"How know you of that, Lakla?" I gasped.

"Oft and oft I came to him there, and to you, while you lay sleeping. How call you *him*?" She paused.

"Larry!" I said.

"Larry!" she repeated it excellently. "And you?"

"Goodwin," said Rador.

I bowed quite as though I were being introduced to some charming young lady met in that old life now seemingly aeons removed.

"Yes—Goodwin." she said. "Oft and oft I came. Sometimes I thought you saw me. And *he*—did he not dream of me sometime—?" she asked wistfully.

"He did." I said, "and watched for you." Then amazement grew vocal. "But how came you?" I asked.

"By a strange road," she whispered, "to see that all was well with *him*—and to look into his heart; for I feared Yolara and her beauty. But I saw that she was not in his heart." A blush burned over her, turning even the little bare breast rosy. "It is a strange road," she went on hurriedly. "Many times have I followed it and watched the Shining One bear back its prey to the blue pool; seen the woman *he* seeks"—she made a quick gesture toward Olaf—"and a babe cast from her arms in the last pang of her mother love; seen another woman throw herself into the Shining One's embrace to save a man she loved; and I could not help!" Her voice grew deep, thrilled. "The friend, it comes to me, who drew you here, Goodwin!"

She was silent, walking as one who sees visions and listens to voices unheard by others, Rador made a warning gesture; I crowded back my questions, glanced about me. We were passing over a smooth strand, hard packed as some beach of long-thrust-back ocean. It was like crushed garnets, each grain stained deep red, faintly sparkling. On each side were distances, the floor stretching away into them bare of vegetation—stretching on and on into infinitudes of rosy mist, even as did the space above.

Flanking and behind us marched the giant batrachians, fivescore of them at least, black scale and crimson scale lustrous and gleaming in the rosaceous radiance; saucer eyes shining circles of phosphorescence green, purple, red; spurs clicking as they crouched along with a gait at once grotesque and formidable.

Ahead the mist deepened into a ruddier glow; through it a long, dark line began to appear—the mouth I thought of the caverned space through which we were going; it was just before us; over us—we stood bathed in a flood of rubescence!

A sea stretched before us—a crimson sea, gleaming like that lost lacquer of royal coral and the Flame Dragon's blood which Fu S'cze set upon the bower he built for his stolen sun maiden—that going toward it she might think it the sun itself rising over the summer seas. Unmoved by wave or ripple, it was placid as some deep woodland pool when night rushes up over the world.

It seemed molten—or as though some hand great enough to rock earth had distilled here from conflagrations of autumn sunsets their flaming essences.

A fish broke through, large as a shark, blunt-headed, flashing bronze, ridged and mailed as though with serrate plates of armour. It leaped high, shaking from it a sparkling spray of rubies; dropped and shot up a geyser of fiery gems.

Across my line of vision, moving stately over the sea, floated a half globe, luminous, diaphanous, its iridescence melting into turquoise, thence to amethyst, to orange, to scarlet shot with rose, to vermilion, a translucent green, thence back into the iridescence; behind it four others, and the least of them ten feet in diameter, and the largest no less than thirty. They drifted past like bubbles blown from froth of rainbows by pipes in mouths of Titans' young. Then from the base of one arose a tangle of shimmering strands, long, slender whiplashes that played about and sank slowly again beneath the crimson surface.

I gasped—for the fish had been a *ganoid*—that ancient, armoured form that was perhaps the most intelligent of all life on our planet during the Devonian era, but which for age upon age had vanished, save for its fossils held in the embrace of the stone that once was their soft bottom beds; and the half-globes were *Medusae*, jelly-fish—but of a size, luminosity, and colour unheard of.

Now Lakla cupped her mouth with pink palms and sent a clarion note ringing out. The ledge on which we stood continued a few hundred feet before us, falling abruptly, though from no great height to the Crimson Sea; at right and left it extended in a long semicircle. Turning to the right whence she had sent her call, I saw rising a mile or more away, veiled lightly by the haze, a rainbow, a gigantic prismatic arch, flattened, I thought, by some quality of the strange atmosphere. It sprang from the ruddy strand, leaped the crimson tide, and dropped three miles away upon a precipitous, jagged upthrust of rock frowning black from the lacquered depths.

And surmounting a higher ledge beyond this upthrust a huge dome of dull gold, Cyclopean, striking eyes and mind with something unhumanly alien, baffling; sending the mind groping, as though across the deserts of space, from some far-flung star, should fall upon us linked sounds, coherent certainly, meaningful surely, vaguely familiar—yet never to be translated into any symbol or thought of our own particular planet.

The sea of crimson lacquer, with its floating moons of luminous colour—this bow of prismed stone leaping to the weird isle crowned by the anomalous, aureate excrescence—the half human batrachians-the elfland through which we had passed, with all its hidden wonders and terrors—I felt the foundations of my cherished knowledge shaking. Was this all a dream? Was this body of mine lying somewhere, fighting a fevered death, and all these but images floating through the breaking chambers of my brain? My knees shook; involuntarily I groaned.

Lakla turned, looked at me anxiously, slipped a soft arm behind me, held me till the vertigo passed.

"Patience," she said. "The bearers come. Soon you shall rest."

I looked; down toward us from the bow's end were leaping swiftly another score of the frog-men. Some bore litters, high, handled, not unlike palanquins—

"Asgard!" Olaf stood beside me, eyes burning, pointing to the arch. "Bifrost Bridge, sharp as sword edge, over which souls go to Valhalla. And *she*—she is a Valkyr—a sword maiden, *Ja!* "

I gripped the Norseman's hand. It was hot, and a pang of remorse shot through me. If this place had so shaken me, how must it have shaken Olaf? It was with relief that I watched him, at Lakla's gentle command, drop into one of the litters and lie back, eyes closed, as two of the monsters raised its yoke to their scaled shoulders. Nor was it without further relief that I myself lay back on the soft velvety cushions of another.

The cavalcade began to move. Lakla had ordered O'Keefe placed beside her, and she sat, knees crossed Orient fashion, leaning over the pale head on her lap, the white, tapering fingers straying fondly through his hair.

Presently I saw her reach up, slowly unwind the coronal of her tresses, shake them loose, and let them fall like a veil over her and him.

Her head bent low; I heard a soft sobbing—I turned away my gaze, lorn enough in my own heart, God knew!

XXV

The Three Silent Ones

The arch was closer—and in my awe I forgot for the moment Larry and aught else. For this was no rainbow, no thing born of light and mist, no Bifrost Bridge of myth—no! It was a flying arch of stone, stained with flares of Tyrian purples, of royal scarlets, of blues dark as the Gulf Stream's ribbon, sapphires soft as midday May skies, splashes of chromes and greens—a palette of giantry, a bridge of wizardry; a hundred, nay, a thousand, times greater than that of Utah which the Navaho call Nonnegozche and worship, as well they may, as a god, and which is itself a rainbow in eternal rock.

It sprang from the ledge and winged its prodigious length in one low arc over the sea's crimson breast, as though in some ancient paroxysm of earth it had been hurled molten, crystallizing into that stupendous span and still flaming with the fires that had moulded it.

Closer we came and closer, while I watched spellbound; now we were at its head, and the litter-bearers swept upon it. All of five hundred feet wide it was, surface smooth as a city road, sides low walled, curving inward as though in the jetting-out of its making the edges of the plastic rock had curled.

On and on we sped; the high thrusting precipices upon which the bridge's far end rested, frowned close; the enigmatic, dully shining dome loomed ever greater. Now we had reached that end; were passing over a smooth plaza whose level floor was enclosed, save for a rift in front of us, by the fanged tops of the black cliffs.

From this rift stretched another span, half a mile long, perhaps, widening at its centre into a broad platform, continuing straight to two massive gates set within the face of the second cliff wall like panels, and of the same dull gold as the dome rising high beyond. And this smaller arch leaped a pit, an abyss, of which the outer precipices were the rim holding back from the pit the red flood.

We were rapidly approaching; now upon the platform; my bearers were striding closely along the side; I leaned far out—a giddiness seized me! I gazed down into depth upon vertiginous depth; an abyss indeed—an abyss dropping to world's base like that in which the Babylonians believed writhed Talaat, the serpent mother of Chaos; a pit that struck down into earth's heart itself.

Now, what was that—distance upon unfathomable distance below? A stupendous glowing like the green fire of life itself. What was it like? I had it! It was like the corona of the sun in eclipse—that burgeoning that makes of our luminary when moon veils it an incredible blossoming of splendours in the black heavens.

And strangely, strangely, it was like the Dweller's beauty when with its dazzling spirallings and writhings it raced amid its storm of crystal bell sounds!

The abyss was behind us; we had paused at the golden portals; they swung inward. A wide corridor filled with soft light was before us, and on its threshold stood—bizarre, yellow gems gleaming, huge muzzle wide in what was evidently meant for a smile of welcome—the woman frog of the Moon Pool wall.

Lakla raised her head; swept back the silken tent of her hair and gazed at me with eyes misty from weeping. The frog-woman crept to her side; gazed down upon Larry; spoke—*spoke*—to the Golden Girl in a swift stream of the sonorous, reverberant monosyllables; and Lakla answered her in kind. The webbed digits swept over O'Keefe's face, felt at his heart; she shook her head and moved ahead of us up the passage.

Still borne in the litters we went on, winding, ascending until at last they were set down in a great hall carpeted with soft fragrant rushes and into which from high narrow slits streamed the crimson light from without.

I jumped over to Larry, there had been no change in his condition; still the terrifying limpness, the slow, infrequent pulsation. Rador and Olaf—and the fever now seemed to be gone from him—came and stood beside me, silent.

"I go to the Three," said Lakla. "Wait you here." She passed through a curtaining; then as swiftly as she had gone she returned through the hangings, tresses braided, a swathing of golden gauze about her.

"Rador," she said, "bear you Larry—for into your heart the Silent Ones would look. And fear nothing," she added at the green dwarf's disconcerted, almost fearful start.

Rador bowed, was thrust aside by Olaf.

"No," said the Norseman; "I will carry him."

He lifted Larry like a child against his broad breast. The dwarf glanced quickly at Lakla; she nodded.

"Come!" she commanded, and held aside the folds.

Of that journey I have few memories. I only know that we went through corridor upon corridor; successions of vast halls and chambers, some carpeted with the rushes, others with rugs into which the feet sank as into deep, soft meadows; spaces illumined by the rubrous light, and spaces in which softer lights held sway.

We paused before a slab of the same crimson stone as that the green dwarf had called the portal, and upon its polished surface weaved the same unnameable symbols. The Golden Girl pressed upon its side; it slipped softly back; a torrent of opalescence gushed out of the opening—and as one in a dream I entered.

We were, I knew, just under the dome; but for the moment, caught in the flood of radiance, I could see nothing. It was like being held within a fire opal—so brilliant, so flashing, was it. I closed my eyes, opened them; the lambency cascaded from the vast curves of the globular walls; in front of me was a long, narrow opening in them, through which, far away, I could see the end of the wizards' bridge and the ledged mouth of the cavern through which we had come; against the light from within beat the crimson light from without—and was checked as though by a barrier.

I felt Lakla's touch; turned.

A hundred paces away was a dais, its rim raised a yard above the floor. From the edge of this rim streamed upward a steady, coruscating mist of the opalescence, veined even as was that of the Dweller's shining core and shot with milky shadows like curdled moonlight; up it stretched like a wall.

Over it, from it, down upon me, gazed three faces—two clearly male, one a woman's. At the first I thought them statues, and then the eyes of them gave the lie to me; for the eyes were alive, terribly, and if I could admit the word—*supernaturally*—alive.

They were thrice the size of the human eye and triangular, the apex of the angle upward; black as jet, pupilless, filled with tiny, leaping red flames.

Over them were foreheads, not as ours—high and broad and visored; their sides drawn forward into a vertical ridge, a prominence, an upright wedge, somewhat like the visored heads of a few of the great lizards—and the heads, long, narrowing at the back, were fully twice the size of mankind's!

Upon the brows were caps—and with a fearful certainty I knew that they were *not* caps—long, thick strands of gleaming yellow, feathered scales thin as sequins! Sharp, curving noses like the beaks of the giant condors; mouths thin, austere; long, powerful, pointed chins; the—*flesh*—of the faces white as the whitest marble; and wreathing up to them, covering all their bodies, the shimmering, curdled, misty fires of opalescence!

Olaf stood rigid; my own heart leaped wildly. What—what were these beings?

I forced myself to look again—and from their gaze streamed a current of reassurance, of good will—nay, of intense spiritual strength. I saw that they were not fierce, not ruthless, not inhuman, despite their strangeness; no, they were kindly; in some unmistakable way, benign and sorrowful—so sorrowful! I straightened, gazed back at them fearlessly. Olaf drew a deep breath, gazed steadily too, the hardness, the despair wiped from his face.

Now Lakla drew closer to the dais; the three pairs of eyes searched hers, the woman's with an ineffable tenderness; some message seemed to pass between the Three and the Golden Girl. She bowed low, turned to the Norseman.

"Place Larry there," she said softly—"there at the feet of the Silent Ones."

She pointed into the radiant mist; Olaf started, hesitated, stared from Lakla to the Three, searched for a moment their eyes—and something like a smile drifted through them. He stepped forward, lifted O'Keefe, set him squarely within the covering light. It wavered, rolled upward, swirled about the body, steadied again—and within it there was no sign of Larry!

Again the mist wavered, shook, and seemed to climb higher, hiding the chins, the beaked noses, the brows of that incredible Trinity—but before it ceased to climb, I thought the yellow feathered heads bent; sensed a movement as though they lifted something.

The mist fell; the eyes gleamed out again, inscrutable.

And groping out of the radiance, pausing at the verge of the dais, leaping down from it, came Larry, laughing, filled with life, blinking as one who draws from darkness into sunshine. He saw Lakla, sprang to her, gripped her in his arms.

"Lakla!" he cried. "Mavourneen!" She slipped from his embrace, blushing, glancing at the Three shyly, half-fearfully. And again I saw the tenderness creep into the inky, flame-shot orbs of the woman being; and a tenderness in the others too—as though they regarded some well-beloved child.

"You lay in the arms of Death, Larry," she said. "And the Silent Ones drew you from him. Do homage to the Silent Ones, Larry, for they are good and they are mighty!"

She turned his head with one of the long, white hands—and he looked into the faces of the Three; looked long, was shaken even as had been Olaf and myself; was swept by that same wave of power and of—of—what can I call it?—*holiness* that streamed from them.

Then for the first time I saw real awe mount into his face. Another moment he stared—and dropped upon one knee and bowed his head before them as would a worshipper before the shrine of his saint. And—I am not ashamed to tell it—I joined him; and with us knelt Lakla and Olaf and Rador.

The mist of fiery opal swirled up about the Three; hid them.

And with a long, deep, joyous sigh Lakla took Larry's hand, drew him to his feet, and silently we followed them out of that hall of wonder.

But why, in going, did the thought come to me that from where the Three sat throned they ever watched the cavern mouth that was the door into their abode; and looked down ever into the unfathomable depth in which glowed and pulsed that mystic flower, colossal, awesome, of green flame that had seemed to me fire of life itself?

XXVI

The Wooing of Lakla

I had slept soundly and dreamlessly; I wakened quietly in the great chamber into which Rador had ushered O'Keefe and myself after that culminating experience of crowded, nerve-racking hours—the facing of the Three.

Now, lying gazing upward at the high-vaulted ceiling, I heard Larry's voice:

"They look like birds." Evidently he was thinking of the Three; a silence—then: "Yes, they look like *birds*—and they look, and it's meaning no disrespect to them I am at all, they look like *lizards*"—and another silence—"they look like some sort of gods, and, by the good sword-arm of Brian Boru, they look human, too! And it's *none* of them they are either, so what—what the—what the sainted St. Bridget are they?" Another short silence, and then in a tone of awed and absolute conviction: "That's it, sure! That's what they are—it all hangs in—they couldn't be anything else—"

He gave a whoop; a pillow shot over and caught me across the head.

"Wake up!" shouted Larry. "Wake up, ye seething caldron of fossilized superstitions! Wake up, ye bogy-haunted man of scientific unwisdom!"

Under pillow and insults I bounced to my feet, filled for a moment with quite real wrath; he lay back, roaring with laughter, and my anger was swept away.

"Doc," he said, very seriously, after this, "I know who the Three are!"

"Yes?" I queried, with studied sarcasm.

"Yes?" he mimicked. "Yes! Ye—ye" He paused under the menace of my look, grinned. "Yes, I know," he continued. "They're of the Tuatha De, the old ones, the great people of Ireland, *that's* who they are!"

I knew, of course, of the Tuatha De Danann, the tribes of the god Danu, the half-legendary, half-historical clan who found their home in Erin some four thousand years before the Christian era, and who have left so deep an impress upon the Celtic mind and its myths.

"Yes," said Larry again, "the Tuatha De—the Ancient Ones who had spells that could compel Mananan, who is the spirit of all the seas, an' Keithor, who is the god of all green living things, an' even Hesus, the unseen god, whose pulse is the pulse of all the firmament; yes, an' Orchil too, who sits within the earth an' weaves with the shuttle of mystery and her three looms of birth an' life an' death—even Orchil would weave as they commanded!"

He was silent—then:

"They are of them—the mighty ones—why else would I have bent my knee to them as I would have to the spirit of my dead mother? Why else would Lakla, whose gold-brown hair is the hair of Eilidh the Fair, whose mouth is the sweet mouth of Deirdre, an' whose soul walked with mine ages agone among the fragrant green myrtle of Erin, serve them?" he whispered, eyes full of dream.

"Have you any idea how they got here?" I asked, not unreasonably.

"I haven't thought about that," he replied somewhat testily. "But at once, me excellent man o' wisdom, a number occur to me. One of them is that this little party of three might have stopped here on their way to Ireland, an' for good reasons of their own decided to stay a while; an' another is that they might have come here afterward, havin' got wind of what those rats out there were contemplatin', and have stayed on the job till the time was ripe to save Ireland from 'em; the rest of the world, too, of course," he added magnanimously, "but Ireland in particular. And do any of those reasons appeal to ye?"

I shook my head.

"Well, what do you think?" he asked wearily.

"I think," I said cautiously, "that we face an evolution of highly intelligent beings from ancestral sources radically removed from those through which mankind ascended. These half-human, highly developed batrachians they call the *Akka* prove that evolution in these caverned spaces has certainly pursued one different path than on earth. The Englishman, Wells, wrote an imaginative and very entertaining book concerning an invasion of earth by Martians, and he made his Martians enormously specialized cuttlefish. There was nothing inherently improbable in Wells' choice. Man is the ruling animal of earth today solely by reason of a series of accidents; under another series spiders or ants, or even elephants, could have become the dominant race.

"I think," I said, even more cautiously, "that the race to which the Three belong never appeared on earth's surface; that their development took place here, unhindered through aeons. And if this be true, the structure of their brains, and therefore all their reactions, must be different from ours. Hence their knowledge and command of energies unfamiliar to us—and hence also the question whether they may not have an entirely different sense of values, of justice—and that is rather terrifying," I concluded.

Larry shook his head.

"That last sort of knocks your argument, Doc," he said. "They had sense of justice enough to help *me* out—and certainly they know love—for I saw the way they looked at Lakla; and sorrow—for there was no mistaking that in their faces.

"No," he went on. "I hold to my own idea. They're of the Old People. The little leprechaun knew his way here, an' I'll bet it was they who sent the word. An' if the O'Keefe banshee comes here—which save the mark!—I'll bet she'll drop in on the Silent Ones for a social visit before she an' her clan get busy. Well, it'll make her feel more at home, the good old body. No, Doc, no," he concluded, "I'm right; it all fits in too well to be wrong."

I made a last despairing attempt.

"Is there anything anywhere in Ireland that would indicate that the Tuatha De ever looked like the Three?" I asked—and again I had spoken most unfortunately.

"Is there?" he shouted. "Is there? By the kilt of Cormack MacCormack, I'm glad ye reminded me. It was worryin' me a little meself. There was Daghda, who could put on the head of a great boar an' the body of a giant fish and cleave the waves an' tear to pieces the birlins of any who came against Erin; an' there was Rinn—"

How many more of the metamorphoses of the Old People I might have heard, I do not know, for the curtains parted and in walked Rador.

"You have rested well," he smiled, "I can see. The handmaiden bade me call you. You are to eat with her in her garden."

Down long corridors we trod and out upon a gardened terrace as beautiful as any of those of Yolara's city; bowered, blossoming, fragrant, set high upon the cliffs beside the domed castle. A table, as of milky jade, was spread at one corner, but the Golden Girl was not there. A little path ran on and up, hemmed in by the mass of verdure. I looked at it longingly; Rador saw the glance, interpreted it, and led me up the stepped sharp slope into a rock embrasure.

Here I was above the foliage, and everywhere the view was clear. Below me stretched the incredible bridge, with the frog people hurrying back and forth upon it. A pinnacle at my side hid the abyss. My eyes followed the cavern ledge. Above it the rock rose bare, but at the ends of the semicircular strand a luxuriant vegetation began, stretching from the crimson shores back into far distances. Of browns and reds and yellows, like an autumn forest, was the foliage, with here and there patches of dark-green, as of conifers. Five miles or more, on each side, the forests swept, and then were lost to sight in the haze.

I turned and faced an immensity of crimson waters, unbroken, a true sea, if ever there was one. A breeze blew—the first real wind I had encountered in the hidden places; under it the surface, that had been as molten lacquer, rippled and dimpled. Little waves broke with a spray of rose-pearls and rubies. The giant Medusae drifted—stately, luminous kaleidoscopic elfin moons.

Far down, peeping around a jutting tower of the cliff, I saw dipping with the motion of the waves a floating garden. The flowers, too, were luminous—indeed sparkling—gleaming brilliants of scarlet and vermilions lighter than the flood on which they lay, mauves and odd shades of reddish-blue. They gleamed and shone like a little lake of jewels.

Rador broke in upon my musings.

"Lakla comes! Let us go down."

It was a shy Lakla who came slowly around the end of the path and, blushing furiously, held her hands out to Larry. And the Irishman took them, placed them over his heart, kissed them with a tenderness that had been lacking in the half-mocking, half-fierce caresses he had given the priestess. She blushed deeper, holding out the tapering fingers—then pressed them to her own heart.

"I like the touch of your lips, Larry," she whispered. "They warm me here"—she pressed her heart again—"and they send little sparkles of light through me." Her brows tilted perplexedly, accenting the nuance of diablerie, delicate and fascinating, that they cast upon the flower face.

"Do you?" whispered the O'Keefe fervently. "Do you, Lakla?" He bent toward her. She caught the amused glance of Rador; drew herself aside half-haughtily.

"Rador," she said, "is it not time that you and the strong one, Olaf, were setting forth?"

"Truly it is, handmaiden," he answered respectfully enough—yet with a current of laughter under his words. "But as you know the strong one, Olaf, wished to see his friends here before we were gone—and he comes even now," he added, glancing down the pathway, along which came striding the Norseman.

As he faced us I saw that a transformation had been wrought in him. Gone was the pitiful seeking, and gone too the just as pitiful hope. The set face softened as he looked at the Golden Girl and bowed low to her. He thrust a hand to O'Keefe and to me.

"There is to be battle," he said. "I go with Rador to call the armies of these frog people. As for me—Lakla has spoken. There is no hope for—for mine Helma in life, but there is hope that we destroy the Shining Devil and give *mine* Helma peace. And with that I am well content, *ja!* Well content!" He gripped our hands again. "We will fight!" he muttered. "*Ja!* And I will have vengeance!" The sternness returned; and with a salute Rador and he were gone.

Two great tears rolled from the golden eyes of Lakla.

"Not even the Silent Ones can heal those the Shining One has taken," she said. "He asked me—and it was better that I tell him. It is part of the Three's—*punishment*—but of that you will soon learn," she went on hurriedly. "Ask me no questions now of the Silent Ones. I thought it better for Olaf to go with Rador, to busy himself, to give his mind other than sorrow upon which to feed."

Up the path came five of the frog-women, bearing platters and ewers. Their bracelets and anklets of jewels were tinkling; their middles covered with short kirtles of woven cloth studded with the sparkling ornaments.

And here let me say that if I have given the impression that the *Akka* are simply magnified frogs, I regret it. Frog-like they are, and hence my phrase for them—but as unlike the frog, as we know it, as man is unlike the chimpanzee. Springing, I hazard, from the stegocephalia, the ancestor of the frogs, these batrachians followed a different line of evolution and acquired the upright position just as man did his from the four-footed folk.

The great staring eyes, the shape of the muzzle were frog-like, but the highly developed brain had set upon the head and shape of it vital differences. The forehead, for instance, was not low, flat, and retreating—its frontal arch was well defined. The head was, in a sense, shapely, and with the females the great horny carapace that stood over it like a fantastic helmet was much modified, as were the spurs that were so formidable in the male; colouration was different also. The torso was

A. MERRITT

upright; the legs a little bent, giving them their crouching gait—but I wander from my subject.[1]

They set their burdens down. Larry looked at them with interest.

"You surely have those things well trained, Lakla," he said.

"Things!" The handmaiden arose, eyes flashing with indignation. "You call my *Akka* things!"

"Well," said Larry, a bit taken aback, "what do you call them?"

"My *Akka* are a *people*," she retorted. "As much a people as your race or mine. They are good and loyal, and they have speech and arts, and they slay not, save for food or to protect themselves. And I think them beautiful, Larry, *beautiful!*" She stamped her foot. "And you call them—*things!*"

Beautiful! These? Yet, after all, they were, in their grotesque fashion. And to Lakla, surrounded by them, from babyhood, they were not strange, at all. Why shouldn't she think them beautiful? The same thought must have struck O'Keefe, for he flushed guiltily.

"I think them beautiful, too, Lakla," he said remorsefully. "It's my not knowing your tongue too well that traps me. *Truly*, I think them beautiful—I'd tell them so, if I knew their talk."

Lakla dimpled, laughed—spoke to the attendants in that strange speech that was unquestionably a language; they bridled, looked at O'Keefe with fantastic coquetry, cracked and boomed softly among themselves.

"They say they like *you* better than the men of Muria," laughed Lakla.

"Did I ever think I'd be swapping compliments with lady frogs!" he murmured to me. "Buck up, Larry—keep your eyes on the captive Irish princess!" he muttered to himself.

"Rador goes to meet one of the *ladala* who is slipping through with news," said the Golden Girl as we addressed ourselves to the food. "Then, with Nak, he and Olaf go to muster the *Akka*—for there will be battle, and we must prepare. Nak," she added, "is he who went before me when you were dancing with Yolara, Larry." She stole a swift, mischievous glance at him. "He is headman of all the *Akka*."

---

1. The *Akka* are viviparous. The female produces progeny at five-year intervals, never more than two at a time. They are monogamous, like certain of our own *Ranidae*. Pending my monograph upon what little I had time to learn of their interesting habits and customs, the curious will find instruction and entertainment in Brandes and Schvenichen's *Brutpfleige der Schwanzlosen Bat rachier*, p. 395; and Lilian V. Sampson's *Unusual Modes of Breeding among Anura*, Amer. Nat. xxxiv., 1900.—W. T. G.

"Just what forces can we muster against them when they come, darlin'?" said Larry.

"Darlin'?"—the Golden Girl had caught the caress of the word—"what's that?"

"It's a little word that means Lakla," he answered. "It does—that is, when I say it; when you say it, then it means Larry."

"I like that word," mused Lakla.

"You can even say Larry darlin'!" suggested O'Keefe.

"Larry darlin'!" said Lakla. "When they come we shall have first of all my *Akka*—"

"Can they fight, *mavourneen*?" interrupted Larry.

"Can they fight! My *Akka*!" Again her eyes flashed. "They will fight to the last of them—with the spears that give the swift rotting, covered, as they are, with the jelly of those *Saddu* there—" She pointed through a rift in the foliage across which, on the surface of the sea, was floating one of the moon globes—and now I know why Rador had warned Larry against a plunge there. "With spears and clubs and with teeth and nails and spurs—they are a strong and brave people, Larry—darlin', and though they hurl the *Keth* at them, it is slow to work upon them, and they slay even while they are passing into the nothingness!"

"And have we none of the *Keth*?" he asked.

"No"—she shook her head—"none of their weapons have we here, although it was—it was the Ancient Ones who shaped them."

"But the Three are of the Ancient Ones?" I cried. "Surely they can tell—"

"No," she said slowly. "No—there is something you must know—and soon; and then the Silent Ones say you will understand. You, especially, Goodwin, who worship wisdom."

"Then," said Larry, "we have the *Akka*; and we have the four men of us, and among us three guns and about a hundred cartridges—an'—an' the power of the Three—but what about the Shining One, Fireworks—"

"I do not know." Again the indecision that had been in her eyes when Yolara had launched her defiance crept back. "The Shining One is strong—and he has his—slaves!"

"Well, we'd better get busy good and quick!" the O'Keefe's voice rang. But Lakla, for some reason of her own, would pursue the matter no further. The trouble fled from her eyes—they danced.

"Larry darlin'?" she murmured. "I like the touch of your lips—"

"You do?" he whispered, all thought flying of anything but the beautiful, provocative face so close to his. "Then, *acushla*, you're goin' to get acquainted with 'em! Turn your head, Doc!" he said.

And I turned it. There was quite a long silence, broken by an interested, soft outburst of gentle boomings from the serving frog-maids. I stole a glance behind me. Lakla's head lay on the Irishman's shoulder, the golden eyes misty sunpools of love and adoration; and the O'Keefe, a new look of power and strength upon his clear-cut features, was gazing down into them with that look which rises only from the heart touched for the first time with that true, all-powerful love, which is the pulse of the universe itself, the real music of the spheres of which Plato dreamed, the love that is stronger than death itself, immortal as the high gods and the true soul of all that mystery we call life.

Then Lakla raised her hands, pressed down Larry's head, kissed him between the eyes, drew herself with a trembling little laugh from his embrace.

"The future Mrs. Larry O'Keefe, Goodwin," said Larry to me a little unsteadily.

I took their hands—and Lakla kissed me!

She turned to the booming—smiling—frog-maids; gave them some command, for they filed away down the path. Suddenly I felt, well, a little superfluous.

"If you don't mind," I said, "I think I'll go up the path there again and look about."

But they were so engrossed with each other that they did not even hear me—so I walked away, up to the embrasure where Rador had taken me. The movement of the batrachians over the bridge had ceased. Dimly at the far end I could see the cluster of the garrison. My thoughts flew back to Lakla and to Larry.

What was to be the end?

If we won, if we were able to pass from this place, could she live in our world? A product of these caverns with their atmosphere and light that seemed in some subtle way to be both food and drink—how would she react to the unfamiliar foods and air and light of outer earth? Further, here so far as I was able to discover, there were no malignant bacilli—what immunity could Lakla have then to those microscopic evils without, which only long ages of sickness and death have bought for us a modicum of protection? I began to be oppressed. Surely they had been long enough by themselves. I went down the path.

I heard Larry.

"It's a green land, *mavourneen*. And the sea rocks and dimples around it—blue as the heavens, green as the isle itself, and foam horses toss their white manes, and the great clean winds blow over it, and the sun shines down on it like your eyes, *acushla*—"

"And are you a king of Ireland, Larry darlin'?" Thus Lakla—

But enough!

At last we turned to go—and around the corner of the path I caught another glimpse of what I have called the lake of jewels. I pointed to it.

"Those are lovely flowers, Lakla," I said. "I have never seen anything like them in the place from whence we come."

She followed my pointing finger—laughed.

"Come," she said, "let me show you them."

She ran down an intersecting way, we following; came out of it upon a little ledge close to the brink, three feet or more I suppose about it. The Golden Girl's voice rang out in a high-pitched, tremulous, throbbing call.

The lake of jewels stirred as though a breeze had passed over it; stirred, shook, and then began to move swiftly, a shimmering torrent of shining flowers down upon us! She called again, the movement became more rapid; the gem blooms streamed closer—closer, wavering, shifting, winding—at our very feet. Above them hovered a little radiant mist. The Golden Girl leaned over; called softly, and up from the sparkling mass shot a green vine whose heads were five flowers of flaming ruby—shot up, flew into her hand and coiled about the white arm, its quintette of lambent blossoms—regarding us!

It was the thing Lakla had called the *Yekta*; that with which she had threatened the priestess; the thing that carried the dreadful death—and the Golden Girl was handling it like a rose!

Larry swore—I looked at the thing more closely. It was a hydroid, a development of that strange animal-vegetable that, sometimes almost microscopic, waves in the sea depths like a cluster of flowers paralyzing its prey with the mysterious force that dwells in its blossom heads![2]

---

2. The *Yekta* of the Crimson Sea, are as extraordinary developments of hydroid forms as the giant *Medusae*, of which, of course, they are not too remote cousins. The closest resemblances to them in outer water forms are among the *Gymnoblastic Hydroids*, notably *Clavetella prolifera*, a most interesting ambulatory form of six tentacles. Almost every bather in Southern waters, Northern too, knows the pain that contact with certain "jelly fish" produces. The *Yekta's* development was prodigious and, to us, monstrous. It secretes

"Put it down, Lakla," the distress in O'Keefe's voice was deep. Lakla laughed mischievously, caught the real fear for her in his eyes; opened her hand, gave another faint call—and back it flew to its fellows.

"Why, it wouldn't hurt me, Larry!" she expostulated. "They know me!"

"Put it down!" he repeated hoarsely.

She sighed, gave another sweet, prolonged call. The lake of gems—rubies and amethysts, mauves and scarlet-tinged blues—wavered and shook even as it had before—and swept swiftly back to that place whence she had drawn them!

Then, with Larry and Lakla walking ahead, white arm about his brown neck; the O'Keefe still expostulating, the handmaiden laughing merrily, we passed through her bower to the domed castle.

Glancing through a cleft I caught sight again of the far end of the bridge; noted among the clustered figures of its garrison of the frog-men a movement, a flashing of green fire like marshlights on spear tips; wondered idly what it was, and then, other thoughts crowding in, followed along, head bent, behind the pair who had found in what was Olaf's hell, their true paradise.

---

in its five heads an almost incredibly swiftly acting poison which I suspect, for I had no chance to verify the theory, destroys the entire nervous system to the accompaniment of truly infernal agony; carrying at the same time the illusion that the torment stretches through infinities of time. Both ether and nitrous oxide gas produce in the majority this sensation of time extension, without of course the pain symptom. What Lakla called the *Yekta* kiss is I imagine about as close to the orthodox idea of Hell as can be conceived. The secret of her control over them I had no opportunity of learning in the rush of events that followed. Knowledge of the appalling effects of their touch came, she told me, from those few "who had been kissed so lightly" that they recovered. Certainly nothing, not even the Shining One, was dreaded by the Murians as these were—W. T. G.

XXVII

THE COMING OF YOLARA

Never was there such a girl!" Thus Larry, dreamily, leaning head in hand on one of the wide divans of the chamber where Lakla had left us, pleading service to the Silent Ones.

"An', by the faith and the honour of the O'Keefes, an' by my dead mother's soul may God do with me as I do by her!" he whispered fervently.

He relapsed into open-eyed dreaming.

I walked about the room, examining it—the first opportunity I had gained to inspect carefully any of the rooms in the abode of the Three. It was octagonal, carpeted with the thick rugs that seemed almost as though woven of soft mineral wool, faintly shimmering, palest blue. I paced its diagonal; it was fifty yards; the ceiling was arched, and either of pale rose metal or metallic covering; it collected the light from the high, slitted windows, and shed it, diffused, through the room.

Around the octagon ran a low gallery not two feet from the floor, balustraded with slender pillars, close set; broken at opposite curtained entrances over which hung thick, dull-gold curtainings giving the same suggestion of metallic or mineral substance as the rugs. Set within each of the eight sides, above the balcony, were colossal slabs of lapis lazuli, inset with graceful but unplaceable designs in scarlet and sapphire blue.

There was the great divan on which mused Larry; two smaller ones, half a dozen low seats and chairs carved apparently of ivory and of dull soft gold.

Most curious were tripods, strong, pikelike legs of golden metal four feet high, holding small circles of the lapis with intaglios of one curious symbol somewhat resembling the ideographs of the Chinese.

There was no dust—nowhere in these caverned spaces had I found this constant companion of ours in the world overhead. My eyes caught a sparkle from a corner. Pursuing it I found upon one of the low seats a flat, clear crystal oval, remarkably like a lens. I took it and stepped up on the balcony. Standing on tiptoe I found I commanded from the bottom of a window slit a view of the bridge approach. Scanning it I could see no trace of the garrison there, nor of the green spear flashes. I placed the crystal to my eyes—and with a disconcerting abruptness the cavern mouth leaped before me, apparently not a hundred feet away; decidedly the crystal was a very excellent lens—but where were the guards?

I peered closely. Nothing! But now against the aperture I saw a score or more of tiny, dancing sparks. An optical illusion, I thought, and turned the crystal in another direction. There were no sparklings there. I turned it back again—and there they were. And what were they like? Realization came to me—they were like the little, dancing, radiant atoms that had played for a time about the emptiness where had stood Sorgar of the Lower Waters before he had been shaken into the nothingness! And that green light I had noticed—the *Keth*!

A cry on my lips, I turned to Larry—and the cry died as the heavy curtainings at the entrance on my right undulated, parted as though a body had slipped through, shook and parted again and again—with the dreadful passing of unseen things!

"Larry!" I cried. "Here! Quick!"

He leaped to his feet, gazed about wildly—and disappeared! Yes— vanished from my sight like the snuffed flame of a candle or as though something moving with the speed of light itself had snatched him away!

Then from the divan came the sounds of struggle, the hissing of straining breaths, the noise of Larry cursing. I leaped over the balustrade, drawing my own pistol—was caught in a pair of mighty arms, my elbows crushed to my sides, drawn down until my face pressed close to a broad, hairy breast—and through that obstacle—formless, shadowless, transparent as air itself—I could still see the battle on the divan!

Now there were two sharp reports; the struggle abruptly ceased. From a point not a foot over the great couch, as though oozing from the air itself, blood began to drop, faster and ever faster, pouring out of nothingness.

And out of that same air, now a dozen feet away, leaped the face of Larry—bodyless, poised six feet above the floor, blazing with rage— floating weirdly, uncannily to a hideous degree, in vacancy.

His hands flashed out—armless; they wavered, appearing, disappearing—swiftly tearing something from him. Then there, feet hidden, stiff on legs that vanished at the ankles, striking out into vision with all the dizzy abruptness with which he had been stricken from sight was the O'Keefe, a smoking pistol in hand.

And ever that red stream trickled out of vacancy and spread over the couch, dripping to the floor.

I made a mighty movement to escape; was held more firmly—and then close to the face of Larry, flashing out with that terrifying instantaneousness even as had his, was the head of Yolara, as devilishly mocking as I had ever seen it, the cruelty shining through it like delicate white flames from hell—and beautiful!

"Stir not! Strike not—until I command!" She flung the words beyond her, addressed to the invisible ones who had accompanied her; whose presences I sensed filling the chamber. The floating, beautiful head, crowned high with corn-silk hair, darted toward the Irishman. He took a swift step backward. The eyes of the priestess deepened toward purple; sparkled with malice.

"So," she said. "So, *Larree*—you thought you could go from me so easily!" She laughed softly. "In my hidden hand I hold the *Keth* cone," she murmured. "Before you can raise the death tube I can smite you—and will. And consider, *Larree*, if the handmaiden, the *choya* comes, I can vanish—so"—the mocking head disappeared, burst forth again—"and slay her with the *Keth*—or bid my people seize her and bear her to the Shining One!"

Tiny beads of sweat stood out on O'Keefe's forehead, and I knew he was thinking not of himself, but of Lakla.

"What do you want with me, Yolara?" he asked hoarsely.

"Nay," came the mocking voice. "Not Yolara to you, *Larree*—call me by those sweet names you taught me—Honey of the Wild Bee-e-s, Net of Hearts—" Again her laughter tinkled.

"What do you want with me?" his voice was strained, the lips rigid.

"Ah, you are afraid, *Larree*." There was diabolic jubilation in the words. "What should I want but that you return with me? Why else did I creep through the lair of the dragon worm and pass the path of perils but to ask you that? And the *choya* guards you not well." Again she laughed. "We came to the cavern's end and, there were her *Akka*. And the *Akka* can see us—as shadows. But it was my desire to surprise you with my coming, Larree," the voice was silken. "And I feared that they would hasten to be first to bring you that message to delight in your joy. And so, *Larree*, I loosed the *Keth* upon them—and gave them peace and rest within the nothingness. And the portal below was open—almost in welcome!"

Once more the malignant, silver pealing of her laughter.

"What do you want with me?" There was wrath in his eyes, and plainly he strove for control.

A. MERRITT

"Want!" the silver voice hissed, grew calm. "Do not Siya and Siyana grieve that the rite I pledged them is but half done—and do they not desire it finished? And am I not beautiful? More beautiful than your *choya*?"

The fiendishness died from the eyes; they grew blue, wondrous; the veil of invisibility slipped down from the neck, the shoulders, half revealing the gleaming breasts. And weird, weird beyond all telling was that exquisite head and bust floating there in air—and beautiful, sinisterly beautiful beyond all telling, too. So even might Lilith, the serpent woman, have shown herself tempting Adam!

"And perhaps," she said, "perhaps I want you because I hate you; perhaps because I love you—or perhaps for Lugur or perhaps for the Shining One."

"And if I go with you?" He said it quietly.

"Then shall I spare the handmaiden—and—who knows?—take back my armies that even now gather at the portal and let the Silent Ones rot in peace in their abode—from which they had no power to keep me," she added venomously.

"You will swear that, Yolara; swear to go without harming the handmaiden?" he asked eagerly. The little devils danced in her eyes. I wrenched my face from the smothering contact.

"Don't trust her, Larry!" I cried—and again the grip choked me.

"Is that devil in front of you or behind you, old man?" he asked quietly, eyes never leaving the priestess. "If he's in front I'll take a chance and wing him—and then you scoot and warn Lakla."

But I could not answer; nor, remembering Yolara's threat, would I, had I been able.

"Decide quickly!" There was cold threat in her voice.

The curtains toward which O'Keefe had slowly, step by step, drawn close, opened. They framed the handmaiden! The face of Yolara changed to that gorgon mask that had transformed it once before at sight of the Golden Girl. In her blind rage she forgot to cast the occulting veil. Her hand darted like a snake out of the folds; poising itself with the little silver cone aimed at Lakla.

But before it was wholly poised, before the priestess could loose its force, the handmaiden was upon her. Swift as the lithe white wolf hound she leaped, and one slender hand gripped Yolara's throat, the other the wrist that lifted the quivering death; white limbs wrapped about the hidden ones, I saw the golden head bend, the hand that held the *Keth* swept up with a vicious jerk; saw Lakla's teeth sink into the wrist—the blood spurt forth and heard the priestess shriek. The cone fell, bounded toward me; with all my strength I wrenched free the hand that held my pistol, thrust it against the pressing breast and fired.

The clasp upon me relaxed; a red rain stained me; at my feet a little pillar of blood jetted; a hand thrust itself from nothingness, clawed—and was still.

Now Yolara was down, Lakla meshed in her writhings and fighting like some wild mother whose babes are serpent menaced. Over the two of them, astride, stood the O'Keefe, a pike from one of the high tripods in his hand—thrusting, parrying, beating on every side as with a broadsword against poniard-clutching hands that thrust themselves out of vacancy striving to strike him; stepping here and there, always covering, protecting Lakla with his own body even as a caveman of old who does battle with his mate for their lives.

The sword-club struck—and on the floor lay the half body of a dwarf, writhing with vanishments and reappearings of legs and arms. Beside him was the shattered tripod from which Larry had wrenched his weapon. I flung myself upon it, dashed it down to break loose one of the remaining supports, struck in midfall one of the unseen even as his dagger darted toward me! The seat splintered, leaving in my clutch a golden bar. I jumped to Larry's side, guarding his back, whirling it like a staff; felt it crunch once—twice—through unseen bone and muscle.

At the door was a booming. Into the chamber rushed a dozen of the frog-men. While some guarded the entrances, others leaped straight to us, and forming a circle about us began to strike with talons and spurs at unseen things that screamed and sought to escape. Now here and there about the blue rugs great stains of blood appeared; heads of dwarfs, torn arms and gashed bodies, half occulted, half revealed. And at last the priestess lay silent, vanquished, white body gleaming with that uncanny—fragmentariness—from her torn robes. Then O'Keefe reached down, drew Lakla from her. Shakily, Yolara rose to her feet. The handmaiden, face still blazing with wrath, stepped before her; with difficulty she steadied her voice.

"Yolara," she said, "you have defied the Silent Ones, you have desecrated their abode, you came to slay these men who are the guests of the Silent Ones and me, who am their handmaiden—why did you do these things?"

"I came for him!" gasped the priestess; she pointed to O'Keefe.

"Why?" asked Lakla.

"Because he is pledged to me," replied Yolara, all the devils that were hers in her face. "Because he wooed me! Because he is mine!"

"That is a lie!" The handmaiden's voice shook with rage. "It is a lie! But here and now he shall choose, Yolara. And if you he choose, you and he shall go forth from here unmolested—for Yolara, it is his happiness that I most desire, and if you are that happiness—you shall go together. And now, Larry, choose!"

Swiftly she stepped beside the priestess; swiftly wrenched the last shreds of the hiding robes from her.

There they stood—Yolara with but the filmiest net of gauze about her wonderful body; gleaming flesh shining through it; serpent woman— and wonderful, too, beyond the dreams even of Phidias—and hell-fire glowing from the purple eyes.

And Lakla, like a girl of the Vikings, like one of those warrior maids who stood and fought for dun and babes at the side of those old heroes of Larry's own green isle; translucent ivory lambent through the rents of her torn draperies, and in the wide, golden eyes flaming wrath, indeed—not the diabolic flames of the priestess but the righteous wrath of some soul that looking out of paradise sees vile wrong in the doing.

"Lakla," the O'Keefe's voice was subdued, hurt, "there *is* no choice. I love you and only you—and have from the moment I saw you. It's not easy—this. God, Goodwin, I feel like an utter cad," he flashed at me. "There is no choice, Lakla," he ended, eyes steady upon hers.

The priestess's face grew deadlier still.

"What will you do with me?" she asked.

"Keep you," I said, "as hostage."

O'Keefe was silent; the Golden Girl shook her head.

"Well would I like to," her face grew dreaming; "but the Silent Ones say—*no*; they bid me let you go, Yolara—"

"The Silent Ones," the priestess laughed. "*You*, Lakla! You fear, perhaps, to let me tarry here too close!"

Storm gathered again in the handmaiden's eyes; she forced it back.

"No," she answered, "the Silent Ones so command—and for their own purposes. Yet do I think, Yolara, that you will have little time to feed your wickedness—tell that to Lugur—and to your Shining One!" she added slowly.

Mockery and disbelief rode high in the priestess's pose. "Am I to return alone—like this?" she asked.

"Nay, Yolara, nay; you shall be accompanied," said Lakla; "and by those who will guard—and *watch*—you well. They are here even now."

The hangings parted, and into the chamber came Olaf and Rador.

The priestess met the fierce hatred and contempt in the eyes of the Norseman—and for the first time lost her bravado.

"Let not *him* go with me," she gasped—her eyes searched the floor frantically.

"He goes with you," said Lakla, and threw about Yolara a swathing that covered the exquisite, alluring body. "And you shall pass through the Portal, not skulk along the path of the worm!"

She bent to Rador, whispered to him; he nodded; she had told him, I supposed, the secret of its opening.

"Come," he said, and with the ice-eyed giant behind her, Yolara, head bent, passed out of those hangings through which, but a little before, unseen, triumph in her grasp, she had slipped.

Then Lakla came to the unhappy O'Keefe, rested her hands on his shoulders, looked deep into his eyes.

"*Did* you woo her, even as she said?" she asked.

The Irishman flushed miserably.

"I did not," he said. "I was pleasant to her, of course, because I thought it would bring me quicker to you, darlin'."

She looked at him doubtfully; then—

"I think you must have been *very*—pleasant!" was all she said—and leaning, kissed him forgivingly straight on the lips. An extremely direct maiden was Lakla, with a truly sovereign contempt for anything she might consider non-essentials; and at this moment I decided she was wiser even than I had thought her.

He stumbled, feet vanishing; reached down and picked up something that in the grasping turned his hand to air.

"One of the invisible cloaks," he said to me. "There must be quite a lot of them about—I guess Yolara brought her full staff of murderers. They're a bit shopworn, probably—but we're considerably better off with 'em in our hands than in hers. And they may come in handy—who knows?"

There was a choking rattle at my feet; half the head of a dwarf raised out of vacancy; beat twice upon the floor in death throes; fell back. Lakla shivered; gave a command. The frog-men moved about; peering here and there; lifting unseen folds revealing in stark rigidity torn form after form of the priestess's men.

Lakla had been right—her *Akka* were thorough fighters!

She called, and to her came the frog-woman who was her attendant. To her the handmaiden spoke, pointing to the batrachians who stood, paws and forearms melted beneath the robes they had gathered. She took them and passed out—more grotesque than ever, shattering into streaks of vacancies, reappearing with flickers of shining scale and yellow gems as the tattered pennants of invisibility fluttered about her.

The frog-men reached down, swung each a dead dwarf in his arms, and filed, booming triumphantly away.

And then I remembered the cone of the *Keth* which had slipped from Yolara's hand; knew it had been that for which her wild eyes searched. But look as closely as we might, search in every nook and corner as we did, we could not find it. Had the dying hand of one of her men clutched it and had it been borne away with them? With the thought Larry and I raced after the scaled warriors, searched everybody they carried. It was not there. Perhaps the priestess had found it, retrieved it swiftly without our seeing.

Whatever was true—the cone was gone. And what a weapon that one little holder of the shaking death would have been for us!

XXVIII

IN THE LAIR OF THE DWELLER

It is with marked hesitation that I begin this chapter, because in it I must deal with an experience so contrary to every known law of physics as to seem impossible. Until this time, barring, of course, the mystery of the Dweller, I had encountered nothing that was not susceptible of naturalistic explanation; nothing, in a word, outside the domain of science itself; nothing that I would have felt hesitancy in reciting to my colleagues of the International Association of Science. Amazing, unfamiliar—*advanced*—as many of the phenomena were, still they lay well within the limits of what we have mapped as the possible; in regions, it is true, still virgin to the mind of man, but toward which that mind is steadily advancing.

But this—well, I confess that I have a theory that is naturalistic; but so abstruse, so difficult to make clear within the short confines of the space I have to give it, so dependent upon conceptions that even the highest-trained scientific brains find difficult to grasp, that I despair.

I can only say that the thing occurred; that it took place in precisely the manner I am about to narrate, and that I experienced it.

Yet, in justice to myself, I must open up some paths of preliminary approach toward the heart of the perplexity. And the first path is the realization that our world *whatever* it is, is certainly *not* the world as we see it! Regarding this I shall refer to a discourse upon "Gravitation and the Principle of Relativity," by the distinguished English physicist, Dr. A. S. Eddington, which I had the pleasure of hearing him deliver before the Royal Institution.[1]

I realize, of course, that it is not true logic to argue—"The world is not as we think it is—therefore everything we think impossible is possible in it." Even if it *be* different, it is governed by *law*. The truly impossible is that which is outside law, and as nothing *can* be outside law, the impossible *cannot* exist.

---

1. Reprinted in full in *Nature*, in which those sufficiently interested may peruse it.—W. T. G.

A. MERRITT

The crux of the matter then becomes our determination whether what we think is impossible may or may not be possible under laws still beyond our knowledge.

I hope that you will pardon me for this somewhat academic digression, but I felt it was necessary, and it has, at least, put me more at ease. And now to resume.

We had watched, Larry and I, the frog-men throw the bodies of Yolara's assassins into the crimson waters. As vultures swoop down upon the dying, there came sailing swiftly to where the dead men floated, dozens of the luminous globes. Their slender, varicoloured tentacles whipped out; the giant iridescent bubbles *climbed* over the cadavers. And as they touched them there was the swift dissolution, the melting away into putrescence of flesh and bone that I had witnessed when the dart touched fruit that time I had saved Rador—and upon this the Medusae gorged; pulsing lambently; their wondrous colours shifting, changing, glowing stronger; elfin moons now indeed, but satellites whose glimmering beauty was fed by death; alembics of enchantment whose glorious hues were sucked from horror.

Sick, I turned away—O'Keefe as pale as I; passed back into the corridor that had opened on the ledge from which we had watched; met Lakla hurrying toward us. Before she could speak there throbbed faintly about us a vast sighing. It grew into a murmur, a whispering, shook us—then passing like a presence, died away in far distance.

"The Portal has opened," said the handmaiden. A fainter sighing, like an echo of the other, mourned about us. "Yolara is gone," she said, "the Portal is closed. Now must we hasten—for the Three have commanded that you, Goodwin, and Larry and I tread that strange road of which I have spoken, and which Olaf may not take lest his heart break—and we must return ere he and Rador cross the bridge."

Her hand sought Larry's.

"Come!" said Lakla, and we walked on; down and down through hall after hall, flight upon flight of stairways. Deep, deep indeed, we must be beneath the domed castle—Lakla paused before a curved, smooth breast of the crimson stone rounding gently into the passage. She pressed its side; it revolved; we entered; it closed behind us.

The room, the—hollow—in which we stood was faceted like a diamond; and like a cut brilliant its sides glistened—though dully. Its shape was a deep oval, and our path dropped down to a circular polished base, roughly two yards in diameter. Glancing behind me I saw that in the closing of the entrance there had been left no trace of it save the steps that led from where that entrance had been—and as I looked these steps *turned*, leaving us isolated upon the circle, only the faceted walls about us—and in each of the gleaming faces the three of us reflected—dimly. It was as though we were within a diamond egg whose graven angles had been turned *inward*.

But the oval was not perfect; at my right a screen cut it—a screen that gleamed with fugitive, fleeting luminescences—stretching from the side of our standing place up to the tip of the chamber; slightly convex and crisscrossed by millions of fine lines like those upon a spectroscopic plate, but with this difference—that within each line I sensed the presence of multitudes of finer lines, dwindling into infinitude, ultramicroscopic, traced by some instrument compared to whose delicacy our finest tool would be as a crowbar to the needle of a micrometer.

A foot or two from it stood something like the standee of a compass, bearing, like it a cradled dial under whose crystal ran concentric rings of prisoned, lambent vapours, faintly blue. From the edge of the dial jutted a little shelf of crystal, a keyboard, in which were cut eight small cups.

Within these cups the handmaiden placed her tapering fingers. She gazed down upon the disk; pressed a digit—and the screen behind us slipped noiselessly into another angle.

"Put your arm around my waist, Larry, darlin', and stand close," she murmured. "You, Goodwin, place your arm over my shoulder."

Wondering, I did as she bade; she pressed other fingers upon the shelf's indentations—three of the rings of vapour spun into intense light, raced around each other; from the screen behind us grew a radiance that held within itself all spectrums—not only those seen, but those *unseen* by man's eyes. It waxed brilliant and ever more brilliant, all suffusing, passing through me as day streams through a window pane!

The enclosing facets burst into a blaze of coruscations, and in each sparkling panel I saw our images, shaken and torn like pennants in a whirlwind. I turned to look—was stopped by the handmaiden's swift command: "Turn not—on your life!"

The radiance behind me grew; was a rushing tempest of light in which I was but the shadow of a shadow. I heard, but not with my ears—nay with *mind* itself—a vast roaring; an *ordered* tumult of sound that came hurling from the outposts of space; approaching—rushing—

hurricane out of the heart of the cosmos—closer, closer. It wrapped itself about us with unearthly mighty arms.

And brilliant, ever more brilliant, streamed the radiance through us.

The faceted walls dimmed; in front of me they melted, diaphanously, like a gelatinous wall in a blast of flame; through their vanishing, under the torrent of driving light, the unthinkable, impalpable tornado, I began to move, slowly—then ever more swiftly!

Still the roaring grew; the radiance streamed—ever faster we went. Cutting down through the length, the *extension* of me, dropped a wall of rock, foreshortened, clenched close; I caught a glimpse of the elfin gardens; they whirled, contracted, into a thin—slice—of colour that was a part of me; another wall of rock shrinking into a thin wedge through which I flew, and that at once took its place within me like a card slipped beside those others!

Flashing around me, and from Lakla and O'Keefe, were nimbuses of flickering scarlet flames. And always the steady hurling forward—appallingly mechanical.

Another barrier of rock—a gleam of white waters incorporating themselves into my—*drawing out*—even as were the flowered moss lands, the slicing, rocky walls—still another rampart of cliff, dwindling instantly into the vertical plane of those others. Our flight checked; we seemed to hover within, then to sway onward—slowly, cautiously.

A mist danced ahead of me—a mist that grew steadily thinner. We stopped, wavered—the mist cleared.

I looked out into translucent, green distances; shot with swift prismatic gleamings; waves and pulsings of luminosity like midday sun glow through green, tropic waters: dancing, scintillating veils of sparkling atoms that flew, hither and yon, through depths of nebulous splendour!

And Lakla and Larry and I were, I saw, like shadow shapes upon a smooth breast of stone twenty feet or more above the surface of this place—a surface spangled with tiny white blossoms gleaming wanly through creeping veils of phosphorescence like smoke of moon fire. We were shadows—and yet we had substance; we were incorporated with, a part of, the rock—and yet we were living flesh and blood; we stretched—nor will I qualify this—we *stretched* through mile upon mile of space that weirdly enough gave at one and the same time an absolute certainty of immense horizontal lengths and a vertical concentration that contained nothing of length, nothing of space whatever; we stood *there* upon the face of the stone—and still we were *here* within the faceted oval before the screen of radiance!

"Steady!" It was Lakla's voice—and not beside me *there*, but at my ear close before the screen. "Steady, Goodwin! And—see!"

The sparkling haze cleared. Enormous reaches stretched before me. Shimmering up through them, and as though growing in some medium thicker than air, was mass upon mass of verdure—fruiting trees and trees laden with pale blossoms, arbours and bowers of pallid blooms, like that sea fruit of oblivion—grapes of Lethe—that cling to the tide-swept walls of the caverns of the Hebrides.

Through them, beyond them, around and about them, drifted and eddied a horde—great as that with which Tamerlane swept down upon Rome, vast as the myriads which Genghis Khan rolled upon the califs—men and women and children—clothed in tatters, half nude and wholly naked; slant-eyed Chinese, sloe-eyed Malays, islanders black and brown and yellow, fierce-faced warriors of the Solomons with grizzled locks fantastically bedizened; Papuans, feline Javans, Dyaks of hill and shore; hook-nosed Phoenicians, Romans, straight-browed Greeks, and Vikings centuries *beyond* their lives: scores of the black-haired Murians; white faces of our own Westerners—men and women and children—drifting, eddying—each stamped with that mingled horror and rapture, eyes filled with ecstasy and terror entwined, marked by God and devil in embrace—the seal of the Shining One—the dead-alive; the lost ones!

The loot of the Dweller!

Soul-sick, I gazed. They lifted to us visages of dread; they swept down toward us, glaring upward—a bank against which other and still other waves of faces rolled, were checked, paused; until as far as I could see, like billows piled upon an ever-growing barrier, they stretched beneath us—staring—staring!

Now there was a movement—far, far away; a concentrating of the lambency; the dead-alive swayed, oscillated, separated—forming a long lane against whose outskirts they crowded with avid, hungry insistence.

First only a luminous cloud, then a whirling pillar of splendours through the lane came—the Shining One. As it passed, the dead-alive swirled in its wake like leaves behind a whirlwind, eddying, twisting; and as the Dweller raced by them, brushing them with its spirallings and tentacles, they shone forth with unearthly, awesome gleamings—

like vessels of alabaster in which wicks flare suddenly. And when it had passed they closed behind it, staring up at us once more.

The Dweller paused beneath us.

Out of the drifting ruck swam the body of Throckmartin! Throckmartin, my friend, to find whom I had gone to the pallid moon door; my friend whose call I had so laggardly followed. On his face was the Dweller's dreadful stamp; the lips were bloodless; the eyes were wide, lucent, something like pale, phosphorescence gleaming within them—and soulless.

He stared straight up at me, unwinking, unrecognizing. Pressing against his side was a woman, young and gentle, and lovely—lovely even through the mask that lay upon her face. And her wide eyes, like Throckmartin's, glowed with the lurking, unholy fires. She pressed against him closely; though the hordes kept up the faint churning, these two kept ever together, as though bound by unseen fetters.

And I knew the girl for Edith, his wife, who in vain effort to save him had cast herself into the Dweller's embrace!

"Throckmartin!" I cried. "Throckmartin! I'm here!"

Did he hear? I know now, of course, he could not.

But then I waited—hope striving to break through the nightmare hands that gripped my heart.

Their wide eyes never left me. There was another movement about them, others pushed past them; they drifted back, swaying, eddying—and still staring were lost in the awful throng.

Vainly I strained my gaze to find them again, to force some sign of recognition, some awakening of the clean life we know. But they were gone. Try as I would I could not see them—nor Stanton and the northern woman named Thora who had been the first of that tragic party to be taken by the Dweller.

"Throckmartin!" I cried again, despairingly. My tears blinded me.

I felt Lakla's light touch.

"Steady," she commanded, pitifully. "Steady, Goodwin. You cannot help them—now! Steady and—watch!"

Below us the Shining One had paused—spiralling, swirling, vibrant with all its transcendent, devilish beauty; had paused and was contemplating us. Now I could see clearly that nucleus, that core shot through with flashing veins of radiance, that ever-shifting shape of glory through the shroudings of shimmering, misty plumes, throbbing lacy opalescences, vaporous spirallings of prismatic phantom fires. Steady over it hung the seven little moons of amethyst, of saffron, of emerald and azure and silver, of rose of life and moon white. They poised themselves like a diadem—calm, serene, immobile—and down from them into the Dweller, piercing plumes and swirls and spirals, ran countless tiny strands, radiations, finer than the finest spun thread of spider's web, gleaming filaments through which seemed to run—*power*—from the seven globes; like— yes, that was it—miniatures of the seven torrents of moon flame that poured through the septichromatic, high crystals in the Moon Pool's chamber roof.

Swam out of the coruscating haze the—face!

Both of man and of woman it was—like some ancient, androgynous deity of Etruscan fanes long dust, and yet neither woman nor man; human and unhuman, seraphic and sinister, benign and malefic—and still no more of these four than is flame, which is beautiful whether it warms or devours, or wind whether it feathers the trees or shatters them, or the wave which is wondrous whether it caresses or kills.

Subtly, undefinably it was of our world and of one not ours. Its lineaments flowed from another sphere, took fleeting familiar form— and as swiftly withdrew whence they had come; something amorphous, unearthly—as of unknown unheeding, unseen gods rushing through the depths of star-hung space; and still of our own earth, with the very soul of earth peering out from it, caught within it—and in some— unholy—way debased.

It had eyes—eyes that were now only shadows darkening within its luminosity like veils falling, and falling, *opening* windows into the unknowable; deepening into softly glowing blue pools, blue as the Moon Pool itself; then flashing out, and this only when the—face— bore its most human resemblance, into twin stars large almost as the crown of little moons; and with that same baffling suggestion of peep-holes into a world untrodden, alien, perilous to man!

"Steady!" came Lakla's voice, her body leaned against mine.

I gripped myself, my brain steadied, I looked again. And I saw that of body, at least body as we know it, the Shining One had none— nothing but the throbbing, pulsing core streaked with lightning veins of rainbows; and around this, never still, sheathing it, the swirling, glorious veilings of its hell and heaven born radiance.

So the Dweller stood—and gazed.

Then up toward us swept a reaching, questing spiral!

A. MERRITT

Under my hand Lakla's shoulder quivered; dead-alive and their master vanished—I danced, flickered, *within* the rock; felt a swift sense of shrinking, of withdrawal; slice upon slice the carded walls of stone, of silvery waters, of elfin gardens slipped from me as cards are withdrawn from a pack, one by one—slipped, wheeled, flattened, and lengthened out as I passed through them and they passed from me.

Gasping, shaken, weak, I stood within the faceted oval chamber; arm still about the handmaiden's white shoulder; Larry's hand still clutching her girdle.

The roaring, impalpable gale from the cosmos was retreating to the outposts of space—was still; the intense, streaming, flooding radiance lessened—died.

"Now have you beheld," said Lakla, "and well you trod the road. And now shall you hear, even as the Silent Ones have commanded, what the Shining One is—and how it came to be."

The steps flashed back; the doorway into the chamber opened.

Larry as silent as I—we followed her through it.

XXIX

The Shaping of the Shining One

We reached what I knew to be Lakla's own boudoir, if I may so call it. Smaller than any of the other chambers of the domed castle in which we had been, its intimacy was revealed not only by its faint fragrance but by its high mirrors of polished silver and various oddly wrought articles of the feminine toilet that lay here and there; things I afterward knew to be the work of the artisans of the *Akka*—and no mean metal workers were they. One of the window slits dropped almost to the floor, and at its base was a wide, comfortably cushioned seat commanding a view of the bridge and of the cavern ledge. To this the handmaiden beckoned us; sank upon it, drew Larry down beside her and motioned me to sit close to him.

"Now this," she said, "is what the Silent Ones have commanded me to tell you two: To you Larry, that knowing you may weigh all things in your mind and answer as your spirit bids you a question that the Three will ask—and what that is I know not," she murmured, "and I, they say, must answer, too—and it—frightens me!"

The great golden eyes widened; darkened with dread; she sighed, shook her head impatiently.

"Not like us, and never like us," she spoke low, wonderingly, "the Silent Ones say were they. Nor were those from which they sprang like those from which we have come. Ancient, ancient beyond thought are the *Taithu*, the race of the Silent Ones. Far, far below this place where now we sit, close to earth heart itself were they born; and there they dwelt for time upon time, *laya* upon *laya* upon *laya*—with others, not like them, some of which have vanished time upon time agone, others that still dwell—below—in their—cradle.

"It is hard"—she hesitated—"hard to tell this—that slips through my mind—because I know so little that even as the Three told it to me it passed from me for lack of place to stand upon," she went on, quaintly. "Something there was of time when earth and sun were but cold mists in the—the heavens—something of these mists drawing together, whirling, whirling, faster and faster—drawing as they whirled more and more of the mists—growing larger, growing warm—forming at last into the globes they are, with others spinning around the sun—something of regions within this globe where vast fire was prisoned and bursting forth tore and rent the young orb—of one such bursting forth that sent what you call moon flying out to company us and left behind those spaces whence we now dwell—and of—of life particles that here and there below grew into the race of the Silent Ones, and those others—but not the *Akka* which, like you, they say came from above—and all this I do not understand—do you, Goodwin?" she appealed to me.

I nodded—for what she had related so fragmentarily was in reality an excellent approach to the Chamberlain-Moulton theory of a coalescing nebula contracting into the sun and its planets.

Astonishing was the recognition of this theory. Even more so was the reference to the life particles, the idea of Arrhenius, the great Swede, of life starting on earth through the dropping of minute, life *spores*, propelled through space by the driving power of light and, encountering favourable environment here, developing through the vast ages into man and every other living thing we know.[1]

Nor was it incredible that in the ancient nebula that was the matrix of our solar system similar, or rather *dissimilar*, particles in all but the subtle essence we call life, might have become entangled and, resisting every cataclysm as they had resisted the absolute zero of outer space, found in these caverned spaces their proper environment to develop into the race of the Silent Ones and—only *they* could tell what else!

"They say," the handmaiden's voice was surer, "they say that in their—cradle—near earth's heart they grew; grew untroubled by the turmoil and disorder which flayed the surface of this globe. And they say it was a place of light and that strength came to them from earth heart—strength greater than you and those from which you sprang ever derived from sun.

"At last, ancient, ancient beyond all thought, they say again, was this time—they began to know, to—to—realize—themselves. And wisdom came ever more swiftly. Up from their cradle, because they did not wish to dwell longer with those—others—they came and found this place.

---

1. Professor Svante August Arrhenius, in his *Worlds in the Making*—the conception that life is universally diffused, constantly emitted from all habitable worlds in the form of spores which traverse space for years and ages, the majority being ultimately destroyed by the heat of some blazing star, but some few finding a resting-place on globes which have reached the habitable stage.—W. T. G.

"When all the face of earth was covered with waters in which lived only tiny, hungry things that knew naught save hunger and its satisfaction, *they* had attained wisdom that enabled them to make paths such as we have just travelled and to look out upon those waters! And *laya* upon *laya* thereafter, time upon time, they went upon the paths and watched the flood recede; saw great bare flats of steaming ooze appear on which crawled and splashed larger things which had grown from the tiny hungry ones; watched the flats rise higher and higher and green life begin to clothe them; saw mountains uplift and vanish.

"Ever the green life waxed and the things which crept and crawled grew greater and took ever different forms; until at last came a time when the steaming mists lightened and the things which had begun as little more than tiny hungry mouths were huge and monstrous, so huge that the tallest of my *Akka* would not have reached the knee of the smallest of them.

"But in none of these, in *none*, was there—realization—of themselves, say the Three; naught but hunger driving, always driving them to still its crying.

"So for time upon time the race of the Silent Ones took the paths no more, placing aside the half-thought that they had of making their way to earth face even as they had made their way from beside earth heart. They turned wholly to the seeking of wisdom—and after other time on time they attained that which killed even the faintest shadow of the half-thought. For they crept far within the mysteries of life and death, they mastered the illusion of space, they lifted the veils of creation and of its twin destruction, and they stripped the covering from the flaming jewel of truth—but when they had crept within those mysteries they bid me tell *you*, Goodwin, they found ever other mysteries veiling the way; and after they had uncovered the jewel of truth they found it to be a gem of infinite facets and therefore not wholly to be read before eternity's unthinkable end!

"And for this they were glad—because now throughout eternity might they and theirs pursue knowledge over ways illimitable.

"They conquered light—light that sprang at their bidding from the nothingness that gives birth to all things and in which lie all things that are, have been and shall be; light that streamed through their bodies cleansing them of all dross; light that was food and drink; light that carried their vision afar or bore to them images out of space opening many windows through which they gazed down upon life on thousands upon thousands of the rushing worlds; light that was the flame of life itself and in which they bathed, ever renewing their own. They set radiant lamps within the stones, and of black light they wove the sheltering shadows and the shadows that slay.

"Arose from this people those Three—the Silent Ones. They led them all in wisdom so that in the Three grew—pride. And the Three built them this place in which we sit and set the Portal in its place and withdrew from their kind to go alone into the mysteries and to map alone the facets of Truth Jewel.

"Then there came the ancestors of the—*Akka*; not as they are now, and glowing but faintly within them the spark of—self-realization. And the *Taithu* seeing this spark did not slay them. But they took the ancient, long untrodden paths and looked forth once more upon earth face. Now on the land were vast forests and a chaos of green life. On the shores things scaled and fanged, fought and devoured each other, and in the green life moved bodies great and small that slew and ran from those that would slay.

"They searched for the passage through which the *Akka* had come and closed it. Then the Three took them and brought them here; and taught them and blew upon the spark until it burned ever stronger and in time they became much as they are now—my *Akka*.

"The Three took counsel after this and said—'We have strengthened life in these until it has become articulate; shall we not *create* life?'" Again she hesitated, her eyes rapt, dreaming. "The Three are speaking," she murmured. "They have my tongue—"

And certainly, with an ease and rapidity as though she were but a voice through which minds far more facile, more powerful poured their thoughts, she spoke.

"Yea," the golden voice was vibrant. "We said that what we would create should be of the spirit of life itself, speaking to us with the tongues of the far-flung stars, of the winds, of the waters, and of all upon and within these. Upon that universal matrix of matter, that mother of all things that you name the ether, we laboured. Think not that her wondrous fertility is limited by what ye see on earth or what has been on earth from its beginning. Infinite, infinite are the forms the mother bears and countless are the energies that are part of her.

"By our wisdom we had fashioned many windows out of our abode and through them we stared into the faces of myriads of worlds, and upon them all were the children of ether even as the worlds themselves were her children.

"Watching we learned, and learning we formed that ye term the Dweller, which those without name—the Shining One. Within the Universal Mother we shaped it, to be a voice to tell us her secrets, a lamp to go before us lighting the mysteries. Out of the ether we fashioned it, giving it the soul of light that still ye know not nor perhaps ever may know, and with the essence of life that ye saw blossoming deep in the abyss and that is the pulse of earth heart we filled it. And we wrought with pain and with love, with yearning and with scorching pride and from our travail came the Shining One—our child!

"There is an energy beyond and above ether, a purposeful, sentient force that laps like an ocean the furthest-flung star, that transfuses all that ether bears, that sees and speaks and feels in us and in you, that is incorporate in beast and bird and reptile, in tree and grass and all living things, that sleeps in rock and stone, that finds sparkling tongue in jewel and star and in all dwellers within the firmament. And this ye call consciousness!

"We crowned the Shining One with the seven orbs of light which are the channels between it and the sentience we sought to make articulate, the portals through which flow its currents and so flowing, become choate, vocal, self-realizant within our child.

"But as we shaped, there passed some of the essence of our pride; in giving will we had given power, perforce, to exercise that will for good or for evil, to speak or to be silent, to tell us what we wished of that which poured into it through the seven orbs or to withhold that knowledge itself; and in forging it from the immortal energies we had endowed it with their indifference; open to all consciousness it held within it the pole of utter joy and the pole of utter woe with all the arc that lies between; all the ecstasies of the countless worlds and suns and all their sorrows; all that ye symbolize as gods and all ye symbolize as devils—not negativing each other, for there is no such thing as negation, but holding them together, balancing them, encompassing them, pole upon pole!"

So *this* was the explanation of the entwined emotions of joy and terror that had changed so appallingly Throckmartin's face and the faces of all the Dweller's slaves!

The handmaiden's eyes grew bright, alert, again; the brooding passed from her face; the golden voice that had been so deep found its own familiar pitch.

"I listened while the Three spoke to you," she said. "Now the shaping of the Shining One had been a long, long travail and time had flown over the outer world *laya* upon *laya*. For a space the Shining One was content to dwell here; to be fed with the foods of light: to open the eyes of the Three to mystery upon mystery and to read for them facet after facet of the gem of truth. Yet as the tides of consciousness flowed through it they left behind shadowings and echoes of their burdens; and the Shining One grew stronger, always stronger of *itself within itself*. Its will strengthened and now not always was it the will of the Three; and the pride that was woven in the making of it waxed, while the love for them that its creators had set within it waned.

"Not ignorant were the *Taithu* of the work of the Three. First there were a few, then more and more who coveted the Shining One and who would have had the Three share with them the knowledge it drew in for them. But the Silent Ones in their pride, would not.

"There came a time when its will was now *all* its own, and it rebelled, turning its gaze to the wider spaces beyond the Portal, offering itself to the many there who would serve it; tiring of the Three, their control and their abode.

"Now the Shining One has its limitations, even as we. Over water it can pass, through air and through fire; but pass it cannot, through rock or metal. So it sent a message—how I know not—to the *Taithu* who desired it, whispering to them the secret of the Portal. And when the time was ripe they opened the Portal and the Shining One passed through it to them; nor would it return to the Three though they commanded, and when they would have forced it they found that it had hived and hidden a knowledge that they could not overcome.

"Yet by their arts the Three could have shattered the seven shining orbs; but they would not because—they loved, it!

"Those to whom it had gone built for it that place I have shown you, and they bowed to it and drew wisdom from it. And ever they turned more and more from the ways in which the *Taithu* had walked—for it seemed that which came to the Shining One through the seven orbs had less and less of good and more and more of the power you call evil. Knowledge it gave and understanding, yes; but not that which, clear and serene, lights the paths of right wisdom; rather were they flares pointing the dark roads that lead to—to the ultimate evil!

"Not all of the race of the Three followed the counsel of the Shining One. There were many, many, who would have none of it nor of its power. So were the *Taithu* split; and to this place where there had been none, came hatred, fear and suspicion. Those who pursued the ancient ways went to the Three and pleaded with them to destroy their work—and they would not, for still they loved it.

"Stronger grew the Dweller and less and less did it lay before its worshippers—for now so they had become—the fruits of its knowledge; and it grew—restless—turning its gaze upon earth face even as it had turned it from the Three. It whispered to the *Taithu* to take again the paths and look out upon the world. Lo! above them was a great fertile land on which dwelt an unfamiliar race, skilled in arts, seeking and finding wisdom—mankind! Mighty builders were they; vast were their cities and huge their temples of stone.

"They called their lands Muria and they worshipped a god Thanaroa whom they imagined to be the maker of all things, dwelling far away. They worshipped as closer gods, not indifferent but to be prayed to and to be propitiated, the moon and the sun. Two kings they had, each with his council and his court. One was high priest to the moon and the other high priest to the sun.

"The mass of this people were black-haired, but the sun king and his nobles were ruddy with hair like mine; and the moon king and his followers were like Yolara—or Lugur. And this, the Three say, Goodwin, came about because for time upon time the law had been that whenever a ruddy-haired or ashen-tressed child was born of the black-haired it became dedicated at once to either sun god or moon god, later wedding and bearing children only to their own kind. Until at last from the black-haired came no more of the light-locked ones, but the ruddy ones, being stronger, still arose from them."

XXX

The Building of the Moon Pool

S he paused, running her long fingers through her own bronze-flecked ringlets. Selective breeding this, with a vengeance, I thought; an ancient experiment in heredity which of course would in time result in the stamping out of the tendency to depart from type that lies in all organisms; resulting, obviously, at last, in three fixed forms of black-haired, ruddy-haired, and silver-haired—but this, with a shock of realization it came to me, was also an accurate description of the dark-polled *ladala*, their fair-haired rulers and of the golden-brown tressed Lakla!

How—questions began to stream through my mind; silenced by the handmaiden's voice.

"Above, far, far above the abode of the Shining One," she said, "was their greatest temple, holding the shrines both of sun and moon. All about it were other temples hidden behind mighty walls, each enclosing its own space and squared and ruled and standing within a shallow lake; the sacred city, the city of the gods of this land—"

"It is the Nan-Matal that she is describing," I thought.

"Out upon all this looked the *Taithu* who were now but the servants of the Shining One as it had been the messenger of the Three," she went on. "When they returned the Shining One spoke to them, promising them dominion over all that they had seen, yea, *under it* dominion of all earth itself and later perhaps of other earths!

"In the Shining One had grown craft, cunning; knowledge to gain that which it desired. Therefore it told its *Taithu*—and mayhap told them truth—that not yet was it time for *them* to go forth; that slowly must they pass into that outer world, for they had sprung from heart of earth and even it lacked power to swirl unaided into and through the above. Then it counselled them, instructing them what to do. They hollowed the chamber wherein first I saw you, cutting their way to it that path down which from it you sped.

"It revealed to them that the force that is within moon flame is kin to the force that is within it, for the chamber of its birth was the chamber too of moon birth and into it went the subtle essence and powers that flow in that earth child: and it taught them how to make that which fills what you call the Moon Pool whose opening is close behind its Veil hanging upon the gleaming cliffs.

"When this was done it taught them how to make and how to place the seven lights through which moon flame streams into Moon Pool—the seven lights that are kin to its own seven orbs even as its fires are kin to moon fires—and which would open for it a path that it could tread. And all this the *Taithu* did, working so secretly that neither those of their race whose faces were set against the Shining One nor the busy men above know aught of it.

"When it was done they moved up the path, clustering within the Moon Pool Chamber. Moon flame streamed through the seven globes, poured down upon the pool; they saw mists arise, embrace, and become one with the moon flame—and then up through Moon Pool, shaping itself within the mists of light, whirling, radiant—the Shining One!

"Almost free, almost loosed upon the world it coveted!

"Again it counselled them, and they pierced the passage whose portal you found first; set the fires within its stones, and revealing themselves to the moon king and his priests spake to them even as the Shining One had instructed.

"Now was the moon king filled with fear when he looked upon the *Taithu*, shrouded with protecting mists of light in Moon Pool Chamber, and heard their words. Yet, being crafty, he thought of the power that would be his if he heeded and how quickly the strength of the sun king would dwindle. So he and his made a pact with the Shining One's messengers.

"When next the moon was round and poured its flames down upon Moon Pool, the *Taithu* gathered there again, watched the child of the Three take shape within the pillars, speed away—and out! They heard a mighty shouting, a tumult of terror, of awe and of worship; a silence; a vast sighing—and they waited, wrapped in their mists of light, for they feared to follow nor were they near the paths that would have enabled them to look without.

"Another tumult—and back came the Shining One, murmuring with joy, pulsing, triumphant, and clasped within its vapours a man and woman, ruddy-haired, golden-eyed, in whose faces rapture and horror lay side by side—gloriously, hideously. And still holding them it danced above the Moon Pool and—sank!

"Now must I be brief. *Lat* after *lat* the Shining One went forth, returning with its sacrifices. And stronger after each it grew—and gayer and more cruel. Ever when it passed with its prey toward the pool, the *Taithu* who watched felt a swift, strong intoxication, a drunkenness of spirit, streaming from it to them. And the Shining One forgot what it had promised them of dominion—and in this new evil delight they too forgot.

"The outer land was torn with hatred and open strife. The moon king and his kind, through the guidance of the evil *Taithu* and the favour of the Shining One, had become powerful and the sun king and his were darkened. And the moon priests preached that the child of the Three was the moon god itself come to dwell with them.

"Now vast tides arose and when they withdrew they took with them great portions of this country. And the land itself began to sink. Then said the moon king that the moon had called to ocean to destroy because wroth that another than he was worshipped. The people believed and there was slaughter. When it was over there was no more a sun king nor any of the ruddy-haired folk; slain were they, slain down to the babe at breast.

"But still the tides swept higher; still dwindled the land!

"As it shrank multitudes of the fleeing people were led through Moon Pool Chamber and carried here. They were what now are called the *ladala*, and they were given place and set to work; and they thrived. Came many of the fair-haired; and they were given dwellings. They sat beside the evil *Taithu*; they became drunk even as they with the dancing of the Shining One; they learned—not all; only a little part but little enough—of their arts. And ever the Shining One danced more gaily out there within the black amphitheatre; grew ever stronger—and ever the hordes of its slaves behind the Veil increased.

"Nor did the *Taithu* who clung to the old ways check this—they could not. By the sinking of the land above, their own spaces were imperilled. All of their strength and all of their wisdom it took to keep this land from perishing; nor had they help from those others mad for the poison of the Shining One; and they had no time to deal with them nor the earth race with whom they had foregathered.

"At last came a slow, vast flood. It rolled even to the bases of the walled islets of the city of the gods—and within these now were all that were left of my people on earth face.

"I am of those people," she paused, looking at me proudly, "one of the daughters of the sun king whose seed is still alive in the *ladala*!"

As Larry opened his mouth to speak she waved a silencing hand.

"This tide did not recede," she went on. "And after a time the remnant, the moon king leading them, joined those who had already fled below. The rocks became still, the quakings ceased, and now those Ancient Ones who had been labouring could take breath. And anger grew within them as they looked upon the work of their evil kin. Again they sought the Three—and the Three now knew what they had done and their pride was humbled. They would not slay the Shining One themselves, for still they loved it; but they instructed these others how to undo their work; how also they might destroy the evil *Taithu* were it necessary.

"Armed with the wisdom of the Three they went forth—but now the Shining One was strong indeed. They could not slay it!

"Nay, it knew and was prepared; they could not even pass beyond its Veil nor seal its abode. Ah, strong, strong, mighty of will, full of craft and cunning had the Shining One become. So they turned upon their kind who had gone astray and made them perish, to the last. The Shining One came not to the aid of its servants—though they called; for within its will was the thought that they were of no further use to it; that it would rest awhile and dance with them—who had so little of the power and wisdom of its *Taithu* and therefore no reins upon it. And while this was happening black-haired and fair-haired ran and hid and were but shaking vessels of terror.

"The Ancient Ones took counsel. This was their decision; that they would go from the gardens before the Silver Waters—leaving, since they could not kill it, the Shining One with its worshippers. They sealed the mouth of the passage that leads to the Moon Pool Chamber and they changed the face of the cliff so that none might tell where it had been. But the passage itself they left open—having foreknowledge I think, of a thing that was to come to pass in the far future—perhaps it was your journey here, my Larry and Goodwin—verily I think so. And they destroyed all the ways save that which we three trod to the Dweller's abode.

"For the last time they went to the Three—to pass sentence upon them. This was the doom—that here they should remain, alone, among the *Akka*, served by them, until that time dawned when they would have will to destroy the evil they had created—and even now—loved; nor might they seek death, nor follow their judges until this had come to pass. This was the doom they put upon the Three for the wickedness that had sprung from their pride, and they strengthened it with their arts that it might not be broken.

"Then they passed—to a far land they had chosen where the Shining One could not go, beyond the Black Precipices of Doul, a green land—"

"Ireland!" interrupted Larry, with conviction, "I knew it."

"Since then time upon time had passed," she went on, unheeding. "The people called this place Muria after their sunken land and soon they forgot where had been the passage the *Taithu* had sealed. The moon king became the Voice of the Dweller and always with the Voice is a woman of the moon king's kin who is its priestess.

"And many have been the journeys upward of the Shining One, through the Moon Pool—returning with still others in its coils.

"And now again has it grown restless, longing for the wider spaces. It has spoken to Yolara and to Lugur even as it did to the dead *Taithu*, promising them dominion. And it has grown stronger, drawing to itself power to go far on the moon stream where it will. Thus was it able to seize your friend, Goodwin, and Olaf's wife and babe—and many more. Yolara and Lugur plan to open way to earth face; to depart with their court and under the Shining One grasp the world!

"And this is the tale the Silent Ones bade me tell you—and it is done."

Breathlessly I had listened to the stupendous epic of a long-lost world. Now I found speech to voice the question ever with me, the thing that lay as close to my heart as did the welfare of Larry, indeed the whole object of my quest—the fate of Throckmartin and those who had passed with him into the Dweller's lair; yes, and of Olaf's wife, too.

"Lakla," I said, "the friend who drew me here and those he loved who went before him—can we not save them?"

"The Three say no, Goodwin." There was again in her eyes the pity with which she had looked upon Olaf. "The Shining One—*feeds*—upon the flame of life itself, setting in its place its own fires and its own will. Its slaves are only shells through which it gleams. Death, say the Three, is the best that can come to them; yet will that be a boon great indeed."

"But they have souls, *mavourneen*," Larry said to her. "And they're alive still—in a way. Anyhow, their souls have not gone from them."

I caught a hope from his words—sceptic though I am—holding that the existence of soul has never been proved by dependable laboratory methods—for they recalled to me that when I had seen Throckmartin, Edith had been close beside him.

"It was days after his wife was taken, that the Dweller seized Throckmartin," I cried. "How, if their wills, their life, were indeed gone, how did they find each other mid all that horde? How did they come together in the Dweller's lair?"

"I do not know," she answered, slowly. "You say they loved—and it is true that love is stronger even than death!"

"One thing I *don't* understand"—this was Larry again—"is why a girl like you keeps coming out of the black-haired crowd; so frequently and one might say, so regularly, Lakla. Aren't there ever any red-headed boys—and if they are what becomes of them?"

"That, Larry, I cannot answer," she said, very frankly. "There was a pact of some kind; how made or by whom I know not. But for long the Murians feared the return of the *Taithu* and greatly they feared the Three. Even the Shining One feared those who had created it—for a time; and not even now is it eager to face them—*that* I know. Nor are Yolara and Lugur so *sure*. It may be that the Three commanded it: but how or why I know not. I only know that it is true—for here am I and from where else would I have come?"

"From Ireland," said Larry O'Keefe, promptly. "And that's where you're going. For 'tis no place for a girl like you to have been brought up—Lakla; what with people like frogs, and a half-god three quarters devil, and red oceans, an' the only Irish things yourself and the Silent Ones up there, bless their hearts. It's no place for ye, and by the soul of St. Patrick, it's out of it soon ye'll be gettin'!"

Larry! Larry! If it had but been true—and I could see Lakla and you beside me now!

XXXI

LARRY AND THE FROG-MEN

L ong had been her tale in the telling, and too long, perhaps, have I been in the repeating—but not everyday are the mists rolled away to reveal undreamed secrets of earth-youth. And I have set it down here, adding nothing, taking nothing from it; translating liberally, it is true, but constantly striving, while putting it into idea-forms and phraseology to be readily understood by my readers, to keep accurately to the spirit. And this, I must repeat, I have done throughout my narrative, wherever it has been necessary to record conversation with the Murians.

Rising, I found I was painfully stiff—as muscle-bound as though I had actually trudged many miles. Larry, imitating me, gave an involuntary groan.

"Faith, *mavourneen*," he said to Lakla, relapsing unconsciously into English, "your roads would never wear out shoe-leather, but they've got their kick, just the same!"

She understood our plight, if not his words; gave a soft little cry of mingled pity and self-reproach; forced us back upon the cushions.

"Oh, but I'm sorry!" mourned Lakla, leaning over us. "I had forgotten—for those new to it the way is a weary one, indeed—"

She ran to the doorway, whistled a clear high note down the passage. Through the hangings came two of the frog-men. She spoke to them rapidly. They crouched toward us, what certainly was meant for an amiable grin wrinkling the grotesque muzzles, baring the glistening rows of needle-teeth. And while I watched them with the fascination that they never lost for me, the monsters calmly swung one arm around our knees, lifted us up like babies—and as calmly started to walk away with us!

"Put me down! Put me down, I say!" The O'Keefe's voice was both outraged and angry; squinting around I saw him struggling violently to get to his feet. The *Akka* only held him tighter, booming comfortingly, peering down into his flushed face inquiringly.

"But, Larry—darlin'!"—Lakla's tones were—well, maternally surprised—"you're stiff and sore, and Kra can carry you quite easily."

"I *won't* be carried!" sputtered the O'Keefe. "Damn it, Goodwin, there are such things as the unities even here, an' for a lieutenant of the

Royal Air Force to be picked up an' carted around like a—like a bundle of rags—it's not discipline! Put me down, ye *omadhaun*, or I'll poke ye in the snout!" he shouted to his bearer—who only boomed gently, and stared at the handmaiden, plainly for further instructions.

"But, Larry—dear!"—Lakla was plainly distressed—"it will *hurt* you to walk; and I don't *want* you to hurt, Larry—darlin'!"

"Holy shade of St. Patrick!" moaned Larry; again he made a mighty effort to tear himself from the frog-man's grip; gave up with a groan. "Listen, *alanna*!" he said plaintively. "When we get to Ireland, you and I, we won't have anybody to pick us up and carry us about everytime we get a bit tired. And it's getting me in bad habits you are!"

"Oh, *yes*, we will, Larry!" cried the handmaiden, "because many, oh, many, of my *Akka* will go with us!"

"Will you tell this—Boob!—to put me down!" gritted the now thoroughly aroused O'Keefe. I couldn't help laughing; he glared at me.

"Bo-oo-ob?" exclaimed Lakla.

"Yes, boo-oo-ob!" said O'Keefe, "an' I have no desire to explain the word in my present position, light of my soul!"

The handmaiden sighed, plainly dejected. But she spoke again to the *Akka*, who gently lowered the O'Keefe to the floor.

"I don't understand," she said hopelessly, "if you want to walk, why, of course, you shall, Larry." She turned to me.

"Do you?" she asked.

"I do not," I said firmly.

"Well, then," murmured Lakla, "go you, Larry and Goodwin, with Kra and Gulk, and let them minister to you. After, sleep a little—for not soon will Rador and Olaf return. And let me feel your lips before you go, Larry—darlin'!" She covered his eyes caressingly with her soft little palms; pushed him away.

"Now go," said Lakla, "and rest!"

Unashamed I lay back against the horny chest of Gulk; and with a smile noticed that Larry, even if he had rebelled at being carried, did not disdain the support of Kra's shining, black-scaled arm which, slipping around his waist, half-lifted him along.

They parted a hanging and dropped us softly down beside a little pool, sparkling with the clear water that had heretofore been brought us in the wide basins. Then they began to undress us. And at this point the O'Keefe gave up.

"Whatever they're going to do we can't stop 'em, Doc!" he moaned.

"Anyway, I feel as though I've been pulled through a knot-hole, and I don't care—I don't care—as the song says."

When we were stripped we were lowered gently into the water. But not long did the *Akka* let us splash about the shallow basin. They lifted us out, and from jars began deftly to anoint and rub us with aromatic unguents.

I think that in all the medley of grotesque, of tragic, of baffling, strange and perilous experiences in that underground world none was more bizarre than this—valeting. I began to laugh, Larry joined me, and then Kra and Gulk joined in our merriment with deep batrachian cachinnations and gruntings. Then, having finished apparelling us and still chuckling, the two touched our arms and led us out, into a room whose circular sides were ringed with soft divans. Still smiling, I sank at once into sleep.

How long I slumbered I do not know. A low and thunderous booming coming through the deep window slit, reverberated through the room and awakened me. Larry yawned; arose briskly.

"Sounds as though the bass drums of every jazz band in New York were serenading us!" he observed. Simultaneously we sprang to the window; peered through.

We were a little above the level of the bridge, and its full length was plain before us. Thousands upon thousands of the *Akka* were crowding upon it, and far away other hordes filled like a glittering thicket both sides of the cavern ledge's crescent strand. On black scale and orange scale the crimson light fell, picking them off in little flickering points.

Upon the platform from which sprang the smaller span over the abyss were Lakla, Olaf, and Rador; the handmaiden clearly acting as interpreter between them and the giant she had called Nak, the Frog King.

"Come on!" shouted Larry.

Out of the open portal we ran; over the World Heart Bridge—and straight into the group.

"Oh!" cried Lakla, "I didn't want you to wake up so soon, Larry—darlin'!"

"See here, *mavourneen!*" Indignation thrilled in the Irishman's voice. "I'm not going to be done up with baby-ribbons and laid away in a cradle for safe-keeping while a fight is on; don't think it. Why didn't you call me?"

"You needed rest!" There was indomitable determination in the handmaiden's tones, the eternal maternal shining defiant from her eyes. "You were tired and you hurt! You shouldn't have got up!"

"Needed the rest!" groaned Larry. "Look here, Lakla, what do you think I am?"

"You're all I have," said that maiden firmly, "and I'm going to take care of you, Larry—darlin'! Don't you ever think anything else."

"Well, pulse of my heart, considering my delicate health and general fragility, would it hurt me, do you think, to be told what's going on?" he asked.

"Not at all, Larry!" answered the handmaiden serenely. "Yolara went through the Portal. She was very, *very* angry—"

"She was all the devil's woman that she is!" rumbled Olaf.

"Rador met the messenger," went on the Golden Girl calmly. "The *ladala* are ready to rise when Lugur and Yolara lead their hosts against us. They will strike at those left behind. And in the meantime we shall have disposed my *Akka* to meet Yolara's men. And on that disposal we must all take counsel, you, Larry, and Rador, Olaf and Goodwin and Nak, the ruler of the *Akka*."

"Did the messenger give any idea when Yolara expects to make her little call?" asked Larry.

"Yes," she answered. "They prepare, and we may expect them in—" She gave the equivalent of about thirty-six hours of our time.

"But, Lakla," I said, the doubt that I had long been holding finding voice, "should the Shining One come—with its slaves—are the Three strong enough to cope with it?"

There was troubled doubt in her own eyes.

"I do not know," she said at last, frankly. "You have heard their story. What they promise is that they will help. I do not know—anymore than do you, Goodwin!"

I looked up at the dome beneath which I knew the dread Trinity stared forth; even down upon us. And despite the awe, the assurance, I had felt when I stood before them I, too, doubted.

"Well," said Larry, "you and I, uncle," he turned to Rador, "and Olaf here had better decide just what part of the battle we'll lead—"

"Lead!" the handmaiden was appalled. "*You* lead, Larry? Why you are to stay with Goodwin and with me—up there, there we can watch."

"Heart's beloved," O'Keefe was stern indeed. "A thousand times I've looked Death straight in the face, peered into his eyes. Yes, and with ten thousand feet of space under me an' bursting shells tickling the ribs of the boat I was in. An' d'ye think I'll sit now on the grandstand an' watch while a game like this is being pulled? Ye don't know your future husband, soul of my delight!"

And so we started toward the golden opening, squads of the frog-men following us soldierly and disappearing about the huge structure. Nor did we stop until we came to the handmaiden's boudoir. There we seated ourselves.

"Now," said Larry, "two things I want to know. First—how many can Yolara muster against us; second, how many of these *Akka* have we to meet them?"

Rador gave our equivalent for eighty thousand men as the force Yolara could muster without stripping her city. Against this force, it appeared, we could count, roughly, upon two hundred thousand of the *Akka*.

"And they're some fighters!" exclaimed Larry. "Hell, with odds like that what're you worrying about? It's over before it's begun."

"But, *Larree*," objected Rador to this, "you forget that the nobles will have the *Keth*—and other things; also that the soldiers have fought against the *Akka* before and will be shielded very well from their spears and clubs—and that their blades and javelins can bite through the scales of Nak's warriors. They have many things—"

"Uncle," interjected O'Keefe, "one thing they have is your nerve. Why, we're more than two to one. And take it from me—"

Without warning dropped the tragedy!

XXXII

"Your Love; Your Lives; Your Souls!"

Lakla had taken no part in the talk since we had reached her bower. She had seated herself close to the O'Keefe. Glancing at her I had seen steal over her face that brooding, listening look that was hers whenever in that mysterious communion with the Three. It vanished; swiftly she arose; interrupted the Irishman without ceremony.

"Larry darlin'," said the handmaiden. "The Silent Ones summon us!"

"When do we go?" I asked; Larry's face grew bright with interest.

"The time is now," she said—and hesitated. "Larry dear, put your arms about me," she faltered, "for there is something cold that catches at my heart—and I am afraid."

At his exclamation she gathered herself together; gave a shaky little laugh.

"It's because I love you so that fear has power to plague me," she told him.

Without another word he bent and kissed her; in silence we passed on, his arm still about her girdled waist, golden head and black close together. Soon we stood before the crimson slab that was the door to the sanctuary of the Silent Ones. She poised uncertainly before it; then with a defiant arching of the proud little head that sent all the bronze-flecked curls flying, she pressed. It slipped aside and once more the opalescence gushed out, flooding all about us.

Dazzled as before, I followed through the lambent cascades pouring from the high, carved walls; paused, and my eyes clearing, looked up—straight into the faces of the Three. The angled orbs centred upon the handmaiden; softened as I had seen them do when first we had faced them. She smiled up; seemed to listen.

"Come closer," she commanded, "close to the feet of the Silent Ones."

We moved, pausing at the very base of the dais. The sparkling mists thinned; the great heads bent slightly over us; through the veils I caught a glimpse of huge columnar necks, enormous shoulders covered with draperies as of pale-blue fire.

I came back to attention with a start, for Lakla was answering a question only heard by her, and, answering it aloud, I perceived for our benefit; for whatever was the mode of communication between those whose handmaiden she was, and her, it was clearly independent of speech.

"He has been told," she said, "even as you commanded."

Did I see a shadow of pain flit across the flickering eyes? Wondering, I glanced at Lakla's face and there was a dawn of foreboding and bewilderment. For a little she held her listening attitude; then the gaze of the Three left her; focused upon the O'Keefe.

"Thus speak the Silent Ones—through Lakla, their handmaiden," the golden voice was like low trumpet notes. "At the threshold of doom is that world of yours above. Yea, even the doom, Goodwin, that ye dreamed and the shadow of which, looking into your mind they see, say the Three. For not upon earth and never upon earth can man find means to destroy the Shining One."

She listened again—and the foreboding deepened to an amazed fear.

"They say, the Silent Ones," she went on, "that they know not whether even they have power to destroy. Energies we know nothing of entered into its shaping and are part of it; and still other energies it has gathered to itself"—she paused; a shadow of puzzlement crept into her voice "and other energies still, forces that ye *do* know and symbolize by certain names—hatred and pride and lust and many others which are forces real as that hidden in the *Keth*; and among them—fear, which weakens all those others—" Again she paused.

"But within it is nothing of that greatest of all, that which can make powerless all the evil others, that which we call—love," she ended softly.

"I'd like to be the one to put a little more *fear* in the beast," whispered Larry to me, grimly in our own English. The three weird heads bent, ever so slightly—and I gasped, and Larry grew a little white as Lakla nodded—

"They say, Larry," she said, "that there you touch one side of the heart of the matter—for it is through the way of fear the Silent Ones hope to strike at the very life of the Shining One!"

The visage Larry turned to me was eloquent of wonder; and mine reflected it—for what *really* were this Three to whom our minds were but open pages, so easily read? Not long could we conjecture; Lakla broke the little silence.

"This, they say, is what is to happen. First will come upon us Lugur and Yolara with all their host. Because of fear the Shining One will lurk behind within its lair; for despite all, the Dweller *does* dread the Three, and only them. With this host the Voice and the priestess will strive to conquer. And if they do, then will they be strong enough, too, to destroy us all. For if they take the abode they banish from the Dweller all fear and sound the end of the Three.

"Then will the Shining One be all free indeed; free to go out into the world, free to do there as it wills!

"But if they do not conquer—and the Shining One comes not to their aid, abandoning them even as it abandoned its own *Taithu*—then will the Three be loosed from a part of their doom, and they will go through the Portal, seek the Shining One beyond the Veil, and, piercing it through fear's opening, destroy it."

"That's quite clear," murmured the O'Keefe in my ear. "Weaken the morale—then smash. I've seen it happen a dozen times in Europe. While they've got their nerve there's not a thing you can do; get their nerve—and not a thing can they do. And yet in both cases they're the same men."

Lakla had been listening again. She turned, thrust out hands to Larry, a wild hope in her eyes—and yet a hope half shamed.

"They say," she cried, "that they give us choice. Remembering that your world doom hangs in the balance, we have choice—choice to stay and help fight Yolara's armies—and they say they look not lightly on that help. Or choice to go—and if so be you choose the latter, then will they show another way that leads into your world!"

A flush had crept over the O'Keefe's face as she was speaking. He took her hands and looked long into the golden eyes; glancing up I saw the Trinity were watching them intently—imperturbably.

"What do you say, *mavourneen*?" asked Larry gently. The handmaiden hung her head; trembled.

"Your words shall be mine, O one I love," she whispered. "So going or staying, I am beside you."

"And you, Goodwin?" he turned to me. I shrugged my shoulders—after all I had no one to care.

"It's up to you, Larry," I remarked, deliberately choosing his own phraseology.

The O'Keefe straightened, squared his shoulders, gazed straight into the flame-flickering eyes.

"We stick!" he said briefly.

Shamefacedly I recall now that at the time I thought this colloquialism not only irreverent, but in somewhat bad taste. I am glad to say I was alone in that bit of weakness. The face that Lakla turned to Larry was radiant with love, and although the shamed hope had vanished from the sweet eyes, they were shining with adoring pride. And the marble visages of the Three softened, and the little flames died down.

"Wait," said Lakla, "there is one other thing they say we must answer before they will hold us to that promise—wait—"

She listened, and then her face grew white—white as those of the Three themselves; the glorious eyes widened, stark terror filling them; the whole lithe body of her shook like a reed in the wind.

"Not that!" she cried out to the Three. "Oh, not that! Not Larry—let me go even as you will—but not him!" She threw up frantic hands to the woman-being of the Trinity. "Let *me* bear it alone," she wailed. "Alone—mother! Mother!"

The Three bent their heads toward her, their faces pitiful, and from the eyes of the woman One rolled—tears! Larry leaped to Lakla's side.

"*Mavourneen!*" he cried. "Sweetheart, what have they said to you?"

He glared up at the Silent Ones, his hand twitching toward the high-hung pistol holster.

The handmaiden swung to him; threw white arms around his neck; held her head upon his heart until her sobbing ceased.

"This they—say—the Silent Ones," she gasped and then all the courage of her came back. "O heart of mine!" she whispered to Larry, gazing deep into his eyes, his anxious face cupped between her white palms. "This they say—that should the Shining One come to succour Yolara and Lugur, should it conquer its fear—and—do this—then is there but one way left to destroy it—and to save your world."

She swayed; he gripped her tightly.

"But one way—you and I must go—together—into its embrace! Yea, we must pass within it—loving each other, loving the world, realizing to the full all that we sacrifice and sacrificing all, our love, our lives, perhaps even that you call soul, O loved one; must give ourselves *all* to the Shining One—gladly, freely, our love for each other flaming high within us—that this curse shall pass away! For if we do this, pledge the Three, then shall that power of love we carry into it weaken for a time all that evil which the Shining One has become—and in that time the Three can strike and slay!"

The blood rushed from my heart; scientist that I am, essentially, my reason rejected any such solution as this of the activities of the Dweller.

Was it not, the thought flashed, a propitiation by the Three out of their own weakness—and as it flashed I looked up to see their eyes, full of sorrow, on mine—and knew they read the thought. Then into the whirling vortex of my mind came steadying reflections—of history changed by the power of hate, of passion, of ambition, and most of all, by love. Was there not actual dynamic energy in these things—was there not a Son of Man who hung upon a cross on Calvary?

"Dear love o' mine," said the O'Keefe quietly, "is it in your heart to say *yes* to this?"

"Larry," she spoke low, "what is in your heart is in mine; but I did so want to go with you, to live with you—to—to bear you children, Larry—and to see the sun."

My eyes were wet; dimly through them I saw his gaze on me.

"If the world *is* at stake," he whispered, "why of course there's only one thing to do. God knows I never was afraid when I was fighting up there—and many a better man than me has gone West with shell and bullet for the same idea; but these things aren't shell and bullet—but I hadn't Lakla then—and it's the damned *doubt* I have behind it all."

He turned to the Three—and did I in their poise sense a rigidity, an anxiety that sat upon them as alienly as would divinity upon men?

"Tell me this, Silent Ones," he cried. "If we do this, Lakla and I, is it *sure* you are that you can slay the—Thing, and save my world? Is it *sure* you are?"

For the first and the last time, I heard the voice of the Silent Ones. It was the man-being at the right who spoke.

"We are sure," the tones rolled out like deepest organ notes, shaking, vibrating, assailing the ears as strangely as their appearance struck the eyes. Another moment the O'Keefe stared at them. Once more he squared his shoulders; lifted Lakla's chin and smiled into her eyes.

"We stick!" he said again, nodding to the Three.

Over the visages of the Trinity fell benignity that was—awesome; the tiny flames in the jet orbs vanished, leaving them wells in which brimmed serenity, hope—an extraordinary joyfulness. The woman sat upright, tender gaze fixed upon the man and girl. Her great shoulders raised as though she had lifted her arms and had drawn to her those others. The three faces pressed together for a fleeting moment; raised again. The woman bent forward—and as she did so, Lakla and Larry, as though drawn by some outer force, were swept upon the dais.

A. MERRITT

Out from the sparkling mist stretched two hands, enormously long, six-fingered, thumbless, a faint tracery of golden scales upon their white backs, utterly unhuman and still in some strange way beautiful, radiating power and—all womanly!

They stretched forth; they touched the bent heads of Lakla and the O'Keefe; caressed them, drew them together, softly stroked them—lovingly, with more than a touch of benediction. And withdrew!

The sparkling mists rolled up once more, hiding the Silent Ones. As silently as once before we had gone we passed out of the place of light, beyond the crimson stone, back to the handmaiden's chamber.

Only once on our way did Larry speak.

"Cheer up, darlin'," he said to her, "it's a long way yet before the finish. An' are you thinking that Lugur and Yolara are going to pull this thing off? Are you?"

The handmaiden only looked at him, eyes love and sorrow filled.

"They are!" said Larry. "They are! Like HELL they are!"

XXXIII

The Meeting of Titans

It is not my intention, nor is it possible no matter how interesting to me, to set down *ad seriatim* the happenings of the next twelve hours. But a few will not be denied recital.

O'Keefe regained cheerfulness.

"After all, Doc," he said to me, "it's a beautiful scrap we're going to have. At the worst the worst is no more than the leprechaun warned about. I would have told the Taitha De about the banshee raid he promised me; but I was a bit taken off my feet at the time. The old girl an' all the clan'll be along, said the little green man, an' I bet the Three will be damned glad of it, take it from me."

Lakla, shining-eyed and half fearful too:

"I have other tidings that I am afraid will please you little, Larry—darlin'. The Silent Ones say that you must not go into battle yourself. You must stay here with me, and with Goodwin—for if—if—the Shining One does come, then must we be here to meet it. And you might not be, you know, Larry, if you fight," she said, looking shyly up at him from under the long lashes.

The O'Keefe's jaw dropped.

"That's about the hardest yet," he answered slowly. "Still—I see their point; the lamb corralled for the altar has no right to stray out among the lions," he added grimly. "Don't worry, sweet," he told her. "As long as I've sat in the game I'll stick to the rules."

Olaf took fierce joy in the coming fray. "The Norns spin close to the end of this web," he rumbled. "*Ja!* And the threads of Lugur and the Heks woman are between their fingers for the breaking! Thor will be with me, and I have fashioned me a hammer in glory of Thor." In his hand was an enormous mace of black metal, fully five feet long, crowned with a massive head.

I pass to the twelve hours' closing.

At the end of the *coria* road where the giant fernland met the edge of the cavern's ruby floor, hundreds of the *Akka* were stationed in ambush, armed with their spears tipped with the rotting death and their nail-studded, metal-headed clubs. These were to attack when the Murians debauched from the *corials*. We had little hope of doing more here than effect some attrition of Yolara's hosts, for at this place the captains of the Shining One could wield the *Keth* and their other uncanny weapons freely. We had learned, too, that every forge and artisan had been put to work to make an armour Marakinoff had devised to withstand the natural battle equipment of the frog-people—and both Larry and I had a disquieting faith in the Russian's ingenuity.

At any rate the numbers against us would be lessened.

Next, under the direction of the frog-king, levies commanded by subsidiary chieftains had completed rows of rough walls along the probable route of the Murians through the cavern. These afforded the *Akka* a fair protection behind which they could hurl their darts and spears—curiously enough they had never developed the bow as a weapon.

At the opening of the cavern a strong barricade stretched almost to the two ends of the crescent strand; almost, I say, because there had not been time to build it entirely across the mouth.

And from edge to edge of the titanic bridge, from where it sprang outward at the shore of the Crimson Sea to a hundred feet away from the golden door of the abode, barrier after barrier was piled.

Behind the wall defending the mouth of the cavern, waited other thousands of the *Akka*. At each end of the unfinished barricade they were mustered thickly, and at right and left of the crescent where their forest began, more legions were assembled to make way up to the ledge as opportunity offered.

Rank upon rank they manned the bridge barriers; they swarmed over the pinnacles and in the hollows of the island's ragged outer lip; the domed castle was a hive of them, if I may mix my metaphors—and the rocks and gardens that surrounded the abode glittered with them.

"Now," said the handmaiden, "there's nothing else we can do—save wait."

She led us out through her bower and up the little path that ran to the embrasure.

Through the quiet came a sound, a sighing, a half-mournful whispering that beat about us and fled away.

"They come!" cried Lakla, the light of battle in her eyes. Larry drew her to him, raised her in his arms, kissed her.

"A woman!" acclaimed the O'Keefe. "A real woman—and mine!"

With the cry of the Portal there was movement among the *Akka*, the glint of moving spears, flash of metal-tipped clubs, rattle of horny spurs, rumblings of battle-cries.

And we waited—waited it seemed interminably, gaze fastened upon the low wall across the cavern mouth. Suddenly I remembered the crystal through which I had peered when the hidden assassins had crept upon us. Mentioning it to Lakla, she gave a little cry of vexation, a command to her attendant; and not long that faithful if unusual lady had returned with a tray of the glasses. Raising mine, I saw the lines furthest away leap into sudden activity. Spurred warrior after warrior leaped upon the barricade and over it. Flashes of intense, green light, mingled with gleams like lightning strokes of concentrated moon rays, sprang from behind the wall—sprang and struck and burned upon the scales of the batrachians.

"They come!" whispered Lakla.

At the far ends of the crescent a terrific milling had begun. Here it was plain the *Akka* were holding. Faintly, for the distance was great, I could see fresh force upon force rush up and take the places of those who had fallen.

Over each of these ends, and along the whole line of the barricade a mist of dancing, diamonded atoms began to rise; sparking, coruscating points of diamond dust that darted and danced.

What had once been Lakla's guardians—dancing now in the nothingness!

"God, but it's hard to stay here like this!" groaned the O'Keefe; Olaf's teeth were bared, the lips drawn back in such a fighting grin as his ancestors berserk on their raven ships must have borne; Rador was livid with rage; the handmaiden's nostrils flaring wide, all her wrathful soul in her eyes.

Suddenly, while we looked, the rocky wall which the *Akka* had built at the cavern mouth—was not! It vanished, as though an unseen, unbelievably gigantic hand had with the lightning's speed swept it away. And with it vanished, too, long lines of the great amphibians close behind it.

Then down upon the ledge, dropping into the Crimson Sea, sending up geysers of ruby spray, dashing on the bridge, crushing the frog-men, fell a shower of stone, mingled with distorted shapes and fragments whose scales still flashed meteoric as they hurled from above.

"That which makes things fall upward," hissed Olaf. "That which I saw in the garden of Lugur!"

The fiendish agency of destruction which Marakinoff had revealed to Larry; the force that cut off gravitation and sent all things within its range racing outward into space!

And now over the debris upon the ledge, striking with long sword and daggers, here and there a captain flashing the green ray, moving on in ordered squares, came the soldiers of the Shining One. Nearer and nearer the verge of the ledge they pushed Nak's warriors. Leaping upon the dwarfs, smiting them with spear and club, with teeth and spur, the *Akka* fought like devils. Quivering under the ray, they leaped and dragged down and slew.

Now there was but one long line of the frog-men at the very edge of the cliff.

And ever the clouds of dancing, diamonded atoms grew thicker over them all!

That last thin line of the *Akka* was going; yet they fought to the last, and none toppled over the lip without at least one of the armoured Murians in his arms.

My gaze dropped to the foot of the cliffs. Stretched along their length was a wide ribbon of beauty—a shimmering multitude of gleaming, pulsing, prismatic moons; glowing, glowing ever brighter, ever more wondrous—the gigantic Medusae globes feasting on dwarf and frog-man alike!

Across the waters, faintly, came a triumphant shouting from Lugur's and Yolara's men!

Was the ruddy light of the place lessening, growing paler, changing to a faint rose? There was an exclamation from Larry; something like hope relaxed the drawn muscles of his face. He pointed to the aureate dome wherein sat the Three—and then I saw!

Out of it, through the long transverse slit through which the Silent Ones kept their watch on cavern, bridge, and abyss, a torrent of the opalescent light was pouring. It cascaded like a waterfall, and as it flowed it spread whirling out, in columns and eddies, clouds and wisps of misty, curdled coruscations. It hung like a veil over all the islands, filtering everywhere, driving back the crimson light as though possessed of impenetrable substance—and still it cast not the faintest shadowing upon our vision.

"Good God!" breathed Larry. "Look!"

The radiance was marching—*marching*—down the colossal bridge. It moved swiftly, in some unthinkable way *intelligently*. It swathed the

Akka, and closer, ever closer it swept toward the approach upon which Yolara's men had now gained foothold.

From their ranks came flash after flash of the green ray—aimed at the abode! But as the light sped and struck the opalescence it was blotted out! The shimmering mists seemed to enfold, to dissipate it.

Lakla drew a deep breath.

"The Silent Ones forgive me for doubting them," she whispered; and again hope blossomed on her face even as it did on Larry's.

The frog-men were gaining. Clothed in the armour of that mist, they pressed back from the bridge-head the invaders. There was another prodigious movement at the ends of the crescent, and racing up, pressing against the dwarfs, came other legions of Nak's warriors. And re-enforcing those out on the prodigious arch, the frog-men stationed in the gardens below us poured back to the castle and out through the open Portal.

"They're licked!" shouted Larry. "They're—"

So quickly I could not follow the movement his automatic leaped to his hand—spoke, once and again and again. Rador leaped to the head of the little path, sword in hand; Olaf, shouting and whirling his mace, followed. I strove to get my own gun quickly.

For up that path were running twoscore of Lugur's men, while from below Lugur's own voice roared.

"Quick! Slay not the handmaiden or her lover! Carry them down. Quick! But slay the others!"

The handmaiden raced toward Larry, stopped, whistled shrilly— again and again. Larry's pistol was empty, but as the dwarfs rushed upon him I dropped two of them with mine. It jammed—I could not use it; I sprang to his side. Rador was down, struggling in a heap of Lugur's men. Olaf, a Viking of old, was whirling his great hammer, and striking, striking through armour, flesh, and bone.

Larry was down, Lakla flew to him. But the Norseman, now streaming blood from a dozen wounds, caught a glimpse of her coming, turned, thrust out a mighty hand, sent her reeling back, and then with his hammer cracked the skulls of those trying to drag the O'Keefe down the path.

A cry from Lakla—the dwarfs had seized her, had lifted her despite her struggles, were carrying her away. One I dropped with the butt of my useless pistol, and then went down myself under the rush of another.

A. MERRITT

Through the clamour I heard a booming of the *Akka*, closer, closer; then through it the bellow of Lugur. I made a mighty effort, swung a hand up, and sunk my fingers in the throat of the soldier striving to kill me. Writhing over him, my fingers touched a poniard; I thrust it deep, staggered to my feet.

The O'Keefe, shielding Lakla, was battling with a long sword against a half dozen of the soldiers. I started toward him, was struck, and under the impact hurled to the ground. Dizzily I raised myself—and leaning upon my elbow, stared and moved no more. For the dwarfs lay dead, and Larry, holding Lakla tightly, was staring even as I, and ranged at the head of the path were the *Akka*, whose booming advance in obedience to the handmaiden's call I had heard.

And at what we all stared was Olaf, crimson with his wounds, and Lugur, in blood-red armour, locked in each other's grip, struggling, smiting, tearing, kicking, and swaying about the little space before the embrasure. I crawled over toward the O'Keefe. He raised his pistol, dropped it.

"Can't hit him without hitting Olaf," he whispered. Lakla signalled the frog-men; they advanced toward the two—but Olaf saw them, broke the red dwarf's hold, sent Lugur reeling a dozen feet away.

"No!" shouted the Norseman, the ice of his pale-blue eyes glinting like frozen flames, blood streaming down his face and dripping from his hands. "No! Lugur is mine! None but me slays him! Ho, you Lugur—" and cursed him and Yolara and the Dweller hideously—I cannot set those curses down here.

They spurred Lugur. Mad now as the Norseman, the red dwarf sprang. Olaf struck a blow that would have killed an ordinary man, but Lugur only grunted, swept in, and seized him about the waist; one mighty arm began to creep up toward Huldricksson's throat.

"'Ware, Olaf!" cried O'Keefe; but Olaf did not answer. He waited until the red dwarf's hand was close to his shoulder; and then, with an incredibly rapid movement—once before had I seen something like it in a wrestling match between Papuans—he had twisted Lugur around; twisted him so that Olaf's right arm lay across the tremendous breast, the left behind the neck, and Olaf's left leg held the Voice's armoured thighs viselike against his right knee while over that knee lay the small of the red dwarf's back.

For a second or two the Norseman looked down upon his enemy, motionless in that paralyzing grip. And then—slowly—he began to break him!

Lakla gave a little cry; made a motion toward the two. But Larry drew her head down against his breast, hiding her eyes; then fastened his own upon the pair, white-faced, stern.

Slowly, ever so slowly, proceeded Olaf. Twice Lugur moaned. At the end he screamed—horribly. There was a cracking sound, as of a stout stick snapped.

Huldricksson stooped, silently. He picked up the limp body of the Voice, not yet dead, for the eyes rolled, the lips strove to speak; lifted it, walked to the parapet, swung it twice over his head, and cast it down to the red waters!

A. MERRITT

XXXIV

The Coming of the Shining One

The Norseman turned toward us. There was now no madness in his eyes; only a great weariness. And there was peace on the once tortured face.

"Helma," he whispered, "I go a little before! Soon you will come to me—to me and the Yndling who will await you—Helma, *meine liebe!*"

Blood gushed from his mouth; he swayed, fell. And thus died Olaf Huldricksson.

We looked down upon him; nor did Lakla, nor Larry, nor I try to hide our tears. And as we stood the *Akka* brought to us that other mighty fighter, Rador; but in him there was life, and we attended to him there as best we could.

Then Lakla spoke.

"We will bear him into the castle where we may give him greater care," she said. "For, lo! the hosts of Yolara have been beaten back; and on the bridge comes Nak with tidings."

We looked over the parapet. It was even as she had said. Neither on ledge nor bridge was there trace of living men of Muria—only heaps of slain that lay everywhere—and thick against the cavern mouth still danced the flashing atoms of those the green ray had destroyed.

"Over!" exclaimed Larry incredulously. "We live then—heart of mine!"

"The Silent Ones recall their veils," she said, pointing to the dome. Back through the slitted opening the radiance was streaming; withdrawing from sea and island; marching back over the bridge with that same ordered, intelligent motion. Behind it the red light pressed, like skirmishers on the heels of a retreating army.

"And yet—" faltered the handmaiden as we passed into her chamber, and doubtful were the eyes she turned upon the O'Keefe.

"I don't believe," he said, "there's a kick left in them—"

What was that sound beating into the chamber faintly, so faintly? My heart gave a great throb and seemed to stop for an eternity. What was it—coming nearer, ever nearer? Now Lakla and O'Keefe heard it, life ebbing from lips and cheeks.

Nearer, nearer—a music as of myriads of tiny crystal bells, tinkling, tinkling—a storm of pizzicati upon violins of glass! Nearer, nearer—not sweetly now, nor luring; no—raging, wrathful, sinister beyond words; sweeping on; nearer—

The Dweller! The Shining One!

We leaped to the narrow window; peered out, aghast. The bell notes swept through and about us, a hurricane. The crescent strand was once more a ferment. Back, back were the *Akka* being swept, as though by brooms, tottering on the edge of the ledge, falling into the waters. Swiftly they were finished; and where they had fought was an eddying throng clothed in tatters or naked, swaying, drifting, arms tossing—like marionettes of Satan.

The dead-alive! The slaves of the Dweller!

They swayed and tossed, and then, like water racing through an opened dam, they swept upon the bridge-head. On and on they pushed, like the bore of a mighty tide. The frog-men strove against them, clubbing, spearing, tearing them. But even those worst smitten seemed not to fall. On they pushed, driving forward, irresistible—a battering ram of flesh and bone. They clove the masses of the *Akka*, pressing them to the sides of the bridge and over. Through the open gates they forced them—for there was no room for the frog-men to stand against that implacable tide.

Then those of the *Akka* who were left turned their backs and ran. We heard the clang of the golden wings of the portal, and none too soon to keep out the first of the Dweller's dreadful hordes.

Now upon the cavern ledge and over the whole length of the bridge there were none but the dead-alive, men and women, black-polled *ladala*, sloe-eyed Malays, slant-eyed Chinese, men of every race that sailed the seas—milling, turning, swaying, like leaves caught in a sluggish current.

The bell notes became sharper, more insistent. At the cavern mouth a radiance began to grow—a gleaming from which the atoms of diamond dust seemed to try to flee. As the radiance grew and the crystal notes rang nearer, every head of that hideous multitude turned stiffly, slowly toward the right, looking toward the far bridge end; their eyes fixed and glaring; every face an inhuman mask of rapture and of horror!

A movement shook them. Those in the centre began to stream back, faster and ever faster, leaving motionless deep ranks on each side.

Back they flowed until from golden doors to cavern mouth a wide lane stretched, walled on each side by the dead-alive.

The far radiance became brighter; it gathered itself at the end of the dreadful lane; it was shot with sparklings and with pulsings of polychromatic light. The crystal storm was intolerable, piercing the ears with countless tiny lances; brighter still the radiance.

From the cavern swirled the Shining One!

The Dweller paused, seemed to scan the island of the Silent Ones half doubtfully; then slowly, stately, it drifted out upon the bridge. Closer it drew; behind it glided Yolara at the head of a company of her dwarfs, and at her side was the hag of the Council whose face was the withered, shattered echo of her own.

Slower grew the Dweller's pace as it drew nearer. Did I sense in it a doubt, an uncertainty? The crystal-tongued, unseen choristers that accompanied it subtly seemed to reflect the doubt; their notes were not sure, no longer insistent; rather was there in them an undertone of hesitancy, of warning! Yet on came the Shining One until it stood plain beneath us, searching with those eyes that thrust from and withdrew into unknown spheres, the golden gateway, the cliff face, the castle's rounded bulk—and more intently than any of these, the dome wherein sat the Three.

Behind it each face of the dead-alive turned toward it, and those beside it throbbed and gleamed with its luminescence.

Yolara crept close, just beyond the reach of its spirals. She murmured—and the Dweller bent toward her, its seven globes steady in their shining mists, as though listening. It drew erect once more, resumed its doubtful scrutiny. Yolara's face darkened; she turned abruptly, spoke to a captain of her guards. A dwarf raced back between the palisades of dead-alive.

Now the priestess cried out, her voice ringing like a silver clarion.

"Ye are done, ye Three! The Shining One stands at your door, demanding entrance. Your beasts are slain and your power is gone. Who are ye, says the Shining One, to deny it entrance to the place of its birth?"

"Ye do not answer," she cried again, "yet know we that ye hear! The Shining One offers these terms: Send forth your handmaiden and that lying stranger she stole; send them forth to us—and perhaps ye may live. But if ye send them not forth, then shall ye too die—and soon!"

We waited, silent, even as did Yolara—and again there was no answer from the Three.

The priestess laughed; the blue eyes flashed.

"It is ended!" she cried. "If you will not open, needs must we open for you!"

Over the bridge was marching a long double file of the dwarfs. They bore a smoothed and handled tree-trunk whose head was knobbed with a huge ball of metal. Past the priestess, past the Shining One, they carried it; fifty of them to each side of the ram; and behind them stepped—Marakinoff!

Larry awoke to life.

"Now, thank God," he rasped, "I can get that devil, anyway!"

He drew his pistol, took careful aim. Even as he pressed the trigger there rang through the abode a tremendous clanging. The ram was battering at the gates. O'Keefe's bullet went wild. The Russian must have heard the shot; perhaps the missile was closer than we knew. He made a swift leap behind the guards; was lost to sight.

Once more the thunderous clanging rang through the castle.

Lakla drew herself erect; down upon her dropped the listening aloofness. Gravely she bowed her head.

"It is time, O love of mine." She turned to O'Keefe. "The Silent Ones say that the way of fear is closed, but the way of love is open. They call upon us to redeem our promise!"

For a hundred heart-beats they clung to each other, breast to breast and lip to lip. Below, the clangour was increasing, the great trunk swinging harder and faster upon the metal gates. Now Lakla gently loosed the arms of the O'Keefe, and for another instant those two looked into each other's souls. The handmaiden smiled tremulously.

"I would it might have been otherwise, Larry darlin'," she whispered. "But at least—we pass together, dearest of mine!"

She leaped to the window.

"Yolara!" the golden voice rang out sweetly. The clanging ceased. "Draw back your men. We open the Portal and come forth to you and the Shining One—Larry and I."

The priestess's silver chimes of laughter rang out, cruel, mocking.

"Come, then, quickly," she jeered. "For surely both the Shining One and I yearn for you!" Her malice-laden laughter chimed high once more. "Keep us not lonely long!" the priestess mocked.

Larry drew a deep breath, stretched both hands out to me.

"It's goodbye, I guess, Doc." His voice was strained. "Goodbye and good luck, old boy. If you get out, and you *will*, let the old *Dolphin* know I'm gone. And carry on, pal—and always remember the O'Keefe loved you like a brother."

I squeezed his hands desperately. Then out of my balanceshaking woe a strange comfort was born.

"Maybe it's not goodbye, Larry!" I cried. "The banshee has not cried!"

A flash of hope passed over his face; the old reckless grin shone forth. "It's so!" he said. "By the Lord, it's so!"

Then Lakla bent toward me, and for the second time—kissed me.

"Come!" she said to Larry. Hand in hand they moved away, into the corridor that led to the door outside of which waited the Shining One and its priestess.

And unseen by them, wrapped as they were within their love and sacrifice, I crept softly behind. For I had determined that if enter the Dweller's embrace they must, they should not go alone.

They paused before the Golden Portals; the handmaiden pressed its opening lever; the massive leaves rolled back.

Heads high, proudly, serenely, they passed through and out upon the hither span. I followed.

On each side of us stood the Dweller's slaves, faces turned rigidly toward their master. A hundred feet away the Shining One pulsed and spiralled in its evilly glorious lambency of sparkling plumes.

Unhesitating, always with that same high serenity, Lakla and the O'Keefe, hands clasped like little children, drew closer to that wondrous shape. I could not see their faces, but I saw awe fall upon those of the watching dwarfs, and into the burning eyes of Yolara crept a doubt. Closer they drew to the Dweller, and closer, I following them step by step. The Shining One's whirling lessened; its tinklings were faint, almost stilled. It seemed to watch them apprehensively. A silence fell upon us all, a thick silence, brooding, ominous, palpable. Now the pair were face to face with the child of the Three—so near that with one of its misty tentacles it could have enfolded them.

And the Shining One drew back!

Yes, drew back—and back with it stepped Yolara, the doubt in her eyes deepening. Onward paced the handmaiden and the O'Keefe—and step by step, as they advanced, the Dweller withdrew; its bell notes chiming out, puzzled questioning—half fearful!

And back it drew, and back until it had reached the very centre of that platform over the abyss in whose depths pulsed the green fires of earth heart. And there Yolara gripped herself; the hell that seethed within her soul leaped out of her eyes, a cry, a shriek of rage, tore from her lips.

As at a signal, the Shining One flamed high; its spirals and eddying mists swirled madly, the pulsing core of it blazed radiance. A score of coruscating tentacles swept straight upon the pair who stood intrepid, unresisting, awaiting its embrace. And upon me, lurking behind them.

Through me swept a mighty exaltation. It was the end then—and I was to meet it with them.

Something drew us back, back with an incredible swiftness, and yet as gently as a summer breeze sweeps a bit of thistle-down! Drew us back from those darting misty arms even as they were a hair-breadth from us! I heard the Dweller's bell notes burst out ragingly! I heard Yolara scream.

What was that?

Between the three of us and them was a ring of curdled moon flames, swirling about the Shining One and its priestess, pressing in upon them, enfolding them!

And within it I glimpsed the faces of the Three—implacable, sorrowful, filled with a supernal power!

Sparks and flashes of white flame darted from the ring, penetrating the radiant swathings of the Dweller, striking through its pulsing nucleus, piercing its seven crowning orbs.

Now the Shining One's radiance began to dim, the seven orbs to dull; the tiny sparkling filaments that ran from them down into the Dweller's body snapped, vanished! Through the battling nebulosities Yolara's face swam forth—horror-filled, distorted, inhuman!

The ranks of the dead-alive quivered, moved, writhed, as though each felt the torment of the Thing that had enslaved them. The radiance that the Three wielded grew more intense, thicker, seemed to expand. Within it, suddenly, were scores of flaming triangles—scores of eyes like those of the Silent Ones!

And the Shining One's seven little moons of amber, of silver, of blue and amethyst and green, of rose and white, split, shattered, were gone! Abruptly the tortured crystal chimings ceased.

Dulled, all its soul-shaking beauty dead, blotched and shadowed squalidly, its gleaming plumes tarnished, its dancing spirals stripped from it, that which had been the Shining One wrapped itself about Yolara—wrapped and drew her into itself; writhed, swayed, and hurled itself over the edge of the bridge—down, down into the green fires of the unfathomable abyss—with its priestess still enfolded in its coils!

From the dwarfs who had watched that terror came screams of panic fear. They turned and ran, racing frantically over the bridge toward the cavern mouth.

The serried ranks of the dead-alive trembled, shook. Then from their faces tied the horror of wedded ecstasy and anguish. Peace, utter peace, followed in its wake.

And as fields of wheat are bent and fall beneath the wind, they fell. No longer dead-alive, now all of the blessed dead, freed from their dreadful slavery!

Abruptly from the sparkling mists the cloud of eyes was gone. Faintly revealed in them were only the heads of the Silent Ones. And they drew before us; were before us! No flames now in their ebon eyes—for the flickering fires were quenched in great tears, streaming down the marble white faces. They bent toward us, over us; their radiance enfolded us. My eyes darkened. I could not see. I felt a tender hand upon my head—and panic and frozen dread and nightmare web that held me fled.

Then they, too, were gone.

Upon Larry's breast the handmaiden was sobbing—sobbing out her heart—but this time with the joy of one who is swept up from the very threshold of hell into paradise.

XXXV

"Larry—Farewell!"

My heart, Larry—" It was the handmaiden's murmur. "My heart feels like a bird that is flying from a nest of sorrow."

We were pacing down the length of the bridge, guards of the *Akka* beside us, others following with those companies of *ladala* that had rushed to aid us; in front of us the bandaged Rador swung gently within a litter; beside him, in another, lay Nak, the frog-king—much less of him than there had been before the battle began, but living.

Hours had passed since the terror I have just related. My first task had been to search for Throckmartin and his wife among the fallen multitudes strewn thick as autumn leaves along the flying arch of stone, over the cavern ledge, and back, back as far as the eye could reach.

At last, Lakla and Larry helping, we found them. They lay close to the bridge-end, not parted—locked tight in each other's arms, pallid face to face, her hair streaming over his breast! As though when that unearthly life the Dweller had set within them passed away, their own had come back for one fleeting instant—and they had known each other, and clasped before kindly death had taken them.

"Love is stronger than all things." The handmaiden was weeping softly. "Love never left them. Love was stronger than the Shining One. And when its evil fled, love went with them—wherever souls go."

Of Stanton and Thora there was no trace; nor, after our discovery of those other two, did I care to look more. They were dead—and they were free.

We buried Throckmartin and Edith beside Olaf in Lakla's bower. But before the body of my old friend was placed within the grave I gave it a careful and sorrowful examination. The skin was firm and smooth, but cold; not the cold of death, but with a chill that set my touching fingers tingling unpleasantly. The body was bloodless; the course of veins and arteries marked by faintly indented white furrows, as though their walls had long collapsed. Lips, mouth, even the tongue, was paper white. There was no sign of dissolution as we know it; no shadow or stain upon the marble surface. Whatever the force that, streaming from the Dweller or impregnating its lair, had energized the dead-alive, it was barrier against putrescence of any kind; that at least was certain.

But it was not barrier against the poison of the Medusae, for, our sad task done, and looking down upon the waters, I saw the pale forms of the Dweller's hordes dissolving, vanishing into the shifting glories of the gigantic moons sailing down upon them from every quarter of the Sea of Crimson.

While the frog-men, those late levies from the farthest forests, were clearing bridge and ledge of cavern of the litter of the dead, we listened to a leader of the *ladala*. They had risen, even as the messenger had promised Rador. Fierce had been the struggle in the gardened city by the silver waters with those Lugur and Yolara had left behind to garrison it. Deadly had been the slaughter of the fair-haired, reaping the harvest of hatred they had been sowing so long. Not without a pang of regret did I think of the beautiful, gaily malicious elfin women destroyed—evil though they may have been.

The ancient city of Lara was a charnel. Of all the rulers not twoscore had escaped, and these into regions of peril which to describe as sanctuary would be mockery. Nor had the *ladala* fared so well. Of all the men and women, for women as well as men had taken their part in the swift war, not more than a tenth remained alive.

And the dancing motes of light in the silver air were thick, thick— they whispered.

They told us of the Shining One rushing through the Veil, cometlike, its hosts streaming behind it, raging with it, in ranks that seemed interminable!

Of the massacre of the priests and priestesses in the Cyclopean temple; of the flashing forth of the summoning lights by unseen hands— followed by the tearing of the rainbow curtain, by colossal shatterings of the radiant cliffs; the vanishing behind their debris of all trace of entrance to the haunted place wherein the hordes of the Shining One had slaved—the sealing of the lair!

Then, when the tempest of hate had ended in seething Lara, how, thrilled with victory, armed with the weapons of those they had slain, they had lifted the Shadow, passed through the Portal, met and slaughtered the fleeing remnants of Yolara's men—only to find the tempest stilled here, too.

But of Marakinoff they had seen nothing! Had the Russian escaped, I wondered, or was he lying out there among the dead?

But now the *ladala* were calling upon Lakla to come with them, to govern them.

"I don't want to, Larry darlin'," she told him. "I want to go out with you to Ireland. But for a time—I think the Three would have us remain and set that place in order."

The O'Keefe was bothered about something else than the government of Muria.

"If they've killed off all the priests, who's to marry us, heart of mine?" he worried. "None of those Siya and Siyana rites, no matter what," he added hastily.

"Marry!" cried the handmaiden incredulously. "Marry us? Why, Larry dear, we *are* married!"

The O'Keefe's astonishment was complete; his jaw dropped; collapse seemed imminent.

"We are?" he gasped. "When?" he stammered fatuously.

"Why, when the Mother drew us together before her; when she put her hands on our heads after we had made the promise! Didn't you understand that?" asked the handmaiden wonderingly.

He looked at her, into the purity of the clear golden eyes, into the purity of the soul that gazed out of them; all his own great love transfiguring his keen face.

"An' is that enough for you, *mavourneen*?" he whispered humbly.

"Enough?" The handmaiden's puzzlement was complete, profound. "Enough? Larry darlin', what *more* could we ask?"

He drew a deep breath, clasped her close.

"Kiss the bride, Doc!" cried the O'Keefe. And for the third and, soul's sorrow! the last time, Lakla dimpling and blushing, I thrilled to the touch of her soft, sweet lips.

Quickly were our preparations for departure made. Rador, conscious, his immense vitality conquering fast his wounds, was to be borne ahead of us. And when all was done, Lakla, Larry, and I made our way up to the scarlet stone that was the doorway to the chamber of the Three. We knew, of course, that they had gone, following, no doubt, those whose eyes I had seen in the curdled mists, and who, coming to the aid of the Three at last from whatever mysterious place that was their home, had thrown their strength with them against the Shining One. Nor were we wrong. When the great slab rolled away, no torrents of opalescence came rushing out upon us. The vast dome was dim, tenantless; its curved walls that had cascaded Light shone

A. MERRITT

now but faintly; the dais was empty; its wall of moon-flame radiance gone.

A little time we stood, heads bent, reverent, our hearts filled with gratitude and love—yes, and with pity for that strange trinity so alien to us and yet so near; children even as we, though so unlike us, of our same Mother Earth.

And what I wondered had been the secret of that promise they had wrung from their handmaiden and from Larry. And whence, if what the Three had said had been all true—whence had come their power to avert the sacrifice at the very verge of its consummation?

"Love is stronger than all things!" had said Lakla.

Was it that they had needed, must have, the force which dwells within love, within willing sacrifice, to strengthen their own power and to enable them to destroy the evil, glorious Thing so long shielded by their own love? Did the thought of sacrifice, the will toward abnegation, have to be as strong as the eternals, unshaken by faintest thrill of hope, before the Three could make of it their key to unlock the Dweller's guard and strike through at its life?

Here was a mystery—a mystery indeed! Lakla softly closed the crimson stone. The mystery of the red dwarf's appearance was explained when we discovered a half-dozen of the water *coria* moored in a small cove not far from where the *Sekta* flashed their heads of living bloom. The dwarfs had borne the shallops with them, and from somewhere beyond the cavern ledge had launched them unperceived; stealing up to the farther side of the island and risking all in one bold stroke. Well, Lugur, no matter what he held of wickedness, held also high courage.

The cavern was paved with the dead-alive, the *Akka* carrying them out by the hundreds, casting them into the waters. Through the lane down which the Dweller had passed we went as quickly as we could, coming at last to the space where the *coria* waited. And not long after we swung past where the shadow had hung and hovered over the shining depths of the Midnight Pool.

Upon Lakla's insistence we passed on to the palace of Lugur, not to Yolara's—I do not know why, but go there then she would not. And within one of its columned rooms, maidens of the black-haired folks, the wistfulness, the fear, all gone from their sparkling eyes, served us.

There came to me a huge desire to see the destruction they had told us of the Dweller's lair; to observe for myself whether it was not possible to make a way of entrance and to study its mysteries.

I spoke of this, and to my surprise both the handmaiden and the O'Keefe showed an almost embarrassed haste to acquiesce in my hesitant suggestion.

"Sure," cried Larry, "there's lots of time before night!"

He caught himself sheepishly; cast a glance at Lakla.

"I keep forgettin' there's no night here," he mumbled.

"What did you say, Larry?" asked she.

"I said I wish we were sitting in our home in Ireland, watching the sun go down," he whispered to her. Vaguely I wondered why she blushed.

But now I must hasten. We went to the temple, and here at least the ghastly litter of the dead had been cleaned away. We passed through the blue-caverned space, crossed the narrow arch that spanned the rushing sea stream, and, ascending, stood again upon the ivoried pave at the foot of the frowning, towering amphitheatre of jet.

Across the Silver Waters there was sign of neither Web of Rainbows nor colossal pillars nor the templed lips that I had seen curving out beneath the Veil when the Shining One had swirled out to greet its priestess and its voice and to dance with the sacrifices. There was but a broken and rent mass of the radiant cliffs against whose base the lake lapped.

Long I looked—and turned away saddened. Knowing even as I did what the irised curtain had hidden, still it was as though something of supernal beauty and wonder had been swept away, never to be replaced; a glamour gone forever; a work of the high gods destroyed.

"Let's go back," said Larry abruptly.

I dropped a little behind them to examine a bit of carving—and, after all, they did not want me. I watched them pacing slowly ahead, his arm around her, black hair close to bronze-gold ringlets. Then I followed. Half were they over the bridge when through the roar of the imprisoned stream I heard my name called softly.

"Goodwin! Dr. Goodwin!"

Amazed, I turned. From behind the pedestal of a carved group slunk—Marakinoff! My premonition had been right. Some way he had escaped, slipped through to here. He held his hands high, came forward cautiously.

"I am finished," he whispered—"Done! I don't care what *they'll* do to me." He nodded toward the handmaiden and Larry, now at the end of the bridge and passing on, oblivious of all save each other. He drew

A. MERRITT

closer. His eyes were sunken, burning, mad; his face etched with deep lines, as though a graver's tool had cut down through it. I took a step backward.

A grin, like the grimace of a fiend, blasted the Russian's visage. He threw himself upon me, his hands clenching at my throat!

"Larry!" I yelled—and as I spun around under the shock of his onslaught, saw the two turn, stand paralyzed, then race toward me.

"But *you'll* carry nothing out of here!" shrieked Marakinoff. "No!"

My foot, darting out behind me, touched vacancy. The roaring of the racing stream deafened me. I felt its mists about me; threw myself forward.

I was falling—falling—with the Russian's hand strangling me. I struck water, sank; the hands that gripped my throat relaxed for a moment their clutch. I strove to writhe loose; felt that I was being hurled with dreadful speed on—full realization came—on the breast of that racing torrent dropping from some far ocean cleft and rushing— where? A little time, a few breathless instants, I struggled with the devil who clutched me—inflexibly, indomitably.

Then a shrieking as of all the pent winds of the universe in my ears— blackness!

Consciousness returned slowly, agonizedly.

"Larry!" I groaned. "Lakla!"

A brilliant light was glowing through my closed lids. It hurt. I opened my eyes, closed them with swords and needles of dazzling pain shooting through them. Again I opened them cautiously. It was the sun!

I staggered to my feet. Behind me was a shattered wall of basalt monoliths, hewn and squared. Before me was the Pacific, smooth and blue and smiling.

And not far away, cast up on the strand even as I had been, was— Marakinoff!

He lay there, broken and dead indeed. Yet all the waters through which we had passed—not even the waters of death themselves—could wash from his face the grin of triumph. With the last of my strength I dragged the body from the strand and pushed it out into the waves. A little billow ran up, coiled about it, and carried it away, ducking and bending. Another seized it, and another, playing with it. It floated from my sight—that which had been Marakinoff, with all his schemes to turn our fair world into an undreamed-of-hell.

My strength began to come back to me. I found a thicket and slept; slept it must have been for many hours, for when I again awakened the dawn was rosing the east. I will not tell my sufferings. Suffice it to say that I found a spring and some fruit, and just before dusk had recovered enough to writhe up to the top of the wall and discover where I was.

The place was one of the farther islets of the Nan-Matal. To the north I caught the shadows of the ruins of Nan-Tauach, where was the moon door, black against the sky. Where was the moon door—which, someway, somehow, I must reach, and quickly.

At dawn of the next day I got together driftwood and bound it together in shape of a rough raft with fallen creepers. Then, with a makeshift paddle, I set forth for Nan-Tauach. Slowly, painfully, I crept up to it. It was late afternoon before I grounded my shaky craft on the little beach between the ruined sea-gates and, creeping up the giant steps, made my way to the inner enclosure.

And at its opening I stopped, and the tears ran streaming down my cheeks while I wept aloud with sorrow and with disappointment and with weariness.

For the great wall in which had been set the pale slab whose threshold we had crossed to the land of the Shining One lay shattered and broken. The monoliths were heaped about; the wall had fallen, and about them shone a film of water, half covering them.

There was no moon door!

Dazed and weeping, I drew closer, climbed upon their outlying fragments. I looked out only upon the sea. There had been a great subsidence, an earth shock, perhaps, tilting downward all that side—the echo, little doubt, of that cataclysm which had blasted the Dweller's lair!

The little squared islet called Tau, in which were hidden the seven globes, had entirely disappeared. Upon the waters there was no trace of it.

The moon door was gone; the passage to the Moon Pool was closed to me—its chamber covered by the sea!

There was no road to Larry—nor to Lakla!

And there, for me, the world ended.

A Note About the Author

A. Merritt (1884–1943) was an American editor and fantastic fiction writer. Born Abraham Grace Merritt in Beverly, New Jersey, he moved with his family to Philadelphia in 1894. Merritt worked as a reporter for *The Philadelphia Inquirer* before joining the staff of *The American Weekly* as assistant editor in 1912. On the side, Merritt—one of the highest paid journalists of his time—found success as writer of popular fantasy tales. He had a run of successful stories and serial novels that appeared in *Weird Tales, Science and Invention,* and *Argosy*, including *The Moon Pool* (1918), *The Metal Monster* (1920), and *Dwellers in the Mirage* (1932). Merritt was a direct influence on such writers as H. P. Lovecraft and Richard Shaver and was recognized for his achievements as a 1999 inductee to the Science Fiction and Fantasy Hall of Fame.

A Note from the Publisher

Spanning many genres, from non-fiction essays to literature classics to children's books and lyric poetry, Mint Edition books showcase the master works of our time in a modern new package. The text is freshly typeset, is clean and easy to read, and features a new note about the author in each volume. Many books also include exclusive new introductory material. Every book boasts a striking new cover, which makes it as appropriate for collecting as it is for gift giving. Mint Edition books are only printed when a reader orders them, so natural resources are not wasted. We're proud that our books are never manufactured in excess and exist only in the exact quantity they need to be read and enjoyed.

bookfinity™

Discover more of your favorite classics with Bookfinity™.

- Track your reading with custom book lists.
- Get great book recommendations for your personalized Reader Type.
- Add reviews for your favorite books.
- AND MUCH MORE!

Visit **bookfinity.com** and take the fun Reader Type quiz to get started.

Enjoy our classic and modern companion pairings!